THE

AMAZON

AND THE

WARRIOR

THE
AMAZON
AND THE
WARRIOR

JUDITH HAND

TOR®

A TOM DOHERTY ASSOCIATES BOOK
NEW YORK

This is a work of fiction. All the characters and events portrayed in this book are either fictitious or are used fictitiously.

THE AMAZON AND THE WARRIOR

A Tor Book
Published by Tom Doherty Associates, LLC
175 Fifth Avenue
New York, NY 10010

www.tor.com

Tor® is a registered trademark of Tom Doherty Associates, LLC.

ISBN 0-765-34936-1
EAN 978-0765-34936-1

First edition: May 2004

Printed in the United States of America

0 9 8 7 6 5 4 3 2 1

This story is dedicated to
Harold, the man who
held my hand.

CAST OF CHARACTERS

Women

Alcmene—Cassandra's lady-in-waiting.

Andromache—wife of the Trojan prince, Hektor.

Bremusa—Penthesilea's chief Amazon commander.

Cleite—Penthesilea's mother.

Clonie—one of Penthesilea's commanders, the companion of Bremusa.

Derinoe (Deri)—Pentha's sister.

Euryclea—a woman who wants her daughter, Marpessa, to be Amazon Queen.

Evandre—one of Penthesilea's commanders.

Gryn—Pentha's adopted mother, magician, storyteller, Bias' teacher.

Harmonia—Hearth Queen of Themiskyra.

Harmothoe—an Amazon expert in making and carrying fire.

Hekuba—wife of Priam, Queen of Troy.

Helen—wife of Menelaus, king of Sparta, who ran off with the Trojan Prince, Paris.

Hippolyta—Penthesilea's step-sister, daughter of Gryn.

Marpessa—an Amazon commander who wants to be Warrior Queen.

Myrina—Derinoe's daughter by Hektor.

Nausicaa—the mistress of Prince Hektor's friend Glaukos.

Penthesilea (Pentha)—Warrior Queen of Themiskyra.

Semele—Priestess of Artemis at Troy.

Men

Achilles—an Achean warrior, son of King Peleus and the nymph Thetis.

Aeneas—second in command to the Trojan prince, Hektor.

Agamemnon—high king of the Acheans, brother of Menelaus.

Ajax—an Achean warrior of great strength and courage.

Automedon—Achilles's charioteer.

Bias—a Themiskyran boy who takes care of Damon's animals.

Damonides (Damon)—Themiskyran man trained as an Achean warrior.

Glaukos—friend of the Trojan prince, Hektor, and lover of Nausicaa.

Grammeron—the Thracian (family) that holds the secret to navigating the Hellespont.

Hattusilis—Hittite ruler on the Amazon southern border.

Hektor—heir to the Trojan throne, husband of Andromache, and lover of Derinoe.

Leonides—Derinoe's son by Achilles.

Menelaus—king of Sparta, and Helen's husband.

Muttalusha—a Hittite merchant.

Nestor—one of the Achean kings who came to Troy.

Noemon—the old man who built Damon's cabin and taught him falconry

Odysseus—one of the Achean kings who came to Troy.

Paris—youngest son of Priam, the lover of Helen.

Patroklos—cousin and companion of Achilles.

Phemios—Hippolyta's lover and the Themiskyran infantry's third in command.

Priam—king of Troy.

Trusis—headman in Themiskyra who becomes the infantry's second in command.

Divinities or Mythological Figures

Apollo—son of Zeus, god of light, music, poetry and prophecy. In Greek mythology the twin of Artemis.

Artemis—at this time in history, an Asiatic goddess of the hunt and of women.

Athena—a daughter of Zeus who had no mother. She sprung, fully formed, from the head of Zeus.

Centaur—a rude, wild race with the upper body of a man and lower body of a horse.

The Fates—three goddesses thought to determine a child's destiny.

Hydra—a monstrous water serpent with nine heads; its blood was poisonous.

Pegasus—a fabulous winged horse, born of the Gorgon Medussa and the god Poseidon.

Zeus—king of all the gods and goddesses of Mt. Olympus and Mt. Ida.

Animals

Gale—Hippolyta's mare.
Dawn—Pentha's mare.
Dia—Damon's hunting falcon.
Valor—Pentha's battle stallion.
Wolf (Little Wolf)—Damon's wolf.

PREFACE

LOVE AND WAR. ETERNAL THEMES. *THE AMAZON and the Warrior* is a love story set against the background of what is arguably the most famous war ever chronicled in myth or the arts.

Nearly three thousand years ago, around 750 BC, the Greek poet Homer composed the *Iliad,* an epic about the "Age of Heroes," a time when weapons were made of bronze because the secret of iron was still not widely known. From our perspective, this phrase seems ironic because our definition of "hero" has evolved. The truth appears to be that in the centuries around 1250 BC, kings from the cities of Greece (Achea) accumulated the wealth to support their lifestyles, and their armies, by sacking cities throughout the Eastern Mediterranean.* These plunderers took booty in the form of gold and gems, horses and slaves. As depicted by Homer, in a thirst for glory, these royal nobles fought their counterparts among their enemies on the battlefield in deadly duels of honorable combat. These were the heroes of their day. Men about whom story spinners wove their tales, great not because they sacrificed themselves for others, but because they fought or lived larger than life.

This was a time, too, of Amazons, whose home, Themiskyra,

See Michael Wood. 1998. *In Search of the Trojan War*. University of California Press: Berkeley and Los Angeles.

lay astride the river Thermodon on the southern shore of the Black Sea.

If we look at the geography of Turkey, the gods seem to have blessed Themiskyra with a relatively sheltered location. A rugged, high mountain range with few passes protected her back from her extraordinarily aggressive southern neighbors, the Hittites. And the Hellespont, the narrow strait that led from the Aegean into the Euxine (Black) Sea, protected her from Achean raiders out of Greece. Strong southern winds swept down the Hellespont almost perpetually from the north, and the currents, too, consistently ran to the south. This is as true today as it was in the Bronze Age. Although a seafaring people, the Acheans did not possess the technology or know-how to sail against the wind. Thus they would have been hard pressed to bring ships through the strait and into position to threaten the Amazon stronghold.

At the mouth of the Hellespont, on the Aegean coast of Turkey, lay the site of the most famous raiding expedition of all—Troy. This is the story of immortal warriors who fought in the Trojan War—men and women.

PROLOGUE

I T IS JUST PAST DAWN AND PENTHA, RUBBING SLEEP from her eyes, shuffles from the sleeping chamber to let out the dog.

A sound. Then a scream! Sudden shrieking and shouting all around the house.

"Raiders!" someone yells.

A warning chill ripples through Pentha, head to toe. She is sixteen, and from memory her mother's frequent warning comes: *Hide at once! Arm yourself!* That is what her mother has always told them.

Pentha snatches up a cutting knife.

"Acheans!" screams the woman from across their narrow street.

Pentha's heart beats wildly. Her eyes dart around the room, seeking a place to hide. *The wicker basket!* Large, waist high, under the window. She dashes to it and flips back the top, climbs in, pushes aside softened deerskins, squats, and yanks down the cover. Wriggling under the skins, she pulls into a tight ball.

Through spaces in the wicker, Pentha sees her sister Deri and their mother running from the sleeping chamber toward her. Three men chase them. Dirty men, hands empty, swords at their sides banging against their legs.

"Artemis strike you dead!" her mother screams. She and Deri run into the street, the men still chasing them.

Pentha thinks, *I should go after them. Help them.* But she can't move.

She hears the sound of horses' hoofs and a wagon. The sounds stop just outside. Should she stand up at the window and look out? But one of the raiders might see her. Instead of standing, she crouches lower.

A husky voice commands, "Leave the women until the men are taken care of."

Who is that? What will they do with the men?

"Yes, Lord Achilles."

Pentha presses her hand over her racing heart. She thinks, *I must stand up now. I must see.*

Then footsteps running back into the house. She peeks again through the wicker to see her mother and Deri rush back in, followed by a huge man fully clothed in leather and bronze armor. "What is a daughter of Artemis and her young doing this far from home?" the man with the husky voice demands of Deri.

Pentha can't see her mother, but she can see Deri staring, like a paralyzed, frightened hare at the big warrior. Deri, just a year younger than Pentha, is terrified too.

"Die!" Her mother appears in Pentha's view, knife in hand and charging at the warrior, blocking Pentha's view of him.

He steps back, bangs into the door, it slams shut.

Her mother and the warrior struggle . . .

PART 1

MEETING

⊰ 1 ⊱

ALONE AND AT PEACE, DAMON HAD SPENT AN
hour checking his traps above Two Sisters Falls. The
hour was late. The midsummer sky looked dark and bruised;
rain would come before nightfall.

Little Wolf, still awkward at eight-weeks old, bounded
along behind him on the narrow trail that, on Damon's left,
sloped gently downhill to a boulder-strewn stream. When
they reached the spot where, from between two great pines,
a man could take a last glimpse of the fall's thundering
waters before the trail turned, Damon stopped to look back,
stroking his beard as he contemplated the water's beauty.
The wolf pup ran under his legs and bumped one of his
feet. Damon tripped. He and Little Wolf went over the side.

Damon slammed onto his back. Pain shot through his
chest. His breath whooshed out, and he rolled head-over-tail
once then twice more like a log until his left side landed in
the water. Little Wolf slid to a stop beside him.

Clearly thinking this was great fun, the pup leaped onto
Damon's chest, wagging his tail. Damon burst into laughter.

The eager young thing leapt back onto solid ground and
bowed, rump in the air, his tail still waving, inviting more
marvelous play. Damon crawled from the water, his linen
trousers and tunic clinging coldly to his skin. He took a similar stance, rear up and shoulders down, and the two of them
tumbled, the pup growling and Damon laughing.

Damon stopped the game by picking up Little Wolf and staring him down with a somber gaze. Then he settled the soft ball into his lap and stared upstream to the waterfall.

For a moment he simply listened, scratching the wolf behind the ears. In Damon's head, the sound of cascading water created an aura of exquisite colors—unending swirls, patterns never repeated—of the deep purples and gentle pinks of a glorious sunset.

"Do you see the colors, too?" he said. He closed his eyes and let the sound of the fall and the swirling purples and pinks pleasure his mind. Earlier he'd been reminded of his difference from other people, of his oddity, by the chattering of squirrels. Their sounds evoked much the same ugly aura and nausea in him that human speech did.

He stood and made a half-hearted effort to wring water from his clothing. A quick search revealed no sign of the leather thong used to keep his hair back from his face, and further searching would likely prove futile. The thong could be hidden in any bush, snagged under any rock, or blended in with the brown litter on the slope.

With Little Wolf under one arm, Damon scrambled back onto the trail. A stone's throw downstream something the size of a deer or even a bear moved on the far bank. Damon froze. Two women approached. Few people, women or men, ever appeared near his cabin.

Their dress—short deerskin tunics with left shoulder exposed and knee-high boots—identified them as Amazons, daughters of the People of Artemis. They carried bows and moved swiftly, silently toward him in a manner indicating they were close on the trail of quarry—and they hadn't seen him. The woman at the front was startling. Her hair, bound in a typical Amazon braided bun at the back of her head, was a color he had never seen before. Not on a person and not on an animal. A brilliant coppery red. And she was uncommonly tall, a full foot-length taller than her fellow hunter.

The redheaded leader reached the path to the stream used by the forest's largest creatures—deer, leopard, lion, wolf, and boar—and turned onto it. Her companion, a woman with chestnut hair, followed.

The rope loop trap. Not two days ago Damon had seen it along that same path. According to the boy Bias, Damon's only regular contact with the rest of the world, the only village within half a day's walk had been losing goats to something large, probably wolves. The villagers had likely set the snare.

Damon barely registered this thought when he heard the distinctive "thwang" and rustle of a sprung loop trap. A woman yelled. He shook his head, and with a wry smile to Little Wolf he said, "Someone has caught himself an Amazon."

He loped down to the stream and crossed, easily balancing on a series of rocks that might have been placed by Artemis for just that purpose. As he approached the women, he saw that the red-haired one dangled upside down, her left ankle in the loop.

Noting long, elegantly-built legs, shapely waist, and taut belly, he smiled. He also noted, as she slowly twirled, that she wore a leather undergarment that was little more than a strap that expanded in front to cover her private hair and in the rear, the upper half of her buttocks. He had never known what, if anything, an Amazon wore under her tunic. Only his mother, herself an Amazon before she had married and become pregnant with Damon, could have told him, but she was dead now many years.

"Just cut it!" the dangling woman called to her friend.

Amazement stopped what he'd intended to say. He shook his head. He must have misheard. Her words didn't create the brown and jagged grey-scummed aura and sickening sensation he experienced from human speech. Her words washed the scene in sunny yellow and his sensation was pleasure.

Her friend, wrestling to untie the rope, secured to the base of a birch tree, said testily, "If I cut it, you'll fall straight down on your head and break your neck." Her voice created exactly the repugnant, filthy aura he expected.

They still hadn't seen him. The redhead tightened her belly muscles and curled her body to raise her hands to her ankle in a futile gesture to grapple with the loop. A look of extreme pain flashed over her face. She immediately let herself hang straight down again.

Her hair had somehow come unbound from the long single braid always worn at the back of the head when Amazons were hunting or in battle, and masses of the extraordinary stuff, red highlighted with gold, rippled toward the ground.

"I can help," he said. He strode under the hung woman, saying to her companion, "Cut the rope. I'll catch her."

After a brief pause, her eyebrows lifted in surprise at this stranger, the chestnut-haired Amazon cut the rope. Damon immediately held in his arms an indignant woman with a flushed face. Whether her color was caused by indignation or from hanging upside down, he couldn't tell.

Damon couldn't suppress a chuckle. "Apart from your dignity, you seem unharmed. Fortunate. But if you are customarily so unaware, maybe you ought not be out in the woods alone."

He felt her stiffen. "Let me stand!"

Her voice flared with irritation, but its sunny aura was still lovely to see. He had never, in his life, experienced such a voice.

He enjoyed the feel of the tight, sleek muscles of her thighs and she put a firm grip on one of his arms. She added, hotly, "And, as is very evident, I am not alone."

True. So she'd also caught him—in an error.

When her feet touched the ground, a look of pain wrinkled a beautiful, high brow.

Regret struck. He'd spoken too soon and too cockily.

Her friend took her hand. "You're hurt."

"I . . . my hip." She felt her left hip, then tried a step. Her tanned skin actually blanched, her lips thinned, and she quickly shifted her weight off the left leg. The hipbone had clearly not been pulled from its socket, but she still wasn't going to be walking in comfort, if at all, anytime soon.

Damon noticed a long scar on her upper left arm and wondered . . . hunting or battle? He said, "Where is your camp?"

The shorter woman replied. "An hour's walk. At least."

Damon looked at the darkening sky and clouds low and thick, as if weighted with a heavy burden. Dusk was little more than an hour away. "Have you others there who can help?"

The injured beauty shook her head. She looked at her friend. "You walk it and come back with Gale and Valor."

"Gale and Valor?" he said.

"Our horses," said the red-head.

Of course.

A moment of silence—a moment of choice. He could leave them to fend for themselves. Their problem was not his problem. He could return to his cabin and his life and they could continue with theirs.

But then, how would he feel sleeping warmly knowing that they were enduring a night of rain in the open? No matter what she said, or hoped, the red-head was not going to be able to walk or ride until she let her hip rest.

He took the leap. "Will you be able to ride any better than you can walk? I don't think so. My home is just beyond the ridge." He pointed to the trail along which he had only a short time ago been walking quite happily in solitude. "Only a short walk." He looked again at the sky. "You can be dry with me for the night."

The red-head studied him. Her color rose still higher. Yes, she was most definitely embarrassed to have been so easily caught. She looked at her friend. He was a stranger, but then this was Themiskyran country and the remote woods at that. Hospitality was the law. The one with chestnut hair seemed pleased at the thought of shelter for the night, but the tall woman still hesitated, her jaw set firm. He guessed she didn't like being dependent—on anyone for anything.

He swept the injured Amazon into his arms and started walking.

. . . BUT . . ." THE WOMAN STAMMERED.

"Can you walk?"

She shook her head.

To the smaller woman he said, "Please. Carry the pup."

It had been longer than he could remember since he'd had a woman in his arms, and never one so beautiful. To the feel of female flesh against his skin, his body responded in male fashion. Fortunately, her friend walked behind him.

His most unusual "catch of the day" touched his tunic, the dry side, then the wet one. His flesh prickled. She quickly said, "Was the trap yours?"

He forced himself to look straight ahead when what he wanted to do was study her face as he would a newly-discovered flower. And her words had tumbled out, as if she had felt the same thrill of contact.

"No. There is a village not far from here."

She was within a finger's width of being as tall as he, her body solidly built, no doubt from hard riding and fighting. Whenever the trail took an uphill slant, he fell into shorter steps and heavier breathing. Near his cabin, the first cool drop of rain struck his cheek.

When he carried her through the thick, whitethorn hedge that surrounded the yard, she nodded at the hedge. "Does it actually work to keep out the lions and wolves?"

He smiled. "It's intended to slow them down."

"And?"

"I'm still alive."

She chuckled. He risked a quick look at her. Lovely green eyes returned his gaze.

His cabin was simple—a single room with a small covered porch on one side—but soundly built of logs with a sloped slate roof and sturdy beams and rafters and snugly chinked with sticks and clay. He felt suddenly glad that he kept a neat home. All the women of Themiskyra were accustomed to elegance and order and fine comforts. These two would be no different. Only when they were young and Amazon did Themiskyran women live every bit as ruggedly as he did. The Amazons themselves though, were a different breed.

At the door he set her on her feet. At the same moment, as the three of them stood on the covered porch, the sky released its hold on the rain.

Her friend, quivers slung over her shoulder, still carried Little Wolf.

Damon opened the wooden plank door halfway and said, "Wait a moment." Inside, he hurried to the perch where, after he worked his Saker falcon, she spent the remainder of her day. He gazed with appreciation at the beauty the two women would soon see: a pale, almost white, head; dark, blue-gray back with deep-black flight feathers; a white, heavily streaked breast; and large, oval, white spots on a brown tail.

The falcon fixed him with her dark, penetrating, and always eerily noncommittal, gaze. "Sorry, Dia. We have guests." He slipped a tiny leather hood with a jaunty tuft of red feathers over her head. Without it she could likely panic. The only other human she knew was Bias, and the boy had only been to the cabin eight times in the three years Damon had owned the falcon.

Back at the door, he gestured the women inside.

"The pup, too?" asked the smaller woman.

He nodded.

Well-packed dirt covered with boar skins served as his

floor. The hearth dominated the room's center, and a covered opening through the roof let out smoke. A small table with two chairs stood several paces from the hearth. He said, "If you'd like to stoke the fire, there is wood against the wall."

Overhead, the solid sounds of heavy rain began thumping on the slate.

From the cabinet next to the single window, he pulled out a fresh set of tunic and trousers and then, having pulled the window's wooden cover shut against the rain, he retreated into the room's darkest corner. With his back to the women, he shucked the wet tunic over his head, listening to the sound of footsteps and of wood being taken from the pile.

He put on the fresh tunic. Little Wolf sniffed the tunic then darted under foot as Damon unlaced and stripped off his wet trousers, wondering as he bent over if the women were looking at his rear. Actually, he decided, his backside would probably not interest them. Amazons did not live with men, but they had plenty of lovers.

Dry and dressed, he turned to find a small fire springing up in the hearth. The wood being dried spruce, it gave off friendly crackles and a soothing smell. As he'd imagined, both women appeared to have been studying it, not him. He suffered a pang of disappointment, and immediately judged his feeling absurd. The dried ingredients for venison stew— meat, onions, carrots, and herbs—had been soaking in the tripod since morning. He fetched the tripod and positioned the pot over the fire.

Both women rose and, with the wounded beauty limping and helped by her friend, they walked halfway to Dia's perch then paused and stared at the bird, slack-jawed.

He said, "Don't move," then slipped the hood off.

The red-head collected herself first and asked softly, "Is it a Saker?" Her face now radiated remarkable gentleness. Her initial embarrassment past, she was relaxing.

"The bird is quite exquisite," said her companion.

"You've not seen a hunting falcon before?"

They both gave him brief, puzzled stares, then looked again to Dia. "A hunting falcon?" they said together.

"An old man named Noemon, who built this cabin, took me in. And he taught me the art of taming and using the Saker to hunt." Damon slipped the hood back onto Dia's head. "It's something he learned in the southeast. It's summer now and Dia's molting. But in winter, the stew we'd eat tonight would likely be a hare she caught. The ferrets that scare prey up for us live in a cage outside."

The women studied him. The green eyes of the red-head were the lovely color of young spruce needles. Her chestnut-haired companion, he now noticed, was also attractive, especially her rich brown eyes and full breasts.

"You," said the red-head, "ferrets, and a falcon. And what very much appears to be a wolf pup, not a dog." She smiled, her lips were inviting, the smile firing her eyes with mischief. "That's it?"

He returned the smile and added a single nod.

They shared a long look. He once more felt a male stirring, and turning away, hurried to say the first thing that came into his mind. "I'll lower the tripod a bit closer to the heat."

The smaller woman said, after settling her friend and herself on one of several bearskin rugs, "Tell us how it is done—with the falcon. A bird so wild."

Little Wolf bounded into the lap of the red-head, and she massaged him behind the ears.

Damon explained. "First I had to capture her when she was young, from the high land to the south."

"Hittite land?" asked the red-head. Little Wolf flopped onto his side and the Amazon tickled his belly.

Damon nodded, envying Little Wolf's position. "She only hunts well in the open." He stirred the stew, then fetched bread from the shelf next to Dia. He cut the bread, found three clean bowls and a ladle and served up supper. Since he had only two chairs, they ate seated on the skins.

"Over three years ago my friend, Noemon, came to the end of his journey." Sadness for the loss of a man who had in many ways saved his life, brought a stifling tightness to his throat. He swallowed hard. Finding his voice again, he continued. "The gods took him in his sleep. A good man. A clever man. He had no family, and this place became mine. I have been here six years."

They finished, and he added a piece of wood to freshen the fire against the night chill. The smaller woman fetched their quivers. Both women dug into one of several pouches.

He blew under the wood a few times until it flickered into flame.

The red-head, who held and was studying three small, oddly chipped pieces of stone—two black and one green—said, "Why a wolf pup? Why not a dog?"

He resettled, cross-legged, on the bearskin. Little Wolf crawled into his lap. The smaller woman began to whittle what he thought might become the figure of an owl.

"I love a wolf's spirit."

"But . . ."

"The Fates brought *him* to me. Not a dog. His family must be dead or they somehow lost him."

"Don't you worry? He's adorable now, but he will grow wild."

By Zeus, this woman was a beauty to steal the breath of any man who laid eyes on her. "You think I should worry?"

"You don't think you should?"

"He will be wild. Perhaps he'll leave me. Probably not. Wolves are fiercely loyal."

"So is a dog, and you don't have a worry about a dog tearing out the throat of your next visitor."

He grinned. "I don't have visitors."

Both women laughed.

He laid the pup on its back and tickled its belly. "It is only essential that in every moment of every day, he never doubts or questions that I am his master."

She returned the two black stones to the bag and fetched out yet another stone, this one larger, a small piece of leather, and a bit of deer antler tine.

After placing the smaller, green stone on the leather in her left hand, to his surprise, she struck it with the larger stone. A green chunk spun off onto the floor. With another deft stroke, another bit of stone joined the first. He watched, fascinated, as in remarkably short time the green piece achieved the rough shape of an arrowhead. Then, working with the antler tine, pressing it just so, she flaked off smaller pieces. Finally, she notched the end. A beautifully crafted arrowhead lay in her palm.

She said, "You learned to work a falcon from your friend. I learned from my mother to make arrow tips as they made them in the days of the old gods."

He held out his hand, and she tossed the arrowhead to him. With it she sent a smile that suggested sharing. Even intimacy. He felt a quickening heartbeat. He rubbed his thumb gingerly over a cutting edge as sharp as any iron Amazon tip he'd ever felt. Perhaps sharper. But of course, it would be far more breakable.

She dug into the pouch and brought out a black piece and began to work it. Now and then she massaged her hip, as if perhaps thinking she wanted to walk out of this odd place as soon as possible.

He set the pup aside, went to his cupboard, and brought back his fine cutting knife and a nearly-finished dress harness. He needed only to inlay the brow and cheek pieces with bronze swirls he'd gotten on his last trip to Themiskyra and the halter would be ready for trade. For added light, he lit two clay oil lamps.

Seeing the harness, the smaller woman said, "I know you. I recognize the fine work. You are Damonides, are you not?"

He sat again, grinned at her. "My many friends call me Damon."

Both women smiled at his bit of irony. The shorter of the two continued. "My mother, our mother, is Gryn. She often mentions trading with you."

"Often?" he said, genuinely surprised.

"Yes, often."

"And your name is . . . ?"

"Hippolyta."

The red-head stopped her chipping to catch his eye, a little puzzled frown creasing her forehead. "Do you never leave this place except to meet Gryn?"

"I'd have to say, I don't otherwise leave."

"Why? Why all alone here, with only animals and the forest?"

Violent images from the past began to crawl up from deep recesses in his mind. His mouth went dry. The fragile construct of tranquility at his core began to unravel, and his mind raced, determined to stave off its undoing.

The confident face across from him cut through the panic and moored him again. Still, he could barely get out the somber words. "Because it gives me some peace."

His words dropped a sudden heaviness into the room. This was all wrong! With determined effort, Damon pushed the past away, forced his voice to the carefree tone that was his natural spirit. "I want my heart to stay light and my life to be simple. Here," he opened his arms, "with my animals, I live without . . ." He stopped himself from saying, "the nausea of voices and the brutality of men." ". . . without care."

"But you are alone," she said, her voice suddenly tender.

He turned his attention to the bridle.

Mercifully, she seemed to understand and let the subject go. "So, what *do* you do with the wolf, the falcon, and the ferrets and whatever else you have out there when you come to Themiskyra?"

"An hour's walk away there is small village. Three families. I trade my leatherwork with them for the help of one of the sons, Bias. He's twelve. It's not a burden to them. I don't need him often."

He cut away a bit of leather where he would inlay bronze. The sounds in the room became those of thumping rain, crackling logs, chipping stone, and the whisking of whittled wood. He found he often had to force his attention to his hands and his intentions for the bridle since his thoughts stubbornly wandered, instead, to the Amazon's hair, the remembered feel of her skin against his, and the fire in her eyes.

❧ 3 ❦

KEEPING HER HEAD BOWED, PENTHA STOLE
glances at this strange solitary, Damon "as his many
friends called him." She couldn't resist the pull of him. How
strange that, for some reason known perhaps only to him, he
had taken up such an isolated existence. He had a delightful
sense of humor and zest for life.

And he was no ugly thing. Quite the contrary. Deep-sea
blue eyes twinkled under strong brown eyebrows. To look
deeply into his eyes gave her a shiver. He had perhaps forty
years or slightly more. Brown, wavy hair, sitting lightly on
his shoulders, shone with good health. His close-cut beard,
she suspected, did not hide a weak chin or miserable complexion. He did not stay here because of any grand flaw she
could see.

He also possessed enormous strength, something she'd
found arousing when he carried her to the cabin. She had not
had a lover for over a month, not since the night after the last
full moon dance.

Hippolyta broke the silence. "There is much talk about
you in Themiskyra. In the Amazon compound as well as
those of the women and men."

Damon smiled, not at Hippolyta but as if to himself, as if
finding her pronouncement vastly amusing. "And what do
they say?"

"They say you are a rebel. That you were always odd.

Only someone odd would choose to leave beautiful and peaceful Themiskrya to 'see the world.'"

"Well, when it comes to odd, I'd say they are right."

Hippolyta laughed and Pentha joined her. Hippolyta, a darling child of Zeus and Curiosity, pressed on. "And did you see the world?"

"I saw it. I learned to love parts of it. I learned to hate parts of it. Now I prefer the woods."

"They say you were a warrior. That you fought with Acheans. They tell amazing tales of Damonides, the Achean fighter from Themiskyra."

"I know war."

Sensing he didn't want to talk of war, Pentha said, "We share something. I've also seen some of the world beyond Themiskyra. My mother—Gryn took me in when I was seventeen—my natural mother was Amazon, but when she was twenty and five she fell in love with a man who came traveling through. Before I was born, she left Themiskyra with him, to live on Tenedos. Do you know Tenedos, the island off Troy?"

He nodded.

Hippolyta said, "They say you never come into the city or the men's compound. Gryn says she has asked you to visit and you say no. Don't you like people?"

"I like people. I just don't like them in large numbers."

What a very peculiar man, Pentha thought, *sitting there so strong, with strong hands doing fine work, and perfectly happy being alone*. He looked up, caught her looking at him. He grinned. "You've not told me your name."

"Pentha."

Hippolyta added, "It's really Penthesilea."

He dropped his hands and the harness to his lap and stared in obvious astonishment. "I am honored to host the Warrior Queen. Somehow I think I should have guessed."

She couldn't hold back a laugh. "The Warrior Queen who gets herself caught in a simple rope-loop trap that a child would have seen."

"I have heard much about you from Gryn, although she failed to mention you are her adopted daughter."

"What does she say of me?"

"Ah, let me think."

He stopped working the leather and gazed a moment over her shoulder, then bent again to work. "She talked of you mostly during the time you did contest with Marpessa to become the Warrior Queen." Without looking at her he said, "Gryn doesn't like Marpessa. She believes her to be your enemy."

Hippolyta stopped whittling and said, heat in her voice, "Some feel that because Pentha wasn't raised in Themiskyra, she was not acceptable to lead our cavalry. But her mother was Amazon, and after Pentha came back to us she trained hard to learn riding and horses and weapons. Pentha won the competition. The issue was settled for good when she saved our troops from a Hittite ambush."

Again he turned his blue-eyed gaze to Pentha. "Did you like living in Tenedos?"

Was Pentha mistaken or was Damon pointedly uninterested in battles? She said, "I was happy. I loved my mother. I saw little of my father. He stayed mostly at sea."

Would Damon ask her why she left? She held her breath, waiting for that blow to fall. It had been a long time since anyone asked why she left Tenedos and why she came back to Themiskyra, a long time since she had to tell them it was not their concern.

Instead he said, "Like your mother, I also found love in that world. I learned that I like living with a woman all the time, not just coming to her at night."

Damon set the harness and the pup aside and stood. He said, "You are probably tired."

The insistent thumping of the rain on the roof continued. She watched him, admiring his strong, sure movements as he made two heaps of furs behind where she and Hippolyta sat. On the opposite side of the fire, he made another pile for himself.

She removed her sandals and crawled between the furs. She never tired of loving the softness of furs on her skin. In Tenedos, life had been more "citified," as her mother called it. They slept between bedclothes made of linen but of coarse texture. She much preferred the furs of Themiskyra.

For a while she watched the fire, listening to dying snaps of protest that produced pops and tiny flashes of light. She could just make out Damon's form beyond the glow. Soon her eyelids grew heavy and closed, and random thoughts replaced coherent ones.

An image of her hanging upside down.

The feeling of Damon's arms and body, his strong muscles, like a stallion in its prime.

Image of Valor running down the beach at full gallop.

Finally, Morpheus took her.

IT IS JUST PAST dawn in Tenedos and she has come from her sleeping chamber to let the dog out when the sounds begin. Screaming all around the house.

"Raiders!" someone outside yells.

Now she is crouching, hiding, shaking in the huge basket, a butchering knife in her hand. Her mother lies dead on the floor. And the warrior lays over Derinoe, grunting and grunting, and Deri is moaning.

Pentha should leap out and sink her knife deep into his side. Honor demands it. Love for her sister demands it.

But she crouches, rigid as stone. A sweating stone. She cannot feel herself breathing, but feels sweat pour down her side. *Let it end!*

Now her sister and the huge warrior, the biggest man she has ever seen, are outside. The Achean monster is dragging Deri away! This is what they do. Kill the men and boys. Makes slaves of the women and girls.

"Deri!" Pentha screams.

Now she runs beside a chariot, thrusting the knife at the huge warrior in his gilded bronze armor. He knocks the knife away as if it is a feather. Through Pentha's tears, the world is a wavery sheet of running colors.

"Deri!" she screams again as she uselessly pummels the man's enormous, outstretched arm.

For a moment that seems timeless and as electrified as if Zeus has shot her with lightening, her gaze connects with his, and then the movement of the chariot pulls him from her and something shakes her.

"Wake up Pentha!"

This was an entirely different male voice. Gentle. Soothing.

She forced her eyes open. Next to her knelt the man, Damon. And she was striking him and crying.

Hippolyta took her hand. Damon let go of her shoulders.

Hippolyta had fetched a cloth. She wiped sweat from Pentha's forehead and said, "You're back."

Pentha took the cloth and wiped at her tears. She looked at their host. "How dreadful," she said. The look on his face seemed a mixture of wonder and concern. She added, "I'm sorry. I've wakened both of you."

He sat back on his heels. "You were thrashing your covers. Can I get you something? Water perhaps?"

"It's nothing." She hugged her stomach, her insides still shaking.

Hippolyta kissed her on the check, then stood. "Pentha's dreams often don't bring her peace." She moved back to her own bedding and wriggled under the skins.

Damon, too, returned to his furs.

Pentha closed her eyes but now she recalled the actual moment when the infamous Achean royal barged into their house. Large chest, fine mouth, powerfully formed arms and legs, head with long, wavy, chestnut-colored hair. A shaft of morning light struck his elaborate bronze-inlaid breast-piece and a reflected beam pierced the room and momentarily dazzled her.

Then Cleite attacked him, knife in hand. When Pentha's mother lunged at him, he backed against the door which slammed shut. He grabbed her mother's wrist and twisted it. And either the man thrust the knife into her mother or perhaps her mother's forward rush forced her onto the blade.

Pentha hadn't been able to see which. But her mother sagged against him, and Pentha remembered the sharp taste of tears and blood mingled because she had bitten herself so hard to keep from screaming. She had watched in horror as a bright spot of red spread across the chest of her mother's sleeping gown.

And she had noted, even in her distress, that the warrior appeared surprised, truly amazed that her mother attacked him. He lowered her to the floor, so gently, and his eyes looked full of regret. Surely, surely he had not thought that an Amazon daughter of Artemis would be taken captive? Would go docilely into slavery, to be taken across the Great Sea to harvest flax, work clay, and weave her life away for men's pleasure and profit.

And then he and Deri were. . . . Tears welled, slid down Pentha's cheeks. She pressed the back of her hand to her mouth to cover any sound. The dream never came exactly the same. She could be hiding in different places. The Achean might take Deri away by some other means. But the dream always carried the essence of the horrible truth. Pentha had not. . . . had not. . . . Tears threatened again and she bit the back of her hand to block thoughts of her shame.

It took a long time, but eventually her thoughts lost focus. She did not dream again, or if she did, she didn't remember.

❧ 4 ❧

DAMON AWAKENED EARLY. FOR A LONG TIME, HE studied the face of the sleeping woman opposite him. Warrior Queen of the Amazons of Themiskyra. Had there ever been another woman, let alone Warrior Queen, so beautiful? The world told tales of Amazon strength and beauty, but this woman's beauty outshone any he'd ever seen.

Finally he rose and fetched water. He woke the women, and while they washed their faces and went outside, he laid down a simple breakfast of pears, figs, and goat's milk cheese sprinkled with white barley meal.

When they finished, he led them into the yard. "Your hip?" he asked Penthesilea. She seemed to be walking fine.

"No worse for the experience."

He nodded. He doubted she would complain even if in excruciating pain.

"I'll walk you to your camp, lest some new calamity befall you."

Her green eyes flashed. "I—we—are perfectly able to make our camp."

He laughed, and quickly realizing the tease, she laughed too.

She described the location of their horses and gear. He knew the place, and since this was his territory, he led the way. But not for one heartbeat did he forget Penthesilea's presence at his back.

The rain ceased sometime during the night, leaving the morning air gauzy with thick fog and rich with the odor of wet earth and leaves. Where the trail widened, they walked three abreast. Watching her he said, "You have the most uncommon voice."

She raised an eyebrow.

He wanted to tell her the truth. Something inside him ached to tell this woman that her voice was the clear, bright yellow of a mountain daisy. Not since his wife's death, twelve years ago, had he felt so strong a pull to a woman. But like all others to whom he had tried to explain, Pentha would think him mad or cursed. After his first mention of it to his wife, and her shocked, uncomprehending response, he had never again spoken even to her of the colors.

Suddenly regretting he'd said anything at all, he managed only, "It's quite beautiful."

That won him a lovely smile. "Well, that's never been said about me before."

When they reached a rise overlooking their camp, he felt he'd come as far as necessary. Time to part. Dia and Little Wolf and his other companions needed feeding.

They exchanged farewells. He watched them stride down the hill. Hippolyta turned and waved. From a pocket on the inside of his trousers, he fetched out the green arrowhead, felt his body warmth on it, thought how perfectly its color matched Pentha's eyes. He held it a moment, then slid it back into the pocket.

❧ 5 ❧

ACHILLES CAUGHT SIGHT OF THE CAMP OF Agamemnon, ahead and to his left, firmly entrenched at the wide mouth of the bay southwest of Troy.

"Finally," he said to Automedon, his squire and driver, loudly enough to be heard over the sounds of the horses' hooves and dirt-churning chariot wheels. Although the spring day itself was pleasant, it had been a long, dusty ride.

Automedon, a taciturn man—a trait Achilles admired—simply nodded.

A flock of sheep, taken as war prize, grazed nearby. To Achilles' right, between the Achean encampment and the Trojan city with its mighty elevated citadel, lay the Trojan plain and the river Scamander. The citadel wall, with its dressed white limestone towers, jutted out of the plain. Achilles could just see in the long distance the tops of the two southernmost of the five towers.

Below that citadel wall lay a once graceful, busy city, now much the worse for eight years of blockade and intermittent battles but still secure. And inside those as yet unbreached walls, a treasure vast enough, along with the booty and slaves he had already acquired from other conquests in these parts, to justify the years of effort. And, of course, the chance to vindicate the honor of Menelaus for the loss of Helen.

Close by on his left stretched an Aegean beach of light

brown sand, and beyond the beach, deep blue water. Boiling whitecaps gave witness to the seemingly eternal, infernal northern wind. He would not want to be a man at sea on this day.

Achean forces controlled all coastal land north and south of Troy, all the way to his own present southern encampment, but it would be foolish to discount the possibility that his party might encounter a Trojan patrol from inland. Only two days earlier, though, in the first battle of this war season, Agamemnon's forces had suffered a stinging defeat, so it was more likely the Trojans would be tending their own wounded and dead. Still, he and Patroklos had fifty of his armored Myrmedon men on foot at their back, just in case.

The two-hour ride had surely been even dustier for Patroklos, whose chariot followed Achilles'. The Trojan roads didn't match the quality of those of Pylos or Mycenae at home. And the war naturally made it difficult to keep them, such as they were in good repair.

It was shortly after the recent defeat that a messenger from Agamemnon arrived with notice of a High Council. Achilles had been in the middle of planning an important raid, and this bumpy trip only added to his vexation at Agamemnon's summons, an irritation that would surely worsen unless the High King presented something truly weighty. The old man was so often indecisive.

They passed two sentry posts before arriving at the long, low wall that protected Achean forces from inland Trojan attacks. Each Achean contingent occupied a strip of the bay's long shoreline, a beach so extensive it took over an hour to walk from one end to the other. Each royal contingent had their own guarded gate. At Agamemnon's gate, the guards recognized Achilles, saluted, and let his party enter.

The place was a bee's hive of workers and warriors, horses and wagons, slaves and artisans. Several hundred shouting men surrounded a boxing match. The boxers' naked bodies glistened with oil, only their hands being covered by leather gloves.

Agamemnon's tent sprawled across the most elevated

ground, a residence grown after so many years to be more cabin than tent. Automedon pulled Achilles' team to a halt. Patroklos' chariot pulled up alongside. A slave bowed to Achilles and then led him, with Patroklos, to nearby quarters.

Their guest tent's sumptuous interior belied the fact that this was a war compound. Thick wool rugs covered the soil. Cushioned chairs welcomed a man to sit and relax. He noted two tables and several wardrobes. Tapestries with scenes of battle even hid the stark walls. From openings on both sides, a short covered path led to separate sleeping tents.

Two male slaves stood ready to serve them. "Other royals are already here," said the first slave. "After you have bathed, a noon meal awaits you in the High King's tent."

"Who else is here?" Achilles asked.

"Nearly everyone. Lord Odysseus, Lord Diomedes, Lord Menelaus, Lord Nestor. Only Lord Ajax, who must come a distance equal to yours, has not yet arrived.

Two more slaves entered, carrying his and Patroklos' travel chests. From outside came the sounds of at least two more chariots. "Perhaps that is Lord Ajax now," said the first slave. He bowed low and hurriedly backed out.

Heated water stood ready.

"So good to clean up," Patroklos said, loosening the belt to his tunic.

Patroklos drew the tunic over his head, revealing his beautiful body. Strong and powerfully built, although not so massive as Achilles'; since leaving childhood, Achilles had never met a man with a body bigger than his. This was no surprise as he was, by his mother Thetis, the grandson of Zeus.

They were cousins, he and Patroklos. Friends since childhood. This man of fair hair was closer to him than any other living being. A man with a fine disposition. Modest. Dependable. Wise. Achilles could not imagine life without sharing its joys and pains with Patroklos.

He washed his face and upper body, then ran his hands through shoulder-length hair.

Patroklos, having dried his face, turned gray eyes to Achilles. He snapped the edge of his towel against Achilles waist and, grinning, said, "The great Achilles is putting on fat."

"Ha! Worry about yourself."

Dressed in fresh clothing, they strolled to Agamemnon's reception room. Music by five of the High King's drummers, sistrum masters, and a cymbalist greeted them. The smell of wine laced with honey scented the air. He needed a good drink.

The royals had been seated on couches so that they formed a circle. Agamemnon's place remained empty. "Achilles! Patroklos!" several men called out in warm tones.

Odysseus said in his usual reflective style, "Our party is now nearly complete." Black-bearded Odysseus, the brilliant, and devious. Achilles nodded a genuine acknowledgment of admiration to him.

Ajax, next to Achilles the largest man present, had indeed arrived. More than once they had fought side-by-side. The warrior with dark, curly hair was unrelenting, entirely single-minded. A terror in battle. And boring. Ajax settled for granting the two newcomers a greeting nod.

Stocky, and usually dignified Diomedes shakily pointed a beef shank at Achilles and said, "Now that you are here, perhaps our host will appear." Clearly Diomedes had already enjoyed several cups of wine.

After extending his arm in a greeting clasp to Nestor—the hook-nosed, wise king of Pylos who always sat for these councils at Agamemnon's right—Achilles took the place to Agamemnon's left. Patroklos sat on his other side. Slaves quickly served wine and with it, sweet onion as a relish.

Directly opposite lounged Menelaus of Sparta, Agamemnon's brother and the betrayed husband of Helen. She had taken off with her lover, Paris, and a good deal of Menelaus' treasury, supposedly the principal reason why they had come across the sea to Troy. They would win back honor for Agamemnon's betrayed brother.

Paris was famed for extraordinary good looks, while some god had given auburn-haired Menelaus only modest looks and stature. Helen's treachery was despicable, but Achilles had always understood how Paris might have seduced the woman.

Diomedes leaned to Achilles and asked softly, "What do you think? Where is he?"

Achilles could only shrug.

After finishing his first cup of wine, he signaled and slaves brought food. He took generous portions of beef and partridge, some fresh clams, a taste of sea urchin—the missing Agamemnon's favorite—and olives.

He half listened to the sounds of music, laughter, food consumption, and male banter about horses and women, his mind back on the raid he was planning. Renon was a large town and should yield not only substantial gold, but perhaps amber as well. And he estimated a take of at least three hundred women slaves to send back home to Achea.

By the time he was finishing cut figs and pears, Agamemnon had still failed to appear.

Ajax said, loud and with angry emphasis, "What are we here for?"

Exactly Achilles' own question.

Diomedes stood. "Call me when he arrives."

At that moment, Agamemnon stepped from his private quarters into the room.

The aging, fair-haired king of Mycenae looked surprisingly tired, the lines in his face more deeply entrenched than the last time Achilles saw him. Perhaps not surprising, given his recent defeat. But then, this long siege had already inflicted many victories and defeats on both sides.

Diomedes, with slow, dignified grace, sat again.

Agamemnon, shoulders slumped, took his place of honor in the circle but remained standing. Close up, his eyes were red, as if he'd been weeping. Disgusted, Achilles sucked in a deep breath.

"I have called you all here because . . ."

They waited. Even if Achilles did not always agree with him, he conceded that when Agamemnon spoke, he spoke with eloquence. The High King continued. ". . . because I believe we must go with what we have already won and take our men home."

Ajax and Diomedes shouted on top of each other so Achilles couldn't make out what either said. He felt Patroklos place a cautioning hand on his arm.

Nestor turned to mutter something to Odysseus.

Menelaus simply sat open-mouthed.

❧ 6 ❧

Raising his voice above the babble, struggling to keep control, Achilles said, "You have called us here to tell us we are to pack up and go home?"

Agamemnon lifted both hands in an attempt to win quiet. When the babble finally sputtered into silence, he said, "It is clear that the Trojans will not give up Helen. Surely it must also be clear that we cannot breach their defenses."

"That's not clear to me," Achilles shot back.

Agamemnon looked at him, his voice rising in anger. "But you are in the south. You do not sit here day in and day out, manning this blockade, suffering the Trojan raids. Suffering the losses."

Achilles bolted to his feet. They stood facing each other but he towered over Agamemnon. "That's not my responsibility," he thundered, his voice vibrating with disgust and anger. "It's yours. Save Ajax and me, you have all the others to help you. And more than once, Ajax and I have also fought here."

He turned to the others. "What of honor? Are we to go home with honor not yet restored? Whipped dogs."

Every man studied him. All remained silent.

"What about you, Odysseus? Nestor? Diomedes? With plenty of booty and slaves yet to win, are we to turn tail and go home? Well, others may choose to leave. I will not." He looked at Helen's husband. "Surely Menelaus, you can't agree."

He collected himself, forced himself down onto his seat. One by one, the other royals spoke their minds.

In the end, they voted, and Agamemnon agreed that they would remain. He conceded that the blockade held fast, that he must simply devise a more ingenious plan to take Troy. Later, in their tent, Achilles, with Patroklos, was stretched out a table to enjoy a good massage and oiling. Achilles said, "I should be the one in charge of taking Troy."

"That would please me well enough, but it's not going to happen. Agamemnon is High King and will keep his place."

"The Trojans can be taken."

Patroklos said nothing. When the massage reached its end, the attendants left, giving him time to relax with Patroklos before dressing for the night.

They enjoyed the quiet, then Patroklos said, "Sometimes I would very much like this all to be over. I'd like to go home. See my family. See familiar places and eat my mother's food. Sometimes I weary of the battles, the raids, the killing."

For Achilles, the sadness in those words summoned a tragic, bitter memory of killing—the woman on Tenedos, nearly eight years ago, at the very beginning. The fiery Amazon who had attacked him so foolishly. The woman with the stunning, exciting daughter. Whenever he thought of Derinoe, which he still did surprisingly often, he would frequently relive the feeling of his knife slicing into her mother.

He spoke the words he said to himself so many times, his tone matching Patroklos' sadness. "There are things that happen in war. Things that even a man of honor doesn't intend. But they can't be helped."

"What are you thinking of?"

"The Amazon. Actually, of her mother. Had I not . . . had her mother not attacked me, with such bad results, Derinoe would not have left me."

"You really think so?"

Achilles sensed the sarcasm and because of their friendship, dismissed it. Patroklos still did not know Achilles' thoughts on the matter of Amazons, something frequently on Achilles' mind of late. "Derinoe was the most exciting woman I've ever known. Fiery. Independent. I've never had another like her. I've been thinking about the Amazons. They do have the most beautiful women. And indisputably the world's best horses. Better than the Trojans'. What an enormous profit they could bring us!"

"True. But aren't they unreachable? Going that far overland in that mountainous terrain would be quite hazardous. Just to get there would take the better part of a month. And I'd say, a steady supply line would be impossible."

"If we could take ships through the Hellespont, we could reach Themiskyra in two days."

"Getting through requires oarsmen in good condition. Actually, they have to be in exceptional condition. And even if you have enough fit oarsmen, you have to have a pilot, and the Thracians won't pilot Achean ships."

"Perhaps no one's offered a big enough bribe."

Patroklos sat up, giving him a hard stare. "Surely you are not seriously considering an attempt to raid Themiskyra."

Achilles rose and donned a sleeping robe. Into golden goblets, he poured wine for the two of them. Patroklos also threw on a robe, and then accepted the offered wine. Achilles continued. "Maybe it would take something more than a bribe. But the prize would be worth it. And I've heard rumors. Some say it's the Amazons who have the secret of iron, not the Hittites, who only trade with them for finished articles. Think of it. The secret of making iron!"

"What is this obsession you have for Amazons? Don't we have enough on our hands with the Trojans and their allies. Would you also bring down Amazons on us?"

Clearly Patroklos wasn't in sympathy with his plans. Not yet. He needed more information. He would need to assure Patroklos that such a raid was not only warranted, but that success was possible.

He grasped Patroklos by the arm, giving him a reassuring squeeze. "I won't do anything without your agreement. You know that."

They sat to finish the wine, their talk of Amazons and their horses and what a strange, and ludicrously womanish notion it was to ride into battle on a beast. Heroes came to the field in a chariot and met each other man-to-man, face-to-face, on the ground. It was said that even the Warrior Queen, Penthesilea, rode horseback into battle.

⇥ 7 ⇤

O N THE FINAL DAY OF THEIR HUNT, PENTHA AND
Hippolyta added several hares to their catch. At the top
of the last hill before home, Pentha knee-signaled Valor to
halt. To Hippolyta she said, "The horses could use a rest."

Stretched out below Pentha lay the plain of Themiskyra, a
rare strip of flatland on this otherwise rugged and rocky
southern coast of the Euxine Sea. The length of a day's
walk, this narrow band of welcoming terrain provided quite
adequate room for breeding and training the horses. Green
fields with grazing mares rested closest to her, the horses
looking like children's toys. Farther on she could see the
Amazon compound, with its training fields, corrals, barns,
and barracks. Beyond it, the fenced men's compound with
its three, high-walled, secure areas for the forges. And in the
far distance, the city of Themiskyra, home of the People of
Artemis, with the river Thermodon, a thin silver ribbon, running through it to the sea.

In Themiskyra, she had found a safe place. Keeping it safe
was her purpose in life.

"This view is always beautiful," she said, stroking Valor's
withers. She leaned down and smelled his hair, a delicious
animal scent of strength. She sat up again and sighed. "From
here all the world seems so peaceful."

"I'm sorry you had the nightmare."

"It's been over a year since the last one."

"Will you ever tell it to me?"

Guilt tightened her throat, and the tears that had overtaken her last night threatened again. Never! Her failure, her shame, would remain her secret. "It's from when I lived on Tenedos. Talking to Damon about my life there probably brought it on."

"Maybe telling me would help make it go away."

"I don't want to talk about it, dear heart. I can't."

"Nothing?"

"It involves Acheans. I hate them, Hippolyta. Especially one man." Lord Achilles, the soldiers in the street had called him, and in the years that followed, the giant Achean warrior's fame had reached even distant Themiskyra. "If I could have one dream come true, it would be to kill him"

"Do you know—"

"Let's not talk about this."

Hippolyta grinned. "Then let's talk about Phemios. I want to stop by the men's compound and invite him to spend the night with me."

"How many times have you invited him?"

"I may someday marry Phemios."

"Marry!"

"He is quite handsome. And an excellent smithy. He would make good children."

"Hippolyta, we are only twenty and four years old. It's another eight years before we can even think of marrying. And you're letting your heart settle on one man?"

"Oh fuss. Of course, you're right. But still. He is sooo handsome. Look, Gale and Valor are rested. I'll race you to the gate of the men's compound."

"Gale can never beat Valor."

Hippolyta grinned and shook her head. "I don't care. I love to race."

With that she touched her mare's side with the cue to gallop, leaned forward, and Gale took off down the hill, running like quicksilver.

"Run," Pentha said to Valor, a horse so intelligent he responded to spoken as well as touched commands.

She felt him gather himself. He shot down the hill, unwilling, she was certain from years of living and working with him, to let any horse, let alone a mare, beat him in any contest.

Pentha hugged his bare back close with her knees and thighs, felt her camp pack and quiver hitting her back and sides, felt through her legs the pull and release of his muscles, felt the wind whipping her hair. Felt freedom!

She and Valor passed Hippolyta and Gale midway to the gate. At a place not too distant from it, Pentha signaled the stallion to slow down. She and Hippolyta arrived more or less together. Still filled with the joy of the race, she thanked Artemis again for Hippolyta.

They let the horses trot a ways, to settle their hearts gradually, and when they slowed to a walk, she brought Valor close to Gale and reached out her hand. Hippolyta took it and they rode that way until they reached the rustic gate. Made from massive birch logs laid horizontally, it stood open during the day.

Pentha said, "I just hope we don't run into Trusis. Such an arrogant ass."

Hippolyta grinned. "A headman needs confidence."

"Confidence, not self-importance."

They rode inside. Only rarely did women come here. At night, husbands went to their wives' homes in the city, so married women had little reason to visit. During the day, the men returned to work, and unmarried men and young boys above the age of eight slept here.

Unmarried women came mostly to invite a man to spend the night. Pentha thought of Damon's comment, that in the outer world he'd learned that he liked to live with a woman all the time. Her own mother had left to be always with a man. The idea must appeal to some people, but she thought it exceedingly odd.

But then, she had not yet settled her heart on any man. Perhaps that might make a difference.

At this time of day, Phemios would be working iron. The furnace and forges hunkered in the center of the camp, well guarded. Equally well guarded was the secret of extracting this astonishing, hard metal from the dark stone that lay in their mountains to the south. Iron, along with fine horses, was the heart of Amazon wealth.

They knew, too, how to shape it, with brutal heat, into small implements—usable tools and weapons. Iron tipped every Amazon arrow. *Iron is our strength with the Hittites, and also our weakness.*

The Themiskyran Hearth Queen three generations removed had made a compact with the king of their notoriously aggressive southern neighbor. The Amazons would trade this precious commodity only with the Hittites. To the present, that compact held, and moreover, the mighty Hittites let the outside world believe that they held the secret of the metal. But for over a generation now the Hittites had been raiding the People of Artemis. Their present king, Hattusilis, evidently preferred to take by force what he now could have only by trading.

Hattusilis claimed the raiders were outliers, not under his control. No one in Themiskyra believed his claims, but no one could prove he lied. So from their high central plateau, the Hittites made yearly, but so far unsuccessful, attempts to take Themiskyra by force. The raids tested Themiskyran strength and determination, but were not an invasion. And fortunately, the mountains on the Themiskyran southern border loomed as a formidable barrier. Only two narrow passes led from Hittite into Themiskyran territory. If well defended, Themiskyra would never be easy to take from the south.

Nor would her people even think of breaking the agreement to trade with none save the Hittites. Losing control of iron would be so devastating to Hattusilis that, no matter how harassed he was on his other borders, especially by the Egyptians and Assyrians, he would turn his full ire on Themiskyra. Even an Amazon force guarding the narrow passes would not be able to defeat the full weight of Hittite power. But as things stood, the people of Artemis could handle the Hittites and, at the same time, the more dangerous raiding Kaskans to the west. Pentha's life here was secure. And Themiskyra would continue to trade iron for luxuries like ivory, silk, fine linen, spices, and fruits which gave life in this isolated place its elegance.

She and Hippolyta passed the men's community house. In front of it, a pack of twenty or more yelling boys with sticks raced after a stuffed leather ball the size of a cooking pot. Each scrambled to hit the ball into a pit not much larger than the ball at one end of the open ground. They lived here with their fathers. None who were playing were over thirteen, when a boy began to learn a trade—perhaps breeding the horses, perhaps digging ore, or hunting, or working iron like Phemios.

As she and Hippolyta approached the ironworks, a pack train of fifteen horses stood ready to leave. Unfortunately she saw Trusis. She also heard him. Yelling. Something he did far too often. Apparently he was inspecting the train.

"The packs are arranged entirely wrong!" This he screamed into the face of a befuddled and blushing man. "The animal is likely to tip over the edge of a cliff at the first big wind."

Hearing the sound of their horses, Trusis turned. Seeing her and Hippolyta dismount, his almost purple face shifted into a smile.

Hippolyta said, "I'll only take a short time, I promise." She passed Pentha a look of sympathy, then headed toward the forge.

8

TRUSIS QUICKLY APPROACHED PENTHA. "IT IS SO difficult to get them to pack correctly," he said. Like a nervous child, he broadened his smile still more, obviously embarrassed that she caught him indulging in such a display of temper. "But I do my best."

"I'm sure you do."

"What brings you here?" He smoothed the front of his tunic, recovering his usual stiff composure. "It's so good to see you. Our Warrior Queen graces this place of men."

"Hippolyta wanted to speak to Phemios." *And I certainly hope she keeps her promise to be quick about it.*

He patted the stallion's nose, never taking his dark gaze from her. He was slender and pleasant enough to look at. A little taller than she. A few streaks of gray were beginning to show at the temples through the dark, black hair. Because he was the leader of the Themiskyran men, she presumed he was reasonably fit, and when she occasionally watched him at games, he seemed remarkably good with a sword. But she never liked the way he looked at her.

Trusis stepped closer, eyeing the score of skins slung across Valor's rump. "I see you've been hunting. It looks as though you were successful. As you always are."

She thought about hanging upside down in a simple loop trap, and smiled. He quickly smiled back. He'd mistaken her smile, thinking it was for him.

Hippolyta hurried up to them. Goddess bless her.

They swung onto their mounts' leopard-skin riding blankets.

"Come again, Penthesilea," Trusis said, as she wheeled Valor. "Perhaps I will see you at the games at the next full moon."

At the gate, they put the horses into a trot. She felt eager, now, to get to the barracks, to bathe and change.

They passed the visiting house, built conveniently on the perimeter of the Amazon compound that bordered the men's compound, an easy walk between them. Here there were rooms for entertaining lovers at night. She thought of Damon. She envisioned herself in one of those rooms in his arms. A smile touched her lips. Perhaps it wouldn't be impossible to coax him down to the plain.

A few moments more and they reached the Amazon compound entry. No visible boundary marked it. The entire area simply occupied most of the western portion of the flat land along this stretch of shoreline. No one other than Amazons could enter. No children came here, at any age.

A cool breeze swept in from the sea, freshened with essence of seaweed and salt. By midday it would be quite warm. In the distance, fifty or sixty women on horseback practiced mounted javelin throwing. A line of similar number stood at the archery range.

She and Hippolyta rode toward the stable. The women she passed nodded to her, an informal salute. A few, close friends or her top commanders, called her name. Their greetings she returned with a nod, smile, or wave.

After dismounting, she and Hippolyta handed their halter reins to the horses' grooms. She stepped to Valor's head and pressed her cheek to his neck. To his groom she said, "Give them both an especially long rub down and brushing. We raced them. And plenty of water."

Hippolyta linked their arms as they headed for the barracks dormitory. "You should probably invite Trusis to spend at least one night," she said.

Pentha could muster only a faint smile.

"He is terribly fond of you."

"There is something about Trusis. So pompous. I can't imagine him as a lover."

"Making love to a man can often show his better side."

Pentha laughed. "You think Trusis has a better side?"

"Everyone has a better side."

She squeezed the hand resting on her arm. "You have a tender heart."

"Well, it's best for peace that the women sleep with as many of the men as possible. And I don't think you'll keep peace with Trusis if you put him off forever."

"I can try."

"Seriously, Pentha, putting him off too long will cause trouble. Besides, I am so looking forward to this night with Phemios. Do you intend to be alone?"

"If I had wanted to make love, I should have stayed with our host of last night. Now Damon is someone I could easily bed.

"But he is sooo strange, don't you think? At least Trusis doesn't live like a wild man."

Halfway to the Amazon barracks with Hippolyta, and still in conversation about their strange rescuer, Bremusa, first commander of the Amazon cavalry, caught up to them. "Gryn sent a message for you," Bremusa said to Pentha. "She's with Harmonia. They ask that as soon as you return, you come to them. It's urgent."

❧ 9 ❧

Pentha nodded a dismissal to Bremusa who strode off toward the nearest corral.

Hippolyta said, "I haven't seen mother for over a week. I'll come too."

Bremusa had said urgent. "I'm going without changing," Pentha said.

Hippolyta grinned. "Mother has kissed me many times when I was dirty and smelling of horse."

They picked fresh mounts, Pentha's Dawn and Hippolyta's Winter, then made for town at a trot. Riding past garden plots and villas, inns and shrines, Pentha felt a renewed love for her beautiful, un-walled city. She thought of Damon, and how he never entered it or participated in its life. He should be very lonely, but he hadn't seemed so.

They passed a pavilion with the statues of Themiskyra's founders. This peaceful refuge on the Euxine Sea had been created in a time lost in the misty past by others who had also suffered at the hand of Acheans. The Queen of Crete, when she fled from Achean invaders, came to the Thermodon accompanied by her lover, Alektrion, and her great teacher, the Nubian, Zuliya. As a young man, Zuliya had served as a horse trainer with the king of the Mittani. He taught the women of Themiskyra to ride. The Queen of Crete, Leesandra, instilled in the People the will to take up arms so that women should not fall prey to enslavement by Acheans, or anyone else. And Alektrion planned Themiskyra's spacious paved streets and squares, fountains, and main buildings. All had lived long and happy lives here.

An odd thought struck her. Would her life here also be long and equally happy? Surely it would. There was no reason it should not be.

All horses and weapons must be left at the city's entry, and so they left theirs. They hurried toward the main square and the Great Hall, the residence of their current Hearth Queen, Harmonia. Beside the Great Hall stood the imposing temple to Artemis. Harmonia, chosen by the People when she was forty, also served as High Priestess.

Twice they had to stop briefly to chat because Hippolyta had lived here all her life, knew practically everyone, and was dearly loved. Children of people close to her were encouraged by their parents to "show the grace of Hippolyta."

In the main square, a throng of young boys and girls galloped back and forth on stick horses, playing horse stickball around a statue of Artemis, who stood straight, with drawn arrow, a stag at her side. Suddenly a boy shouted, "It's Penthesilea!"

Play stopped. Full of childish giggles, they rushed to her and Hippolyta for a hug or a pat on the head from either sister. How happy these children were. Carefree. As Damon had said he was. Someday, when her duty to Themiskyra was fulfilled, she wanted as many children as the goddess would grant. She would marry and stop using the fennel potion and sponges that usually prevented conception. At this moment, the children's closeness suddenly made her rather wish she had taken time to bathe.

Hippolyta tugged Pentha's arm. Pentha turned to find herself looking into the disapproving face of Euryclea, who had just come out of the Great Hall. Along with Gryn and eight other women, Euryclea served as a member of the Women's Council. The children, perhaps seeing Euryclea's cross look, scampered back to their game.

"What a scandalous way to dress," said the woman who

had passionately wanted her own daughter, Marpessa, to win the contest to be Warrior Queen.

The tall, gaunt woman wore a lovely ankle-length, yellow linen gown, bare over one shoulder and clasped at the waist with a green and yellow girdle. Dark hair swirled in curls on top of her head, the tresses bound with ribbons matching the girdle. And she blocked their path.

Pentha stiffened.

Euryclea actually appeared to sniff in their direction. "Clearly you've been hunting. The two of you, you look like you've come right off the mountain."

Hippolyta said, "If we hadn't been summoned to Harmonia, I would love to hear about Marpessa. I have not seen her lately. But we are expected. Urgently."

This won a smile. "It's nice of *you* to notice, Hippolyta, that Marpessa has been away. She is still serving on the southern border." She frowned again as she looked at Pentha. "A Warrior Queen needs to set a good example. What will all these children think, Pentha, when you show no respect and come here in such a state?"

Euryclea didn't wait for explanation or answer. She clasped and twitched her skirt in a show of pique, passed them both, and strutted off.

Pentha looked at Hippolyta. They chuckled.

From the temple came the sweet sound of priestesses singing a familiar paean to Artemis. They entered the Great Hall and moving swiftly down a long side corridor, came to the living quarters of the High Priestess, Themiskyra's Hearth Queen.

The woman attending the chamber's entry bowed her head and said, "Go in, Pentha. They've been hoping you might arrive in time."

Pentha respected Harmonia who, like her room, always projected a confident welcome and flawless taste. The room was a long rectangle with a round hearth at its center. A clerestory let in light and let out smoke. In winter, the hearth blazed continually, but now, in summer and with the day already warming, the heart of the room lay at rest. Bearskin rugs warmed and softened the gray, slate floors. Murals in earth tones with splashes of bright reds and yellows gave the walls life, scenes of Artemis hunting—deer, lion, and boar.

The real leopard always found at the side of a Themiskyran Hearth Queen reclined next to the hearth, the tip of its tail twitching. Seeing it, Pentha's thoughts flew again to the mysterious Damonides and his own animal companions—falcon and wolf. *I want to see him again.*

Gryn sat before an ivory-inlaid oak table upon which sat a slate draughtboard. She held an ivory playing piece in her hand, but she was watching Harmonia. Harmonia paced, head high and back stiff, holding an ebony playing piece.

Harmonia stopped and looked at Gryn. "I simply cannot imagine what Priam was thinking!" Their Hearth Queen spoke with a slight lisp. "Surely Hekuba had no part in such a folly. I have been told repeatedly by Semele that Hecuba is a clever woman."

Priam. Hekuba. Troy's king and queen. A flicker of buried rage warmed Pentha's cheeks. Did this sudden meeting somehow involve the Acheans? Eight years now the Acheans had blockaded Troy, the royal Achilles among them. And only a short time ago she had imagined the pleasure of killing him.

Harmonia wore a simple linen gown of white with a blue shawl over her shoulders. At her ripe age of fifty and five she often found it difficult to keep warm. Her dark hair, shot with gray, was let down in a simple style one would have in private with a close friend. Nevertheless, she wore the tiara of interwoven arrows, the symbol of Artemis, that indicated her status as Hearth Queen of Themiskyra.

Gryn answered, "The Trojans, so I've been told, don't listen much to their women, wives, or mistresses. So for Hekuba, being queen may not give her words much weight. Besides, they say Helen is not just beautiful, but charming. They say she's won the hearts of both Priam and Hekuba."

Pentha's pulse quickened. Yes! This was definitely about Troy!

⊰ 10 ⊱

WITH HIPPOLYTA BESIDE HER, PENTHA ENTERED Harmonia's chamber. The two older women turned to them.

Gryn wore a long simple gown of dark green. Her chestnut hair, once the same color of chestnut as Hippolyta's, was now nearly white. She usually wore it bound at the back of her neck, but it hung to her waist, as if she had spent the night with Harmonia.

She was thick in the middle with the age of fifty and four and with having delivered four children, but otherwise still fit and agile. Strong, high cheekbones and clear, gray-green eyes composed a face that radiated the good will at her core.

Pentha strode with Hippolyta to their mother and kissed her.

"I'm so very glad you came in time," Harmonia said, looking at Pentha.

Harmonia called to the woman at the door. "Go fetch that little Hittite merchant at once!" The woman set off briskly.

Harmonia strode to the table, slapped the ebony piece next to a game board, and looked back at Pentha with fire in her eyes.

Pentha approached the leopard. The beast yawned, showing glistening white fangs. Pentha squatted beside her, cupped both hands behind her ears and rubbed hard on the soft fur to massage the muscles of her neck. For reward,

Pentha received a wet, scratching swipe of tongue across the wrist.

"The merchant, Muttalusha, has brought word from Troy," Harmonia said. "I want you to hear it from his own lips if he hasn't already started back."

Harmonia was rarely out of sorts, but clearly at this moment, she was in high dudgeon.

"How was the hunting?" Gryn asked.

Hippolyta arched an eyebrow and smiled. "Pentha got caught."

"Caught?" Harmonia gave Hippolyta a sharp look.

Would Hippolyta now tell everyone they met how she had foolishly been trapped, hung upside down for all the world to gawk at, even if the world had only been one man and her woman friend?

She cast a glare toward Hippolyta.

With a positively wicked grin, Hippolyta said, "She stepped into a loop trap, and the most unusual man came to our rescue to help me cut her down." She turned to Gryn. "It was Damonides, mother."

"That recluse?" said Harmonia.

"The very same," Hippolyta answered.

Before this exchange could become even more embarrassing, with Hippolyta graphically describing how the poor, wounded Pentha had been carried to safety in Damon's arms, the merchant hurried into the room.

The small man sported a long, gray-streaked beard. Tiny, close-set eyes of a weasel took in the room. Pentha knew him so far only by reputation. Although his name was Hittite, he claimed no country, only to be a seller of wares. Because of the nature of his life, traveling widely, he was privy to all sorts of information. And he'd never yet been caught claiming to know something that later proved untrue.

"You know our Warrior Queen," Harmonia said.

He bowed low to Pentha.

"I want you to tell her exactly what you told us. Leave nothing out."

He nodded to Harmonia. "As you wish, great Queen."

"We have been hunting for days," Pentha said. "I prefer to sit."

She took a place next to the draught table. Hippolyta and Harmonia took seats by the hearth.

"Speak," Pentha said to him.

"There has, off and on, been discord among the Achean kings laying siege to Troy."

Pentha felt the skin at the back of her neck prickle. She reached next to the game board and picked up an ebony draught piece shaped like a three-quarter moon and began to roll it.

Muttalusha hesitated.

"Go on," she said.

"Their High King, Agamemnon, apparently wished to end the war. Before this war season's first battle, Agamemnon sent a page to Priam. Agamemnon offered to convince his forces to take their ships and leave those lands and return to their homes if the Trojans would meet three conditions. They must give back the wealth that Helen and Paris took with them when she left her husband, the Spartan king Menelaos. They must pay a rather hefty tribute to the Acheans. And they must surrender Helen to Menelaos." He paused.

"And?"

"Priam refused."

"Can you imagine," Harmonia burst in, leaping once more to her feet. "Priam must be the world's greatest fool. All this bloodshed and waste could have ended."

The merchant continued. "The Acheans subsequently lost the first engagement. Rather badly. Although their encampment in the bay south of Troy was still quite secure when I left."

Pentha had the strangest feeling. The merchant claimed that Agamemnon offered to go home and take his thousands of warriors with him—and she had felt a jolting stab of disappointment. Almost anger.

If the Acheans went home, Achilles would surely go with them. And then, under no circumstances she could imagine, could she enjoy a bloody revenge. She could never make him pay for her mother or for Derinoe. Of course, there was no way she could do that now, but this strange disappointment made clear that a place in her heart clung to the possibility of revenge.

She asked, "Do they continue their blockade of the Hellespont?"

"Yes, Queen Penthesilea. No one passes into the straits without paying the Acheans now. Including myself. They are enlarging their coffers quite nicely."

Harmonia asked, her dark eyes burning, "Have the Acheans learned the secret of its navigation from the Thraceans?"

He shook his head, a nervous jerk, as if he expected that Harmonia might hold him personally to blame should this disaster have occurred. "The secret of that great feat," said the merchant, "still lies with the Thracian family of Grammeron. Only their clan knows how to guide a ship so as to defeat the winds, the treacherous currents, the shoals. This very last trip. I will tell you. It was the worst ever! The rocks. The waves." He put his hands to his head, a gesture dramatically emphasizing alarm and thus his own bravery. "I was certain the Furies were coming for me."

Pentha felt no worry about an Achean attack by land. Long distance and rugged terrain separated the Acheans from Themiskyra, the reason the People of Artemis had been spared the eight years of Achean savagery inflicted on cities and kingdoms along the Aegean coast. And although passage south through the straights was easily done, passing north, without whatever secret the family of Grammeron possessed, was impossible. But if the Acheans could bring their ships through the straits and the Sea of Marmora and then into the Euxine Sea itself, no more than a few days stood between them and Themiskyra.

Muttalusha continued while looking around from chair to bench as if hoping someone would invite him to sit. "The Acheans seem willing to let it remain the Grammerons' secret, so long as it's the Acheans, not Priam, who collect the taxes from ships allowed to pass. And so long as the Grammerons don't pilot any ship in league with Troy."

Harmonia sat again by Gryn, who put a comforting hand over Harmonia's.

Pentha stood, and still turning the draught piece, took Harmonia's place at pacing.

To the merchant she said, "Have the Thracians broken their vow to Priam? Are they piloting Achean ships?"

"Not to my knowledge, most honored."

So Themiskyra was still safe. A weight like a boulder of iron oar lifted from her shoulders, and that pleased her. At least her desire for revenge didn't extend so far that she would have Achilles and his horde attack here just so she could enjoy the personal satisfaction of killing him.

Harmonia asked, "Have you further questions, Pentha?"

She shook her head.

To Muttalusha, Harmonia said, "You are dismissed."

He bowed deeply, turned, and scurried out.

Harmonia stood again. "I have never liked Priam. He opposed us and supported Bellerophon against us." Her voice expressed grief now, not anger. "He was very young then, but I doubt he's changed much. He does not like me, and I think that now I must detest him. Why didn't he give back the woman and her wealth? Why not end this nightmare for his people and for all the country that surrounds Troy?"

Gryn sighed. "For us, at least, the news is good. The Acheans still have no access to the Euxine Sea. Although I am tempted to say something that may sound shocking."

Hippolyta patted her mother's hand. "Say it."

"Sometimes I almost long for serious battle. I remember glorious days when I was young, when Iobates set Bellerophon on us and we ventured with our men out of Themiskyra."

Pentha felt a jab of surprise. *What a strange thing for mother to want. To fight alongside men!*

"I admit we had terrible losses," Gryn continued. "That's why, of course, I say my feelings are shocking. But . . ." Her eyes had a wistful look. "I think I miss the excitement. I miss the tight companionship we had with the men. Now our horsewomen are enough to police the western and southern borders, and we still have peace in the east. The men are left to their lives, and we to ours."

Harmonia shook her head. "Dear Gryn, I'm indeed amazed that you should think such a thing. The whole point is that by our defense we live at peace. We don't need our men to waste themselves on war."

Gryn sighed. "Yes, I know. It was just so. . . ."

With only half her attention, Pentha followed what the two women shared about the "glorious days." Finally a nagging fear found its voice. "Do you think Muttalusha is telling the truth? That the Acheans are still barred from the Euxine?"

Both gazes fixed on her.

To Harmonia she said, "What word does Semele send you from Troy with the pigeons?"

"Messages come weekly. It has been some time since she has sent any word concerning the matter of the Hellespont, but if there were any significant change, she would have informed me at once."

Semele served as priestess of Artemis at Troy. Once the most honored of all the divinities in Troy, Artemis had fallen from that high pinnacle. Sadly, Trojans once faithful to Artemis had accepted the horror of the submission of women, an evil common now in much, perhaps most, of the outside world. So they strayed from worship of the goddess who was women's greatest champion. Semele served faithfully, but to only a handful of worshippers. Apollo's temple sat now in the Trojan citadel's most honored place. And another temple by the palace honored Athena. The same Athena the Acheans claimed as *their* greatest champion among the gods.

Pentha stared at the floor, a beautiful day having somehow slipped into gloom. To no one in particular she said, "I pray that Grammeron and his family remain faithful to their oath to Priam. I pray they continue to refuse to bring Acheans into the Euxine Sea. But oaths, as we all know, even ones taken by good men, can be broken."

❧ 11 ❧

THE DRESSMAKER FITTING HER FOR A NEW DANC-
ing gown of an exquisite golden color had been delayed
so Derinoe, dressed in a suitably conservative dark blue
gown that matched her eyes, hurried uphill on Troy's main
thoroughfare toward the citadel, dodging heavy foot traffic
and the curtained and gilded litters of the wealthy.

Troubled thoughts crowded her mind as she passed
through the citadel's southern gate and into the royal
precinct. One of the few donkey carts allowed inside clut-
tered noisily past. Empty clay wine jars rattling in it bore the
mark of the palace stores.

The owner lashed the poor donkey with a willow rod and
cursed. Derinoe would curse too if she thought it would do
any good. Instead, she was meeting on this early summer
day with Cassandra to pray.

The wine vendor headed downhill over the cobble toward
the gate and the city beyond. His residence and warehouse
would be there, as were her two modest rooms. She passed a
royal bakeshop and her mouth watered at the smell of fresh
bread.

After so many years of the Achean blockade, the general
air she always felt from the Trojans when passing along
Troy's streets or visiting shops was somber. The sad mood
lifted for short periods after Trojan forces struck a victory,
but sunk again when the war went badly. In three days, Hek-

tor would once more lead his men against the Acheans. She and Hektor's sister, Cassandra, would sacrifice at the temple to Athena for Hektor's success. Or if not success, she thought, at least his safe return. He must come back safe.

The bronze gate of the home of Cassandra, daughter of Priam, king of Troy, stood twice as tall as a man. Its builders had affixed owls to the bronze work, perched solemnly or in flight and rendered in silver. Owls were Athena's symbols, and Athena the goddess who owned Cassandra's passionate devotion.

Today the gateposts, faced with polished white limestone, reminded Derinoe of whitened bones. She entered the reception courtyard and immediately heard children's laughter. Her son and daughter would be playing with them.

Cassandra let Derinoe's children spend their days with the children of Cassandra's lady-in-waiting because Cassandra was Derinoe's mentor and friend, and because Derinoe's daughter by Hektor was Cassandra's niece. Derinoe had shared the secret of her pregnancy with Cassandra as soon as Derinoe knew she carried Hektor's child. She owed her very life to Cassandra. She would not have lied even if she had wanted to. Fortunately, Cassandra had been pleased, not at all alarmed or distressed, by the news.

Cassandra loved her brother dearly. For that matter, so did everyone in Troy. Priam's oldest son, the heir to Troy's throne, was widely regarded as a man of high honor and great courage. So it wasn't surprising that Cassandra wanted his child—even if a secret child got of a mistress—to be well cared for. Derinoe had often heard Hektor express gratitude to Cassandra for her thoughtfulness to Derinoe and both of her children.

Derinoe headed for the children's garden, hurrying down a narrow flagstone path and through the shoulder-high hedge that separated the children's area from the entry. Yellow, red, and blue flowers lined the perimeter. A black and white marble dolphin, big enough for children to ride on hot summer days, leapt from a fountain in the garden's center. Such a cheerful place, so unlike Derinoe's troubled spirit.

Seven laughing youngsters vied to catch and throw a red ball at each other, the point of the familiar game to be the one hit by the ball the least number of times. Seeing Derinoe, Alcmene, the lady-in-waiting, smiled but, having a crying one-year-old in her arms, did not rise.

Derinoe's son, Leonides, and her daughter, Myrina, ran to Derinoe. Leonides, almost eight this year, hugged her around the waist while two-year-old Myrina hugged her leg. The feeling of their eager young bodies passionately clutching her own made her forget her worry for a happy moment.

After receiving a pat on the head and a smile, Myrina ran back to her playmates. But Leonides held one of Derinoe's hands and stared at the ground.

"What is it, love?" she said.

He already looked so much like his own father. The same wavy chestnut hair and dark eyes. And although Leonides was a year younger than Alcmene's oldest boy, Leonides was already the taller of the two.

"Who is my father?"

Derinoe sucked in a surprised breath.

"And who is Myrina's father?"

"Leonides. What . . . what makes you ask?"

"You've never told me."

She really should go to Cassandra, but Derinoe tilted his chin up. The look in his eyes told her she must make some answer to his question, now. She led him to a bench well away from the others. She sat and he stood in front of her, looking her straight in the eyes.

"I understand that you want to know. Even that you feel very deep in your heart that you must know. But my sweet, I cannot tell you."

"Why not?"

"Can you not just trust me? Can you just believe that if I could, and if it would be a good thing to do, I would tell you?"

He stared at her, and the look was not one of trust.

"Why are you asking?"

"Today Lady Andromache visited Lady Cassandra. And

she did something very strange. She came here to the children's garden."

Andromache! Derinoe felt her heart thud and then begin to race. While her greatest safety in Troy lay with Hektor, her greatest danger in Troy lay with Hektor's wife, the famously jealous Andromache.

She said, "It is a bit strange for such a grand lady. But maybe she likes to watch children playing."

"She didn't pay attention to anyone but Myrina."

A faint rush of nausea struck. "What did she do?"

"She walked right up to Myrina and said, 'You're the daughter of the dancer Derinoe, aren't you?' She touched Myrina's hair and then said, 'What a pretty child. Tell me, who is your father?' But she didn't ask me."

Derinoe forced a laugh, pathetic even to her own ears. "What a strange thing to do, indeed. Myrina can barely talk let alone answer such a question." But Myrina also had her father's hair—in her case, that hair that was black and curly. She also had Hektor's eyes.

Derinoe's mind raced forward. *I should not panic.*

"So you won't tell me who my father is. Or who Myrina's is."

She hugged him, to reassure him, and from his warmth to reassure herself. When she pulled away she said, "I love you. And I promise you that when you are older, when you are a man, I will tell you. But I simply cannot tell you now."

He studied her, hesitation in his eyes.

"I give you my solemn promise."

He gave her a stern look.

She stood, her heart a tight fist in her chest. "I am late. I must go."

He turned and walked back to the children. How beautiful he was. And ultimately, how trusting.

⇥ 12 ⇤

ERINOE SPED FROM THE CHILDREN'S GARDEN
to Cassandra's dressing chamber. "Andromache went
to see Myrina today," she said at once.

Cassandra posed before a polished cedar wardrobe inlaid
with sprays of olive branches in ivory. The fragrance of
dried cherry blossoms hung heavily, ominously, in the air.
She wore a rusty-red gown that matched her auburn curls. A
golden girdle caught the gown at the waist, and her sandals
were of gold inlaid leather.

Of only moderate stature, Cassandra stood several fingers
shorter than Derinoe. She'd piled her waist-length hair onto
her head, much as Derinoe had done with her own dark curls.
A garland of white hyacinth wound through and bound the
tresses.

Cassandra smiled, and her light brown eyes, as always,
flashed with vitality. "Deri, worry lines are creasing your
forehead. They will dig tracts there. And I saw just this
morning, in my washbasin water, that today will be a day of
good news. We needn't worry."

"Cassandra, dear. Didn't you hear? Andromache went to
see Myrina today."

"Myrina? Andromache came to me with a message from
Hektor."

She picked out a gauzy shawl of light brown wool and,

throwing it over her shoulders, studied the effect in a polished copper mirror next to be wardrobe.

"But," Derinoe persisted, "she stopped in the garden. And she asked Myrina who her father is."

"Then, perhaps she suspects. It's very hard to keep a secret in our small world."

"You know what she did to the other woman."

Cassandra replaced the brown shawl and took a dark-red one. "Which woman?" she said, draping the shawl over her shoulders.

"I will always believe Andromache had the woman and her two children killed."

Cassandra turned and stared at her, then stepped to her and took her by the hand. "The woman disappeared years ago. There is no way to know that Andromache was responsible. Perhaps the woman simply decided to leave Troy."

"I don't believe that. And I doubt you do either. Andromache is fiercely jealous of Hektor. She wants to live in the fantasy that he is steadfastly devoted only to her."

Cassandra drew them to a couch so they could sit. She said, "I won't lie to you. Hektor does love Andromache. Never doubt it. And he adores his children. But he also loves you. Andromache would not dare to make a move against you while Hektor lives."

"Things can be done—in secret."

"As I just said, it's very difficult to keep any secrets in Troy." She hugged Derinoe. "Besides, I have seen your future. You will live happily into great old age, Deri. Don't worry."

"What of my children? What of Myrina?"

"I've not seen their futures."

"If anything happens to either of my children, I can assure you that I will not live into old age, happily or otherwise."

"Then you should be at peace. I have foreseen that you will be happy." Cassandra stood. "So, I'm ready. Let's us go and honor Athena and pray for my brother's victory."

As they linked arms, Derinoe said, "I would love to have peace."

But she would worry. Her life from the moment of her mother's death had never been free from worry.

She thought of Achilles and what she had had to do to escape him. And the degrading things she'd done in order to survive when she reached Troy without family or resources. Years of terror and worry had passed before the fates crossed her path with Cassandra's and some small light touched her life.

But that small light had not brought peace.

❧ 13 ❧

DAMON STRODE TO THE CABIN'S OPEN WINDOW. His gaze turned, as it did many times a day, to the green arrowhead Pentha had fashioned and tossed to him casually, but with that questioning, perhaps even suggestive, look in her eyes. It still hung by a leather thong in the window's center where he placed it the day she left. It had dangled there for nearly two moon cycles.

He took the arrowhead in hand, ambled into his front yard, and sat on a stump by the door. Little Wolf followed, flopped down and laid his short muzzle on Damon's sandaled toe.

Damon rubbed the arrowhead's surface with his thumb while inhaling a deep, reflective breath. Ash smoke from his hearth, friendly and familiar, filled him briefly with a sense of belonging and calm. But then the empty feeling of longing settled in his chest again like a stone.

"I suppose I should have sufficient will to put her out of my mind."

He thought a moment, than looped the thong over his head and let the arrowhead rest on his chest.

He glanced at Little Wolf and grinned. "What? Don't look at me like that! It's good luck to carry something strong. You can't blame a man for wanting good luck."

Damon stood. The pup scrambled to its feet. Growing fast, Little Wolf easily kept up now when they went out together.

"Time to check traps. Let's see what we've caught for dinner."

As they walked through the gate of the thornbush barrier he said, "Maybe another Amazon?"

❧ 14 ❧

ACHILLES POURED ANOTHER HALF A GOBLET OF wine, sipped it, paced to and glanced over a tapestry on his tent wall showing the sack of Thebes, then paced back to the table. He was quite certain he had found the perfect source for the information he needed, and anxious for that source to arrive.

A male slave entered, and behind him a man wearing odd, brown leggings, black boots, and an elaborately embroidered, multi-colored tunic. "The merchant, Muttalusha, Lord Achilles," said the slave, who then backed out of the tent, leaving Achilles alone with the Hittite.

Achilles took a chair and gestured for the nervous-looking merchant to take one as well. A man with small, dark, eyes, Muttalusha's greeting smile had been thin-lipped, the cue that made him appear so on edge.

"I understand you have traveled often through the Hellespont and to the lands to the east along the coast of the Euxine. How long before your next trip?"

"Yes, Lord Achilles. I make the journey regularly. I leave again within the week."

The merchant spoke Achean, as did the Trojans and many of the people of this region, but Muttalusha's accent had a peculiar Hittite lilt to it. "You and I are going to become partners."

"I do feel honored, sire, but I take no partners."

"Partners is, actually, the wrong word. You are going to work for me."

The merchant's face paled.

"I am not proposing to take a portion of your profits. Set your mind to rest on that account."

Muttalusha twisted a ring on the small finger of his left hand.

"I am going to pay you for information. And I expect you to keep our agreement secret."

"I am most happy to supply you with information, Lord Achilles. You need not pay me."

"I am going to pay you. Because I am going to ask you to get information for me that will be—sensitive. It's only right, since sharing such information with me may entail some risk on your part, that you be paid. I will pay you in gold and amber three times what you make on one of your circuits to the east. I will send you a down payment tomorrow, after we have agreed."

Muttalusha continued to twist the ring, which appeared to be a ruby. Apparently this Hittite did quite well for himself.

"What kind of information?"

"I want to know, first of all, the numbers and names of all the members of the Thracian Grammeron family who know the secret of piloting through the Hellespont."

The merchant nodded. *Good!*

Achilles explained further that he wanted to know the details of the layout of Themiskyra. How far it lay from its harbor, the nature of its defenses, where the Amazons were barracked. He asked for a detailed description of the merchant's last trip up the Hellespont, and midway through the description he poured himself more wine. He made no offer of drink to the merchant.

When the telling was over, Muttalusha said, "My lord, may I be so bold to ask, exactly why you would want this information?"

"I should think that would be obvious, even to a peddler."

At the word "peddler," he sensed that Muttalusha stiffened, pride offended. The man was not the total rabbit he appeared to be.

"I want Amazon horses. And I want Amazon slaves."

"I certainly can understand your interest in their horses. They are wonderfully bred. But as for taking Amazons for slaves. All such women are good for is to look at. They are ready mankillers. They would never accept the harness of a slave."

"I had one once. She was surpassingly beautiful." In his mind he saw Derinoe's raven-dark waves of hair, fair skin, fine features, and deep blue eyes. And those long, firm but slender, legs. "Full of fire."

"Were you able to sell her at a good price?"

"Sadly, no. I don't know her fate. The clever little thing escaped."

"Not at all surprised, my lord."

"They will sell, and at a great price, for men who want fire and novelty."

"I defer to your judgment."

"One more thing. Possibly the most important. I have heard rumors that it is not the Hittites who know the secret of making iron but the Amazons. Do you think that's true?"

"My lord, I have not heard this. It seems unlikely."

"I want you to find out."

"This would be . . . I can't imagine . . . I cannot promise."

"You are to try, and if the rumor is true, I will double what I've said I would pay."

"I understand. I will do what I can."

"You are dismissed, Mutallusha."

The Hittite stood, bowed low. He turned and started for the tent opening. Achilles rose and strode quickly to him and spun him around. Holding him by his tunic, pulling him onto his toes, and fixing his gaze with a fierce look he said, "You agree that what I have said I will pay for this information is generous."

Mutallusha nodded quickly.

"Then remember this. If you reveal to anyone else the nature of the information I have asked you to gather, if you reveal you are gathering *any* information for me, I will personally cut off your balls and feed them to my dogs, along with your heart." He paused. "Understood?"

Again Mutallusha nodded.

Achilles released his hold and watched the little man scurry out. Tomorrow he would send the down payment. He did not expect it to be returned. All men loved one thing above all others, and for Muttalusha, that loved thing was wealth.

❧ 15 ❧

HOLDING A DEAD QUAIL AND TWO DEAD HARES, Damon stomped into his cabin, followed by Little Wolf. He flung his catch onto the table, then strode to the washbasin and filled it with water.

He scooped some over his face and the back of his neck. The water smacked him with a late September chill. He untied the leather thong holding his hair, ran his fingers through the strands. He dried his face, tossed the towel next to the basin, then retied the leather.

He should be happy. He'd caught all he needed. His days were filled with activities—checking and setting his traps, caring for Dia and his other animals, working with leather, keeping the cabin in good repair. By the gods, though, he was bored.

Maybe worse than bored.

He had created a life that had no reminders of war or killing, his own or those by others. He didn't have to deal with people or the nausea of the morbid colors their speech thrust on him. But all that had been upset one late afternoon when the cursed Amazon blundered into a trap.

This longing for her was hugely impractical. Wildly unrealistic.

He stretched out the leg of a dead hare, and with the chopping knife, lopped the leg off at the joint with more than necessary force. Hare fur made particularly good roughage for

Dia. He took it to her. She clamped the cut leg to her perch by stepping onto it with the talons of one foot. With razor sharp beak, she broke the skin and started feasting.

Damon stared at her foot, watched her ripping fur and flesh.

With one hand, he grabbed the green arrowhead still hanging by the leather thong around his neck. One great tug and he ripped it from its resting place. He stared at it, elegant and deadly, then walked out the door into the courtyard. Holding the thong, he spun the arrowhead once over his head and then let go.

The arrowhead sailed up and almost, but not quite, over the whitethorn hedge.

Despite his intention never to lay eyes on it again, he noted where within the hedge that it fell.

Feeling unburdened, but also strangely disappointed, he returned to the cabin. Once more he stood in front of Dia, watching her reduce the hare's leg to bloody shreds. She had finished her molt and he was flying her again. That, at least, pleased him

He touched the place on his chest where the arrowhead had lain but quickly pulled his hand away. He returned to the table, picked up his catch, and walked outside, intending to clean them and feed Little Wolf. The quail and the hares hung heavy in his hand, like the weight pressing on his heart.

Little Wolf sat watching him, head cocked to one side. Damon dropped his catch and turned to where the arrowhead struck the hedge.

"Damn the woman!"

After finding a good long stick, he approached the hedge at the place closest to where the arrowhead had disappeared. The barrier—its span four feet and its height six feet—was still quite leafy. He squatted, hoping to glimpse the arrowhead on the ground at the base of the scrub where he could fish it out with the stick. Nothing.

Walking backward to the place where he'd stood when he threw it, he checked once more where he was certain it had disappeared. Sure that he had the right spot, he returned, dropped onto his hands and knees, and using his elbows and arms to keep thorns from his face, trusting that his long-sleeved tunic and trousers would give his skin protection, forced his way in a foot or so.

He shoved, wriggled, and searched the bush and ground and finally caught sight of it dangling arm's length above the dirt. Using the stick, he stabbed at the thong until the arrow-head dropped. He dragged it closer, clutched it, then slowly backed out of the hedge.

With Little Wolf sitting beside him, watching him intently, Damon studied his prize. His forehead burned, so he touched his hand to it. His hand came away bloody. For that matter, both hands bled from scratches. His shirtsleeves were even pushed up so that his forearms bled.

He started laughing. Tears came to his eyes. Still laughing, he flung himself backward onto the ground, arms outstretched, and stared into the blue sky. Slowly, his laughter subsided.

No doubt remained. The peace he had created was shattered.

But maybe this kind of peace wasn't what he wanted. He would go into Themiskyra. He could buy supplies for the winter. He certainly needed figs and barley for bread. He could also use some raising of spirits with fermented mare's milk, something he didn't know how to make and couldn't store if he did.

And he would find out what Pentha was doing and where she was.

He leapt to his feet and retied the arrowhead around his neck. With revived spirits, he lopped off the hare's other leg and tossed it to Little Wolf.

"I'll probably live to regret it. But I'm going to fetch Bias to take care of you. Then I'm going into Themiskyra. I'm going to find Pentha."

He stared at the hedge, not seeing it but instead seeing Pentha standing at his gate in front of it. "I want to hear and see her voice again."

❧ 16 ❧

THE NARROW, TWISTING, AND SOMEWHAT DANGER-
ous trail Damon chose to reach Themiskyra seldom saw
travelers. Virtually everyone from the territory around his
cabin used a broader, gently curving path that led out of the
high country in a gradual descent until it joined the
flagstone-paved road coming from the bay at the mouth of
the Thermodon. Damon chose the high "back door," faster
by two hours or more.

Providing, of course, that one did not plunge over the
side of several cliffs through which it cut. Or did not encounter, as he had just done, a rockfall that must be
cleared.

He studied the rubble. Not really too bad. Only fist-to
bucket-sized stones.

Standing patiently behind him was the donkey he bor-
rowed from Bias's family for supply and trading trips. Bias
brought the donkey to the cabin. Damon gave the boy in-
structions for the care of Dia, Wolf, the ferrets, chickens, and
goat, and when Damon returned, Bias took the donkey home.

Bias called her Pleasant. That pretty much described her
nature. She was also sure-footed, which meant she could not
be hurried. Since Damon rarely hurried anywhere, that usually suited him. On this trip, though, he wanted to see Pentha
as quickly as he could manage. Several times he urged
Pleasant to make an exception—to no avail.

He secured her lead rope around a boulder, made quick work of the debris on the path, and they were off again.

He reveled in a clear, bright day that seemed the very essence of his own mood. Now and then he saw the red flash of a linnet or heard the pugnacious calls of jays. From occasional patches of deep woods came the tappings of woodpeckers at work.

Within the hour he caught a glimpse of a rainbow of bright colors not far ahead on the trail—reds, greens, and yellows mostly—the coat of a man leading three donkeys. How peculiar to see anyone here.

The narrow trail had few places that would allow two donkeys to pass. He stopped Pleasant and backed her. By the time he found a wide enough spot, the man had reached him.

"Thank you so very much for backing," the short little man said. "I fear I took a wrong turn. But this trail will lead me to the mouth of the Thermodon, will it not?"

"It will."

"Well that, at least, is fortunate."

"I see you carry pigeons."

"Ah, yes. I am Muttalusha. A merchant. And I supply the Hearth Queen with signal carriers."

Damon watched the man, who had a Hittite lilt to his Achean, as the man and his three pack animals moved on. Very peculiar. How could anyone possibly make a mistake and take this trail?

Damon turned and set off again. Perhaps he had lived alone too long. Was he now suspicious of people for no good reason?

A little over an hour later, at shortly past midday, he turned a corner and there, spread out below, at the end of a trail that descended steeply in tight switchbacks, lay the Thermodon valley. Although the sun shown brightly, the north wind blew cold, especially on this elevated and exposed ridge. It whistled through a narrow spot in the rocks behind him, and the whistling created a shimmering, not unpleasant, green aura.

Damon stopped. Directly below, lay the grand city, home

to three times as many people as the ten thousand residents of Troy. Damon had seen Troy three times, and while its white walls and proud towers jutted in magnificence above the Trojan plain, the vast expanse of unwalled Themiskyra, with its white fountains and colorful gardens, easily matched Troy's beauty.

Above the city, staggered at various levels, circled half a dozen birds—Black Kites, suspended unmoving, using a strong midday rising air current to lift them, without effort on their part, to high elevation.

Far off to the left, the Amazon compound and training grounds stretched along the coast, brown pastures and fields extending as far as he could see. In this compound, the barracks for what he estimated must be three thousand women, drawn from all the cities, towns, and villages of the Thermodon, stood closest to the city. Damon had made this trip once in spring and remembered now that when grasses were fresh and high, the Amazon grounds had been a long strip of vivid green.

Between the city and Amazon compound lay the men's compound, with its perpetual black smoke rising from the forges.

Descent took only half an hour. The home of a carpenter and her family nestled against the bottom of the hill. When he came on these trips, this family let him spend the night bedded down in their barn, allowing him to meet Gryn while avoiding Themiskyra. A daughter, a fifteen-year-old dressed in winter trousers and tunic, ran out to greet him.

"Damon," she said, smiling as if the sun had risen after a week of foggy days. She planted a kiss on his cheek. "Shall I take word to Gryn that you're here?"

Her voice reminded him again what it would mean to go into the city. "No." He led Pleasant to a water trough and tied her, then sat on a stump with a good view of the wide dirt road.

"Would you like mare's milk?" the girl asked.

"It's a bit early in the day for that. Later tonight. For now, just water."

She brought water and began chatting about a piglet. His thoughts wandered. He must have winter supplies. And he had come here determined to see Pentha. But going into Themiskyra would be a descent into Hades.

He stood and paced, uncertainty gnawing at his stomach. *Why have I been cursed with these colors! Why must I suffer a lifetime affliction that makes it so hard for me to be with people or to have friends?*

The girl watched with wide-eyed surprise.

He said, "I'm going into town."

He would give much, suffer much, to see Pentha again. He reached where the arrowhead still lay against his chest and felt its shape under his tunic.

"Care well for the donkey. I should be back by evening."

AT THE CITY'S MASSIVE oak gate, decorated with carvings of stags, boars, and hunting dogs, the crush of people and talk began the assault on Damon's senses. He squared his shoulders, took a steadying breath.

He had barely passed inside when the babble finally did its work. He backed into a doorway, closed his eyes, and covered his ears. Sweat rose on his forehead. He sucked in several great gulps of air.

With one or two people, deep breathing sufficed. But deep breathing didn't touch this nausea. He ran to the alley beside the building, ducked two steps down it before he knelt and threw up. When he'd finished, he stood and wiped sweat from his forehead and face with his sleeve.

"Blessed Artemis, I need to see Pentha again, but this is a horrible price."

From experience he knew that if he remained surrounded with many people, the severe response would eventually pass—it took a day or two. In fact, throwing up had made him feel better already.

He returned to the main thoroughfare, plowed ahead, craving something to drink so he could wash his mouth. At a taverna he asked for a cup of water. He took it out the back, rinsed his mouth, and spat into the gutter.

The directions to Gryn's house were exactly as she had described. But once more along the way, he stopped to withdraw for a few moments into the relative quiet of an alley.

Gryn had said that after her husband died, she looked for another, but couldn't find any man that pleased her so much. So she settled for inviting a man to visit at night, until she or the man tired of each other. Her housemaid, a sun-browned crone with a cloud of white hair was dressed in a red woolen gown. She informed him that Gryn was ill. "Perhaps something she ate. She will want to see you. Do you want to wait for her to dress?"

"No. Tell her I'm glad it isn't serious. Tell her I will meet her tomorrow."

His pulse raced at the mere thought of seeing Pentha. He felt fifteen again, with hands and feet too large for his body. "By any chance, is the lady Penthesilea here?"

"You can find her at the parade grounds. This morning she and her women put on a show for the Honorable Harmonia. This afternoon, anyone who wants to may visit the Amazons and their horses."

Having received directions, he set off. He soon found himself on the western edge of the city. In a large, oval field, women, men, and horses mingled. The Amazons stood out because they wore trousers and tunics and had their hair braided and bound simply at the back of their necks while the ladies of Themiskyra wore fall gowns and shawls and their hairstyles ranged through a variety of elegant efforts favoring curls. Gay music—drums, sistrums, flutes, cythera— set a festive tone. Themiskyrans loved their music. And he realized this was perhaps the greatest pleasure he missed by living in isolation.

He looked for startling, gold-tinged red hair, but didn't at once locate his quarry. Then the head and chest of a gray stallion rose above the crowd, his front hooves pawing the air. And right in front of the magnificent beast, Damon saw the red hair.

He walked, slowly, toward her. Would she be surprised? Pleased? Maybe not pleased. He felt gazes from the crowd on him. He heard whispers. Hippolyta had said that he was talked about here, that he was considered a rebel and odd. Were the whispers hostile? Or just curious?

Pentha and her horse commanded the center of attention. She looked radiant. At least thirty people stood watching, including Hippolyta and two other Amazons. These two stood nearly as tall as Pentha, one with huge chest and arms and fair-colored hair, the other equally fair-haired and marked by a long scar on her right cheek. Closest to Pentha stood a slender, fit-looking man, a little taller than she. Streaks of gray showed at the temples of his dark black hair. He wore no coat, just winter trousers and a tunic. But his tunic was every bit as impressive as the coat of the merchant Muttalusha. Rather dandy for the average man of Artemis.

With a flick of a long birch prod, Pentha urged the stallion to rise again. The crowd clapped and breathed sounds of awe and delight. Then she saw Damon.

She broke into a huge smile. By the goddess, what a smile.

He walked up to her, nodded, then said, "Your mother's housemaid said I might find you here."

❧ 17 ❧

"Damonides! Damon." Pentha gestured to the two Amazons beside her. "Let me introduce Bremusa and Clonie. These are my head commanders, my great strength. Indeed, they are like one."

Bremusa possessed the impressive arms and chest. Clonie bore the scar. And Pentha's clear yellow voice cut through the murky aura around the whole scene. He bowed his head in greeting, and both women touched the back of their clenched fists to their forehead, the Amazon salute.

All this talk— He sucked in a breath, hoped very much he wouldn't throw up again. The yellow color could not blot out all other sensation.

"You know my sister, Hippolyta."

He nodded to Hippolyta, who mercly smiled back, a warm smile. "And this," Pentha said, turning to the man beside her, "is Trusis, our headman. Trusis handles all things involving the men."

Damon gazed at a man who looked as if he had just eaten something sour. Puckered lips. Creased brow.

Remembering the look of pleasure on Pentha's face when she'd first seen him moments ago, Damon knew that this Trusis, if he did not already possess Pentha, wanted her every bit as much as Damon did. The headman did not appreciate her warm response to an intruding stranger.

"Trusis," she said, "Damonides once did me a great favor."

"I know you," Trusis said. "You are the recluse who lives with *animals* in a *cabin* in the mountains."

The words "animals" and "cabin" oozed with the same sourness that wrinkled the man's face.

Damon returned the smile with one of his own. "Yes, I'm quite partial to animals." A pile of fresh horse manure lay just behind Trusis' left foot. Just how arrogant was the man? Damon added, keeping his tone friendly, "Speaking of animals, don't step backward."

The headman shot Damon the look of a man who would not be told what he should or should not do, and stepped back. He planted his foot in the dung. Slipped. Plopped on top of it. The rich aroma rose around him.

The crowd burst into laughter. Pentha, Damon noticed, fought to smother hers. Damon reached down toward the headman, to give him a hand up.

Trusis ignored Damon's hand. He pushed himself off the manure and sprang to his feet. Face red, the man rushed off.

Pentha stepped close and laid her hand on Damon's arm. She smelled of horse sweat and sea. He wanted to make love to her, as soon as he or the gods could arrange.

He pushed his thoughts back to Trusis. "There are many ways to get close to animals."

She and her commanders and Hippolyta dissolved into laughter. When Pentha had caught her breath, he said, "Your horse is astonishing."

She stroked the gray's dark muzzle. "My Valor—there is none like him. Few horses have the great-heartedness of spirit and strength in the legs to do the rise."

A dark-haired woman wearing a golden wreath of intertwined arrows approached. She walked with the dignity of a leader, and only the Hearth Queen would wear such a wreath. This must be Harmonia.

Pentha introduced him. Harmonia accepted the bow of his head with a smile. She had a calming air about her, but when she said, with a faint lisp, "I have seen your workmanship. I'd say there is no finer work in leather," the aura surrounding her voice was the usual dirty, gray-brown.

Pentha said, "It is our good fortune, Damon, that you chose to come today. I have a great favor to ask."

Damon was inclined to do Pentha any favor she might possibly imagine. He waited.

"We Amazons are experts with bow, axe, and javelin. But I'm convinced our skill with the sword does not match the skill of some others. Of the Acheans, for example." She spoke the word Achean with lips twisted suggesting not respect, but distaste. "You fought with the Acheans. Rumors often came back to Themiskyra of your daring and skill in battle."

Did rumors also come back telling how many people I killed? Including women and children?

Pentha turned to Bremusa. "Fetch us a pair of swords and shields," she said. Then turning back to Damon, "I want you to test me. I've been practicing, but I have only other Amazons. Clonie is good," she smiled at her cheek-scarred commander, "but you," she looked at him again, "you are Achean-trained. I'm willing, right now, to have you make a fool of me if you can."

Bremusa returned with two swords and shields. He looked at them, then at Pentha. "I have no desire to make a fool of you. I doubt I could."

"Please, Damon. You will be doing me the greatest favor. I want to see your moves, feel your manner of attack."

How could he tell her, how could he make any of the men and women now gathering around them understand how profoundly he loathed even the thought of touching a sword? Frowning, he shook his head.

Harmonia said, "Do indulge us, Damonides. I, too, would like to see an Achean-trained swordsman in action."

Hippolyta laughed. "I am taking bets. I think Damon will either land the first skin touch or will disarm Pentha."

Smiling, Pentha said to her sister. "I'm not so bad that you should feel safe betting against me."

He could do it. It wouldn't kill him. And Pentha clearly would be amazed and perhaps insulted if he refused. She had asked as a favor . . . still. "A long time ago I gave up the life of the sword."

She grinned, a wicked grin that put fiery sparks in her eyes. "Then when I best you, you will have a good excuse to feel no shame."

She took one of the swords and then held out the other.

He simply looked at it.

She frowned. "I need to be as good as any Achean alive." There was a touch of anger and urgency in her tone. "I need your experience."

He took the sword. Tested its weight. It felt at home. He was ashamed at how good it seemed to have his fingers wrapped around the hilt. Years fled and he was in Samos where he had fought his last battle. And where he had promised himself he would never fight again.

Bremusa gave them shields. They were the larger, heavier Achean ones of wood, hide, and bronze, not Amazon wicker and hide. He wondered, did Pentha have some notion that the Acheans at Troy might, somehow, come as far as Amazon territory? Was she preparing to do battle with Acheans?

She took a position of readiness. "The rules are, first touch to any part of the body except arm wins. First one to disarm the other, of course, wins."

He took his own position of readiness, the first difference between them. She held the Achean shield too high and too far from her body. She at once shifted to the position he had taken.

He didn't want to do this.

She charged him and swung. He took the blow with his shield, amazed that he was forced a step back. Her upper arm was well muscled, something quite evident, but he had underestimated the power possible in the superbly exercised arm of a woman.

She struck again, and this time when he deflected the blow, he came in low with his own sword, attempting to land a touch to her leg. He would end this quickly. But she dropped her shield and blocked him.

They both stood tall again, and exchanged chops and counters. The clang of metal created the sharp white light in his mind that he had almost forgotten. And all sense of nausea vanished.

He let her back him up, testing her strength. Then he put more force into his blows. She backed.

"Watch out Pentha!" someone shouted.

He focused, looked for weakness. She might not be able to parry. He rushed her, slashing left and right. She blocked him, left and right with sword and shield.

He switched to a low, backhand stroke, but quick as a ferret, she swung her sword down in time to check him.

Again they exchanged blows and counterblows, circling left, protecting their exposed right sides. He had the sense, now, that if he tried to kill her, he might be able to. Might. He wasn't certain. She was so strong. So fast.

She tried his own backhand stroke, but aimed high—she learned quickly. Her blade whistled close to his head.

"You have him now!" a female voice cried.

Again he tried to overpower her with fast, heavy blows. They overran the gathered crowd, which parted around them.

His arm muscles burned. If she felt fatigued, she showed no signs. No lowering of her shield. No lessoning of the power of her blows. She rushed him, came in low. Switched to high. He closed on her and their swords crossed, slid together until their hilts collided, and he and she stood so close he felt her breath on his face. He looked into green eyes, deadly with determination. They were both gasping.

"I declare a draw," Harmonia said imperiously.

The crowd broke into cheers, "Well done!" and "Grand display!"

He felt letdown. His blood was running hot. He wanted to know if he could beat her. Then he smiled at the same moment that she smiled at him. What would it be like to cover her mouth with his own? To mingle the sweat of their struggle?

They disengaged and stepped back. Clonie took his sword and shield. Hippolyta took Pentha's and the two Amazons, grinning and bantering, walked away.

"Thank you, Damonides," Harmonia said, then she followed after them.

The crowd dispersed. Bremusa stepped up, two bronze cups in hand. "Mare's milk for the champions," she said, and then she, too, left them.

His heart still raced, but not just from fighting now. He took a long drink of the milk.

She said, "I suspect it was a draw because I spend nearly all of my time practicing with weapons. If you were in good form. . . ." She sipped at the milk.

"You are fast. And daughter of Artemis, you are incredibly strong." He studied her with open admiration.

"Hard work." She turned toward benches. "Come. Sit with me."

They sat and she said, "I think now that you didn't want to duel. I think I shouldn't have insisted. I apologize."

He grinned. "Why is it that you are always so serious? And now I see, determined?"

"That's how you see me?"

"Those are good traits."

"But you, you prefer to keep things light."

"If I can."

"My life, my responsibility, is to protect my people. I imagine that makes me serious. Or then, maybe it's the other way around. Maybe I took on this responsibility because you are right, and I am much too serious."

"I didn't say 'much too,' I just said serious." By the goddess, he had come all this way to see her, and here he was seeming critical. "I came to see you after I learned that Gryn was ill."

"I'm glad you did."

Did he see a hint of blush on her cheeks? He remembered the glowing smile she gave him when she saw him. He felt encouraged.

She said, "Will you come with me to the festival this evening?" She lifted her cup of milk. "Lots of mare's milk and positively nothing serious. A lot of singing and wild dancing. And fine food."

"You already know I don't enjoy the company of a lot of people. I have been away from town and crowds for a long time."

"But you came here."

He looked directly into her eyes. "I wanted to see you."

She paused, looked directly back, then said, "And I've wanted to see you."

They sat that way, suspended.

She broke the spell. "I planned to go hunting one last time before the heavy snows fall. Tomorrow, with Hippolyta for three days. But I could ask her to stay behind. Would you go with me?"

"I should return home tomorrow. My animals need care."

She tilted her head and smiled. "You said there is a boy who cares for them. Bias, isn't it? Wouldn't he care for them until you return if you sent him word?"

Without thinking, his hand went to his tunic where the arrowhead lay next to his skin. A powerful insight seized him. This was like the moment he decided to leave Themiskyra, like the moment he asked his wife to marry him, like the moment he killed the woman and her son in a senseless battle. This moment, this decision, came to him from the Fates.

PART II

TOUCHED BY THE FATES

❧ 18 ❧

Damon followed Pentha down a narrow ani-
mal trail, the cool smell of damp earth like a comforting living presence around him. This was territory familiar
to her, new to him. A shifting breeze rustled the leaves as if
the woods now-and-then shuddered at the approach of winter. Both he and Pentha wore warm trousers and heavy tunics. Each carried a quiver, arrows, and a hunting knife. The
sun, were he able to see it, would announce mid-afternoon.

What am I doing here? The thought startled him. And so
did the answer. He wasn't here to have a desirable woman
for the first time in years. He walked behind Pentha fired by
the hope that she might, like her mother, love a man enough
to give up her Amazon life.

They gingerly crossed a stream on a fallen log coated with
gray-green moss. On the far side, they stopped. They studied
fresh scat. "Leopard," he said. "No older than a day."

She nodded. A look farther along the bank revealed a paw
print.

He said, "I'd say a good-sized male."

Again she nodded. She turned upstream.

They soon found a fresh break in the undergrowth.
Silently they nocked an arrow to their bowstrings and followed the trail. Ten steps and he stopped and pointed to the
dead body of a hind draped in the lowest branch of a tree

where the leopard had hauled it up to keep less agile predators from eating it.

He and Pentha backed off and squatted behind low brush, peering over it to study the leopard's catch. He said, "Artemis favors us. He's away."

They settled in. From a pouch in her quiver, Pentha fished out a tiny jar made from a single piece of hollowed, white quartz. Oddly shaped, not round but flattish on two sides, it had an unusually wide mouth.

"I'm going to share a secret with you," she said. From the mouth she pulled out a plug made from bees wax covered with layers of linen. "It's not that there is an oath against telling, it's just something we keep to ourselves, and if I tell you, I'd prefer you tell no one else."

"You can trust me."

She nodded. "Yes, I believe I can. I like the feeling. Give me your arrow."

He handed it to her. She brushed his fingers with hers, and gooseflesh prickled his sides. She dipped the arrow's tip partway into the jar. When she drew the tip out, a thin, grayish-white liquid clung to it. She handed it back. "Blow until it dries."

"What is it?"

"Poison. Gryn says it is the blood of the great serpent, Hydra. We use it for hunting, especially large game. But it works on anything with a warm body. So only one of us needs to hit the leopard. He will run. We follow. It won't take long before the poison fells him."

"It kills?"

"No, no! It's difficult and dangerous to make the brew strong enough to kill. We only use it to bring the animal down. When weak, the concoction only puts them painlessly to sleep."

She signaled for him to dip the arrows remaining in his quiver. He set to work, and asked, "Why don't I know of this?"

"It's part of the Amazon way. It's not something we share

with others." She gave him a gentle smile. "But I wanted to share with you."

"But why haven't I heard of this effect on Amazon enemies?"

She frowned. "To use it in battle is forbidden. There are ways to fight a person with honor, and ways that would dishonor Artemis."

He finished dipping the arrows, then they settled once more into quiet waiting. Time trickled past. He thought of making love to her tomorrow. Anxiety hit and he clenched his fist. It had been a very long time since he'd bedded a woman.

Pentha fished another something from her quiver and unwrapped it. The gut-turning smell of polecat slapped him so hard his head jerked back. The revolting scent reminded him of the nausea that struck him only two days before, when he'd first entered the town. She quickly explained that foul smell would be their main protection from the dangers of the night. And their disguise when the cat returned. He rubbed the greasy stuff on his face and arms.

When she'd returned it to its wrapping and her quiver, she moved close to him. She scooted around so that their backs rested against each other.

Dusk brought darkness and a change in the forest's voices. Bird twittering ceased. Twice he heard owl hooting.

A leopard pelt was prized for its warmth and beauty. Also because killing a leopard was difficult. The big cats tended to be out only at dusk or, even more likely, in the dead of night. A man exposed at night courted all kinds of dangers. Damon's wife would never have done such a thing. But Pentha? Part of his attraction to Pentha had to be her courage and stunning independence. And apparently, fearlessness.

Her body warmth and her slow breathing brought on another surge of physical response. He could see only one small patch of sky. He concentrated hard on the stars. Profoundly mysterious points of light. Marching solemnly across the heaven, night after night, ever faithful, never understood.

He said what he had often wondered when watching them for long hours. "So where do the stars come from?"

She said. "Where do they go?"

From her tone he imagined he saw an ironic smile on her lips.

Something, perhaps a twig, snapped. They straightened and took knives in hand.

❧ 19 ❧

DAMON STRAINED TO HEAR ANOTHER SOUND. Pentha remained rigidly alert beside him. A faint rustling from their right. Then nothing.

Shortly he heard the leopard's claws digging into tree bark. Not too much later, the crunching noises of bones being broken. Pentha sat tight to his side, and they listened to the leopard feed until what Damon felt might be close to midnight. Then once more, silence.

Twice they heard wolves calling their mournful yet beautiful wails, but never any hint of the leopard moving. Artemis still favored them.

A loud scraping sound startled him from sleep. Pentha, too, snapped to full alert. In the early light of day the leopard stood boldly on the tree limb. A huge male. The cat stretched, arching his back, then yawned, flashing his killing fangs, long tongue, and wide mouth.

They leapt to their feet, fixed their arrows. The cat saw them and even as their arrows flew, he lunged to the ground and bounded off. Both arrows whished into empty space.

Damon sprinted in pursuit, nocking another arrow, Pentha close behind.

Had the leopard had a fainter heart, he could have escaped, but when they reached the river, the animal stopped, turned, yowled. When he turned to run, Damon's arrow hit him in the flank, Pentha's in the shoulder.

The leopard raced downstream, but quickly abandoned the trail for dense undergrowth. Damon, Pentha now beside him, followed, dodging trees and crashing through bushes.

Just as Pentha described, the chase did not last long. They found the beast, standing still and breathing hard.

It turned and sprang at Pentha. She dodged it, and when it landed, it took only a few steps more before sinking to the ground. His mouth gaped open and his long tongue rolled out. His eyes closed as he seemed to fall into a deep sleep. His sides rose and fell with great gasps.

"Beautiful," Damon said.

"Do you need meat?" Pentha asked. "Do you need a skin?"

"I'm here because I can always use meat and skin before winter sets in." That wasn't the reason, of course. She was the reason.

She smiled. "Amazons always let their first strike live. It is our thank offering to Artemis. You and I have both killed before, but not with each other. We can let him live. Our first hunt together."

He nodded. "I'd like that." He looked at the arrows sticking out of the cat's side. "But the poison? The wounds?"

"The poison not only weakens, it keeps wounds from going sour. If we remove the shafts, he will carry our tips. But he will heal."

"Then let's offer him to the Goddess. Something beautiful."

They removed the shafts up to the skin—Pentha had obviously done this more than once—then they left quickly, wanting to be well away when the cat regained his senses.

Damon led back to their camp. The first thing he wanted to do was get rid of the polecat smell. And if he undressed to bathe, she would see the arrowhead hung around his neck and know how deeply she'd hooked him. He pulled out the arrowhead, undid the knot, and tucked the charm and thong into his trouser pocket.

They reached the place where they had put down bedding and laid stones for a fire, a spot with a good view next to a swift river. The far bank, twice the distance he could throw a stone, presented a solid wall of mixed forest, mostly oaks. All of it was ablaze in shades of red, with here and there some orange and yellow, as much on fire with life as he felt in Pentha's presence. Off their bank, about halfway across the river, a mound of boulders split the water. He imagined fishing just below the boulders tomorrow and taking at least one big trout for their dinner.

The two packhorses, hobbled in a grassy clearing, whinnied a greeting. Along the near bank, the water ran shallow enough to wade into, and an eddy formed a natural pool.

He said, "This smell kept me on the edge of nausea all night."

"Go ahead." She walked to their things and searched through one of the packs.

He stripped, waded in, grimaced, and sucked in a deep breath. The frigid water made even the hair on his head feel as though it were standing on end. Where the pool dropped off to waist height, he let himself completely under, leapt back up, running his hands through his soaked hair.

He turned, and there walking toward him was Pentha, as naked as Artemis at her bath. He had never seen anything more beautiful. She had let down her hair. It fell over her shoulders to her waist. Her woman's hair matched its coppery red.

He watched, fascinated, as she followed the path he'd taken into the shallows and then into the small pool.

"The polecat stink is bad, but it works," she said. She laughed. "Usually."

She strode to where the water came to just below her breasts and they floated, pointing directly at him. She held something. His heart was pounding, his pulse throbbing in his throat. If he hadn't been standing in ice water, he would surely have had the biggest erection of his life.

"This will not only take away the stink, we'll smell lovely."

She thrust the cube under his nose and he smelled mint. She washed his chest and back. She had him dip into the water and then worked the stuff into his hair. When he'd rinsed it, she washed very private parts under the water. He pulled her to him, then, and kissed her.

"Wash me," she said.

He started with her breasts, and then her back, then her hair, and then, as she had done, he finished with private parts under the water, and when he touched her there, she kissed him.

"We're clean," she whispered.

He laughed. "And freezing!" He took her hand and led her to the bank. They ran, hand-in-hand, to the pile of furs. These had been sewn together to make sacks that could be laced up, with the fur on the inside and outside.

He slicked off what water he could, but she pulled a cloth from one of the packs and dried her body and her hair a bit, then handed the cloth to him. He dried as best he could, then they crawled into one sack together.

Their bodies soon warmed each other, and he kissed her as he had dreamed of kissing her for what had seemed like an age of restless nights. When she returned his kisses and began to touch him and run her legs along his, he stopped her and said, "Let me wait. I need to wait a moment."

"Don't wait," she said. "A man who lives alone can't wait."

So he didn't. He entered her, her hands guiding his. Weeks of longing and fantasy drove animal passion. His skin seemed on fire.

Her powerful fingers dug into his buttocks.

Stroked his back.

Pulled at his hair. Caressed his beard.

He exploded into hot, searing ecstasy. Too soon! Too soon. But glorious!

They lay together for some moments, Pentha with her head on his chest. Damon traced the bones of her face. Drained and yet complete, he let himself drift.

She woke him with a rain of kisses—his forehead, his cheeks, his neck—and finger caresses to match the kisses.

Seeing he was awake, she took his hand and laid it on her belly. "Have you learned other ways to please a woman?"

He had, and soon her cries said he had succeeded, and finally she stiffened, clenching his wrist with that astonishing, powerful grip.

They rested, then he opened her hand and kissed the palm. "I have never felt more at peace in my life."

"Gryn says that the sense of peace is one of coupling's greatest gifts."

This was not the peace of coupling. This was far more profound. "Say something," he said.

"What?"

"Anything. I like to hear you talk."

"That's the second time you've said you like my voice. No one else has ever said that. What is so special about my voice?"

He tensed. Should he risk exposing his strangeness? He moved onto one elbow so she could see his face. He wanted to share everything with her. "You've shared a secret with me, about the poison. Now I'll share a secret with you."

"Remember you said I could trust you? Well, you can trust me."

"I don't experience the world like other people do."

She frowned.

"It took me a long time to figure it out. I think I had fifteen years when something my mother said made it clear that I'm different."

"Different?"

"You hear sounds. And you see colors. So does everyone else I have ever met. But I see them mixed together. When I hear a waterfall, I can close my eyes and it's not only sound that is there, I see a shimmering aura of pinks and purples."

She shook her head.

He said, "Close your eyes!"

She did.

"What do you see?"

"Blackness."

"Well, if I closed my eyes, and you said the words, 'Damon, what do you see?' I would tell you I see a lovely yellow color."

She opened her eyes and stared at him, still not understanding.

"And I see the colors even if I don't close my eyes. When you talk to me, a yellow aura surrounds everything."

"Yellow. Like sunflowers."

"Your voice is prettier than sunflowers."

"That sounds, well, odd, but nice."

"The problem is, most voices, and a few other sounds, like donkey braying or reed flutes, are not. They create a sickening color I can only describe as filthy gray-brown. And the sound nauseates me. For me, being around people is like being awash continually in polecat smell. After a few days with people, I can tolerate it, but it's still unpleasant."

"I've never heard of, or even imagined, such a thing."

"I've only told a few people. They either didn't believe me, or they didn't understand. When I told my closest friend that the sound of his voice made me sick, he decided I was cursed. He never talked to me again."

"This is why you live alone, isn't it?"

"It's one of the reasons."

"Yes, there must be others. I can't imagine living so alone when you say you can at least bear the sickness. Will you share the other reasons?"

He shook his head and lay back down. The killings were a place he would go with no one, not even Pentha.

❧ 20 ❦

PENTHA TOOK ONE OF DAMON'S HANDS AND opened it. His hands were large with long, sturdy fingers. She felt great power in those hands. Beautiful hands.

Hearing sounds and seeing colors. Colors and sounds making Damon sick. She said, "I'm glad you told me. It explains much, although in a way, you remain just as mysterious. Maybe more so. I like mysteries."

He grinned. "Speaking of mysteries, there is something I want to tell you. The day I came to Themiskyra, I came by the back door. I met a man on the trail, a Hittite. He said his name was Muttalusha."

"I know him. A small man with dark, black eyes."

"I find it extremely unusual that he took the back door."

She sat up and looked down at his strong face and gentle eyes. "So do I. What business would an outsider have on such a dangerous path?"

"He said he'd been distracted and made the wrong turn. That makes no sense. Before he got very far, he would have known he was going wrong."

"As soon as we return, I will tell Harmonia."

He played with the ends of her hair. "Those were my thoughts, too." And then, "You are astonishingly beautiful."

"And you please me." It surprised her how much this strange, gentle man pleased her.

She bent down and kissed him. They made love again—

slowly, deliciously, resoundingly. She fell into contented sleep with the warmth of his body along her back and his hand cupping her breast.

DAMON AWOKE AT MIDDAY and his first thought, after he remembered where he was, was how beautiful life could be when a man had a companion. Over these last solitary years, he had actually forgotten the joy that comes from sharing.

Pentha appeared to be asleep. He laid his arm outside the bag and the sun's heat soaked his skin. She snuggled closer. He said, "I feel like a bear just out of hibernation. I'm starving."

While they dressed, he made no secret of watching her every move. When this time was over, he would want to remember everything about her to the smallest detail.

They fetched cooking supplies from the packs. He arranged the kindling they had collected so it would draw air, added bits of linen fluff, and used flint to set the lot to burning. She carried a tripod and two cups to the stream. She filled the tripod, then he watched her pull up the water-proofed goatskin of fermented mare's milk sunken on a line, just beneath the surface to keep it cool, and pour them both a cup. They downed their first. She poured them another. He felt himself relaxing under the drink's influence.

With the fire well caught, he sat the tripod filled with water over it. She poured in a mixture of dried meat and vegetables and stirred. They settled on a log he dragged to the fire, eating apples and sipping.

She said, "You know, I have already broken one rule by hunting with a man. I'm willing to break another. Tomorrow, if you'd like, rather than hunt, I will teach you to ride. One of the pack horses will do."

A man riding an Amazon horse! He laughed.

"You don't want to?"

"Actually, it's a fine idea."

"I've often wondered. Why don't the Acheans have cavalry? I know their women don't fight. And certainly women are much better on the horses because their bodies are lighter. But why don't the Achean men have a cavalry?"

He didn't want to talk fighting with her, but then, fighting was her life. "At first I wondered the same thing. But the fact is, fighting on the ground is what they have always done. In their minds, the idea of riding, except in a chariot, seems ridiculous. I've heard commanders poke fun, saying only women, the Amazons, would do something so foolish as to waste manpower on the back of a horse. I think if they once understood the advantages, they would ride. But so far, strong force on the ground has worked for them and worked very well. They have sacked and raided and conquered towns and cities all around the Great Sea. Their manner of doing battle has made the Achean royals powerful and rich. They have no reason to change."

"They still have not taken Troy."

"No, and maybe they won't. Troy's defenses are formidable. And she has the support of all the cities in the Troad and many powers beyond. The Hittites especially are generous with supplies. They want the Acheans out of this part of the world."

"The Acheans are a plague. Maggots in a wound. Achilles is the worst. What a farce to claim he is the greatest warrior ever to live. That he is the grandson of Zeus. That he's invincible."

Her face had taken a dark look, brow creased, eyes hooded. She hissed the name Achilles with breathtaking venom. She dropped her hands to her side, as if Damon didn't exist, as if she wasn't here in this place with him. He'd never imagined Pentha's face capable of so fierce a look.

What was it in her that stoked such white-hot fire? She wasn't angry at him, but with something else. Perhaps something in herself.

The Fates were playing with him. He wanted her. Beyond all reason, he wanted this magnificent woman as his mate. Walls he had so painstakingly built to keep away pain and despair had been breached.

❧ 21 ❦

THEY SPENT THE NEXT DAY RIDING. AND THE next. He would have sworn that he fell off more than he rode, and they laughed more than he had laughed in eight years. Last night, while he slept with Pentha in his arms, the winter's first snow arrived. The trees and ground lay lightly spread with a crisp white blanket, and flakes like tiny white leaves still fluttered down in slow glides from a gray heaven, cloaking the land with peace. Damon's breath rose white from his mouth.

He hoisted the last pack onto the horse, and she held it while he secured it. She had bundled herself in a coat of black sable and her red hair, once more braided at her nape, made a startling contrast with the dark fur. Sadness squatted heavy as a millstone on his heart. He must make a hard decision, and he thought it unlikely he would ever again see Pentha's magnificent hair flowing freely to her waist.

Taking a lead rope each, they started for Themiskrya. She stopped and looked back.

He asked, "What are you thinking?"

She smiled. They started walking again. "We've had three days I want to remember."

"I'm glad you asked me to come."

"It's fun, hunting with a man." She gave him a mischievous grin. "You can do more than just hunt and tell stories."

He wished he could believe that their coupling meant she

loved him as he now knew he loved her, but he was quite certain it did not. A man could tell. "I think I told you once that I liked living with a woman all the time. That's one of the reasons."

"If a man and woman were together all the time, they would soon bore each other."

"I didn't find that to be so." A silent pause, then he said, "Wouldn't you like to live with a husband, as other people do? As they do in Troy?" *Couldn't you want to live with me*?

"What did your mother say to you about leaving Themiskyra for a man?"

"She never talked about him except to say that she loved him. He was away most of the time, and I think she was lonely. If she had stayed in Themiskyra, she would not have been lonely. Besides, living with a man isn't the Amazon way."

"If a woman were to live with me, I would never leave her to be lonely." *I would never let you be lonely.* "Surely your mother wasn't too unhappy. She had you. Don't you want to have children?"

"Of course. But I can't now. When my service is over, I will consider marriage. It's only seven more years."

"Actually, seven years is a long time. Many things can happen to a woman who regularly goes into battle."

"It's my duty."

"I was a warrior. I did my duty. It didn't make me happy. Don't you think being happy, being truly at peace, is more important than some duties?"

"I don't deserve to be happy."

Stunned, he stared at her. But she just kept walking. Since he could think of no sensible reply to such an astonishing pronouncement, he let the silence draw out.

AS PENTHA APPROACHED THE Amazon encampment a feeling of emptiness settled on her. Very shortly she was going to say goodbye to Damon. He would not be going to the men's compound where she might expect to see him again soon if she chose to. He would return to his isolated mountain world. Being with a man for three days had unsettled her—especially being with a man like Damon, who at every instant made her feel valued in a way she'd never felt before.

At the Amazon encampment, he could go no further. He handed her the lead rope from his packhorse. She said, "I think if you kept at it, you might someday make an outstanding horseman."

"Two days of lessons aren't much to judge by."

"Ah, but it is. You have a feeling for the animal. Most men don't realize how very skittish they are."

An uncomfortable silence vibrated the air between them. She felt certain he was as reluctant to part as she was.

"Whenever I can," she said, "I will invite you to come to me."

He shook his head.

"Then, let's leave it that you can come to me when you choose. I'm often gone, though, so it might be difficult for you to know when we can be together."

"I am going to be truthful, Pentha. I prefer that you not send for me, and I will not come to you."

She was unsure she'd heard him correctly.

He continued. "I care for you as I have cared only once before. And to see you now and then for a night will frustrate rather than gratify me." He tilted his head and looked deeply into her eyes. A muscle along the edge of his jaw clenched. She thought he might reach out and touch her, but instead he said, "I don't think that if I asked, you will come to live with me?"

He stopped and waited, motionless.

The request, the very idea, was. . . . She couldn't think what to say.

The silence between them threatened to explode. He continued. "And I cannot come and live with you. It's not 'the Amazon way.' So our situation is impossible."

He stepped to her and wrapped her in that bear-hug of an embrace. His breath brushed her cheek. She felt secure there, in his embrace, as if her burdens had been reduced by half. But he stepped back and the full weight of her life settled again. "I care for you, Pentha," he said. "And not in the Amazon way."

He turned and strode off, shoulders straight.

"Damon," she said. This was all wrong.

He did not look back.

She fought the urge to call out to him again. Instead she said softly, "If you change your mind, send word and I will have you come to me at any time."

Finally, when it felt foolish to continue to stare after him, she led the horses into the compound and to the stable where Ino, Valor's groom, quickly appeared, ready to serve. "See that they are unpacked and well cared for," Pentha muttered out of sheer habit. *I could take Valor this minute and ride after Damon.*

"My lady, you are to go at once to see Bremusa," Ino said, her voice charged with excitement.

Pentha walked blindly toward the barracks, stopped in place. *What does he mean? What does he find so wrong with our way?*

Bremusa caught up to her. "The Kaska mounted a raid on Lockruos," she said. "Word came half an hour ago. They fielded a surprisingly large force and have overwhelmed the local patrol. I sent a messenger to fetch you. Apparently you missed each other."

A raid! She must focus. She must think. "Preparations to ride?" She resisted the urge to turn and look to see Damon again.

"Already under way. We can leave with the horses in perhaps another half an hour. The supply wagons will follow shortly."

❧ 22 ❧

ON BOARD THE *PROUD LION*, ACHILLES LISTENED
to the steady drumbeat of the oarmaster and the rhyth-
mic rise, fall, and swish of forty oars in the calm sea. His
fleet of fifty ships had finally reached Goat's Head bay,
Troy's spacious main harbor. It lay opposite Tenedos.

Achilles had a brief vision of Derinoe struggling with
him eight, or was it nine, years ago now, when he had carried her away from her home there. He pushed the unpleasant image away.

What he needed was good anchorage—and the bay
looked already full to overflowing. Today he would settle his
fleet. Within days the remainder of his camp—men, women,
and what booty still had not been sent home—would arrive
overland from the south.

Spring had come at last. This was the first week of April
and the beginning of a new battle season. The High Council
had agreed that this year the entire Achean contingent—the
ships and all their men—would assemble at Goat's Head.
Along the shoreline he saw impressive signs of massive construction. The encampment was now a small town, filled
with not only the soldiers and those craftsmen who serviced
them, but many more women and camp followers.

The trench in front of the wall had been widened and deepened since his last visit. In preparation for this season,
Agamemnon had directed that the wall be made twice as high

and twice as thick. It loomed up from the beach now, a giant edifice of stone and earth and timber. A string of six wagons piled with massive timbers, presumably cut from Mount Ida, crawled along the shoreline road. In the far distance, behind a rise in the land, he could see the two southernmost white towers of Priam's citadel.

This year they would take Troy. Its treasury and its location at the hub of the vital Hellespont trade routes would bring not only greater riches but a steady income. He could go home with enough wealth to secure his kingdom not only for himself, but also for his sons and their heirs.

Patroklos joined him at the bow. "Look at the size of that wall!" He swept a graceful hand across the panoply of anchored vessels, each carrying their king's banner. "And that sight is astonishing. Not since we all rallied at Aulis, at the beginning so many years ago, has the entire force been together."

Achilles' anxiety about good anchorage hitched up a notch. Agamemnon alone had come to this campaign with a hundred ships. Menelaus had brought sixty from Sparta. Nestor from Pylos and Idomeneus from Crete had each mustered eighty ships, and few had been lost. Ajax and others had lesser numbers of ships and men, but the grand total came to over one thousand vessels. Still, Agamemnon had assured Achilles that Goat's Head Bay would have room for all, in part because many ships had early on been pulled to shore and dismantled, awaiting reassembly for the final trip home.

Achilles' mind returned to the wall, then to the nature of this exceptional gathering. He shook his head. "Agamemnon has decided to make an all-out effort. After all of this labor, all of this planning, he will feel no one can claim he didn't make a supreme try. But my sense of things is that if we don't take Troy this year, Agamemnon is going home, no matter what anyone else wants, thinks, or says."

They passed the southern edge of the bay's wide mouth. Frowning, Patroklos said, "Shouldn't you turn the fleet in? Didn't you say Agamemnon directed that we put in at the south end?"

"You've seen the south end. It's more exposed to wind. It's plagued more by submerged rock. I expect the north end is still open."

"Isn't Ajax assigned to the north?"

"I'll wager Ajax hasn't arrived yet. He's very brave and very bold, but rather slow when it comes to thinking ahead. And my rule is, first to arrive gets the prize."

Patroklos gave him that familiar, you're-stirring-up-trouble-again, look.

Achilles laughed and slapped his cousin, his companion, on the shoulder. "When you want something, Patroklos, you really should have learned by now that you have to take it."

FIFTEEN DAYS AFTER ARRIVING at the bay, their united forces, under Agamemnon, attempted to take the citadel. The battle was a disaster. Reaching the security of his encampment, exhausted and furious, Achilles called to Patroklos, whose chariot had pulled up beside his own, "You go yourself to Odysseus' encampment. I thought I saw him go down. And I don't want lies others might offer."

Automedon was bleeding from a superficial cut on his forearm. "Get that wound cleaned right away," Achilles said to his charioteer, giving his friend a thump of gratitude. Automedon was nothing short of brilliant with the horses.

Achilles leapt down from the chariot's car. Patroklos joined him and they strode into their tent. Achilles continued. "After you're bathed and rested, I want you to see whether Odysseus is alive and what condition he's in so I can rest tonight. The 'Sacker of Cities' is my strongest ally against Agamemnon's endless vacillations."

Patroklos shook his head. "We can be grateful to Athena, to Zeus himself, that the Trojans didn't breech the wall."

Two slaves rushed to remove their armor.

As Patroklos' man unstrapped his cuirass, Patroklos nodded toward the bleeding cut on Achilles' leg. "You're wounded," he said. Concern softened his voice.

Achilles remembered the javelin's glancing strike. "It's not serious."

"Master Achilles," came a voice from the corner to his left.

Achilles swung around to find the Hittite merchant, Muttalusha, bowing, almost cringing.

"What are you doing here?" he bellowed at the little man.

"You summoned me, sire."

Ah yes, he had. The battle had distracted his thoughts. He dropped one foot on a footrest and the slave removed his greave. When the other was also off, he strode to a chair, saying to the slave, "Wine."

With a sigh, Patroklos took another chair and put both feet on the footrest. Achilles gave the merchant a hard stare. "So, you have returned from your first trip this year to Themiskyra. What news do you bring me?"

Something was definitely wrong with the merchant. When Achilles first saw him, he exuded an overweening confidence often displayed by men of his trade. The second time had been just before winter set in, and Muttalusha confirmed the rumor about iron, something Achilles had turned over in his mind all winter long. But now the merchant's shoulders drooped, as did the lines of his face.

"Speak up!"

"I fear I cannot add much beyond what I have already provided." Muscles in Muttalusha's cheek quivered, putting Achilles in mind of the twitchings of a cornered mouse.

"Nothing?"

"I have not been able to gain access to the men's compound and it is the men who work the ore. The truth is, while the women at least seem friendly and open, the men of Artemis are a closed bunch. I've not been able to successfully befriend even one so as to bind him into my debt."

"I don't want you to befriend them, by Zeus! What about a bribe? What about a man with a weakness who can be blackmailed?"

The little man actually wrung his hands as he shuffled his feet. God's blood! It was beginning to look like he'd get little more than minnows from this pond. "Knowing that they have the secret of making iron will not help me take the city.

I need something useful. Like exactly how many women they have under arms."

"I'm sorry, sire, . . ."

"I don't require sorry. I can't use sorry. Where do they keep their weapons?"

"The town women are talkative, but never the Amazons. I have only three times spoken with one."

Patience exploded. Achilles leapt to his feet, strode to the merchant, grabbed the man by his coat, and pulled him close. "I did not pay you for nothing. When you return from your next trip, I will expect results."

He felt the man shaking, crown to sole. Muttalusha nodded.

"There has to be some inner weakness, some jealousies among them that I can exploit." He spun the man toward the tent entrance and then shoved him with the force of the disgust he felt, causing the little weasel to stumble. Muttalusha quickly scrambled back into balance.

"I assure you," the merchant said, "I will return with what you require." After bowing low, he darted from the tent like a chased hare.

With the irritating, and seemingly ineffective, merchant gone, Achilles returned to his chair. Wine awaited him. He took a long swallow, felt its smooth, comforting slide to the center of his stomach. "I may have thrown away valuable property on that Hittite."

"I'll repeat myself," Patroklos said. "Why stir up the hornet's nest Themiskyra is likely to be? Is it that the little Amazon burrowed so deep into your mind that her escape fuels this crazed urge to take on the whole race?"

Crazed! Achilles tightened his grip on his wine cup. "It's a case of profit, nothing more. Don't try to make it personal."

Patroklos shrugged, then downed another swallow.

Achilles pressed on. "Not all the news is bad. I have captured ten sons of the Thracean family of Grammeron. I've informed the family head that they *will* pilot my ships to the Euxine from now on or lose a son at every refusal."

Patroklos simply took another swig.

A powerful need seized Achilles. He felt his pulse

quicken. He must bring Patroklos into favor with his desire to reach the Euxine Sea and eventually the Amazons. He and Patroklos were almost always in agreement. They had been since childhood. His friend's good will was more valuable than gold.

Perhaps Patroklos' attitude came from jealousy of a sort. Achilles had cared for Derinoe more profoundly than any other of the many female war prizes he'd taken or been given. Perhaps Patroklos sensed the difference. Perhaps for the time Derinoe was present in their camp, Patroklos had felt shut out. Achilles hadn't intended any change in their relationship. Patroklos had never before been jealous of a woman. But then, the Amazon had been very different in spirit from other women.

Patroklos stood. "I need to bathe." He strode to the door leading to his own tent and turned. "I presume you have considered that even though the Thraceans may bend to your will and act as pilots, we may not be able to muster enough rowers with sufficient strength to take very many ships through. Maybe not enough to mount effective raids. Even if we can find exceptionally fit men in sufficient numbers, man-eating demons live beneath the waters. Many rowers refuse to attempt the passage."

Achilles felt himself warming. Patroklos had used the word *we*. He smiled. "We need to think not on the problems, but on the possibilities. I've already set our best rowers to strength and endurance training. Twelve ships are enough for a successful campaign." In reality, until he had better information, he could not be certain how many ships would be needed. But the information would eventually come, he felt certain. "We will get enough men through—and in battle force. By mid-summer, early fall for certain, we will be in the Euxine Sea."

❧ 23 ❧

ONLY A LIMITED NUMBER OF PLACES MADE FOR good hunting with Dia. Her wings weren't built for quick turns required for forest hunting. Hers were long and narrow. She needed open space bordered with woods, the hiding places for her avian prey, and plenty of open land for the burrows and warrens of her favorite catches, rabbits and hares.

So Damon, with Bias and Wolf, had hiked to this ideal spot, not far from the Euxine Sea and the Themiskyran border with Kaska country. They stood on a hill overlooking a wide valley. Dense stands of oak flanked the valley's floor. At mid-morning, the early September day felt calm and warm, but the chill in this morning's washstand water hinted at an early fall.

At the valley's far end, streams of smoke from a Themiskyran settlement's home fires curled upward into a sky full of towering cloud palaces. Now and then whiffs of burning wood reached their hill.

Dia sat on Damon's arm. Bias carried her travel cage, just in case, but when she was put into it, she ruffled her feathers in a way that indicated she didn't like it. Whenever possible, Damon carried her.

"Put on the glove," he said to the boy.

Bias' face glowed with anticipation. "I've waited a long time." At thirteen, he had shot up at least the length of Damon's thumb in just the last several months. Apparently his appetite hadn't been enough to match his growth. His arms and legs were too thin and too long for the rest of him. In time, he would probably grow as tall as Damon.

"You see how I'm holding her," Damon instructed. "Keep your arm level, and steady."

"I'm ready."

Damon brought his arm up behind Bias' arm, then slid his slowly under, forcing Dia to step onto the boy's gloved wrist. The two small bells attached to the base of her tail jingled. The bells made it easier to find her when she took prey in dense grass or brush. Damon placed the leather jesses into Bias's hand.

"Royally fearsome!" Bias said, his eyes fixed on the falcon in wonder. "How long before I can fly her."

"That depends on how hard you are willing to work. What we will do, come next spring, is capture a smaller bird. One easier to handle, so you can learn for yourself everything necessary to train and care for a hunter."

"Thank you, Damon. I give you all the thanks in the world."

"The person you should thank is your mother. She is generous to agree to let you live with me."

"Guess some good has to come from having three brothers."

For some months, the boy had begged and begged, with both determination and yet respect for Damon's privacy. Bias even went to the great length of swearing he would never set foot in Damon's house and would sleep outside in the shed with the nanny goat if Damon would only teach him how to hunt with a bird. Damon laughed then and gave in. How could he say no to such passion. "You will sleep in the cabin," he had said. "And I will teach you what Noemon taught me."

He asked Bias, "How does her weight feel?"

"For her size, it doesn't seem much. But I don't think I could have carried her here all this way, like you did."

"Your arm will get stronger and used to staying at that angle."

To Wolf, Damon said, "Sit!" then "Lie down."

Wolf immediately obeyed. He was over a year old, no longer a pup. More than a year had passed since Damon had watched a little wolf pup sitting happily in Pentha's lap. He lingered a moment on that sweet image, then forced his thoughts to return to now. The Warrior Queen was never going to be a part of his life. Better that the memories of her be allowed to die.

He rubbed Wolf behind the ears. The pack hunter learned fast and was keen to please. If directed, he followed at Damon's heel, and waited without moving when Damon left him.

Damon put his arm in front of Bias's and slid the boy's arm under his own. Dia stepped once more onto Damon's wrist.

"Feel the muscles here in her breast," he said, and showed Bias how.

"You must learn to keep her at the right weight. And you best judge her condition by knowing how the breast feels. Not too fat. Not too lean. She must be exercised daily. You have to keep on muscle for flying and killing. But she must always be lean and hungry. Otherwise, she won't return. She'll just take off and disappear into the distance." He ran two fingers down the soft, dark-streaked white breast. "Because they are so beautiful and so courageous, we love them. But they do not love us." That was the very first lesson that Noemon had taught him.

In a swift, practiced move, he slipped off her hood. The membranes keeping her eyes moist flicked over her black, piercing stare. Damon let the jesses hang loose and lifted his arm, coaxing her into the sky. She took off. Her wings created a great whirring and stirred up their own wind, which ruffled Damon's hair.

At first she headed down the valley, but quickly banked several times to gain elevation.

"You will learn that she doesn't see the world the way we do," he said.

Bias waited for an explanation.

"She will see prey too small and too distant for me. She'll swoop on something, strike it, and go to ground while I'm thinking I've seen absolutely nothing. It's a bit frightening, but also exciting. Maybe one of the reasons I am so attached to her is because she's like me. She experiences the world differently."

"Like you?"

He thought about telling Bias about the sounds and colors. Decided not to. "She's a loner."

He sat beside Wolf to watch and wait for Dia to find a target.

Bias dropped down beside him. "You will go into Themiskyra soon?" Bias asked.

Damon nodded. "I think next week. You will have to go home to get Pleasant for me."

Themiskyra. Pentha. He touched his tunic, felt the arrowhead beneath it.

"Got ya!" Bias said, a huge grin lighting his face.

"Got me?"

Bias pointed to where Damon had touched the arrowhead. "The fearless woman, right? The one you said made the arrowhead. You're dreaming of seeing her."

"I'm not!" Damon's neck was actually warming. The heat spread to his face.

"Yes, you are."

He returned Bias' grin and boxed the boy's ear. "You are way too smart, do you know that?"

"Smart enough."

"I should keep all my thoughts to myself."

"Let me spend this winter with you and Dia and I won't tell your secret."

"Very smart, indeed. Except, to whom would you tell it? The goat? The ferrets? Wolf?" Damon stroked Wolf's head.

"Mmm. Well." Cocky grin turned sheepish. "Right."

Damon stared over the valley. He *was* dreaming of Pentha.

"Look," Bias said, his finger aimed off to their right.

One valley over, black smoke rose from the forest.

They watched, and the amount of rising smoke grew quickly.

Damon stood and studied the horizon. Bias also jumped up. "You know," Bias said, "that's about where the Kaskan village is."

They watched in silence, then Bias added, "It could just be a fire in the woods."

"Maybe." Damon's scalp prickled. "But I think your first guess is right. Too much smoke, and too quickly."

"Shouldn't we go see?"

"I don't get involved with people, Bias." They continued to watch a few moments more. The smoke grew thicker. "Demon's piss!"

Damon carried a leather pouch slung from one shoulder, his falcon kit. From it he fished out the wolverine-bone whistle and blew it. He also took out and unwrapped a bit of raw squirrel and held it in the glove.

He whistled again and searched the sky.

"There," Bias said, pointing at the black form against white clouds.

She came in high, then tightened into her startling dive. Beside him, he heard Bias exhale an "Ooohhh!" as she hurtled toward Damon's gloved hand, and then as she landed, the boy said, "Royally fearsome!"

Damon quickly hooded her again and as he put her in the travel cage, said to Bias, "We have to run."

❧ 24 ❧

DAMON ESTABLISHED A LOPE THAT HE KNEW would let a fit man run a long time. Dia was too valuable to leave alone and unprotected, so he carried her in her cage. Wolf ran to his right, and Bias stuck close on Damon's heels. He wondered if Bias had the stamina to make it all the way to the village.

A trail led from this valley to the Kaskan village, which hugged a bay along the coast. Damon slowed only slightly when they went uphill. Bias gradually fell behind.

Damon's breathing came with labored effort, sweat stuck his tunic to his chest, and his arm ached from carrying Dia when he reached the ridge that overlooked the Kaskan site. The village straddled a small stream. His breath caught, as if he'd been punched in the stomach.

Flames ate at more than half of the structures. He could hear screams. Soon Bias trotted up and stopped, panting hard.

Damon didn't have to guess about the fires' origin. He counted five ships at sea, moving west. He squinted at the ships, took in the shape of the prow and aft deck. Still panting hard, he felt a sickening twist in his gut.

"Achean," he said to Bias, who was bent over beside him, gasping huge gulps of air.

Achean!

The screams from the village drove out all other thoughts. Damon set Dia's cage on the ground.

"Stay here!" he commanded.

He bounded down the hill, Wolf at his side.

Nothing but empty homes met him at the village's outer boundary, but as he raced toward the screams—he knew those sounds well, the sounds of men in terror and pain—he quickly found scattered bodies. Five men here. Seven there. Several old women.

The screams came from the village's center. He passed a long hut, it's wooden roof ablaze. It most likely had been the women's meeting place because he raced past the dead bodies of infants. Nursing infants and very young children were nothing but a nuisance to Achean raiders. That, too, he knew well.

At the village center he reached the source of the sounds searing his mind, tearing at his heart. Leaping and crackling fire tongues engulfed half of a large, rectangular wooden structure, doubtless the community meeting hall. Around him, in pools of darkening blood, lay the dead bodies of some twenty men and boys.

Kaskans built their buildings so that openings placed high up, one on each side, let in light and let out smoke. These openings would be too high for the men inside to reach without something to climb on, and when Damon raced around the front, he found what he knew he would. All the wooden tables and chairs were outside, most laid up against the only door. Wolf darted frantically back and forth, frightened yet unwilling to leave Damon.

Damon dashed to the pile, grabbed a chair, tossed it backward. The sound of fists beating on the door, male voices yelling, screams of pain, all fired his body. Many screams he could now tell were those of boys. He grabbed a table, too big for him to lift but with strength beyond normal, he dragged it backward.

Bias suddenly appeared beside him. "I told you to stay away from here," Damon shouted. This was something no one should see, no one should hear. Bias would never be the same.

Bias ignored him, and together they dragged away yet another table. Then each threw a chair off the pile. Two ale barrels, still half filled and heavy, they tipped on their sides and rolled away.

The screams were subsiding. Fingers of fire licked around the door's edges. The flames fully engulfed the roof. Damon felt and smelled heat singing hairs on his arms.

"Faster!" he urged.

Together they shoved away another table.

The beating on the door stopped.

They stood side-by-side and stared at the last table, which flames from the door had set afire and which was untouchable, burning from one end to the other.

He took Bias by the shoulders and walked the boy backward, away from the rectangle of fire and death.

He slumped onto the ground, Bias beside him.

He sat silent, and felt the water of his grief and remorse running down his cheeks. When he was young, when he was ignorant, he had let others lead him on just such raids. And then he killed the boy's mother, whose final gesture was to reach out to her dying son, a gesture that tore at Damon's heart. And when he returned to his home at last, two months later, he was told that a raid by Thracians had taken the loves of his life. That day he grew old.

Wolf crawled on his belly to Damon's leg and placed his muzzle there, seeking comfort. Damon laid a hand on his head.

To Bias he said, "Where is Dia?"

"I left her on the hill."

"You were brave to come. I'm sorry for what you have seen. For what you will see. I need to check now, if anyone yet alive can be helped. You can help me, or not. As you chose."

Damon stood.

Bias jumped up. "I can help."

Using his two thumbs, he wiped tears from Bias' cheeks. "Then find anyone alive, and call me to come check them. I will be able to tell if anything can be done. Move quickly."

With Bias's help, he made a survey. None of the men in

the central courtyard were alive. They checked the first home next to the burning central building. No men or women there. Nor in any of the next four homes. It quickly became evident they would find no women or young children. The Acheans were utterly thorough, ruthlessly expert at what they did. That was, of course, why they were so successful. He found no one who could be saved. No one who could breed a grudge.

He strode down to the beach and found a fishing boat with a sail of a size he could manage alone. To Bias he said, "I want you to take Dia and Wolf home. The Acheans have breached the Hellespont."

A chill of horror raised the hairs at the back of his neck as he thought of Pentha, and how she would take this news. How all of the People of Artemis might soon be affected.

He had only seen five vessels. Could the Acheans be planning things even bigger? Pentha would be in the middle of anything that happened.

"Going by boat is the fastest way for me to take word to the Hearth Queen. This boat will do."

He put both hands on Bias's shoulders, looked into his eyes. "You have seen for yourself, now, the evil men do to each other. I can't take the memory away." He wanted to say something that would heal the boy's spirit, but couldn't think of anything that would touch this horror. "I can say, the pain will grow less with the years."

He gave the boy what he hoped was a reassuring squeeze, and said, "Go!"

⇥ 25 ↤

At Themiskyra's harbor, Damon found a farmer with an empty mule-cart and asked for a ride. Fortunately, the man felt no urge to chat. At the Amazon compound entry, the farmer said, "You can't go in."

"I know."

"Just tell the girl what will come scamperin' up what your business is."

Damon nodded. The farmer flicked his mule's flank with a long pole.

A girl of perhaps thirteen galloped up on a mare with white socks. The girl had raven black hair, bound in the Amazon way at her nape. She wore the leather trousers of winter. This was probably her first year here. She pulled up in front of Damon and waited.

"I've come to see Queen Penthesilea," he said. "Tell her it's Damon. And tell her I bring news of Achean ships in the Euxine Sea."

The girl displayed no visible reaction. *Too young to know what this means.*

"You can meet her there," she said, pointing to a long, single story building a short walk away to his right. The girl wheeled the horse, already expert at it, and trotted toward a stable.

He walked to the building, and despite the disturbing news he carried, he found curiosity rising. Amazons spent nights here with the men of their choosing. Had he agreed to her arrangement, he might have been spending nights here with Pentha.

One step up brought him onto a long, covered porch, finished with finely polished pine planks. A number of chairs, also of finely worked woods with animal designs carved into the backs, invited a person to sit and rest. The view down the coastline presented at least a hundred women engaged in either archery or practice with a slingshot. Beyond the warriors, mares and their young grazed in a fall pasture.

Inside he found a spacious reception room. Nearly every speck of floor lay hidden under carpets with brilliantly colored designs—spirals, rosettes, diamonds, zigzags. His feet seemed to sink into the carpets like walking on fresh moss. He had seen rooms in some fine homes, but never more lush carpets. Red, green, and deep blue tones dominated. The one on which he stood probably originated somewhere far to the east of the Hittites. Perhaps the Mittani. Perhaps even as far as Assyria.

He eased himself into a cushioned chair. This was late afternoon. He was alone. He imagined quite a different scene at night.

Curiosity struck more forcefully. He stood again and looked down the hallway that led from the room's center to the building's other end. Door after door lined the corridor. He looked around to be certain he was alone. Then he walked to the first door, opened it, and peered inside.

Clean and comfortable. Two large chairs cushioned in green sat against one wall with a low table holding a bronze basin and a lamp. The bed was larger than any he'd ever seen, something royalty might insist on. A black, mink-pelt cover invited one to come and touch. A washing basin occupied one corner, and a cabinet stood in the other. A man could curl up or stretch out in pleasure here.

Curiosity satisfied, he backed out, returned to the reception room, and sat.

Soon Pentha strode in, accompanied by two of her commanders—Bremusa and Clonie. And Hippolyta. Hippolyta rushed to and embraced Damon. Her spirit always impressed him with an uncommon gentleness.

Pentha simply stood still before him—but he felt as if the lightening of Zeus jumped between them.

The room and the other women blurred. His heart seemed to rise to his throat. He ached to hear her speak so that he could see the yellow light. He had dreamed for a year of hearing her speak again.

"It pleases me to see you, Damon."

❧ 26 ❧

A ND THERE IT WAS, THE YELLOW LIGHT, IN Pentha's voice exactly as Damon remembered it. No. Better. Like the brightest golden sunrise.

And did he detect a hint of caring, a bit of wistfulness?

He said, "I'm sorry. I carry bad news."

"Tell us."

"I was out with the boy I told you about, Bias. We saw smoke and I feared it was at a Kaskan village. When we arrived, the village had been sacked. Achean ships had put back to sea."

Her gaze seemed to bore into his skull. "Can you be sure they were Achean?"

"I know them well, Pentha. There were five Achean warships."

"Who was leading them? Was it Achilles?"

"Why do you ask specifically about Achilles?"

She snapped back, "Was Achilles there?"

"The pennants were those of Achilles, but it would be impossible to say if he was there. The ships were too far away to see individuals. I saw only five ships. They may have been an expeditionary force, without the king."

She let out a long breath. "The villagers?"

"Killed the men, boys, old women, infants. Took women able to work and breed."

Hippolyta sank into a chair, bowed, and shook her head.

Pentha turned to the broad-chested Bremusa. "Take this news to Harmonia. Tell her, I call a Grand Council, and it must be this night." Bremusa struck the back of her clenched fist to her forehead in salute, turned, and strode out.

Pentha paced. Clonie stood still, watching her commander.

Abruptly, Pentha stopped. She looked at him. "You say there were five ships. What direction were they moving?"

"West."

"I am calling for a Grand Council. Tonight. You and I have talked of this before. It's my worst fear, but I've felt in my bones it was coming. It changes everything." She went back to pacing.

"Sadly, I agree."

"Good. Then you will stay the night, and describe for the council what you saw."

"No."

"Of course. You must."

"You don't need me. I've told you everything I know."

She stopped and stared at him, as if not quite understanding, or not wanting to understand. The shocking vibration in the air sprang back to life between them.

"Hippolyta. Clonie. Leave us. I'll join you shortly in the barracks."

Hippolyta stood, and they left, Clonie following Hippolyta out the door.

"Why won't you stay? I want you to stay. I may need your help."

He touched the place where, beneath his tunic, her arrowhead lay and fought the urge to cross the chasm between them, take her in his arms, and take one more kiss from her mouth. "You will be talking of war, preparing for war. War is not my life."

"I ask only that you describe what you saw."

"I repeat, you don't need me to do that. I need to return to my animals."

"This news is earthshaking, Damon. Why won't you stay? Perhaps there will be some who question that the ships truly were Achean."

He didn't want to argue with her. He said nothing.

Her face, which had been so intense and angry, relaxed. The fire in her eyes softened. "Is it me? Are you for some reason angry at me?"

He shook his head, could not suppress a rueful smile. She had no idea how much it was her, but certainly not in anger. "Of course not. I remember our days together with nothing but pleasure."

She said softly, "I have missed you.

I have missed you. The words snatched the breath from his lungs. "And I missed you."

"Then stay."

"War is not my business. And nothing has changed my feeling that you also are not my business. I can't be with a woman only now and then. At a whim. If I spent the night here in Themiskyra, I would want to spend it only with you. And certainly not in talk of war."

"Stay, Damon."

"I cannot." He bowed his head to her. "I ask your leave."

"I'll not order you to stay. I'll not keep you if you don't want to stay."

Fire burned where his heart should be. "I'm glad to see you again. Glad to hear, and see, your voice."

She smiled at that.

He added, "I will have you and your people in my prayers."

With an effort so mighty he felt his heart might burst open, he turned and walked out the door.

❧ 27 ❧

A YOUNG, FEMALE VOICE SAID, "YOUR TAMBOURINE, mistress."

Derinoe let the curtain close and turned to face the hazel-eyed girl of perhaps fifteen holding the tambourine Derinoe had forgotten and left behind when changing clothes. Derinoe wore three silk garments, the outmost dark blue one essentially a veil covering most of her body but not her arms, face, or head. To the girl she said, "You need not call me mistress. I'm a servant too."

"Oh, mistress. That's certainly not so. No dancer in Troy compares with you. I doubt there's a better dancer in the world."

Derinoe smiled. "Kind words make a heart happy."

The girl nodded at the curtain, which Derinoe still held closed, and said, "May I look?"

Derinoe once more pulled the heavy, gold silk curtain back so that she and the girl could peek into the Great Hall of Priam. This dinner for one hundred of Troy's elite was a dinner of joy. Hektor had returned, and not only safe. In this last battle of the war season, he had fought the Achean royal Ajax—a huge man—and their duel had ended in a tie. In recognition of their respect for each other, the warriors even exchanged armor. Tonight, long after the evening's celebrants snuffed out their last candle, Derinoe would be in

Hektor's arms. She hoped to catch a glimpse of him before she danced, to assure herself he was truly uninjured.

Together she and the girl contemplated the lavish scene. Despite years of siege, Troy's control of her landlines enabled these assembled elites to receive the goods necessary to feast in opulence. A head table occupied the end of the room to her left. Two side tables ran from the head table to the room's other end. Wood blazed in the great central hearth as the season, now in early September, had turned cold.

Gold plates, candleholders, goblets, and platters flickered in the light of candles on the tables and lighted bronze cressets on the walls. The mouth-watering smell of cooked beef and partridge, boar and hare permeated air and clothing. Heavy red wine flowed fast and in abundance, like the Scamander River in early spring. And in the room's center, between the hearth and Priam's table, six acrobats in body-tight costumes of red and yellow entertained, twisting themselves into the most remarkable positions, doing astonishing flips, then piling one onto the shoulders of another.

The girl said, "Isn't our Queen elegant? I know a woman who sews Hekuba's gowns. That purple. Purest silk from Cos." She put a hand to Derinoe's outermost covering. "This is silk too, isn't it?"

Derinoe nodded, still gazing into the room. Would Hektor come? Surely he would. The banquet was for him. Would Andromache arrive with him?

The thought of Andromache soon studying every tiny bit of Derinoe's exposed body gave Derinoe a chill that tickled the back of her neck. The last time she had danced for the royals Andromache had pretended interest in Derinoe's costume, but then had said, "I hear you have a little girl. And a boy. Where is your husband?"

Afterward, Derinoe couldn't even remember how she had replied, but her fears for the children had leapt once more into full flame.

"I'm more fascinated by the monkey," she said to the girl, something to divert her mind. "See! There. Behind the king's throne. The ambassador from Nubia's king Memnon just gave it as a gift."

The monkey sat on a perch behind Priam, a remarkable little thing with a black body, white nose, and long, white beard. With tiny, busy hands, it peeled skin from a yellow fruit and then took delicate bites from the white center.

The monkey wasn't the only animal present. A bronze cage—of a man's height—displayed four almost entirely white Little Egrets with startling, bright yellow feet. Long, snowy plumes crested their heads. A hand-raised pair of cranes, as tall as a man's chest and resplendent in white with gorgeous black necks, strutted freely between the tables.

Behind another curtain, musicians created a festive mood with music of reed flutes, tambourines, and sistrum. Soon the musicians would play for her.

The girl said, "Do you get to eat from the table after the banquet?"

She shook her head. After the banquet, she would join Cassandra in the palace rooms reserved for the king's daughter. Cassandra didn't enjoy large public dinners. They would dine there together before Derinoe went to Hektor's quarters. He rarely slept the whole night with Andromache. Derinoe put her hand to the curls piled onto her head, as if checking that everything about her was perfectly in place to meet him.

The guests leapt to their feet, thumping on the tabletops in applause. Hektor strode from the main door to the head table with Andromache the customary pace behind him. At least from here, Derinoe could see no wound on him.

Aphrodite had surely kissed Hektor in his mother's womb. He was so stunningly handsome. Not pretty like his younger brother, the fair-haired Paris, who sat next to Helen. No, Hektor had strong features and a character to match.

His light skin contrasted sharply with black curly hair, very like her own light skin and dark hair. His close-cut beard emphasized the strong jaw, and under a high forehead, his dark blue eyes most often bespoke thoughtfulness.

He went first to his father and kissed Priam on both cheeks, then embraced his mother and kissed her too. He sat to his father's right with Andromache behind and to his left. Derinoe counted eight of Priam's other legitimate sons also seated at the head table with their wives.

"When do you dance?" the girl said.

"The musicians will wait until Andromache serves Hektor food. Then they begin the music for me."

"Aren't you nervous?"

Irony seized her and she smiled, hugely amused. This young woman could have no idea how nervous. With her dancing, Derinoe had attracted Hektor. She did not think he would abandon her or their child if she ceased to please the court. On the other hand, what would happen when she grew old? Too old to dance and please. This worry never ceased to plague her. And now, what if Andromache did know the truth for certain? "Very," she said.

The music changed. Conversation diminished. A hush gathered around the guests. Derinoe straightened. The girl took hold of the curtain. "Now," Derinoe said.

The moment she stepped into sight, the hush became complete. Only the music filled the space. Making no movement except with her hand, she rattled the tambourine, then touched it to her thigh. Sudden silence.

When she once again rattled it, the music commenced, drums and flutes. She moved her hips side to side, keeping her body still from the waist up except for moving the rattling tambourine in a wide circle.

She glided forward into the room's center. Sliding around the blazing hearth, she headed straight for Priam. When she reached him, the music changed again, and she began undulated both upper and lower body, then twirled, one way and then the other, all the time varying the tambourine's insistence. Now soft, now loud.

She dared to glance at Hektor, only a glance. His intense gaze met hers, but the practiced skill of an heir to a throne kept his face unreadable.

She did not have the courage to look at Andromache.

She stepped close to the front of Priam's table, undid the especially designed and lengthened end of the dark blue outermost garment, and handed the end to Priam.

He tugged on the silk, and the garment pulled away from her body. Priam let it ripple to the floor. The white silk beneath it exposed not only her arms but was cut low across her breasts, and deep slits up both sides let her viewers see flashes of the light blue, sheer gown beneath. And flashes of her long legs.

She danced alongside the front of one side table, and up the front of the other, all the time working the tambourine. When she once again reached Priam, her heart beat against her throat. The music possessed her now.

Hot, her skin tingling, she gave Priam the specially lengthened end of the white silk. He pulled that garment from her body, leaving her draped only in a light blue that revealed the shadow of all beneath it. The fabric barely covered her breasts, completely exposed her waist, and hung seductively in front of her legs and directly behind.

She undid the large pin that held up her black hair so that its waves fell to her waist. In a final twirl and with loud tambourine rattle, she sank to the floor, her back arched and one hand pointed toward the ceiling. She lost herself in a fantasy of Hektor's gaze on her. Imagined herself soon in his arms, his lips on hers.

The music stopped. Slowly the moment released her. She registered the loud sounds of thumped applause on the tables and voices of men and women calling out "Well done," and "Beautiful," and "Derinoe!"

She rose and curtsied to Hekuba and bowed low to Priam. She dared not risk another glance at Hektor.

Surrounded with applause, she ran from the room. It took only moments to change back into a light woolen green gown. Gradually her heart slowed. She cooled off.

She tucked her dancing things into an embroidered satchel, a gift from Cassandra, and after wrapping a woolen shawl over her shoulders, strode toward one of many private passages. She had been Cassandra's friend for over six years, and Hektor's lover for four. She knew many, if not all, of the citadel's private and secret passages.

❧ 28 ❧

W HEN DERINOE REACHED CASSANDRA'S HOME, Alcmene greeted her. "The Lady Cassandra went for a stroll on the wall. She asks you to meet her there."

Many shops in the citadel backed up against the thick, massive stone structure that ringed Troy's inner heart. These buildings gave added protection to the fortification. In earlier times of quiet, the citadel's elite walked along the top to enjoy the view, the activities in the city, or the sunset. Now, since the invasion, they could often watch battles on the plain below when the clashes surged close enough.

Some homes within the wall's embrace stood near it, but none were connected to it. A narrow wooden footbridge spanned a gap of ten steps between Cassandra's top floor garden and the wall's walkway. Derinoe crossed, and seeing Cassandra standing not far from the tower guarding the southern gate, she strolled to join her.

She embraced Cassandra, who said, "So how did it go?"

"If applause is a true gauge, it went well."

Cassandra linked their arms. "The signs today indicate we should not eat fowl, so I changed our dinner slightly."

She turned to look southwest again, past the lights of the oil lamps in the city windows, southwest toward the mouth of the bay where the Acheans squatted on Trojan land. For years, Achilles had encamped south and Ajax north of Troy;

the lands surrounding the city could not possibly supply food and fuel for the entire Achean force for any lengthy period.

Derinoe had arranged her escape from Achilles early in the siege, when he was still encamped at Troy. She often wondered where she might have ended up had she not been able to escape before he moved south.

Cassandra sighed. "I used to come here to look at the stars. Now I find myself staring with sick fascination at their campfires."

To Derinoe, the enemy fires, strung in a long sweeping curve, seemed like a goddesses' necklace laid out against a black cat's fur. She spoke her thoughts. "In the night darkness, the fires seem beautiful. They make me think of the peace of home and hearth. But then I think, thousands of barbarians huddle around them. Savages who would like nothing better than to kill every man in Troy. Then they would cheerfully rape the women."

Cassandra said, "Let's walk. Let's put our minds on other things. Will you go to Hektor tonight after we dine?"

"Yes. He must have sent his message almost the minute he returned from the fighting."

The eternal wind had quieted for the night, but the air still nipped her skin with a cold bite. Derinoe slipped the woolen shawl higher across her shoulders. To circle the citadel once made for good exercise.

Cassandra said, "I am very upset with Paris."

"What has your little brother done now?"

Any talk with Cassandra about Paris always distressed Derinoe. Despite his physical beauty and often entertaining ways, Derinoe despised him from the first time they met. He had rebuked her for interrupting something he was saying. Paris, like most Trojan men, thought women should be kept in their place. Her Amazon mother would have slapped his disrespectful face.

"He and Hektor had an enormous fight. Not physical mind you. But Hektor is furious that Paris rarely joins in when the Trojans launch a battle. He told Paris so. I was there. So was Helen and Andromache. What a scene."

"Paris is an outstanding archer and would be a great asset in any battle. But it's obvious he's is a man interested only in the hunt and making love, not fighting."

"I hear the disgust, even in your voice."

"Do you want me to say sweet things about him even if I don't believe them?"

"People just don't understand him."

"He seduced another man's wife and managed to convince her to abscond to a foreign land with much of her husband's wealth."

"Why don't people blame Helen? Instead, Hektor supports her. So do Priam and Hekuba."

Derinoe felt a sharp stab of pity for Helen who, not unlike herself, lived essentially alone, cut off from her family and former life. With shocking vividness, the image of Derinoe's mother, on the floor and with blood spreading across her white sleeping gown, sent a shiver down Derinoe's arms. She clutched the shawl tighter.

And Pentha? Pentha was doubtless dead as well, because she, too, would never have surrendered to the Acheans.

"I suppose I do blame Helen in a way," Derinoe replied. "She did, after all, leave Menelaus of her own will to come here. But mostly I feel sorry for her. Those beautiful blue eyes. It's not hard to see why Paris was smitten. Her temperament is gentle and she is quite without guile." *All so unlike that venomous Andromache.* "Really, when you know her you can hardly help but like her, and he took her away from her home."

"Still, to put all the blame on Paris—"

Cassandra could not see that her brother was an essentially weak and debauched man. Derinoe continued. "Paris is physically beautiful. He has a charmed tongue. Everyone can easily imagine him casting a spell on so simple a woman. But what makes people angry with Paris is that although he has brought war to Troy, he's not willing to fight to drive the enemy away."

What gloomy talk! Better to think of other things. "You must visit Priam," she said, "and see the monkey he received today."

"A monkey?"

Their chat turned to monkeys, Nubians, silk, and the next festival to Athena. By the time they completed the circuit, Derinoe felt warm enough to let the shawl drape loosely over her shoulders.

They crossed the bridge onto the roof garden, and before reentering her rooms, Cassandra led them to a niche holding the image of her patron goddess.

They knelt. Derinoe joined Cassandra in a prayer of praise. But for some reason, perhaps her recent thought of her mother, the words came out stilted with guilt. How this sight would have shocked and saddened her mother. Her prayers should be to Artemis, protectress of Amazons.

But then, could she really think of herself as Amazon now?

Not for the first time she felt dissatisfied. Trapped. And riddled with fear for Myrina and Leonides.

⊰ 29 ⊱

WHEN DERINOE FINISHED PRAYING WITH CAS-sandra, she said, "I've not told you much about my former life." They went inside and walked down one story. She continued. "My mother prayed to the huntress, Artemis."

Cassandra cast her a sharp look.

Derinoe hurried on. "Of course, I honor Athena so I have no trouble following your example."

Cassandra put her hand on Derinoe's arm. "Don't let anyone in Troy hear you express any desire to follow that wild woman of the woods."

Derinoe waited, unsure what to say. But perhaps she shouldn't be surprised at Cassandra's advice. Shortly after meeting Cassandra, Derinoe had learned that to openly worship Artemis in Troy was considered not only rather low class, but a possible sign of disloyalty. Since the days when, in his youth, Priam sided with Bellerophon against the Amazons, Artemis worshippers had become suspect. Clearly, Cassandra's thin lips and creased brow made evident her contempt for anyone attracted to the Huntress.

Cassandra led into the sitting room, tossed off her shawl, and moved to a table that held wine. She poured, then handing Derinoe wine and shaking her head, she said, "I have recently seen things. Evil things. I have great fears for the people of Troy. Some days I grow quite frantic."

She sipped, and her mood seemed to shift. "I have never asked anything about your former life. When I was hurt and alone, you tended me even though you didn't know who I was. And for that, I will always be grateful. We are friends. I don't need to know anything else. I don't even need to know who Leonides' father is."

Derinoe's heart skipped a beat. Was this actually a request? Did Cassandra in fact want to know?

Mercifully, two servants interrupted the uncomfortable moment, bringing light dinner. Derinoe lingered over a whitefish, redolent with thyme, her thoughts far from Cassandra's talk of how desperately Athena's statue in the temple needed refurbishing.

When fruit was served—golden apples and grapes—a man entered carrying a lyre. His cheery round face bore twinkling dark brown eyes and a wispy froth of white hair ringed a bald top.

"We will have our own entertainment," Cassandra said, with a glowing smile. To the man she said, "So, teller of tales and singer of songs, begin."

"Wise high priestess of our divine Athena, I am greatly honored to devise a pleasure for you and your friend."

He strummed the lyre and played a popular paean to Zeus. That completed, he recited a poem in which Athena, born straight from the head of her father, Zeus—a goddess untouched by any woman, not even in birth—granted a bit of her wisdom to mortals. "And now," he said, "a story that teaches us some of that wisdom.

"One day a young hunter named Actaeon finished his hunting. And he suddenly realized that he was lost."

Derinoe knew this story well. Her mother had told it to Derinoe and Pentha many times. A sharp edge of grief struck. She shoved her memories down into the deep places where she hid all her troubles, and settled back to enjoy a familiar tale.

"Actaeon tried first one path, and then another. Then he heard women's laughter. He made for it, and burst into a clearing. There, bathing nude in a spring was the huntress goddess, Artemis."

The storyteller's voice turned ominous. "She was surrounded by her nymphs. Actaeon saw her beauty and forgot her vengeful nature and her hatred for men, and he lingered. Too long. Artemis saw him. She was certain he would boast that he had seen her naked."

Derinoe felt warm blood of protest rising under her skin.

The teller of tales continued. "The very thought that Actaeon might boast enraged Artemis. Actaeon turned to flee, but too late. Her quiver was not at hand, so the goddess cast a spell on the water, scooped it up, and flung it onto him.

"With the speed of lightning's flash, he transformed into a great, beautiful stag.

"He ran, and his hunting dogs gave chase. Terrified, Actaeon ran for his life, knowing what the dogs would do if they caught him. And they did. They brought him down and devoured him alive.

"Artemis is a goddess who hates men, and to worship her is to be seduced by her and leads to destruction of the most violent, horrifying kind."

Her back rigid, Derinoe felt her heart beating a wild pulse in her throat. The man had changed the story to please the high priestess of Artemis's rival in Troy, the high priestess of Athena. This was the kind of lie that led men to think they could rape women as Achilles had raped her. "Your story isn't right!"

White eyebrows lifted.

"Artemis did not punish Actaeon because she hates men." The heat in her heart showed in her voice. "Actaeon knew that the goddess was bathing, and did not respect her. He felt he had every right to enter the clearing and gaze upon her. If he could have, he might have raped her. Artemis does not hate men. What she hates is men who do not respect women. For that that she punished him. Why do you change the story?"

He took a step back. Looking at Cassandra he bowed and said, "I am profoundly sorry if my telling has offended, My Lady."

Derinoe looked at Cassandra, who turned blazing eyes on Derinoe.

Derinoe rushed to explain. "My mother told me the story many times, Cassandra. He tells it wrong."

Cassandra waved her hand in dismissal. The storyteller vanished on quick feet. With a voice as chilled as ice, Cassandra said, "Should I think your loyalty to Athena is in doubt?"

A cold breath of fear prickled Derinoe's skin—she must not offend Cassandra. Then a pang of guilt—she should, in fact, be honoring Artemis as her mother would have wanted. But then above all, a warming rush of gratitude—this woman had saved her life.

She rose and knelt in front of Cassandra and took her hand. "I love you, my dear friend. You are the high priestess of the goddess Athena, and for you I honor Her. You have protected me and my son and my daughter. I am forever in your debt."

"And I love you," Cassandra said, slipping her arms around Derinoe. "So let us not argue. Just, please, Derinoe. Let's not speak, ever again, of Artemis. If you were to take up the worship of that disrespectful Artemis, our friendship would suffer. Quite seriously"

Derinoe held Cassandra in an embrace a moment longer, her heart slowing from relief. They were still friends. Hektor was Derinoe's first source of security, but Cassandra was her critical second source. Their friendship should not, must not, ever be damaged.

Still, she seemed to have taken one more step from her past. To survive, she had lived in denial of so many things for so many years. Now it seemed she must finally, permanently, deny even her memories of Amazon pride and freedom.

She forced a smile. "I should go to Hektor now."

She should take Hektor a happy heart, not this crushing sadness. He didn't like to see her unhappy. But perhaps just seeing him would lift her spirit.

They exchanged a kiss to the cheek. Cassandra said, "Give my brother my love."

❧ 30 ❧

"THE PROPOSAL YOU HAVE JUST HEARD IS A PER-
fect example of why Penthesilea is unsuited to the position of Warrior Queen."

Euryclea paused, obviously for effect as she scanned the
Grand Council Chamber, attempting to capture the attention
of every one of the fifty most important women and men of
Themiskyra. The central hearth blazed and torches on the
walls added more light. It was night and their gloomy subject was war, but the room itself couldn't have been more
cheerful.

Pentha clenched a fist in her lap. She forced her expression to remain impassive, but her mind had reeled during all
of Euryclea's diatribe. Pentha had expected some disagree-
ment at this meeting, some questions, but not this vitriolic
attack on her authority.

Euryclea made an imposing figure, tall and dressed in a
formal gown, as were all the women except Pentha and her
Amazons. She and they would not wear gowns until they left
service as Amazons, but for Grand Council they were for-
mally dressed in silk, trousers and long-sleeved, high necked
tunics. And Pentha wore the golden girdle that was the symbol of her authority, the golden girdle worn by all Warrior
Queens for as long as there was memory in Themiskrya. In
battle it held her sword's sheath and her ax. When the time

came, she would pass it to her successor. And Euryclea had just made clear she thought that time should be now.

Harmonia sat at the head of the room on a dais. Pentha sat to her left. At Harmonia's right side sat Trusis and four other men of the men's council. To Pentha's left sat Bremusa and three women from the women's council.

Euryclea, as currently recognized speaker, stood in the center of the semicircle. From there she could turn to address either the members on the dais or the remainder of Themiskyra's elite.

Pentha felt a sudden urge to leap up and wring Euryclea's neck. *The woman has basically declared war on me.* Instead she looked to the front row of seated dignitaries, at Hippolyta. Hippolyta looked back and shook her head, her full lips pursed in disgust. Gryn, sitting beside Hippolyta, simply stared at Euryclea with a composed, unreadable expression.

"In short," Euryclea said, "we have defended our borders against Hittites and Kaska for years. Rather than stir ourselves to an ill advised preparation for war with an enemy that has not yet so much as threatened us, we need to reconsider who should be setting policy and leading our troops."

Euryclea bowed to Harmonia, then returned to her seat in the front row:

Harmonia said, "We have now heard the news of the attack on the Kaskan village from Penthesilea. We have heard her urge the People of Artemis to arm themselves in preparation for an Achean attack of unprecedented magnitude. And now we have heard from the honorable Euryclea, who takes a contrary position. Pentha, I would like to hear any rebuttal you might wish to offer."

Many heads had nodded while Euryclea talked. Pentha must touch deep places in their hearts if she hoped to win this battle. She drew a steadying breath, then rose and moved in front of the hearth and faced the majority.

"The People of Artemis are free. We are famous for our saying, 'A mother bear is deadly in defense of her young.' We live here, secure within our borders because we maintain a defense second to none. At least, it has been second to none until now." She paused and locked eyes with Euryclea. "But the Acheans are warriors born and bred. They live for battle. It is their meat and drink, the air they breathe." She shifted her gaze to embrace the majority. "They are ruthless predators, interested only in what they can take in booty and slaves. You heard what Damonides saw. Not one person in the Kaskan village was spared. Many men and boys were burned alive."

She paused to let that sickening image work its way into their thoughts. She turned and addressed the dais.

"Euryclea believes they will not come here for fear of us. I assure you, she is wrong. They may respect us. But they do *not* fear us. If they find us in any way vulnerable, they will come. We must ensure that we're not in any way weak. Our men must make ready once more, as they have done in past emergencies, to fight. And all women of suitable age, even those who might have chosen otherwise, should be trained to the horse and bow."

Harmonia said, "I would hear Trusis speak to this matter of the men."

Pentha saluted and returned to her seat.

Trusis stood and with an air of delighted importance, strutted to the hearth. "What is it you wish to know?" he said to Harmonia.

Her voice touched with impatience, Harmonia said, "What do you think of this idea that we should arm the men and fit them for battle?"

"I couldn't agree more."

To Pentha he looked stunned and excited, like a man whose self-important mind had suddenly burst into flames of desire. If the People of Artemis were to prepare the men as warriors, Trusis' position would inflate to perhaps match the size of his own imagined significance. The involvement of their men in battles was rare—Pentha could think of only five times in all their history that it had been necessary—and as their leader, Trusis' name would live forever in Amazon memory.

He continued, alternately pressing his palms together and then spreading his arms dramatically as he made a point. Finally, "Our men are eager to participate in any preparations that our Warrior Queen recommends. We see the threat. We agree we must prepare to meet it." He smiled at Pentha, and she felt sure that he thought his speech of support was endearing him to her. "I concur with her wise judgment in such matters."

Harmonia ended his moments of glory saying, "Thank you, Truisis." He bowed, and strode back to his seat with straight shoulders and glittering eyes.

Harmonia asked, "Would anyone else speak?"

Marpessa rose. Like her mother, she was tall and gaunt. Were the age difference not evident, they could have been twins. In a sweetly oily tone she said, "I do feel it's important to add something. This scheme Penthesilea has suggested will take us in entirely the wrong direction. We prosper and thrive because we do *not* spend our resources on conquest. And this grand scheme of Pentha's comes close to suggesting we go outside of Themiskyra to fight. Didn't she say, 'If the Trojans cannot expel the Acheans, it may be necessary for us to rid our shores of this foreign plague?' Reaching outside of Themiskyra would be a great mistake." Her tone hardened. "This is not our way. Pentha was raised outside, and it would seem that her heart is still with the outside."

Pentha stiffened. *How dare the viper accuse me of lack of loyalty to the People!* She gathered herself to protest. Bremusa laid a hand on her arm.

Harmonia said, "Thank you, Marpessa." She turned to Pentha, her brow creased and her eyes questioning. "Marpessa makes a good point. I, too, believe I heard you saying something that goes beyond just being strong in our defense."

What could she say to open their eyes and embolden their hearts? She again took place before the hearth. Her mother's face flashed before her, her mother telling her stories of the Amazon past. Glorious stories that had informed her childhood and created in her marrow a white-hot passion for freedom.

"Sometimes history touches a People with a moment when reaching out is essential, for honor and for life. Only one generation ago men came from Athens to Themiskyra, led by Herakles. They stole from us not only this girdle I wear today, but took away Antiope and gave her to one of their kings, Theseus. We did not ignore this wrong or turn our backs. We did not stay at home wringing our hands. Led by Hippolyta, my sister's namesake, Amazons went to Athens and mounted a siege that returned the girdle to us. Now these same barbarians are again raiding the coast of lands that are not theirs and have come to our door. Will we turn our backs, wring our hands, fail to prepare?

She turned to Harmonia. "And true, I *am* convinced that we must be prepared to do more than simply defend Themiskyra." She drew a slow breath. If she completed this argument, she risked giving Euryclea and Marpessa the weapon they needed to bring her down, because without Harmonia's good will, Pentha's position would become precarious in the extreme. But to remain silent . . . No. She must lay it all out. "The stalemate between Troy and the Acheans has gone on nine years, and during that time, the Acheans have brought death, rape, grief, and enslavement to one village and town after another. Priam has been unable to expel this rotting evil. What I said was that it may be necessary for *us* to rid these shores of the foreign plague. And what I mean by that, honored Queen, is that we must be able and willing to offer aid to Priam."

She heard a nervous stirring from the assembly behind her, and Harmonia's face darkened, her brows drew together, her lips thinned.

Pentha plunged on. "It is true that when he was young, Priam took up arms against us and sided with Bellerophon. We are not now and for a long time have not been on good terms with Troy. But I urge this council," she gave Harmonia a long look, then turned to face the majority, "I urge the People of Artemis, to look into the future and see that if we do not act now, we may live to see our way of life destroyed, our men and boys slaughtered, and our women and girls sold into slavery.

"We are great warriors. Indeed, our security in part depends upon our reputation as fierce and uncompromising. Let me prepare us to defend Themiskyra. Let me also prepare us to give aid to Troy. Do not turn away from our greatness."

She turned and faced the dais. "Because if I cannot make the preparations I consider essential, it *is* best that someone else take my place."

A hush fell. Pentha saw shock in the faces of both Gryn and Hippolyta as she returned to her seat.

Behind her she heard Euryclea. "Honored Harmonia, I really . . ."

"You have already spoken," Harmonia said, her hand raised to cut Euryclea off. "Does anyone else wish to speak?"

Pentha sat. No one rose.

"According to custom then," Harmonia said, "we will retire for discussion for two hours. At that time, a vote will would be taken. And then I will give my decision."

With Bremusa, Clonie, Hippolyta, and Gryn, Pentha spent the time in a corner of a nearby garden, sipping mare's milk and talking. All agreed that since this was essentially the end of war season, and Damon had said the ships were headed west, there would be no clash with the Acheans this year. "We have the whole winter to prepare," Breumusa observed

The clusters of friends and acquaintances in the garden spoke in muted tones that gave no clue as to how the matter was evolving. She did note that none who passed close by went out of their way to catch her attention and bow, the usual treatment she received.

They returned together to the Council Chamber where the vote was taken in secret—a blue token dropped into the leather sack signifying that Pentha should be given full discretion, a white token signifying that they should prepare only to defend Themiskyra, a green token signifying that Harmonia should announce a contest to determine a new Warrior Queen.

The tokens were counted so that all could observe. Harmonia then stood. "I have no love for Priam. But logic and honor require that personal feelings be set aside. I have voted as have the overwhelming majority of you." She turned to Pentha. "You have the support of this council and of myself to prepare the women and men of Artemis to defend Themiskyra and to give aid to Priam of Troy if he will accept it."

The room burst into male whistles and female clapping. Euryclea and Marpessa and their friends pointedly refrained.

Later, when she and Hippolyta and Gryn reached the place where Gryn would go to her home, they stopped to embrace. "The first thing I will do," Pentha said, "is put out spies to find out exactly where those five ships are and where they will winter."

Gryn took her hand, gave it a firm squeeze. "There is something else even more important."

Pentha waited.

"I assume you are serious about preparing to fight and kill the Acheans at Troy."

"Yes."

"Then we must know all we can about Achean fighting. You saw how differently Damon held the Achean shield when the two of you dueled. He will also know about the construction of their weapons. About their tactics. The first thing you must do is convince Damon to help us."

❧ 31 ❧

THE SMELL OF A FIR-SCENTED WOOD FIRE REACHED Pentha well before she spotted the small wooden shed where Bias said she could find Damon. She walked resolutely, determined to convince him. His help was critical. Nothing would deter her.

This morning, when she'd reached the mountains, she found them mantled with a light snow. Her breath came out in little white puffs. Given the leaden grayness of the sky and the somber quiet in the woods, she imagined the arrival of more snow soon. She caught sight of a hind amidst the fir trees. It caught sight of her and bounded away.

The narrow, but well-worn, trail from his cabin wound sharply downhill over kettle-sized rocks and through the dense stand of firs. Generations of dropped needles lent a gentle spring to her stride.

Black smoke curled out of a clay pipe stuck through the shed's sod roof. She tapped on the closed door. Silence. She lifted the wooden latch and took a quick look inside.

Logs burning in an iron brazier provided toasty warmth. Three shelves held blankets and food items: bread, a clay pot of what was probably olives, and some apples. Unlike his cabin, which had a packed dirt floor, someone had taken the time and effort to craft wood planks for the shed. The bearskin that covered the planks came from a beast that, standing upright, would have towered over any man.

Pentha closed the door and proceeded down the trail perhaps twenty steps to a tiny glen. Cut branches indicated that it had been hacked out by hand. There in the center lay a pool, perhaps three times the size of her bathtub. In the pool's center, Damon stood waist deep with his back to her, steam rising around him.

She suddenly realized she would surprise or even frighten him when she spoke. She cleared her throat, then said, "Bias told me I would find you here."

Damon spun around, splashing water in a great arc, some of which hit her leg. Exceedingly hot water!

His face broke into a smile of joy that would live with her the rest of her life. This was what his heart thought of her, undisguised by rationality or guile or worry or doubts. A smile at once deeply humbling and also frightening. She couldn't imagine feeling so intensely happy at simply seeing someone, and all this happiness focused on her.

He quickly recovered and said, "You have discovered my one luxury." He held a sponge in his right hand.

She said, "The water's very hot."

"I enjoy it most in the winter."

In a long silence, she studied him and he studied her.

Then he said, "Take off your clothes."

She hesitated.

"Join me." He lifted the sponge over his head and squeezed. Water streaked down his face and dripped onto his chest. Around his neck, a green object hung on a leather thong.

She was here to ask him to do something he had said many times he did not do. Perhaps bathing with him was not— No. Perhaps it would actually be good to begin with something fun and pleasurable, to ensure an agreeable mood.

She unlaced the neck of her tunic and shucked it over her head. He watched, his face unreadable.

She stripped off boots and trousers.

The hot water felt like a lover's embrace.

When she reached Damon, he squeezed water first on one

shoulder and then the other. She stared in fascination at the object dangling from the thong. The arrowhead she had made.

She touched it.

He flinched as if she'd touched him with a hot iron and wrapped his hand over the arrowhead. Slowly, a grin lifted the corners of his mouth. "And now you know another one of my secrets."

She covered his hand with her own. "I'm honored, Damon. I have nothing of yours to keep, but I keep thoughts of you in my heart."

With his thumb he rubbed the faceted face, then traced the sharp edge. "It reminds me exactly of you. It's the color of your eyes. It is exquisite. And it's fashioned to kill."

The heat rising inside her plus the heat of the water brought sweat to her upper lip. Moisture also beaded his face. He pulled her to him and kissed first her eyes, and then her lips. She molded her body to him and felt him, erect and hard. The fire to couple stirred in her belly. He used his tongue to part her lips and enter her mouth, and with her whole body, she wanted to melt into him.

He broke off the kiss, which she could have made last forever, and taking her hand, led her to the edge of the pool, and then out of it, heading for the shed.

"Let me bring my clothes," she said. "They'll be frozen if I leave them out here." She snatched them up, then placed her hand back into his and let him lead her.

They made love. The tenderness she remembered from him was still there, but edged with iron. He wanted her. She was certain he was also angry with her. She felt a roughness, a barbed challenge even in his kisses. She refused to rise to the goading and kept her spirit soft.

Afterward he added logs to the fire. They shared goat cheese and apples. Then they made love again. And this time, his voice, his touch, his entry into her body, his caresses after— from no man had she ever felt such passion to please her.

While she lay in his arms he said, "You know, I believe I have only once before felt so at peace."

"Were you alone then? You said being alone gives you peace."

He frowned. "No. I was married. I had a wife and son."

Under the cover, he ran his fingers over her breast. She felt her nipple tighten.

He continued, his voice quite sad. "They were killed. We lived in a dangerous place. I once visited a beautiful place. Ephesus. Rich land. Sunny weather. They don't hold with war. I spent a great many years wishing every day that I had taken them there."

"I am so sorry."

"Why is it you wanted so much to be a warrior? You were already sixteen when you returned. You didn't have to choose the Amazon path."

"I honor my mother. She was Amazon. And I could ask you, why did you give up the life of the sword?"

His hand fell still and he stared at the roof. "War is evil. I've had my fill of it."

"It's possible for you, as one man, to decide that, but life isn't so simple.

"That's what the leaders who start every war always say. 'Life isn't so simple.' They always have a good reason for going at it." She had never heard Damon sound bitter, but she could not miss that sharp edge now. "Well, their reasons no longer convince me."

She sat up, stared hard at him. "We are raided regularly by Hittite and Kaska. Do we just give up and let them enslave us? We don't invade homes and kill innocents."

She waited in a long, strained silence, both of them unblinking. Then he said, softly but firmly, "Amazons never take prisoners. Do you ever wonder about the families of the men you've killed?"

"How dare you ask me such a question!"

He did not flinch. He did not look away. The hard question was still there in his eyes.

"We Amazons have a saying. 'A female bear is deadly in defense of her young.' If we lose our reputation for ferocity, we'll invite worse treatment."

He pulled her down against him and stroked her hair. In spite of herself, some of her anger drained away.

He said, "I don't want to argue with you. My feelings are my own. They come from my life. But I can respect that you feel different."

"No slaving, raping barbarian will take Themiskyra while I live."

She lay quiet for a while longer in his arms. It was now late afternoon and all the logs had been consumed. He said, "Sadly, we can't spend the night unless we fetch more wood. I'll go to the cabin."

"I'll come with you. We can talk better there."

They dressed. She would remember that under his tunic, not far from his heart, lay her arrowhead.

They stepped outside to find quiet snow dropping a veil of white over everything. Bathing with him was one thing, but making love to him might have been a mistake. He'd not asked why she'd come. Perhaps he assumed that she had changed her mind about remaining Amazon until her duty was completed. If so, her purpose here would be more complicated.

"I think I may have misled you. I didn't come to make love. I let my heart run away. I've come to ask you something. Something important." They passed through the thorn hedge.

He put his arm around her shoulder. "Ask me anything."

"I think I should have spoken sooner."

"Ask!"

They reached the door. He opened it and she followed him inside.

The boy, Bias, sat at the table. Arranged before him were several simple clay bowels holding different colored, pea-sized stone beads. He was fixing the beads in a fancy pattern onto a harness. He jumped up, all arms and legs, and said, "I see you found him."

Damon clapped him on the shoulder. "How about you warm us some soup."

Bias headed to the cupboard by the window. The falcon

perched hooded, where she had been when Pentha spent the night in his room. The wolf, which had been lying at the boy's feet, rose and came to Damon, who roughly scratched him behind the ears. The beast had grown considerably. How huge he was. He probably wouldn't get much bigger, he would just fill out. His gold-yellow eyes seemed to look past her surface, into her mind, gauging her strength or her possible weakness. She swallowed nervously and looked away.

She took a seat at the table. Damon sat, took up the harness, and inspected it with his eyes and this thumb. "Looks good."

The boy returned having ladled soup into an iron pot. He stared at Pentha. "You're the fearless woman of the arrowhead, aren't you?"

"Bias!" Damon barked, his brow deeply creased in a frown of dismay.

Pentha laughed.

A slow grin warmed Damon's face. "Have I no privacy at all?"

Bias added, "He said you were quite tall."

Damon shook his head, and Bias hung the pot over the fire.

Continuing to examine the harness, and without looking at her, Damon said, "So what is it you want to ask?"

"It's about the Acheans."

"And?"

"I have been given the task of preparing the People of Artemis to defend Themiskyra against an attack, one likely to come next season."

"I don't see any alternative. An attack will surely come."

"I'm here because we need your help."

❧ 32 ❧

PENTHA ALMOST FLINCHED AS DAMON SHOT HER a glance like a hurled javelin. "What kind of help?"

She wanted him to agree to come to Themiskyra, but clearly she was going to have to approach the idea slowly. Indirectly. "For one thing, we need to know what you think it would take to defeat them."

He sat the harness down, took a handful of beads and rolled them in his palm. "If they come in sufficient force, your horsewomen will lose. The Acheans will kill the horses and then overwhelm you by sheer brute strength. And they will not come unless they are prepared to take you down."

"We know that. I have decided that we will arm and train the men."

He raised an eyebrow, surprised. "That's a move in the right direction. But if your men use Amazon shielding, they will still be outmatched. Both the cavalry and the infantry need body shielding like the Acheans'."

"That won't work for the cavalry. The weight is excessive for the horses. And my women's movements would be restricted. But I agree, making bronze cuirass's and greaves and better shields and helmets for the men is a good idea."

"Then your women must at least adopt a heavier corselet. Heavily padded linen or leather."

"Perhaps. We could try it. Damon, this is exactly why I've

come to ask you to return with me to Themiskyra. To oversee what needs to be done."

He poured the beads back into their bowl. "You know I won't do that."

"Why?"

He took her hand. She saw pleading in his eyes. And to her amazement, fear. "Is there anything I could say to you that would convince you to stay here with me? To never return to Themiskyra? We could even leave here and go somewhere else."

"I don't even know what to think of such a question. It's absurd. I am Warrior Queen."

"Do you think that only you can serve as Warrior Queen? You're free to choose otherwise. Let someone else take on the Acheans. I see disaster ahead." He studied her hand, then once more looked at her with such tenderness. "Come live with me."

She pulled her hand away.

He spoke firmly. "I love you. I want to live my life with you. And I believe that maybe you love me. Perhaps not as profoundly yet as I love you. But I tell you, we could be happy."

Bias, embarrassed at the turn in the conversation, left the table to stir the soup now smelling richly of onion.

"I can marry in a few years. But at this moment, my duty is to protect my people."

"Even if your duty leads to your death."

"You're being overly dramatic."

He stood, his chair scraping across the floor so that hair raised on the back of her neck. He walked away a few steps, then walked back to the table and stood over her. His face was drawn and stern. "You come to me because I know Acheans. Because I know how they practice war. And when I tell you I see nothing but disaster ahead, you accuse me of being overly dramatic. Which is it? You trust my judgment or you don't?"

"Sit down, Damon. I do trust your judgment. But every

creature has its destiny, the thing it's meant to be. My destiny is to be Warrior Queen at this time and in this place."

"Destiny!" He spat out the word.

"Yes, destiny." She pointed to the falcon. "Have you never thought about Dia? She is your captive. Perhaps you should set her free to find her destiny. I know I have to be free to seek mine."

He bent close. His voice soft again. "Listen to me. No good comes from war."

She rose so she could look him in the eye. Her heartbeat throbbed, a great lump in her throat. Fighting growing anger, she kept her tone firm and tight and controlled. "We Amazons are free women. We do not serve men. All other women, soft women, become little more than another convenience for men. I'm asking you to help us keep our freedom. Help us keep Themiskyra safe and at peace."

He drew back, shook his head. "Let me tell you something you might find surprising. Fighting doesn't bring peace."

"Neither does hiding here in the woods!"

The room fell silent. The muscles of Damon's neck bulged, his face flooded red with blood. He roared. "I have had my fill of killing."

He grabbed up the closest bowl of beads and hurled it at the wall. It struck close to Dia. She panicked, lunged off her perch and hung upside down from her jesses, her wings thrashing up a great noise. Bias ran to set her upright.

"You don't know all the reasons I'm here," Damon shouted again, his gaze terrifying. "So why spit out accusations of hiding?"

She shouted back. "You are hiding, aren't you?"

He turned his back and, clenching his fists, walked away, then turned to face her again. Fire still blazed in his eyes and the muscles at the angle of his jaw clenched and unclenched, but his voice was back in tight control. "I, too, want peace. And I've come here to find it."

"Well, with the Acheans, I don't know of any other way to find it or keep it than by fighting. And I do know that I will *never* have peace until Agamemnon and Achilles and their pillaging scum are rotting in Hades."

The air between them vibrated with things said—and things unsaid.

"So, you will not help us?"

Silence.

She drew a deep breath, shaking but regaining control. She finished. "I will be leaving you now. To your peace."

Bias rushed up to her. "It's too late for you to leave. You will be riding half the way in the dark. And it's snowing."

The boy turned to Damon, expecting Damon to back him up.

Maybe he will ask me to stay.

Damon simply continued to glare at her.

He did not care for her safety. He would be happy were she gone. She turned and walked out, sick with hurt, sick with failure.

❧ 33 ❧

A LONG WITH SEVERAL HUNDRED RESIDENTS OF
the citadel out for an early evening stroll, Derinoe
stood on the citadel wall, one of five women in their party.
The other four women were the mistresses of Hektor's
friends. With nervous fingers, she checked that her veil hung
securely. She glanced at Hektor, walking with his four companions just far enough away that the two groups of five—
five men, five women—should not look connected.

In Derinoe's mind, this public outing was wildly dangerous. Hektor was becoming ever more reckless, almost as if
he didn't care if their relationship was discovered. The
wives of Hektor's friends might not know or care if their
husbands were truly out with men, but Andromache would.
Was Hektor having problems with Andromache? Did he
want to hurt his wife? Was Andromache already certain of
his infidelity so he no longer cared what he did? Why this
recklessness that held so much potential danger for
Leonides and Myrina?

Derinoe had suggested that she preferred not to go to the
wall. "So long as you are veiled," he insisted with a frown,
"there is no reason for us not to enjoy the evening. We'll circle the citadel once, then come back for dinner. Humor me."
It had been a command, not a request.

They stopped walking, the men pausing to watch other
men at archery practice in a garden below the wall.

Looking into the far distance, Derinoe imagined the Achean compound at the bay with all its massive construction. She remembered Achilles in one of his tender moods. They were in bed and he had proclaimed that he loved her. Love. What did he know of love? A killer. A rapist. A slaver. And he had had the arrogance to speak to her in all seeming seriousness of love. Had there been some way to kill him before she escaped from him, she would have.

Nausicaa touched her arm and pointed to the men in the garden. "There's Paris." Nausicaa was the mistress of Hektor's oldest friend, Glaukos, the only one of the women Derinoe knew. "Isn't he handsome?" Nausicaa asked.

He's dissolute and irresponsible. "He has beautiful features. But I prefer Hektor's strength." She took Nausicaa's hand in hers. "I think this is very dangerous, for us to appear in public with the men this way. Even veiled. Anyone with keen eyes and a vicious tongue will start talk about Hektor and the others being out with women."

"You worry about Andromache?"

"If she finds out, she'll be furious. She'll want to know who the women were. Especially who was with Hektor."

"We're veiled. We're safe. Don't fret."

Laughter erupted from the men. Hektor continued walking, his men following, and with the other women, she followed at a distance.

Later, in his quarters, she joined the women in a dressing room to remove their veils, fix their hair, and touch up the dark kohl that brought out the color of their eyes. Hektor's servants would pour wine and place food on the sideboard and then depart. Their party of ten could dine, and converse, in private.

Peering into the copper mirror, she discretely studied the other women's reflections. Nausicaa wore a shimmering gown of green silk shot through with lavender swirls. Derinoe was certain the dress was so expensive that Glaukos must have bought it. As far as Derinoe could tell, Glaukos treated Nausicaa with kindness. Derinoe had early on concluded that Hektor's best friend was essentially a good and brave man.

Two of the women were fair of skin and hair and quite young. Derinoe was twenty and four. She guessed the young women could be no older than sixteen. They were chatting about the price of rose perfume. The embargo had long ago made it so expensive that only the immediate royal family could afford it. The fourth woman, whose hair was red, stood to Derinoe's left, sharing the mirror.

Derinoe caught the woman's gaze and smiled. "Your hair reminds me of my sister."

In the dining room, the men already reclined on cushions at low tables, drinking wine and eating onion. Hektor smiled at her, and she felt immediate warmth and let her fears melt. At least here in his rooms, in his presence and in privacy, she was safe.

From the side tables, she and the other women selected delicacies they knew their men liked. For Hektor's first course, she chose squid marinated in oil and boiled eggs split in half from which the yolk had been removed and blended with finely chopped olives and garlic and then spooned back into the hard whites. The bread, made of corn and barley, was his favorite.

Carrying it to him, she thought again of Pentha. And of their mother. And of being Amazon. And that here she was, serving food to a man. How her mother would be frowning in dismay that her daughter had been reduced to such a state. Perhaps frowning in disapproval that she had accepted such a state. But what alternative did she have? The brief sense of peace she'd felt seeing Hektor's smile retreated once more as the guilt she worked hard to ignore rose to replace it. *I have only done what is necessary.*

❧ 34 ☙

DERINOE'S ATTENTION, WHICH HAD BRIEFLY BEEN lost in thoughts of the past, rushed back to Hektor's room, the dinner, and his friends when Glaukos asked, "What do you propose to do about the wall, Hektor?"

Listening intently, Derinoe returned to the sideboard and selected foods for herself.

She returned to sit slightly behind Hektor. He said, "It is truly formidable. I sent word to Hattusilis telling him we need Hittite forces now. Supplies from them are no longer enough. We need warriors. And I sent word to the Nubian king. I believe he will come. I hope with substantial forces."

Hektor's youngest commander, Poulydamas, said, "You should consider contacting Harmonia. The Amazons have been highly successfully defending their borders. Their ability to fight, I hear, is extraordinary."

At the sound of her Queen's name, Derinoe's heart skipped a beat. And to her astonishment, she felt her throat tighten and the welling of tears behind her eyes.

Hektor took a drink, then said, "We all hear the same talk about Amazon fighting. And where there is talk, there is usually truth. They are strange women. Unnatural. And no one doubts their ferocity. But Priam is not about to ask for help from Harmonia. He has been at odds with the Amazons since he was young."

The conversation turned to the buying and breeding of horses, and her mind wandered.

After the dinner she accompanied the other women to the dressing room where they donned veils. Nausicaa spoke in a hushed voice, so only they two could hear. "We do need the Amazons to help us. Couldn't you convince Cassandra to talk to Priam. I know you are close to her."

"What do you think of the Amazons?"

"Glaukos speaks highly of them."

"Well, Cassandra is not only High priestess of Athena, she doesn't take kindly to any followers of Artemis, and especially she seems to hate the Amazons." *And I, to my shame, have sacrificed my devotion to Artemis to please her.* "She would never have any part of asking them here. Besides, Priam rarely pays serious attention to anything she says. She thinks her father considers her slightly mad, with all her portents and warnings and visions."

"Better then that you convince Hektor. We must draw everyone we can to help us."

"When an opportunity arises, I'll try."

Later, alone with Hektor, Derinoe sat on a cushioned stool at a dressing table, preparing to let down her hair. He placed his hands on her shoulders, bent down and breathed on the back of her neck, then kissed it. A shiver of delight ran over her arms. She looked into the mirror and smiled at him.

He let go of her shoulders and said, "I like to watch when you take the pins out."

She proceeded to do just that as he stood behind her, arms crossed. When her hair tumbled down, he bent and kissed the top of her head.

She swiveled and took both of his hands in hers, always deeply pleased by their symmetry and strength, and touched by two deep scars that still could not hide that beauty. She looked up at him. "I owe you so much."

"Don't talk of owing."

"I'm sick with worry for you."

He pulled her to her feet and kissed her. She lingered on

the kiss, willing that it should replace this quivering sickness inside her with peace. But it didn't. When the kiss ended, she drew away, walked toward his bed, turned. "If something should happen to you, and if Andromache should ever discover what is between us, . . ."

He quickly closed the distance between them, drew her against him, and one hand gently pressed her head against his chest. "My beautiful Derinoe. Nothing is going to happen to me. And Andromache is a good woman."

He was so oddly blind to his wife's jealousy. He must love her in some way. Cassandra had said more than once that he loved Andromache. Was it really possible to love two people at the same time? "The Acheans are—"

"Agamemnon is growing tired, Deri. Reliable informants tell me so. We have survived this long. I am confident that during next battle season, if we just hold on, this monstrous siege will end."

"But there will be battles."

"Of course."

"And you will always be there, leading.

"I will always come back to keep you and the children safe. I promise."

"But what if—"

He silenced her question, but not her fear, with a kiss, then smiling, picked her up and tossed her onto the bed.

☙ 35 ❧

A NOISE FROM OUTSIDE—THE BLEATING OF LONE-some, his nanny goat—jerked Damon from sleep. He raised his head from the table and felt a shooting pain from a stiff back. In his hand he still held Pentha's arrowhead. He'd obviously fallen asleep, finally, at the table.

He glanced behind him. Bias still slept soundly on his pile of skins.

Damn Pentha! Damon thought. But he nevertheless retied the arrowhead by its thong around his neck.

He rose and grabbed up his woolen cloak from the floor where he had thrown it last night. Wolf, too, rose and stretched. Twice last night Damon had wrapped himself in the cloak and started out the door to go after Pentha and bring her back. Twice he had changed his mind. To worry about her, as he would have worried about his wife in similar circumstance of falling dark and snow, was ridiculous. Pentha was as competent to care for herself in the woods as he was to care for her. And since he had no intention of help-ing fight the Acheans, what point would there be in fetching her back.

He crossed to the door, Wolf at his heels, and stepped out-side and close the door behind him. He threw the cloak around his shoulders and studied the gloomy, gray sky. Pentha was either back in her barracks or she had bedded somewhere for the night and would now be rising herself.

Damn Pentha!

Wolf began his rounds, checking the cabin's boundaries, sniffing and marking. Lonesome bleated again. Damon had once asked Bias, shortly after Damon traded a harness for the goat, why Bias' father had named the goat Lonesome. Bias had simply shrugged.

Damon strode to a fresh spot at the thorn hedge and relieved himself, creating a bright yellow streak in the new, white snow. Marking my territory, he thought, just like Wolf or a polecat.

He threw chunks of meat caught yesterday to the two ferrets, then entered the shed and placed a couple of handfuls of hay on the ground for Lonesome. She quickly lipped some up and started chewing.

Yes, there was nothing Damon could do to protect Pentha in a wood at night that she couldn't do for herself, but she was right that there was much he could do to protect her if she chose to fight Acheans.

"Damn her!" He grabbed the milk jug from the shelf, squatted next to Lonesome, and gripping a teat, squeezed. Warm, white fluid whizzed into the jug. Lonesome kicked his milking hand.

"Sorry," he muttered, and his next strokes were more careful.

Pentha shouldn't have come. She shouldn't have undressed in front of him. She shouldn't have made love with him. She shouldn't be beautiful. Or courageous. Or determined. And she sure shouldn't have asked him to leave the peace he had created to make war!

Lonesome kicked his hand again, harder.

"I really am sorry," he said.

Damon stopped milking. So was this what he wanted? Did he even have peace here any more?

After he finished milking, he patted the goat and said, "You know what? I'm lonesome, too."

☙ 36 ❧

Except for Wolf and Dia, Damon took his animals—Lonesome, the rooster, and the hens—to Bias' parents. The ferrets he'd released. The cabin stood quiet, covered in snow, prepared for its owner's leaving.

He had told Bias' mother, "If you don't hear from me within a year, the cabin is yours. I hope you give it to Bias, when he's old enough." He thanked her for letting the boy come to assist him and care for Wolf and Dia, and then said, "I swear on my own life, no matter what happens to me, I will see that your son lives to return to you."

The cabin door burst open. Bias rushed in, excited and eager. "Wolf and Dia and me, we're ready. Let's go!"

Damon put his arm on Bias' shoulder. They walked outside, and Damon shut the door. At the gate in the thorn hedge, he turned and one last time studied the home that had sheltered him when he had crawled up the mountain like an animal that had chewed itself free from a trap.

"I had peace here," he said, "but it was the peace of the half-dead." He gave Bias a friendly shake. "You brought life into that peace. And so does Pentha."

"You don't want to leave. So why do you?"

"Sometimes we don't get to do what we want to do, but what needs doing. You heard Pentha. I can't convince her to quit, so I have to do what I can to protect her. I don't want to live with more guilt than I already have. How would I feel if this mess kills her and I did nothing but sit in the cabin?"

❧ 37 ❧

THINGS VERGED ON THE EDGE OF OUT-OF-CONTROL.
"Let's avoid shouting," Pentha said. She spoke firmly to
Evandre whose voice had been climbing to an ever higher
pitch and who had interrupted Clonie for the third time.

Four days after Damon rejected her plea for help, Pentha
and her twelve commanders sat for their second day in the
barracks meeting room, struggling with how to proceed. The
stark benches set the perfect mood for sharp words and dire
circumstances. Evandre was furious that Clonie seemed
convinced that without Damonides' help, the People of
Artemis could not hope to meet the Achean challenge.

But Pentha's internal fire raged with fury at Damon. He
had refused them aid when he knew so much and they knew
so little. Twice she'd nearly shouted herself, something that
would have been so shockingly out of character it would
only have upset these confused proceedings even further.

And the time for talk was about up. Shortly, she must
make the hard decisions on which they would all live or die.

"This discussion is pointless," Clonie continued bitterly,
her face flushed and her eyes on Pentha, "if we don't have
better intelligence. What difference does it make who trains
the men if we don't know what nature of enemy we must defeat? What difference does it make who is in charge of de-
veloping better arms and protection if we don't know what
kinds of arms we must protect against?"

Hippolyta added, "The only Achean arms we have are forty years old. It is certain they have made changes. Improvements."

Damon, curse him, had always avoided discussing anything military. Certainly not details of battle and strategy. Pentha said, "I'm afraid I agree with Clonie, Evandre. We are woefully without adequate information.

"Well then," Evandre huffed, "do we prepare to concede defeat?"

"First, there is a way for us to get current information. The priestess of Artemis at Troy, Semele, has long since planted a spy in the Achean camp. I am sending you, Clonie, to Troy. By boat. That's fastest. You will meet with Semele's spy. Gain what knowledge you can of the Achean encampment, manpower, abilities, and tactics. No more than three months and you must be back so we can put what you learn to good use. It would be to our advantage if we had that information now." They knew she was thinking of Damon, because she had told them about her failed attempt to recruit him. "But we will do the best we can."

Heads nodded. Clonie gave her a broad smile.

Pentha rubbed the back of her stiff and aching neck. "Now we return to the question of who will train the men. I have decided first of all that, contrary to what many of you have suggested, the heads of each of the men's divisions must be a man."

Several women stiffened, faces doubtful or displeased. Bremusa frowned and crossed her arms. Pentha quickly raised her hand to silence the open mouths, and then explained. She would announce a series of testings. Based on the results, she would assign group leaders among the men, and providing that Trusis held up well, she would make him Chief Commander of the Infantry. He would help her make other choices involving the infantry. "The men must have great pride in what they will do. This is the way it was done when our men served in the past. That's how it will be now."

Slowly, Bremusa uncrossed her arms. She nodded. Pentha

watched other bodies relax, the other warriors taking their cue from Bremusa. Thankfully, determination was replacing chaos.

Hippolyta said, "When do we begin?"

❧ 38 ❧

THE AMAZON ENCAMPMENT SMELLED OF WOOD
fires, rain-soaked ground, and horse piss. Snow had not
yet reached the plain. Damon had left Bias and the animals
with the carpenter's family because he must first know if he
was accepted. If Pentha agreed to his help, he would insist
on moving into quarters in the men's compound, and then
fetch the boy. Damon would have to become part of the
world of Themiskyra, no longer separate.

He strode into the Amazon compound and headed for the
barracks. He was halfway to the gray, weathered wooden
building when a girl trotting on horseback arrived at the same
moment as two women with spears dashed up. The two Amazons crossed their spears, blocking his path. "It is against
custom for men to enter here," said the taller one, who reminded him vaguely of Pentha's commander, Bremusa.

"I come by order of Queen Penthesilea." He met the tall
woman's gaze without blinking.

She returned his gaze with an unblinking one of her own.
"Men are not allowed, Damonides."

So she knew his name. He was recognized. The women
probably knew also that he had refused to give them aid. "If
Penthesilea accepts my help, many customs are going to be
turned upside down. We might as well begin now." He
reached out a hand, pushed against the crossed spears, and
walked past the guards.

The women hesitated a moment. One ran ahead. The taller one followed him to the barracks.

He walked inside. Hearing voices, he headed for them, sucking in several deep breaths against nausea. Pentha sat at a round table, her back to him. As the women opposite Pentha stared at him with various amazed expressions, Pentha turned and then jumped to her feet.

"Damon," she said, almost a whisper. Then louder, "Companions, you all know the warrior Damonides. You all know I asked him to help us." She shook her head, and to him said, "To see you here, Damonides, is to say the least, startling."

Profoundly glad he made this decision, he said, "Amazons, if you wish to use the knowledge I have of Achean warfare, I am at your service. In whatever way Penthesilca thinks best."

Hippolyta stood and saluted him, clenched fist to brow. The other women, without exception, followed her example. He broke another tradition. He, a man of Themiskyra, did not bow. He returned their clenched-fist salute. That earned him a barrage of grins and smiles.

Pentha, too, saluted him. Relief coming in waves off her body warmed his heart. She said, "My commanders have made it clear they welcome your help."

She ordered that a chair be brought and a place made for him. The place she indicated lay directly opposite her. Bremusa remained to her right. He felt himself sweating, but the nausea was surprising light, perhaps because Bias had been living with him.

She said, "My women understand your value to us. To the strong infantry we will create. But none of this generation of Themiskyran men of fighting age have fought a single battle. My first decision is to appoint you infantry commander." She paused long enough for him and the women to absorb her choice. Then she said, "Very likely at first the men may not understand my decision. You were born here, but initially the men will see you as an outsider. I expect rough going. With time, though, your experience and knowledge will win them." She folded her hands on the table. "So tell us, how does our new infantry's chief commander intend to proceed?"

Thus began an intense fall and winter. He explained that he would arrange trials for all men of warrior age, to determine their level of fitness and skills. She had planned to do the same, and her one recommendation was that, if at all possible, it would be prudent to select Trusis, their current headman, as his second in command. "The less you upset the current hierarchy among the men," she said, "the less friction will likely develop."

He agreed, and in the days of testing he found that Trusis was intelligent and physically fit. Damon did as Pentha recommended, although he would have preferred a man whose spirit more matched his own. Hippolyta was fond of a smithy, Phemios, and because Damon also liked him, Phemios would have been Damon's first choice. Instead, Phemios became third in command.

When Pentha first presented Damon to the men, he particularly watched Trusis. Trusis turned bright red in the face and looked as though he might explode from the effort to keep his protests stuffed inside. Since he had no option but to accept Damon's authority, Trusis had, by the end of the hour, put on a bright smile. From that point he cooperated. Still, his spirit was essentially a sour one. He had a ferocious temper that Damon occasionally needed to curb when it was directed improperly toward the troops.

Damon did insist on his own quarters in the men's compound, where he and Bias made themselves comfortable. The boy struck up a friendship with Gryn, who had moved from the city to the camp, something quite uncommon for a retired Amazon but to which Pentha agreed. Damon first discovered Bias' attraction to Gryn when Wolf hurt a paw. Damon went looking for Bias to have the boy soothe Wolf while Damon tended the cut. Clonie said, "You'll find the boy in the barracks dining hall with Gryn."

He found them sitting opposite each other at the end of a long trestle table. Between them, lying on the table, was an assortment of round, blue stones, the size of dove eggs. Seeing Damon, Gryn said, "Come. Let me use you."

She stood, walked to Damon, and showed him empty hands. She then reached beside his head, near his ear, dramatically pronounced the incantation familiar to children and adults—"Badimus Flax!"—opened her hand, and there lay four blue stones, apparently conjured from his ear.

"Royally awesome!" Bias exclaimed.

And Gryn was just that—awesome—as conjurer and storyteller. Damon had already seen her pull a hare out of an empty pot. And one night around a campfire he had listened, fascinated, as she told the story of Artemis and Actaeon to a hardened lot of Amazon archers who cheered when his own hunting hounds tore the disrespectful Actaeon to shreds.

Still beaming Bias said, "Gryn's going to teach me."

It eased Damon's mind that Bias found something to do that amused him besides caring for Dia and Wolf.

Damon suffered his greatest unhappiness because Pentha would only spend the night with him every four days or so. So close to her, and yet so very far. He had argued, "I'm here. You're here. Why can't we be together at least at night. I see you so rarely during the day."

"It's not the Amazon way to become too attached to a man. We would set a bad example. Morale would suffer. You can change some things, Damon. But not all things."

The moon cycled again and yet again and as he watched Pentha with her troops, he came to understand that this was, indeed, her destiny. With bow and spear, she was strong and accurate. With the ax, she had no peer. Horses and women responded with the desire to please her when she worked with them to learn skills like lying quiet for long periods, coming from full gallop to abrupt halt, pivoting and changing direction, and charging at a gallop down a steep incline. Twice, villagers who had suffered attacks from rogue leopards begged for her to come to their aid. She was famed for killing these dangerous predators.

Her intensity and dedication evoked similar passion in others. He sometimes worried about this fever driving her because he could not understand where it came from. Now and then he would think of her odd statement, "I don't deserve to be happy." The secret to Pentha lay there somewhere.

But whatever drove her, she was a primal element, like the wind from the north. Nothing would stop her. And his destiny was to help her achieve the goal of protecting her people.

Sometimes, though, he felt choked with the urge to take her away, by force if necessary, to protect her from what would come.

❧ 39 ❧

When Clonie returned from Troy, she re-
ported no changes in Achean tactics and weaponry
from Damon's own days that he thought of major significance. The measures he had already taken had been the
right ones.

Clonie's assessment of the numbers of Acheans gathered
at Troy, however, stunned him. "They have roughly five
thousand fighting men." If even half such a hoard descended
on Themiskyra, nothing the People of Artemis had at the
moment would stop them.

When their own fifteen hundred men reached satisfactory
fitness and had mastered the basics of their weapons—
swords, spears, and bows for most, but also some trained in
sling and ax—Damon moved to something new, something
that might help counter any potential Achean superiority in
numbers. In more than one battle in the past, he'd felt that
the Acheans might have been defeated had their victims
been more organized. He trained the Themiskyran men to
fight in teams, staying tight together, not in the Achean or
Trojan every-man-for-himself way.

In early spring, the Hittites mounted three almost simulta-
neous incursions. In two instances, the local Themiskyran
cavalry proved adequate. His male infantry would, in any
event, have taken too long to arrive to be effective, but still

he regretted that his men missed the chance to gain first-hand battle experience.

But in a third encounter, the local Amazon border troops requested Themiskyran reinforcement, and he and his men accompanied the cavalry. This battle brought him two great surprises. Just seeing Pentha fighting unsettled him profoundly, but at the end of the battle, the Amazons were killing the wounded, a practice he once told her he would never do, and there she had been, standing over a wounded Hittite. For some reason she saw Damon or sensed him watching. She looked him hard in the eye. And then she slit the man's throat, and without giving Damon a second look, moved on to the next fallen warrior.

"Amazons do not take prisoners," she had told him. More than once he had heard Amazons shout, as a rallying cry, "The female bear is deadly in defense of her young!" Their fierce reputation was more valuable to them than gold. But for several moon cycles he could not watch Pentha doing even the simplest things without seeing that killer look in her eyes.

His second surprise involved Trusis. He found himself fighting side by side with Trusis and, even in the midst of the chaos, he saw that Trusis excelled with the sword. He was as good, if not better, than Damon. At one moment, a Hittite attacked them both. Together they struck the man two deadly jabs to the stomach. As the warrior fell at their feet, Damon's gaze met Trusis' in a shared moment of victory. Trusis had, at last, won Damon's grudging respect.

Soon after these incursions, the People of Artemis gathered to celebrate the earth's reflowering. They would sacrifice to the goddess, pray, and then feast.

Damon walked to a large natural amphitheater in the foothills with Trusis and his other infantry commanders. Pentha walked with the Amazon commanders. Themiskyra's people paraded, leading the sacrificial bulls and sheep. Cymbals and drums roused spirits. The happy mood reflected the earth's own joy in the rebirth of plant and animal life.

Harmonia offered the first sacrifice of fifty white sheep to the Goddess, and then Pentha rose before the crowd. "As we celebrate the return of the sun, let us also offer thanks to our protectress, the divine Artemis, for bringing Damonides to us. Because of Damonides, the People are ready to meet any foe."

An explosion of male whistles and female clapping followed.

Even as he expressed his appreciation for their enthusiasm, Damon wasn't exactly sure how he felt. He hadn't taken on this task with pleasure, so its accomplishment brought only modest satisfaction. But the acceptance of the People warmed his heart, a strange, forgotten, unanticipated feeling this—acceptance.

As the crowd's attention returned to Harmonia, Pentha came up close. "They love you," she said.

"They love feeling secure."

"Consider it what you will." She touched his arm. "I haven't forgotten your reluctance to get involved. And I'm grateful. For myself, and for the People."

"The troops are fit. They're ready. I've done what you wanted, but to exactly what end? Our strength is well beyond anything required for our defense here. Only a limited number of Achean ships could ever make it through the Hellespont."

"You know the plan has always been to go to Troy."

Go to Troy. The old anger, the old fear, tightened his chest. With more heat of concern than he intended to show, he said, "If we combined our forces with those of Troy, we might achieve your goal. Breach the Achean wall. Burn their ships. Slaughter them. Perhaps. But no word has come from Troy asking our help, has it?"

She said nothing.

He pressed her. "You sent word to Priam that we would give them aid. You haven't heard from him. You may very well not hear from him. Do we go uninvited? Unwelcome?"

Again she said nothing. She simply gave him a long, hard stare.

❧ 40 ❧

TWO LAMPS SOFTLY LIT HEKTOR'S BEDROOM. Lyre and flute music drifted in through an open window. To Derinoe's ears, they seemed mournful sighs.

Yet another battle was past. Hektor had returned, unharmed. He sat in a dressing gown in front of her on a cushioned stool. His eyes were bloodshot, and rimmed with red. She was certain he had been weeping before she arrived. Just the thought of Hektor weeping stunned her. She had been rubbing his neck. Now, she wrapped her arms around his chest. "Glaukos is dead, Hektor. Your dear friend is dead. I am terrified."

"My beautiful Deri."

"Nausicaa is so grief-stricken she can't get out of bed."

He pulled her around and took her into his lap. "So beautiful but always troubled."

She pulled close to him, drew his head to her breast. "Tell your father he must give Helen back."

She felt his head shake. "You know this war isn't about Helen. It isn't even about Achean honor, no matter how dramatically the scum posture that it is. Maybe for Menelaus honor plays a part. But for the others, it's strictly about treasure, slaves, and control of the Hellespont. Sending Helen back wouldn't end it."

"How do you know? Priam could try."

He pulled back and studied her. "Dishonor his own son by

tossing out his son's wife? Helen came here freely with Paris. Priam won't force her to leave. For that matter, neither would I."

"What about asking aid from the Amazons? Nausicaa asked me again if you have spoken to your father. Did you? What did he say?"

He pushed her off his lap, stood, and took her hand. "Come. I want to show you something."

To Derinoe's alarm, he led her outside his rooms into a common hallway. She tried to pull him to a stop. "Should we leave your quarters? Andromache. . . ."

He just kept walking. "The servants are below. Andromache is partying in Hekuba's quarters with Hekuba and other royal ladies. She won't return until late tomorrow."

He led up the stairway to the roof garden. There he drew her to the southwest corner and nodded toward the bay. "Look at those fires. From here we see only a few dozen, but there are hundreds. The Achean camp has been struck by plague, Deri. Glaukos may be dead, but the gods favor us. The Archeans are burning their dead. They die like bees in a fungus-infected hive. We are going to destroy them, and soon. Calling on Amazons isn't needed."

She threw herself against him, pressed her face against his chest. She tightened her hold as if to prevent him ever leaving.

"We are together," he said. "We can't change what the Fates will do with us. So let's go downstairs and make love. I want you to make me forget war and plague and death."

She locked her arm in his and pressed close to him. "Glaukos is dead," he said, "but the Acheans will pay."

❧ 41 ❧

DAMON ARRIVED AT THE AMAZON COMPOUND and found Hippolyta, Clonie, Bremusa, and Evandre outside the stable. This was three days after the spring festival and their horses stood ready to ride. He had not been aware of any plans for travel. His own plans might have to be changed.

Each woman's second lingered nearby. These young women of eighteen or nineteen years had been accepted with full honor as a warrior but must serve as a second for ten battles. Each rode beside her warrior and carried extra arrows, javelins, and spears and, if her warrior was a commander, her commander's pennant.

Damon didn't see Pentha. The group of nine was fully geared for something, though, so the meeting of commanders he had come to propose would clearly have to be put off. To Hippolyta he said, "I'm looking for Pentha."

"In the stable."

Bias came around the building's corner, and, seeing the group, rushed up to them. He started to address Damon, but changed his mind. Turning to Clonie he said, "I think you have something in your ear."

Clonie stared at him.

Bias reached up beside her head, intoned "Badamus Flax!" and when he brought his hand down, four green stones rolled out of his shirtsleeve onto the ground.

With the Amazons, Damon burst into laughter.

Bias, his face red, snatched up the stones and hurried off.

Damon entered the stable and found Pentha fastening Valor's halter. Always struck with awe at the stallion's strength and beauty, he stroked the arched neck. "Something's happening?"

"A rogue lion. In Ramatha. It's killed two children."

"How long will you be gone?"

"The town is half a day's ride. The people are prepared for us. They will have beaters waiting and someone following the lion's spoor. If we have good luck, we should be back late tomorrow. Perhaps the next day."

Hearing footsteps, he turned toward the stable door. One of Harmonia's pages scurried in.

The page bowed to Pentha. "We received a message from Troy, from the High Priestess Semele."

Pentha nodded.

"There was a devastating plague in the Achean camp. And also a falling out between Achilles and Agamemnon. Achilles withdrew to his ships and refused to participate further in their campaign."

Pentha looked at Damon, his own rising excitement mirrored in her eyes. "If Achilles has dropped out," Pentha said, "they will suffer a tremendous blow to morale."

He nodded. "The perfect opportunity for Hektor to act decisively. He has a physically weakened enemy and they are without their great warrior."

The page said, "There is more. Hektor did attack, and the Trojans breached the Achean wall. They even burned some Achean ships. The Acheans, though, rallied and ultimately held ground and the plague has passed."

Damon snapped, "Is there any good news?"

The page shook her head. "When these messages were sent, Patroklos, Lord Achilles' companion, decided to rejoin the battle. The Achean royals hope Achilles will also do so."

"Achilles!" Pentha said with the venom he always heard her use when the Achean royal's name was mentioned.

"One last thing," the page said. "A rumor is being spread

throughout Troy that the Amazons have not come to their aid because the people of Themiskyra have grown weak and afraid."

Pentha smacked Valor's stall. "Foul lie! And dangerous! Our reputation must not be questioned." She looked hard at the girl. "More?"

"No, Penthesilea."

"Go back to Harmonia. And have her send this message to Priam. 'Penthesilea, Warrior Queen of the Amazons of Themiskyra once more offers the aid of the People of Artemis to Priam, king of Troy. We are prepared to lend our lives to your cause. Let none say that Amazons fear the Acheans. Rather that we are eager to spill their blood.' "

The page bowed and left.

His fist clenched, the heat of anger rushing from his chest to his face, Damon said, "I don't understand you."

She turned to him. "What don't you understand?"

"Why? Why can't you let the Trojans deal with their own mess. Why suffer the humiliation of offering troops to Priam yet again?"

Her brow furrowed and her lips hardened into a straight line. "My task, our task, is to keep the People of Artemis secure. Now and for the future."

"That's not it." He knew he was just short of shouting but he couldn't stop. "There is much more here. Why in the name of all the gods are you so eager to take on the Acheans?"

She skewered him with a look as unbending as iron. "If Priam asks for help, Damon, we will give it."

⊰ 42 ⊱

THE BEATING OF PENTHA'S HEART MADE HER EARS buzz with the rush of blood. Clonie and Hippolyta formed a line to her left. To her right walked Evandre and Bremusa. All carried spears at the ready.

Well behind them, their seconds carried extra spears. In such close conditions, bows were ineffective, and worse, dangerous. A lion that had lost its fear of humans could bring down and kill any one of them before any poison could immobilize it.

The brush directly in front of Pentha grew both tall and thick, but just beyond lay a small clearing. And Pentha could smell big cat. The lion hid somewhere nearby.

The line of five continued slow forward movement. In the near distance to her right, sounds of yelling and clubs struck against trees marked the passage of the beaters. In moments, she and her companions reached the edge of the clearing, a space not much bigger than a small house.

Let the lion bolt into the clearing!

To her dismay, Clonie stepped into the open.

The lion crashed out of the brush, a large male with full mane. He bolted across the clearing and sprang toward Clonie. Pentha pulled back her arm, sensing as she did that Evandre and Bremusa did likewise. She hurled the spear toward the spot where it should meet and strike the leaping lion.

Two screams and a great roar raked the air at the same

moment. The lion struck Clonie, knocking her to the ground. He fell, two spears that Pentha could see stuck in his side, his legs thrashing. One of the screams had come from Clonie, who struggled to push the lion off her arm.

Hippolyta stood in the clearing—but with a spear sticking out of her side. With dawning horror, Pentha realized the second scream had been Hippolyta's.

Hippolyta went down on her knees, then fell sideways, the spear pointing into the air.

Bremusa ran to Clonie. Pentha ran to them and leapt over Clonie and the lion's body to reach Hippolyta. She dropped on her knees beside her sister. Horror followed horror! The spear in Hippolyta's side was her own.

Pentha gasped. Blood ran from Hippolyta's mouth.

Evandre knelt on Hippolyta's other side, staring at the bright red stain spreading into Hippolyta's tunic.

Pentha leapt to her feet, her hands tearing into her hair. She shrieked, "No!" Her entire body shook.

"Pentha."

Hippolyta's soft voice brought Pentha again to her knees. In desperation she grabbed Hippolyta's hand.

Staring blindly at the sky, Pentha prayed. "Merciful Artemis." She swiped tears away.

Evandre stood, watching. Bremusa joined them with Clonie, whose arm was bleeding. Pentha heard their seconds rush up. Tears still flooded her vision. She brushed them away.

"I love you," Hippolyta said.

"You are my bright star. Don't leave me."

"And you are a great Queen. The Goddess honored me when she brought you to us."

"We will, we will . . ."

"It hurts," Hippolyta whispered. "Take it out."

"I can't." Another great rush of tears clouded Pentha's vision. Again she brushed them away.

Hippolyta's eyes weren't focused, simply staring. "Dear sister," she whispered. Pentha felt a gentle squeeze from Hippolyta's hand. "It hurts so much. Take it out."

"I can't. You'll die."

Hippolyta struggled to move her head, then looked Pentha hard in the eyes. "Yes. You can. For me."

"Don't, Hippolyta. Don't ask me."

"Quickly."

Numb, Pentha kissed Hippolyta's hand. She felt the gazes of her women, understood that they knew as well as she what must be done. *Why Hippolyta? Why? She has never had an evil thought!*

"Tell mother I love her."

Pentha nodded. *Why Hippolyta and not me?*

She looked to Evandre, who stood closest. Biting her lip, she nodded again.

Evandre grasped the spear and pulled. With a sickening fleshy sound, the tip came out, covered with gore. A great rush of blood followed it.

In only moments Hippolyta drew a last breath and the unmistakable stillness of death settled on her.

"Please come back," Pentha moaned, tears choking her speech. She wrapped her arms around Hippolyta and rocked her sister's body.

⇥ 43 ⇤

A SOUND FROM OUTSIDE THE SMALL ROOM IN THE
Temple to Artemis startled Pentha from sleep. She listened. The sound was the ringing of the lead sheep's bell
from a flock passing on the street.

She had fallen asleep on the dark green carpet. An attendant must have come in because lamps were lit, and by now
they would otherwise have gone out.

Gathering herself onto her knees, she stared at the altar.
Somehow she had dragged herself through Hippolyta's funeral. More correctly, Bremusa dragged her through it. But
as yet she had not been able to bring herself to make sacrifice. Not here. Not near to the Goddess.

Her green silk trousers were wrinkled with having been
lived in for, how long was it now? Perhaps three days. At
some point she must either kill herself or she must leave this
room to face Gryn and all those who loved Hippolyta. Some
people said suicide was cowardly. Did it make any difference? Honorable. Cowardly. Who could know? Once more
she studied the knife and its deadly blade.

She stood and walked up the alter steps. The attendant had
placed several cuts of lamb, burning charcoal, and a bronze
basin there. Pentha placed the lamb into the basin, sprinkled
it with oil, set it afire. The familiar smell of burning flesh
filled the room. In another basin lay cold ashes from previ-
ous sacrifices. She placed her hands into them, then streaked

dark lines of mourning across her forehead and down her cheeks.

She returned to the base of the altar and knelt in front of the knife.

On the wall in front of her hung a fine weaving. She studied the face of the Goddess bathing in a pristine pool to cleanse herself.

Pentha's hair had come loose from its braid. Beginning now, she would make amends in the only ways she could think of. Taking the knife in one hand and a length of hair in the other, she cut the hair off at chin length. She continued the task until a field of bright red surrounded her.

❧ 44 ❧

"SHE GAVE ORDERS THAT NO ONE IS TO ENTER," SAID one of the two young Amazons guarding the door to the small sanctuary where Damon knew Pentha agonized, alone and grieving.

"Let me pass!"

They uncrossed their spears and stepped back.

He opened the door and stepped inside, squinting as his eyes adjusted to the dim interior. She was kneeling before the alter. He walked to her and stopped at the sight of cut hair encircling her.

"By the gods!" he blurted out. How could she do such a hideous mutilation?

She turned, but didn't rise.

He moved to her and squatted. "Why did you do it?"

"Do you need to ask?"

"The funeral is three days over. You've not been seen. To my knowledge, you've not eaten."

"Why would I eat?"

"Pentha. Gryn is stricken. Her one daughter is dead and the other avoids her."

She nodded. "Yes. I must go to her."

"She knows you are in great pain. She is here in the city, waiting for you."

Pentha said nothing.

"Did you wish Hippolyta dead?"

"You know I didn't."

"Was there a thought in your heart that she die?"

"It was my spear."

"This is the working of the Furies, Pentha. I know what you're thinking. I even know what you're feeling. That it's wrong for you to be alive when she is dead." *I lived for years with that burden.* "I killed once, horribly, when I didn't intend to. A boy. He looked so much like my own son. I didn't intend it, but I came to him in a raid, with my heart set to kill. But killing was not in your heart. You are *not* to blame."

"At the funeral I heard what they were whispering. 'Surely it's a punishment that Pentha killed Hippolyta.' They think I'm not fit for anything. Certainly not to be Warrior Queen."

He touched her arm, worrying that she might flinch from him. She didn't. "It's only Euryclea and Marpessa who say such things." An ember of hope leapt to life in his chest. "But everyone would understand if you chose to step down out of grief."

Pentha looked at him, a blank, uncomprehending stare.

"The army is as ready as it ever could be to defend Themiskyra. You have done that. But you could chose now to—" He stood and drew her up with him. Holding her arms, he said, "I want to live with you Pentha, and love you, and share life with you. There are others who could lead. Bremusa is a great warrior."

She wrenched herself free. "You think I should abandon our people?"

"You wouldn't be abandoning them. You've given them an army that ensures that no one can harm them here."

"Not now. But what if Troy ultimately falls? What if the Acheans learn the secret of the Hellespont? What of the future?"

"Marpessa could—"

"Marpessa! Bremusa! I have killed my sister! You think I could leave now? Go look for peace while others still face uncertainty?"

The tiny flame in his chest flickered out. Nothing he could

say would touch her. Her straight back, the fire in the green
eyes, the twist of disgust on her lips, all said it was still un-
thinkable to her to be anything other than Themiskyra's
Warrior Queen. He'd been foolish with hope. "I want you to
be happy, Pentha. And I will do whatever I can to give that to
you. I had only wished you might feel as I do."

She took his hand. Looking into his eyes she said, "I do
care for you, Damon. You surely know that. But—"

"Then, so be it."

She squeezed his hand. "I need to see Mother."

During the walk from the Temple to Gryn's home, Pentha
seemed oblivious to the stares and murmurs of everyone
they passed, all of whom looked at her ash-smeared face,
crumpled trousers and tunic, and especially her jaggedly
butchered hair, with open-mouthed astonishment.

At Gryn's door a page from Harmonia approached
Pentha. She waved the page off and went inside. "What is
the message?" Damon asked.

PENTHA ENTERED AND WENT straight to the weaving
and sewing area where Gryn spent most of her time. Her
mother sat in a chair, a blue silk tunic and an embroidery
needle in her hands, but staring into space.

Pentha rushed to her and knelt beside the chair. She tried
to speak, but tears blocked off words.

Gryn patted her head.

Pentha looked up. Her mother was crying. "Forgive me,"
Pentha whispered. "I beg forgiveness."

Gryn, lips trembling, only shook her head.

"I have done a great evil. And more than once." Now
words tumbled out of her mouth. "This is the gods' punishment, and I have to accept it. But I can't bear to live if you
don't forgive me."

"Pentha, my sweet. What foolishness is this?"

Damon came in. Gryn wiped away Pentha's tears, then
said to Damon, "She thinks she has done so much evil that
this accident is the gods' way to punish her."

He moved across the room and to her surprise, dropped to

the floor and sat cross-legged opposite her. He touched her cheek and with such tenderness she felt her heart break. "What could you ever have done for which the loss of Hippolyta at your own hands would be fair punishment?"

"My heart knows."

"Well, I don't believe that. This is the Furies. Or the Fates, blind and cruel. These senseless things don't come to good people as punishment. They just happen."

She wanted to believe he was right, and that she was somehow not to blame. She wanted to believe. But something in the deep place where she hid her secret wouldn't let her.

The gentle lines of his faced shifted, and he clenched his jaw. "The page brought news you've wanted. Priam has answered at last. His words are, 'Priam, besieged king of Troy, asks that the great Hearth Queen of Themiskyra send to us troops under the command of the Warrior Queen Penthesilea so we may destroy the Achean invaders encamped before my people.'"

At last!

Damon continued. "Semele also sends word. Her spy in the Achean camp assures her that Acheans cannot have rowers ready in any great numbers to take on the Hellespont for another two or three moon cycles."

Mind racing. Pulse racing. She leapt to her feet. Damon rose, facing her. He did not want this, she knew. But he would be at her side. That she also knew.

She looked to Gryn and said, "We can be, must be, at Troy before the next full moon."

❧ 45 ❧

SLUMPED IN A CHAIR IN HIS TENT IN THE LATE afternoon, Achilles took a swig of wine from the jewel-encrusted golden cup he kept at hand. He'd been doing a lot of drinking, maybe too much drinking, since withdrawing from the alliance. He was probably half drunk already.

But at least this afternoon he had good reason. Patroklos had insisted on returning to the battle.

So here he sat, half drunk, worried for Patroklos.

Demon's piss, I hate Agamemnon!

This whole mess was Agamemnon's fault. And all over a woman awarded as a prize to Achilles. Agamemnon's be-lated taking of Briseus back for himself, the most prized woman Achilles had lately been awarded, simply demanded strong action. Honor required that Achilles withdraw his forces from the siege. No man, no leader, could accept such humiliation.

For weeks now, though, he'd decided he must find some way to reenter the struggle while keeping honor intact. With-out him and his forces, the Acheans took loss after loss. And a spy inside Troy had informed him that the Amazons were marching on Troy. If only he could find a way to attack Themiskyra now. Curse the blasted Hellespont!

A sudden hue of many voices and the sound of chariots flooded the tent. Automedon swiftly followed the noise.

Tears streamed down Automedon's cheeks. Stunned at the sight, Achilles dropped the cup.

"Achilles, come," Automedon sobbed. "Patroklos."

Achilles leapt from the chair. Outside, four litter bearers walked toward him, a body covered in a white linen cloth laid out between them, entirely covered in linen, including the face.

He stopped, his feet suddenly sunken into the ground like two great stones. When the bearers reached him, they halted.

Odysseus and Ajax came up, one on either side of the litter. "I am profoundly sorry," Odysseus said. The sunlines on his weathered faced were deeply dug with sorrow.

Pulling his feet from where they had taken root, Achilles forced himself to the litter, next to Ajax. He wanted to reach out to pull back the thick linen, but his hand was not only shaking, his arm seemed paralyzed because blood shown through the cloth in so many places.

"This is the work of Hektor," Odysseus added. "Patroklos fought well. Brilliantly. He killed many. But then he ventured so close to the Trojan wall that he caught Hektor's attention. Hektor challenged him."

As if lifting the weight of the world itself, Achilles raised his arm and reached toward the linen. Ajax gripped his wrist. "You don't want to look, Achilles. Hektor went mad. He dishonored himself."

"What do you mean?"

Ajax looked to the ground.

Odysseus said, "To do something like this." He shook his head as if amazed. "For any man of honor to defile a warrior's body. This is not like the Trojan prince, to behave so. Some great evil seized Hektor today."

Achilles shook off Ajax's grip, grasped the linen sheet, and thrust it back. His dearest friend and companion lay nearly naked, his body soaked in blood, and there were wounds—the slashes of spear wounds everywhere. The top of Patroklos' head was missing. The ground beneath

Achilles' feet tilted. So much blood covered his cousin's beautiful face, Achilles could not, in truth, recognize him.

Achilles legs failed, he went to his knees. Nausea brought up the wine and his last meal. This was not battle, this was defilement.

When the vomiting ceased, Automedon helped Achilles to his feet. Achilles' body shook and he could only draw in short, gasping breaths.

"We had to fight to reclaim the body," Odysseus added. "I think Hektor would actually have allowed the hoard to feed Patroklos to the dogs. As his chariot retreated, he shouted, 'That's for Glaukos!'"

Ajax said, "We took many captives. Four are Priam's sons."

"Good," Achilles said. "Good."

Achilles looked to Odysseus. "I want the biggest funeral pyre this camp has ever seen. You see to that for me, won't you?"

Odysseus nodded.

"And then afterward, we will have games. In Patroklos' name, I shall give great prizes to the winners."

He bit the inside of his lip to stop tears welling at the back of his eyes that would shame him. They could come later. But not now. "And we will have sacrifices. Oh, yes. We will have sacrifices."

FULLY DRESSED FOR THE funeral, Achilles lay on his bed. Over an hour earlier a slave completed dressing him, and for that hour, he waited flat on his back. The past two days had passed with the unreal feeling of a horrific dream you can't stop and can't escape. Last night, with his troops and the other royals, he spent a nightlong vigil at Patroklos' pyre. Now, at midday, he must preside over last rites for the only person he had ever really loved.

No, that wasn't exactly true. He had loved others. But only Patroklos had truly loved him.

A slave entered, stopped inside the door and said, "It is time, Lord Achilles."

Time. Time to get up. Time to say farewell. Time to face an empty future.

The slave said, "You've not eaten for two days, sire. Are you certain you don't want me to bring something before you go?"

"I have no need to eat."

Achilles sat up. His muscles felt like stiff boards. He finally got his soles on the floor and, fighting weighted feet, he walked outside.

Automedon waited with the chariot. Achilles stepped into the car, and they began the half-hour journey to the funeral pyre. At Achilles' direction, the pyre sat on a rise in the plain where it could best be seen from Troy. He would have Hektor see this day. And Priam. Both of them would see the rage of Lord Achilles for the mutilation and dishonor of Patroklos.

He had forced himself to watch slaves wash Patroklos' body. Watched as they filled the brutal wounds with unguents. The body had then been dressed and laid on a bier and draped with a white shroud. All the chariots of Patroklos' fellow warriors had been driven three times round the bier, and then Achilles had accompanied it, with his troops, to the site of the pyre. There every man cut off a lock of hair and cast it onto the body.

Now, as they once more approached the site, his Myrmedon men lined the road, all with ashes on their forehead, all fully armored. They raised their swords in salute as he passed. Behind them, in eerie silence, stood the troops of the other kings.

Achilles had never seen so huge a pyre. Great logs framed the bottom, topped by smaller ones that would burn hotly. On top of it all lay Patroklos, his mutilated body covered with white linen, in a corral stood a hundred sacrificial bulls, their gilded horns shining in the sun. Achilles would thank Odysseus. He could not have done a better job himself. Sometime during the morning the body had been wrapped in the fat of slaughtered cattle, to speed the reduction of the flesh to ashes.

Achilles stepped from the chariot and, with Automedon

beside him, took his place as the head of the assembled royals. He could not bring himself to acknowledge any of them. Status and courtesy. What point had these things to him now?

Twelve men were bound to stakes around the pyre's base. Twelve Trojan captives.

Odysseus crossed from where he stood with his troops. Frowning, he stopped in front of Achilles. "The Trojan warriors, Achilles. This is not wise. It is unprecedented. You will not be remembered well for it."

"Don't tell me what to do," Achilles bellowed.

Odysseus bowed his head, turned, and returned to his men.

Lamentations rose from the crowd, a deep wailing accompanied by the beating of swords against shields. As the mourning cries continued, the sacrifices began, performed by the priests. They slit the throats of two of Patroklos' hunting dogs. Their blood ran red on the ground. Their bodies were added to the pyre. Four of Achilles best horses were led up a ramp to the top of the pyre and similarly slaughtered.

He asked Automedon, "Which of the twelve are Priam's sons?"

"The four at Patroklos' feet, where they are closest to Troy."

One after the other, the priests slit the Trojan prisoners' throats. The cries of the assembled warriors changed to a shouted, "Patroklos! Patroklos! Patroklos!" Achilles prayed that Priam and Hektor were watching.

He signaled, and four priests set torches to the prepared wood. At first the fuel did not catch. Achilles ordered libations of wine thrown onto the fire. A blaze sprung up, encouraged by the northern wind.

The sight of the flames drove home the ceremony's finality. His throat tightened. This time tears could not be stopped. He offered his final salute. "A good and honorable man, Patroklos. A great warrior and loyal friend. There will be no other like him."

The heat from the blazing pyre was so great now that it put shame to the sun. "May the greatness of this warrior's spirit never be forgotten. May some part of that great spirit live forever in our hearts."

He wanted to say more. He did not dare, lest he completely break down.

He turned and strode to his chariot. When the fires burned themselves out, Patroklos' ashes would be gathered by the priests, placed into a golden bowel, and into the shelter built for it. When the time came, the ashes of Patroklos would be retrieved, and they would be mingled with his own ashes, so that he and Patroklos might share eternity as they had shared life.

To Automedon he said, "Tomorrow I make peace with Agamemnon. I will rally the Acheans to an attack on Troy like no other. And I will kill Hektor."

"All of the royals will welcome you back."

"My mother came to me in a dream last night. She told me that if I challenge Hektor and kill him, I will die here."

Automedon looked at him, eyebrows raised in surprise. "Then surely—"

"I will have my revenge. If I am to die, so be it. I will die in battle. I can accept dying in combat, in a struggle to the death with a worthy opponent. That's the way a warrior should be remembered."

❧ 46 ❦

SEATED NEXT TO ALCMENE IN CASSANDRA'S CHIL-
dren's garden, Derinoe finished retying the ribbon in Myrina's hair and then gave her daughter a hug. The ribbon
didn't need tending. Derinoe just needed something to keep
her mind off of raging fear gnawing her insides. "Now go
play." Myrina scampered to a group of girls dressing dolls.

To Leonides Derinoe called out, "Leonides, don't jump
from there. It's too high."

Alcmene, carding wool while watching the children, said,
"He's a daring one, that boy. I have to keep my eye on him
every minute."

"You are wonderful with the children."

Cassandra rushed into the garden. She grabbed Derinoe's
hand and pulled her away from Alcmene. "I am going to
watch the battle. It is by the northwest wall and close. Come
with me!"

Derinoe pulled free. "I have never watched one. I won't
watch this one. I am too sick with fear to watch."

Cassandra nodded. "You must pray for Hektor, then. Pray
to Athena."

Cassandra draped her shawl over her head and swept past
Derinoe and out of the garden.

Derinoe returned to Alcmene. She picked up wool and a
carder and set to work, her hands moving almost frantically.

She let Alcmene chat on about a recipe for a yellow dye,

only half listening. In what seemed little more than a heartbeat, a young girl rushed into the garden. "Derinoe," the girl said, pausing to gasp for breath, "the Lady Cassandra says you *must* come to the wall. The Lord Hektor is fighting with Achilles."

Shivers prickled her sides. Derinoe stood, her hands clenched together, her will undecided, torn. Hektor and Achilles. A nightmare come to life.

She followed the girl, needing to see but her heart thumping with dread.

She found Cassandra alone, but not far from the royal ladies: Hekuba, Helen, Andromache and other wives of Priam's sons, all of them wearing black robes of recent grief.

Of a sudden, a great envy of Helen stabbed her heart. If Derinoe lost Hektor, she and her children could be in mortal danger. She would have only Cassandra to rely on for protection from Andromache. But there stood Helen, whom the Trojans loved in spite of pretty Paris' being such a silly, trivial man. Even Hekuba and Andromache staunchly defended Helen.

Scores of elites clustered together, rigid and watching in fascination. Cassandra grabbed Derinoe's arm and pulled her to the wall's edge and pointed to a confusing mass of men and chariots who struggled close enough to the wall that the nearer men could be recognized.

Clashing of metal upon metal, shrieks, groans, and screams. The sound lifted the hair on her scalp. Her stomach knotted.

Bronzed swords and shields and helmets gleamed like a myriad of setting suns on still water. Pennants of dazzling gold, red, blue, green, and purple flapped in the neverending breeze or lay trampled in the dirt. And everywhere, bodies lay in pools of blood. The breeze shifted, and a whiff of a strange, feral stench of earth mixed with urine and blood and bowels sent bile up the back of her throat.

She turned away, swallowing hard to keep her insides down.

Cassandra yanked her arm and spun her around. "There," she said, pointing.

Derinoe saw Hektor. He and another man fought each other in a clearing in the middle of the massed bodies, their chariots standing off to the side, and all the men around them watching, their hostility temporarily suspended.

Achilles!

Derinoe's heart turned to ice. He was exactly as she remembered him. Huge. Even taller and bulkier than Hektor. The deep chill gave way to a hot flush of rage.

Hektor held only his sword. Achilles had spear and sword. Neither was helmeted. Hundreds of warriors, from both sides, had parted to make room to watch the battle between these two famed enemies.

Her trembling arm clutching Derinoe, Cassandra rambled. "My parents tried and tried to make Hektor stay inside the walls, but he wouldn't listen. He went out. He accepted Achilles' challenge. Like a madman he raced around the wall in his chariot. He must have hoped to draw Achilles close enough to a place where archers on the wall could kill him. It didn't work. Now this!"

Achilles thrust his spear toward Hektor's legs. Hektor rushed forward and took a mighty swing toward Achilles head. Up came Achilles' sword. Hektor swung his sword again. Achilles countered with his spear.

She wanted to turn away, but fear and fascination rooted her to the wall.

Hektor rushed Achilles, forcing the Achean backward so many steps that the watching men cleared more space. She prayed, a whispered prayer: "Kill him, Hektor! Kill him quickly!"

Achilles threw himself against Hektor. Hektor stumbled backward with Achilles pressing against his body. Twisting to his right, Hektor broke free

Achilles raised his spear, snapped his powerful spear arm forward, and drove the tip into Hektor's throat.

A great roar rose from the watching warriors and the assembly on the wall. Derinoe heard a woman's shriek and was certain it was Andromache's.

Hektor stood a moment, and then fell backward like a great tree.

Cassandra started moaning. And Derinoe stood unable to move, her mind detached from her body.

She watched, as fascinated as she had been the first time she watched a snake swallow a mouse, as the men around the two warriors struggled over Hektor's body. The Trojans intended to retrieve the body so Hektor might be buried properly. Without burial, his spirit would never find peace. But they were driven back. Finally they fled toward the wall.

Achean warriors pounded Achilles on the back. He drew his sword and raised it toward Priam, thrust it into the air, full of his triumph.

He signaled to two men to help him. They stripped Hektor's armor from his body to take as trophy. Each piece Achilles waved in the air toward Priam. Derinoe could only imagine what Priam had to be feeling, seeing his magnificent son so disrespected.

Achilles signaled again, and a length of rope was brought to him. "What is he doing?" Cassandra grabbed Derinoe's arm. Her hair hung loose in a mess. Her eyes were red with tears.

Derinoe looked to where she had last seen Andromache. To her horror, Andromache turned and stared back with a look of raw hate.

Derinoe whipped her gaze once more to the battleground. Achilles had bound Hektor's feet together. He handed the rope to his charioteer. The charioteer took it to the chariot and tied it to the back of the chariot car.

"What is he doing?" Cassandra screamed.

As suddenly as the detachment of her mind from her body had taken her, it released her. Derinoe screamed, "Hektor!"

Achilles stepped into his chariot and took the reins himself. He turned to the wall and yelled, "For Patroklos!"

He flicked the reins, the horses lunged forward. Achilles dragged Hektor's body by the heels.

"Hektor!" she screamed again, and tears burned themselves down her cheeks.

His body bumped across the ground. His head struck a rock. The chariot went ever faster. Derinoe grabbed her head, closed her eyes.

She was surely going mad. His beautiful body was being dragged through the dirt. Ripped. Torn. His beautiful body. She sank onto the wall, shuddering, crying, rocking.

❧ 47 ❧

STANDING AMONG PENTHA'S COMMANDERS, DAMON waited for her to step from her tent. Beside him stood Trusis and Phemios.

Phemios had been deeply shaken by Hippolyta's death, but his loyalty to Pentha never wavered. The men liked Phemios. They merely respected Trusis, primarily for his skill with the sword, although they also extended grudging admiration for his tenacity in pursuing any goal. Grudgingly, because his means could include stepping on others.

Close on Damon's right, Bias fidgeted with the excess energy of youth.

After a thirty-four day march and three days of hard work, the forces of Themiskyra were well entrenched outside Troy. The site had access to water, a view of the surroundings, and high ground where Pentha could place her tent. Priam had suggested the location. Four days earlier the Trojan king sent an advance message of welcome and indicated where they might be most comfortable and secure. He said that Troy, although still in deep mourning for his son, Hektor, eagerly awaited their arrival.

Bremusa and Clonie appeared at the tent's entry. They took up positions on either side of it.

Pentha stepped out in battle gear, dressed in short tunic, knee-high boots, and golden girdle. She lacked only her white fur hat and her weapons. Her butchered hair, although so short Damon often felt like weeping at the look of it, crowned her head in red-gold waves. The men bowed their heads. The Amazons saluted with fist to brow.

"We've had a long march," Pentha said. "We made it to Troy in even better time than I hoped. I thank every one of you for what you have accomplished."

Trusis called out, in what Damon considered a fawning tone, "It is you who led us and gave us the encouragement we needed."

The commanders let out a cascade of whistles, the sound treating Damon to a fabulous pink and green aura.

When the whistles stopped, she said, "Tomorrow we enter the city. And soon thereafter, with the blessing of Artemis, we will join with the Trojans and finally overwhelm the Achean forces. Rest well tonight. Enjoy tomorrow." She gave them a mischievous smile. "You can be sure that even though the Trojans are in mourning, there will undoubtedly be feasting and some fun."

She saluted them and then walked toward Damon. She drew him aside, so only he could hear, "Tomorrow is the beginning of the end of this thing."

"I'm not thinking about tomorrow. I'm thinking about tonight and about how I haven't been able to make love to you for so long I can't remember."

"No Amazon on duty or campaign—"

"I know. No lovers. Only after victory. Making love weakens resolve."

She clapped him on the shoulder, as she might any man, but her gaze reached the depth of his soul. "And within weeks, perhaps within only days, we will have our victory and this campaign will be over, and you and I will have each other again."

He smiled, but he felt fear, not hope. Not once during their entire march to Troy had she expressed any doubts to him. Not once had she acknowledged that they were going to attempt something Priam had been unable to do in nine years. Not once had she confessed the possibility that one or both of them might die.

She left him and returned to her two commanders. They reentered her tent, and he began walking with Trusis, Phemios, and Bias back to his own.

Suddenly Trusis said, his voice hot with accusation, "What are you doing?" He stared at Bias.

There in Bias' hand lay Trusis' knife, obviously pilfered from the sheath on Trusis' belt. Trusis had caught the boy in the act.

Damon laughed. "Bias, you are impossible. And terrible at lifting."

Trusis, still angry, said to Damon, "Doesn't he have something better to do with his time? Seems you could put him to better use."

To Bias Damon said, "It *has* been two days since you exercised Dia. Tomorrow, when I am in Troy, take her to the hill overlooking the valley I pointed out yesterday. Work her well."

"But Damon!" The boy turned around, half skipping and half walking backward while looking into Damon's eyes with pleading. "I want to go to Troy with you."

"She has to be worked regularly. You know that."

Trusis said, "I have often admired your falcon, Damon." Trusis actually sounded sincere.

"Please Damon," Bias persisted. "Let me go with you."

"We won't leave until mid-morning. You could come if you rise very early and work her and be back in time to help me do what I have to do before we leave."

Bias turned back around, grinning. "Done!"

Damon added, "Day after tomorrow we'll work her together. I want to see her condition for myself." He slapped the boy's shoulder. "Just to see that you've been doing right by her."

They reached the tent used by Trusis and Phemios. Trusis put a hand on Damon's arm. Bias had gone a few steps further but also stopped.

Trusis offered a warm smile. "I would like to see how it's done. And maybe, when we have time, perhaps you could teach me how to man a hunting bird. Could I perhaps accompany you when you next go with Bias to fly her?"

Behind the backs of Trusis and Phemios, Bias made a sour face, waved his arms frantically, and shook his head with great exaggeration.

Damon grinned. He looked back at Trusis' quite eager gaze. "Of course, you are welcome to come."

Bias used his thumbs to pull back and corners of his mouth in a demon's grin, and quickly let them go and pasted on a smile as Trusis turned to him and said, "So, Bias. Let me know the next time you and Damon will fly the bird."

After Trusis and Phemios walked into their tent, Bias said, "The man is a right good fool."

"Trusis has his good points."

"Are you really going to let him come with us?"

"There is no harm in letting him come once. He will see how much work is involved. He will quickly lose interest."

"So I really should tell him the next time we fly her?"

"Yes." Damon had another thought. "And I strongly suggest you don't use Trusis for lifting practice. He has no sense of humor."

❧ 48 ❦

CARRYING A WARM CUP OF APPLE JUICE, PENTHA crossed from her tent to the small one beside it. Today the forces of Themiskyra would enter Troy. All around she heard carts and horses being prepared for the parade and restless men and women chatting with eager animation as they put last minute touches on their clothing or weapons. She must also make final rounds to be sure that all was in order, but first she must check on Gryn.

The smell of wood fires and warm breakfasts momentarily buoyed her spirits. She lifted Gryn's tent flap and stepped inside.

Gryn, sitting on her bed, bare feet on the rug and still dressed in her sleeping robe, looked up.

Pentha said, "How do you feel?"

"Dreadful."

"I thought you might like a warm drink to start the day."

Taking the cup, Gryn offered a weak smile. "You are a good girl." She took a sip, then another. "Could you rub my head again? It helped last night."

Pentha stepped behind Gryn and used both thumbs to rub her temples.

"That does feel so good." Gryn patted Pentha's hand. "I can't come with you today, and I am devastated. It will be a grand parade. Priam will heap honor on you, and I would love to have seen it."

"This trip has been hard for you. I'm sorry I couldn't somehow make it easier."

"My dear daughter. I am the one who insisted that I would not remain in Themiskyra. It is age, not you, that is at fault."

"Well, I'm grateful to have you with me. Your company gives me strength. I worry, mother. All the time."

"When you sacrifice to Artemis today, I want you to offer a pair of white doves in my name."

"There will be no sacrifice to Artemis today."

"But there must be."

"Not today."

Gryn's eyes narrowed with disapproval. "Why not?"

"You know as well as I that many Trojan elites not only don't worship Artemis, they are hostile to her."

Gryn stood. "What, my daughter, does that have to do with whether we offer sacrifice?"

"I want this day to go well. I want our leaders to meet the Trojans and establish good will."

"And to serve that end you will not honor the source of our strength?"

"I have prayed, mother, and the Goddess has spoken to me. She sees wisdom in waiting. That way the Trojans will see that we respect their feelings. Day after tomorrow we will sacrifice to Artemis in Troy."

Gryn nodded. "I misunderstood. I thought you meant not to sacrifice at all." She lowered herself slowly back onto the bed. "Yes. What you say is best. It almost always is."

"I prepare now to meet the Trojan king." Pentha knelt by Gryn's knees. "Give me a hug and your blessing."

Strong, warm arms embraced Pentha. "I am honored to be your mother," Gryn said, her breath warm on Pentha's ear.

The next hours passed swiftly. Pentha made only one significant change. She decided that a display of the infantry, led by Damon and his commanders under their pennants, should enter Troy first, behind the war drums, not the cavalry. The infantry would be followed by a cavalry display. She strode from her tent, in full battle gear, and headed for Valor.

Her warhorse's halter was encrusted with bronze, inlaid by Damon. And Gryn had woven a riding blanket of scarlet wool that was also emblazoned with bronze images of Artemis, stags, boars, and axes. Pentha's battle pennant was a scarlet field against which two golden stags reared against each other with antlers engaged and below them a pair of crossed battle axes. "The blanket matches the pennant," Gryn said upon offering her gift, the comment being a sort of female logic suggesting that a woman should never go into battle to kill people unless all her gear matches. Pentha had laughed out loud, as did Gryn when she saw the irony.

Pentha vaulted onto Valor's back and then heard Damon's voice. "Pentha!" he called. "Pentha. Wait."

He strode up to her and gestured for her to dismount. Drawing her aside, he said, "The scouts returned from the Achean moat and wall. It can be breached. We can take the Acheans down."

A hot rush of anticipation warmed her throat.

He continued, his own fast breathing exposing an excitement like her own. "It's as we hoped. The horses will make the difference. They will let us bring big enough logs to the moat swiftly enough to span it and let the infantry pass quickly across, under the cover of archers. And we won't make Hektor's mistake and breach the wall in the center. We will hit them from both ends, and once inside their perimeter, we can kill them from both sides at once."

She grabbed him, squeezed him. She fought to keep from kissing him in front of her troops. Now she could show the Trojans how to win. She could lead the Trojans. She could kill Achilles.

She let him go. "Say nothing yet to anyone. You and I must talk more details before we meet tomorrow with the Trojan commanders."

He led her back to Valor, grabbed her at the waist and lifted her to the stallion's back. She leaned down to him. "We'll fight, and we'll win."

❧ 49 ❧

D AMON TOOK HIS PLACE AT THE HEAD OF THE COL-
umn of milling men, women, and horses, Trusis to his
right and Phemios to his left. For a moment he felt a strange
embarrassment. He was a fraud. He had not sought this battle. He felt no excitement. No joy. Not even anticipation of
winning. Just resignation.

Phemios said, "Soon we will enter Troy again as victors."

"Perhaps."

Phemios cast him a wide-eyed, shocked look. Damon realized he had spoken true but not wisely. 'Perhaps' was not a
word that would animate men soon to follow him into battle.
He amended, "Or we may just rush back to the city to celebrate and skip the parade."

Phemios grinned, satisfied.

But in fact, "perhaps" was the right word. The right
thought. Perhaps, if they were very fortunate, their efforts
would give the People of Artemis the security Pentha so passionately wanted. Perhaps. But no guarantee existed. In his
experience, one war simply begat another. One act of revenge bred yet another round of passionate hatred.

He nodded to the head drummer. The man signaled, and
the fifty drummers set up a marching beat and advanced.
The vibration from the drums reached into Damon's chest.

The infantry commanders' pennant bearers followed the

drummers. Then Damon was swept into a grand display of force.

Bias came running and fell in, with Wolf tethered by a long leather strip to his arm. Although Wolf obeyed all of Damon's and Bias' commands, they agreed that the animal's wild spirit was a risk, and that Wolf must be tethered around other people, especially strangers.

Trusis frowned and looked to Damon, perhaps expecting him to banish the boy to walk with the foot soldiers. Damon simply smiled back.

They quickly reached the edge of the town where a Trojan delegation in ten chariots awaited them. The Trojans turned the chariots around and led them through the city. As they passed along the central street leading to the citadel's southern gate, the crowds grew, and so did their cheering. And virtually every Trojan face had a smear of ash on the forehead, a sign of mourning for Hektor.

Gone were the encampment's smells of horses' flesh and urine. Damon smelled incense and freshly baked bread.

At first the city seemed no different than he remembered, a place of fine workmanship, like the expert white stucco of the buildings, many of which were three and four stories high. But at closer inspection, signs of the long siege showed everywhere—walls needed repair, he saw only limited selections of vegetables in street vendors' bins, and unrepaired damage marred almost all community water fountains. Still, the street was as he remembered it: remarkably wide and well laid out, as good as any in Themiskyra, which he thought the finest he'd ever seen.

At the citadel wall, the head of the Trojan reception directed the Themiskyran troops to a nearby park. Damon imagined the space customarily being used for Trojan military training and for festivals. Here the Themiskyran rank and file would spend the day and then celebrate with the people of Troy through the night. Themiskyran commanders and their aides had been invited inside Priam's famous wall.

Damon waited beside the chariot of one of their hosts as

the infantry marched to the park. Only a small portion of the infantry was on display, and a still smaller portion of their cavalry. The nature of their full strength must not be revealed lest spies take the information back to Agamemnon. Most particularly, the numbers of horses must be kept secret.

Then, as the first of the Amazons began arriving on horseback, he heard, in the distance, a great noise. It grew, came closer. Clapping, shouting, stomping, whistling, pounding on pots and drums and their wooden shutters, on anything they could find, the people of Troy welcomed Pentha.

And in spite of all his misgivings, his own heart was pounding in anticipation. Yes, even hope.

Finally, he caught sight of her pennant.

❧ 50 ❦

NOT FAR OUTSIDE THE CITADEL'S SOUTHWEST gate, Derinoe waited with Nausicaa to watch the Amazons. Leonides, now nine, and Myrina, now four, stood in front of her. Nausicaa's daughter, a girl the same age as Myrina, stood beside them. Nausicaa had given bone whistles to the children, to use when they saw something that particularly pleased them.

The Amazons had arrived at Troy with a surprise. Men serving as infantry.

"Aren't you glad, Deri, that you came with me?" Nausicaa said as fit men paraded past and war drums lent their strides a determined air. "Doesn't seeing fresh troops give you at least a little feeling of hope?"

"For me, it is too late. They should have come before Achilles killed Hektor."

Nausicaa took Derinoe's hand and squeezed it gently. She had the good sense not to offer empty words of comfort for a love lost. Her own suffering for Glaukos was still fresh and crushing. Instead she said, "Andromache is deep in grief. When she comes out of it, she will have forgotten you and the children. Don't worry."

But Derinoe did worry. She hadn't been invited to dance tonight in Priam's court for the Amazons, something she was certain would have been the case had Hektor been alive. And the first day she left her children with Alcmene at Cassandra's home, doubt nearly paralyzed her. Should she act as if nothing had changed or should she never let the children out of her sight? But the children begged to go. So she worried during the day and could not sleep at night.

The last of the infantry passed, their bronzed cuirasses, shields, greaves, and helmets gleaming from the touch of a mid-afternoon sun slanting to the ground from behind tall, gray-lined clouds. Four lines of pennants, of all the colors of the most magnificent double rainbow, passed by, snapping sharply in the breeze.

The children blew on their whistles. The crowd yelled, clapped, or pounded on whatever object they had at hand as the first line of mounted Amazons, preceded by more drummers, trotted into view, their horse's hoofs beating on the street like clattering hail.

The sight snatched Derinoe's breath. She put her hand over her chest and felt her heart's quickened pulse. Line after line of tanned and lean women rode past, backs straight, eyes vibrant, throwing smiles of confidence to the throngs.

They wore the short battle tunic of Amazons, bare over one shoulder, and all were fully battle dressed: sword, ax, quiver and bow, javaline and shield. And behind each Amazon rode a younger women, her second, carrying spare weapons.

Derinoe suddenly discovered tears flooding down her cheeks. She brushed them away, but the crying didn't stop.

"What is it?" Nausicaa said, her forehead creased with concern.

"I have paid a terrible price."

"For what, Deri dear?"

She shook her head. "For peace. For security. For what I thought was security."

The two of them continued to stare at the passing women and horses.

Derinoe envisioned her mother astride such a mount. She remembered her mother's pride. "We Amazons are free," she had told Pentha and Derinoe so many times.

Something inside snapped. She brushed away the tears.

With each passing moment, Derinoe felt a stiffening inside. She said, "Look at them! Fierce. Unafraid. My mother was Amazon."

Nausicaa turned wide eyes to her.

"Yes. I was born to be Amazon, but the Fates played with me. But they have played with me long enough. I'm going to take my children away from Troy."

"How can you possibly do that? Without means. Without a destination."

"I don't know. But I've escaped before from much worse. I will make a way."

She paused as the impact of her intent settled in. "And I have a destination."

"Oh, mommy, look at the beautiful horse!" Myrina said, tugging on Derinoe's gown. She pointed toward a woman beneath a scarlet and gold pennant who rode a magnificent gray stallion.

Nausicaa said, "By Zeus, the horse *is* a beauty. But so is the woman. That must be the Amazon Queen. They say she is beautiful. And she comes last, a place of honor."

Stunned, Derinoe could barely whisper. "I thought the name of the Amazon Queen was Harmonia."

"Perhaps Harmonia is their Hearth Queen. This woman is surely the Warrior Queen. And Deri, except for her hair, she looks remarkably like you."

The world tilted, then spun. She grabbed Nausicaa's arm. The afternoon lurched into something entirely unreal, as if she must be falling into a dream.

She said, her voice infused with her own amazement, "The woman. Unless I have gone mad, she is my sister."

❧ 51 ❧

D AMON COULD NOT TAKE HIS GAZE OFF PENTHA AS she rode up, wrapped in the exuberant cheers of Trojans in desperate need of salvation. He waited, as did the other Themiskyran commanders, to enter the citadel with her.

Chariots gaily decorated with cloth streamers of red, blue, gold, and green waited at the tall gate to carry the Amazon Warrior Queen and her commanders into the citadel's heart and up to Priam's door. Atop their bridles, the chariot horses sported festive blue and gold feather plumes.

Also waiting for Pentha was the man Priam had appointed as Trojan supreme military command in place of Hektor, a stocky man a head shorter than Damon, with auburn hair, an eloquent voice, and courteous manner. He introduced himself as Aeneas. His black eyes twinkled as if he were perpetually amused.

Pentha dismounted. Aeneas ambled to her and gave her the Trojan salute of a fist placed over the heart. She returned with the Amazon salute, fist to brow.

"In the name of Priam, King of Troy, I welcome the great Amazon Queen," Aeneas said. "I am Aeneas, newly appointed supreme commander of the forces of Troy." He gestured to waiting chariots. "These are double chariots, honorable Penthesilea. I have assigned one for every two of your commanders. They will bear us all to the great King.

Your commanders first, and then you and I will share this one." He gestured to the biggest and finest of the lot, one pulled by not two but four horses.

Damon chuckled and noticed that most of the other Themiskyran commanders were also smiling. Clearly, Aeneas did not know Pentha.

There was the briefest pause as she studied the Trojan. She then gave the commander one of her warmest smiles—a smile Damon knew sped like fermented mare's milk straight to the head of any man within its range—and then she said, "I am honored by your welcome, Aeneas. And by your offer to share a chariot with me. You may proceed me, or follow me, as you feel best. But I ride alone."

With the rest of the Themiskyran commanders, Damon waited for the man's response. Hostile or accepting? What would it be?

Aeneas returned her smile and with slow dignity, saluted her again. "As you choose. The King's chariot is yours. It will be my pleasure to follow you."

Damon quickly assigned the various infantry and cavalry commanders to cars, putting himself and Trusis just in front of Pentha. With drummers still leading, they entered the Trojan citadel, Damon's first glimpse inside.

What he saw left him momentarily stunned. Never had he seen streets this wide. Nor buildings, except for palaces, with entrances so tall. Or possessed of so many windows. All the stucco here still blazed white and perfect. Flowers of red and yellow, orange and gold, brightened windows and doorways.

Where he would have expected displays of expensive statues of marble or lintel decorations in bronze or gold, he found none. But obvious marks indicated where such objects once rested. Presumably the objects themselves were hidden away against the dire possibility that the citadel might fall.

The street led uphill. They passed Athena's temple. Within, he glimpsed the image of the Goddess. Lamps burned brightly in the dark interior. The image gleamed as if entirely made in, or at the very least covered with, gold.

They passed a Temple to Apollo, of equal size. He couldn't see inside.

And then beyond Apollo's Temple, the palace of Priam, dominating the citadel's highest point. In several places the structure rose to four stories.

A series of broad steps led up to a long portico, which Damon guessed was ten times the distance from his door to his thornhedge. On it stood thirty or so people, the welcoming party.

The chariots stopped. The passengers dismounted. When Pentha stepped out of the King's chariot, Aeneas gestured for her to ascend the steps. Damon and Bremusa followed a good ten paces behind her and Aeneas. At the top stood an elderly man with dark complexion wearing a scarlet, ankle-length robe, a gold crown, and draped in a purple robe richly embroidered in gold designs.

Priam's hair and beard, neatly trimmed, were white. The ruler of Troy stooped notably. To his left stood a woman, stout of figure but with a beautiful face of dark complexion, presumably Hekuba. She had equally white hair but straight back. A purple cloak also covered her white robe.

Damon had little idea who most of the others were. Priam was said to have many sons, recognized and unrecognized. An extraordinarily handsome man, the youngest present, stood to Priam's right. He seemed to actually glow from good health. Tall, fair hair, sky-blue eyes, and a strong jaw and curved mouth that Narcissus might envy, he wore full battle gear of short tunic with greaves. An eye-catching leopard skin draped over his broad shoulders. This, Damon thought, must be the notorious Paris.

Damon's brief euphoria had already evaporated in the face of thoughts of the reality of killing that lay ahead. And he thought sadly about Hektor. He would have liked to have met the man so many loved.

"We are here, at last," Bremusa said. "Pentha is close to the vision that drives her so hard."

Yes. At last in Troy.

He endured the greeting ceremonies—muddy brown talk-talk.

At last the pleasantries ceased. The Trojan royals departed and servants scurried to show the Themiskyran guests to quarters where they might freshen themselves for the evening's festivities.

As soon as he could, he would join Pentha. He needed, desperately needed, to be embraced by the sound and color of her voice.

⇥ 52 ⇤

H IS SWORD FLASHING, THE SOUND OF CLASHING metal creating a blood-stirring ringing in his ears, Achilles thrust and struck at first one and then another of his four practice opponents. All their moves were many times rehearsed. No blood would be drawn. But the power of his blows sent a thrilling shock up his arm and into his shoulder.

The only thing terribly wrong was that Patroklos was not one of those opponents. After this practice, Patroklos would not share a rubdown with him. Patroklos was dead. And killing Hektor, though a triumph in the eyes of all Acheans, was pitiful compensation.

The two men opposite him looked away, over his shoulder.

He turned. Between two armed guards, the merchant, Muttalusha, shuffled toward him. Achilles gestured that his men should resume without him, and then turned to the business of the Amazons.

"Lord Achilles—" the merchant began quickly.

Achilles took him by the arm and pulled him roughly away from the soldiers. "I shouldn't have to send men to find someone I have paid well."

"I assure you, I was only momentarily delayed. I was coming—"

"Don't offer excuses!"

"But really, I—"

"I expect you to come when I say you should come, not

when you find it convenient. But for the moment set that aside." He jabbed his sword tip into the ground, let go of it, spread his legs and crossed his arms. "Do you have the information or not?"

"Now, please let me explain."

"Yes, do. Apart from your very helpful information on the Thracian Grammerons, I have thus far found you to be a dry well."

"I tried. I really tried. But since my first trip to Themiskyra, since we first, uh, made our agreement, the people there have treated me differently. I mean to say, I, uh, I sense that perhaps—"

Achilles snapped out his arms, grabbed Muttalusha's tunic, pressed his face close to the merchant's so that his breath, not only his words, would strike him. "I tell you, I sense an excuse coming on. And what I got from you last time was no better than an excuse. For the impressive sum I have paid, I need information." He thrust the man backward a handful of steps.

"I am truly sorry. But I think Harmonia knows or suspects, or well, I simply think she no longer trusts me, and my movements while in Themiskyra have become very limited."

Achilles looked to the senior man of the two guards that had brought the merchant to him. "Take him away and kill him. Make him useful. Feed him to the hunting dogs."

"No, no!" Muttalusha whined. He rushed to Achilles and would have fallen to his knees had the guards not caught him between them.

They dragged him backward. "Please. I do have something you can use. Not in Themiskyra. But here."

"Stop," Achilles said to the guards.

Muttalusha hurried on. "The Amazons have come to Troy, with infantry."

"Do you think I don't know that?"

"If you could capture the Warrior Queen, you could certainly find out from her everything you want to know about the defenses of Themiskyra. You could kill her, even, and perhaps totally undermine the Themiskyran morale."

"And how do you propose I do that?"

"Well, first you need to know that she is vulnerable. She has a lover."

"All Amazons have lovers."

"Not ones that they care about enough to affect their fighting. They do not live with men. And they don't take husbands until they are thirty-two."

"Is the Warrior Queen any different."

"Yes. Oh, yes, she is. Her lover is the head of their infantry, Damonides. They apparently do not sleep together now, while in the field. But they were lovers before. She is said to care deeply for him."

"I fail to see how I can use this peculiarity in Penthesilea's character."

"Well, I am not sure myself. But there is more. I believe you could, ah, come to an arrangement with one of their commanders."

"An arrangement?" He signaled the guards to release Muttalusha's arms.

The merchant shrugged, and with shaking fingers, resettled his fancy tunic. "I know that their second in command of the infantry, a man named Trusis, detests Damonides. And it is said that Trusis is quite ambitious. I don't presume to tell you how to do it, but Trusis is a weakness you can also exploit."

"In what way is he ambitious?"

"My source says he has been heard to speak ill of Damonides and believes that he, not Damonides, should have been head of the infantry."

"Why?"

"This Damonides, although born in Themiskyra, has lived many years in the outside world. He is, in fact, Achean trained. And Trusis believes their infantry commander should not have been an outsider."

Achilles put up his hand to halt the merchant's rush of words as his mind grappled with their implications. "Achean trained," he said aloud. "And you say his name is Damonides? Now that is useful information."

Unsettling information. A famous Damonides had fought some years back at Chios and Samos and elsewhere for the king of Iolkos. If this was the same renowned man, it would give the Amazons an enormous advantage he hadn't counted on. He must let Agamemnon and the other royals know at once. "Go on."

"Also, Trusis is besotted with the Warrior Queen. He would do anything to get rid of Damonides. Trusis could be induced to betray Damonides, of this my source is certain."

"Just who is your source?"

The merchant grinned, tight lipped and sly and nervous. "She is a nobody who cooks for the soldiers. She owes me a great deal of money."

"Debt is a great inducer."

"Yes, sire."

"Perhaps I will let you live. If this information proves true."

"I assure you, sire, you will find it's true. But I must warn you, or remind you. This Trusis is deeply taken with the Warrior Queen. He would not do anything to harm her. Should he think you mean to harm her person, he will not help you."

"Escort our guest Muttalusha out of the camp," Achilles said to the senior guard.

And then to Muttalusha, "If what you say proves false, I will find you."

❧ 53 ❧

THE GREAT HALL IN KING PRIAM'S COURT WAS twice the size of the Great Hall in Themiskyra. Seated at Priam's head table and surveying the scene, Damon couldn't remember having ever been in a bigger room.

He wouldn't have been able to say what struck him as most overwhelming. The exotic birds and beasts? Something called a mandrill, a huge, monkey-like creature, had an enormous face of the wildest purple and pink. The food? He had been offered every delicacy he could think of, from squid to pheasant to whale to sweetened snow from the top of Mount Ida.

His dominant thought, though, was how to escape as soon as possible. He rubbed the back of his neck. The day grew long, and the press of people and the hum and dirty aura had finally shoved him to the brink of illness. He feared the least thing might tip him over.

Paris lounged beside him. The streak of ashes on Paris' forehead, like those on the foreheads of all Trojans in the room, indicated mourning, but still Damon sensed a genuinely festive air in the room.

Paris's exquisite wife, Helen, had gone to fetch her husband a second course of delicacies. Because the custom here was for wives to sit away from the table, slightly behind the men, and for unmarried men to be served by pretty girls, Penthesilea and her commanders had posed an interesting etiquette problem. It amused Damon that while the Amazons sat at the table with the men, their food servants were not handsome young men, but young girls. Trojan men were like almost all men, who weren't slaves, that he'd met outside Themiskyra—jealous guardians of their dominance. They did not serve a woman, not even an Amazon. It would set a bad precedent.

Paris said, "Since my brother's death, the people have suffered great sadness. I was on the wall just before coming here to our banquet. I saw many celebrations in the city. Singing. Dancing. Penthesilea has brought great hope with her."

"Without hope, Lord Paris, no battle can be won. I will convey your thoughts to Penthesilea."

"Your Warrior Queen is remarkably beautiful."

"I assure you, she is also quite deadly."

A contortionist, a long thin man wearing bright yellow baggy pants and matching turban, folded himself into one unbelievable position after another. Helen walked up and placed before Paris a plate heaped with fresh sea bass covered in white cream sauce that smelled of dill, "My dear Helen," Paris said to her. The glowing smile he gave her spoke of affection that oddly reminded Damon of the way Wolf sometimes looked at him.

Helen's skin was like fresh milk with a natural rose to her cheeks so that she used no rouge. Her lips formed a sweet bow. At the corner of one of her sparkling deep-blue eyes lay a beauty mark that lent distinction to a face so perfect she might otherwise have seemed bland. And when she rose to get Paris's food and her gown clung close to her body, Damon particularly noticed that curved buttocks flowed into long, shapely legs.

She took her seat just as Damon's serving girl arrived with a similar plate of bass and a fresh cup of wine. The girl gave Damon a shy smile and sat the plate and cup on the table, but as she took her seat, Paris snapped, "Idiot girl! Commander Damonides asked for pheasant, not fish. *I* asked for the fish."

The girl blushed to her hair's roots, leapt from her chair

and picked up Damon's plate. "F-forgive me," she stammered, and hurried off before Damon could say fish would be fine.

Damon had to this point made no assessment of Paris's nature. Now, to mask his disgust, he took a sip of the wine. The pretty young prince sadly lacked grace of spirit.

Perhaps to cover her husband's outburst, Helen said sweetly, "How long do you think it will be, Commander Damonides, before our joined forces fight the Acheans?"

Paris answered. "It will be soon." He stuffed a bit of fish into his mouth.

Damon said, "We meet with your military staff tomorrow. After assessing the strength of both armies, we will pick a set of days suitable to us. We will send our choices to Agamemnon. If he behaves according to custom, he will respond with whichever one of those days suits him. Presumably not too soon, as he will be working hard now to assess what we have brought with us. But also not too far into the future. Perhaps no more than a week, because he won't want to give us much time to practice together."

"My husband is Troy's finest archer."

The sound of familiar laughter, a female voice, rose above the general noxious din. Startled, Damon looked to where Pentha sat beside Priam. She wore a formal set of scarlet silk pants and tunic. The only woman in the room to even come close to her beauty was Helen.

Priam said something to her, and again she laughed so loudly it carried throughout the hall. Then she lifted her wine glass and took a long drink.

By Zeus! Pentha was drunk.

At that moment she stood, wine cup in hand. "I want to make a pledge to the people of Troy and to her great King," she said. Her voice was strong, and it immediately commanded everyone's attention. Only if you knew her well would you know how much such a tone and behavior felt wrong.

She sat down the cup, then put out her hands to gather

even more attention, as if that were necessary. Damon held his breath.

"I take an oath. I swear that the People of Artemis will help the People of Troy destroy the Acheans. We will not leave here until we kill Agamemnon. Until we kill Ajax. We will not rest until all of the Achean royals are dead or running for home with tails between their legs like the dogs they are." She swayed a bit, then finished. "And I swear by my life that I will kill Achilles."

The room, which had been hushed, fell utterly silent except for the twittering of birds.

Hubris! The word struck Damon like a lightening bolt. Not just hubris. The Furies within her. And certainly the wine. His heart beat hard in his ears.

Pentha slumped into her seat. The hum in the room slowly resumed as four boys dressed in blue, their skin painted blue, ran into the central open space and began an acrobatic performance with eight blue balls.

Damon stood. He bowed to Paris and then Helen. "Excuse me."

He rushed to Pentha. She was talking with Aeneas. "Forgive me." He looked at Pentha. "I need to speak with you."

Aeneas smiled agreeably, and Pentha rose, to Damon's eyes a bit unsteadily. He took her elbow and steered her far enough from the table that no one could overhear them. "Pentha, you're drunk."

Her back stiffened.

"It's my fault. I should have warned you about wine."

"I like the wine."

"You've never had wine before. It's much stronger than the fermented mare's milk you're used to."

"I am not drunk."

"Unfortunately, you are."

Green eyes glittered dangerously. "What is the matter with you?"

She moved to return to the table. He grabbed her by both elbows. "Listen to me. The wine has gone to your head. Did you listen to what you just said? Do you know what you just said?"

"Certainly. I said we'd get rid of the Acheans."

"But you made it a pledge."

"And why not?"

"You took an oath. In front of this entire Trojan assembly."

"I meant it."

"But such bragging tempts the Fates."

She hesitated.

"An oath, Pentha!" He shook his head, trying to clear it. "Look. I am tired. The sounds of all these voices are too much. I'm leaving." He let her go. "You will do what you choose. But I tell you, drink no more wine. You are speaking nonsense. Dangerous nonsense."

She stared at him. He couldn't tell if he'd reached her or not.

Damon left, enormously relieved physically when he reached cool, open air, but profoundly agitated by troubled thoughts. One should never tempt the Fates.

❧ 54 ❧

"TIME TO RISE, MY BEAUTIFUL QUEEN."

Pentha felt the shaking of her shoulder, recognized Damon's voice, but refused to open her eyes. For many minutes she had been awake, but the room was spinning. Her bed kept tilting backward. She kept clutching the bed covers to keep from sliding off onto her head.

And the headache! Demon's piss. She had never had such a headache!

He yanked her coverlet back, and a rush of cool air sent goosebumps flying across her skin.

"I've brought a bath."

"Leave me be!" She forced one eye to open a slit. The man stood fully dressed in his armor and grinning, missing only his helmet and sword. They sat on a nearby table. She pinched the eye closed.

A rough, wet tongue stroked her hand. Her eyes flew open. Wolf stood beside his master, staring at her.

"Damon, I feel terrible. Go away!"

"Can't."

He grabbed her hands and pulled her into a sitting position. Her head threatened to fly off her shoulders.

"Ohhh," she moaned, praying he would take pity and desist.

"In very few hours we meet the Trojan High Command. You have to be in top form. It's going to take some work."

He swept her legs off the bed and her feet onto the floor. "Can you walk? Your bath awaits." He gestured to a tub on the far side of the room where a young girl stood ready.

"How can you always be so horrifically cheerful? You and Bias. The two of you never take anything seriously." She gave him what she hoped was an intimidating stare. "I am seriously sick. I can't crawl let alone walk."

He cocked his head and grinned still more.

He pulled her upright, and even as she struggled to push him away, he used both hands to shove her sleeping gown up her body and over her head, leaving her naked.

"Damon!"

He swept her into his arms, tramped across the room, and deposited her into the tub.

Warm, lovely warm water, smelling of night jasmine. She closed her eyes.

"And I don't find everything amusing," he continued. "For example, last night I did not find your speech amusing."

"What speech?" The girl put a warm sponge to her back.

"So you don't remember?"

She wrestled with images of the banquet, Priam, Hekuba, Aeneas. And of herself standing in front of a sea of attentive faces. She looked up at him. He had pulled a stool not far from the tub and was happily watching the girl bathe her. "What did I say?"

"I hesitate to repeat it, Pentha. You made outrageous boasts in the form of oaths."

"Boasts."

He nodded.

"What boasts?" Shocking that she couldn't remember a thing. The girl lifted her arm and washed it.

"Well, let's see. You took an oath that the People of Artemis would not leave Troy until we had killed or driven out every Achean. And I quote you further, "I swear by my life that I will kill Achilles."

She pulled her arm from the girl and studied his face. He was not smiling, nor grinning. He was telling the truth. She sat silent, stunned.

He nodded. "It was the wine talking. Mostly."

They remained silent as the girl finished her task, although when the bathing became most intimate, he stood and retreated to a chair by the table.

She stood to be rinsed. The girl brought the customary large jar of water and climbed up on a stool. "Are you sure?" the girl said to Damon.

Without looking, he said. "Yes."

The girl poured.

Icy water hit Pentha with a stunning splash. She sucked in her breath and shrieked, a howling "EEeeee!"

"You demon!" she hurled at him.

She leapt from the tub, snatched up the waiting robe and threw it on, and strode to her pillow. From under it, she took out the dagger and dashed to the chair where he sat. She stepped behind him and placed the dagger at his throat. "That water is melted snow. I should kill you for your disrespect."

With calm he said, "Take care! I will sic Wolf onto you."

Wolf *was* watching them both most intently.

She pressed the knife closer against his skin. "Why ice?"

"It's the best thing for curing the ills of too much wine." He took the wrist of the hand holding the knife, pulled her around and into his lap. "You're especially beautiful when you're angry."

He kissed her. She let herself relax. When he let go of her wrist, she wrapped her arms around him. She pressed her mouth to his mouth, let his tongue explore inside her, thrust her tongue into him.

All thoughts slipped from her mind. For now, for this moment, there were only Damon's lips, his intoxicating male scent, and the divine touch of his hands on her body.

✥ 55 ✥

USING A SECRET CORRIDOR, DERINOE ARRIVED at the point where, if she, Leonides, and Myrina stepped outside into the public corridor, they would be close to where Alcmene had assured her Priam's chamberlain had quartered the Amazon Queen.

"This is fun," Myrina said.

Derinoe straightened the dark blue ribbon in Myrina's hair.

Leonides said, "Why do we come a secret way, mother?"

"Because, if we tried to reach my sister through regular corridors, we'd be stopped. You both wait a moment."

She stepped into the small alcove that lay behind a tall tapestry. Through two eyeholes, she peeked into the public corridor. Seeing no one, she reached behind and taking Myrina's hand, said, "Keep close, Leonides." She slipped from behind the tapestry.

They arrived at the end of the corridor just as a serving girl, flustered and grinning, came running toward them. They turned the corner, and halfway down the hall an Amazon guarded a door. "Just do what I say."

At the door, she said to the guard, "I and my children are here to visit the Warrior Queen, Penthesilea."

"Penthesilea is not seeing guests."

"Tell her that her sister is here to see her."

The Amazon gave Deri a hard stare. "Well, that's a remarkably unconvincing lie. Are you the only person alive who doesn't know that only months ago she killed her sister?"

"I don't know what you are talking about. I am her sister."

"Go away, crazy women, before you get into trouble."

"Just tell her that her sister is here."

"Go away!"

Derinoe leaned down and said softly to Leonides, "You stay here with Myrina." Without straightening, she shoved her way past the guard, and bolted into an antechamber. Another room lay beyond. With the guard scrambling behind her, she plunged into the second room.

There, on the lap of a man dressed in battle gear sat Pentha in a dressing gown, her hair wet, her arms around the man's shoulders.

The guard grabbed Derinoe's arm with fingers that felt like metal pincers. "I am sorry, Pentha," the guard said.

Pentha jumped to her feet. Derinoe stood speechless, partly from simply seeing Pentha so close and so alive and partly from huge embarrassment at barging in on such an intimate moment.

FOR SEVERAL HEARTBEATS, PENTHA simply stared. She pulled her robe tighter. Finally, comprehension dawned. She shook her head. Then the spell holding her broke. Joy, like the arrival of a thousand springtimes, exploded in Pentha's chest. She rushed across the room and threw her arms around the vision from the past. "Deri," she cried, as Deri hugged her back.

Without letting go, they swung each other around in a circle, stopped, and Pentha clung to Derinoe for fear she would wake from this dream and Deri would be gone.

But no. The woman in her arms did not disappear.

She stepped to arm's length, held Deri by the hands. "You are alive. Artemis has granted me the greatest kindness I could imagine."

The guard left them. Behind her, Pentha heard Damon rise.

Deri said, "And you are not only alive, you are Warrior Queen. The world is surpassing strange."

Pentha gestured to Damon, "Come," she said.

He joined them.

"Deri, this is Damonides. Damon. My friend. Commander of my infantry." Pentha still couldn't believe it. "I don't yet know how, Damon, but somehow my sister, from Tenedos, is alive."

Damon bowed his head to Deri.

Pentha thought how Deri had grown exceptionally beautiful. Deri studied Damon a moment and gave him a lovely smile. Deri was not the young girl Pentha remembered, but a stunning woman.

"I have more surprises," Deri said. She turned and went back toward the entry.

Pentha turned to Damon. "She's here in Troy, safe. She's alive and not with . . . she is not a slave." He put his arm around her.

Deri reappeared and with her, two children. She stood them in front of Pentha and said, "Pentha and Damon, this is my son, Leonides. And my daughter, Myrina."

Pentha felt for a brief moment like she ought to sit down.

The boy, Leonides, looked past Damon to where Wolf stood beside the chair Pentha and Damon had so recently shared. "Is it a real wolf?" the boy asked. He was handsome, with chestnut hair and big hands that suggested he would grow into an impressive man.

Damon smiled. "Full blooded."

The little girl, Myrina, hugged Deri's leg as she gazed shyly at Pentha. She looked very unlike her brother. Delicate, with dark hair and dark blue eyes.

"Come," Pentha said. "Let's sit." Before Deri could take a chair, Pentha grabbed her, hugged her again, and whispered in her ear. "I should have tried to help."

Deri shook her head. "There is nothing you or I could have done to change anything. We won't talk of it."

"Lie down," Damon said to Wolf, who gave Damon an

adoring look and immediately circled, tucked his haunches, and flopped to the floor.

"I never knew anyone who had a pet wolf," the boy said, his eyes on Damon, wide with wonder and admiration.

"The Fates delivered him to me when he was young. He lost his family, and I was the fortunate person destined to take him in. If you'd like, you can pet him."

Leonides made no move to pet Wolf. Pentha certainly understood. Wolf was full grown, and sometimes she even felt a shiver of awe when he stood close to her.

Damon looked at Deri, studying her with what appeared to be surprised interest. "You know the two of you look alike. But you also have an unusual voice? It is like your sister's."

"How so?"

Pentha said, "Is it true, Damon? Is her voice also yellow?"

"Exactly like yours."

To Deri, Pentha said, "Damon has many wonderful traits. One of them is that sounds have colors to him."

Deri frowned.

Feeling pleasure in talking about this extraordinary man that she loved, Pentha said, "When Damon hears sounds, almost all sounds, he can close his eyes and see colors. He even sees a halo of colors when his eyes are open and there are sounds. And he likes my voice because, so he tells me, when I talk, I create a pretty yellow aura. Apparently you do too."

Deri looked to Damon, and he nodded, his arms crossed and one of his characteristically happy smiles on his face.

Myrina had made her way close to him, specifically to his sword. It lay in its scabbard on the table. She touched the scabbard.

Damon said to her, "Do you like pretty things made of leather?"

She smiled at him and nodded.

"So do I."

Myrina stepped to him and raised her arms, wanting him to take her into his lap.

To Pentha's surprise she realized she had never before

seen Damon in intimate contact with children. With Bias, yes. But Bias was a boy of fourteen years. And children always followed Damon when he walked any place in Themiskyra. But never had she seen him in a room, as a man would be with his family.

And Damon, too, was apparently struck by the moment's strangeness, because he smiled at Myrina awkwardly. Then he carefully lifted her into his lap, as if his big hands might break her if he squeezed too hard. Myrina reached onto the table and used her small fingers to trace the bronzework of the scabbard.

Pentha said to Derinoe, "How did you find me? And how could you reach me here?"

"I saw you yesterday. In the parade. And I know all of the secrets of the Trojan citadel."

"How is that?"

Leonides finally worked up the courage to approach Wolf. He petted the broad head.

Bias stepped into the room. Seeing Damonides, his mouth went slack, apparently feeling the same amazement Pentha felt at the sight of a little girl in Damon's lap.

"So Bias. What is it?" Damon asked.

Recovered, Bias said, "I'd like permission to go into town."

"You have it. But first, do me a favor. Pentha has a visitor. I think the women need to talk in private. Take the children onto the roof garden with Wolf and show them the things he can do. If that is agreeable to their mother." He looked at Derinoe.

"Are you sure the wolf is safe?"

"With Bias and me, he is safe."

"That would be exceptional," Leonides said.

Damon set Myrina on her feet, and she smiled at Bias, apparently happy enough to go with the two boys and the wolf.

Bias walked up to her and said, "You know, I think you have something in your ear." He paused, took a depth breath, and intoned, "Badamus Flax!" then reached beside Myrina's ear. He pulled his hand back, and there in his palm lay four pale blue, red-speckled robin's eggs. One, though, had broken.

Myrina's eyes popped wide. Then she looked, little mouth ajar, at Bias. Damon chuckled.

Pentha said, "You are improving, Bias. But—well, you still clearly need some work."

As Bias shepherded the children out, Damon stood. "I will also give the two of you privacy." He was uncertain whether to stay or go. He wanted to stay. But offering to leave felt right.

"You don't need to leave," Pentha said, and it sounded more like a serious request that he stay than a casual pleasantry. The thought occurred to him that perhaps such a sudden appearance of her sister had shaken Pentha somehow. She wanted a buffer. Some time to absorb the shock.

The beautiful, dark-haired sister then said, "And I am also happy to have you stay."

That settled it. Listening and seeing the sound of the two of them talking was like watching a fluttering of yellow butterflies in a sunny room.

He sat again. He was also thinking that this visit could not last much longer in any case because he and Pentha must meet with the Trojans.

As if she had read his mind, the guard, Saya, entered and said to Pentha, "You must begin dressing soon. Shall I send a girl in?"

"Not just yet. I will call you."

Saya retreated to her post.

Pentha said to Derinoe, "So, how did you know I would be in these quarters?"

"My life has been . . . unusual. You will learn that I have been a dancer here, for many years. But, I was also the mistress of Priam's son, Hektor. I know most, if not all, of Troy's back passages."

Hektor's mistress! Damon thought. She had said her life was unusual. Unusual would appear to be a grand understatement. She was admittedly attractive. And maybe even an exceptional dancer. But what extraordinary things must have transpired to take a young girl from Tenedos into the very highest levels of Trojan society?

Pentha exclaimed, "You have been living here, at Troy all these years? As Hektor's mistress!"

"Not all. But for a long time. I am also close to Cassandra."

Pentha stood and took several steps from the table, and then turned back to face her sister. Her smile had vanished. "I've seen how they treat women here. You accepted this?"

"It's not a case of accepting."

"So you never accepted all this fawning on their men. Serving their every whim?"

Derinoe hesitated. She stiffened. Distress lines creased her brow and her shoulders drooped. Pentha's words pained her.

"Hektor cared for me and protected me," she shot back.

Pentha persisted. "Cassandra you say. She is the high Priestess of Athena. Have you gone so far as to abandon Artemis? Please don't tell me—"

"Sisters," he interjected, alarmed at the building acrimony. "This is perhaps not—"

Pentha said testily, "Let her answer, Damon." She looked back at her sister. "Have I grieved for years for a woman who would shame our mother and the Goddess."

"I shamed no one."

"Then how could you have become the mistress of a prince of Troy?"

Derinoe leapt to her feet, her face without color and her hands shaking. "It was a great mistake for me to have come here."

Without another word she left swiftly, following the route Bias had taken with her children.

"Pentha," Damon said, "what in Hades has possessed you? The woman is your sister. You thought her dead or worse for years. You grieved for her."

She strode up to him. "I know what it means to be the mistress of one of these men. It means collaboration."

"Collaboration is an ugly word. And it shouldn't come out of your mouth when you speak of your sister."

She slapped him. His cheek burning, his heart having

skipped several beats, he shook his head and gave her a smile of sad disappointment.

They stood in silence a moment. Pentha clenched her fists, turned away from him, walked three paces, and spun back to face him. He watched her shoulders droop and she unclenched her fists. She bit her lip and her eyes glistened, on the verge of tears. "I'm sorry I hit you."

"You should be equally unhappy with yourself for attacking Derinoe. You gave her no time or opportunity for explanation."

"For an Amazon, there can be no explanation—excuse—for collaboration."

"Derinoe is not an Amazon."

"Her mother was. Her heritage is."

He wasn't going to reach Pentha on this matter. Not now. And maybe not ever. "Not everyone, Pentha, has your iron will. I love you for it. But don't let it rob you of a sister who very likely merits understanding, not criticism."

Saya entered the room. "You must dress at once, Pentha, or you will be late. Shall I send in the girl."

Pentha nodded. Damon said, "I will see you when you're dressed. We can go to meet Aeneas and the others together."

❧ 56 ❧

ACHILLES SAT, LEGS STRETCHED BEFORE HIM, IN the shade of an olive tree. His bulk nearly overflowed one of two high-backed camp chairs placed in this secluded olive grove, a site carefully chosen for this meeting. With approval he watched the Themiskyran commander, Trusis, as Automedon brought the chariot to a halt. Apparently this Trusis was a punctual man, a trait Achilles admired. He had not been waiting long.

The meeting required secrecy, so Achilles had sent Automedon to fetch Trusis, who would be on foot. They met outside Troy, well away from the Themiskyran camp. And as instructed, Trusis had come alone. The man had courage.

Trusis stepped down from the chariot and the breeze fluttered the edges of his cloak. He drew the cloak tighter, protection against any chill, but also a sign he felt vulnerable, so far from his own forces. It seemed that the Hittite Merchant had been right. Trusis was a man of ambition, and apparently willing to take risks, but not stupid. He must be relieved that only Achilles waited for him. On the other hand, while Trusis was armed with dagger and sword, Automedon had met him unarmed. The agreement had been that the moment Trusis caught sight of any Achean soldiers or more than one other man, he could kill Automedon.

Achilles rose. He said, "I appreciate your willingness to risk meeting in an isolated place."

"Your terms were convincing. Automedon is well known in Troy. As is your reputation as a man of your word."

Achilles gestured toward the chairs. They sat. Achilles let Trusis study him.

Finally, Trusis spoke. "Your messenger said that if I wanted to rule Themiskyra, you could make it happen. I am here. But for all you know, I may learn your plans and take the information straight back to my Warrior Queen."

"I mean no harm to your Queen. Let me assure you of that."

Trusis simply stared at him.

"What I propose is an alliance. I want two things. To ensure that the Trojans do not win this coming battle. To do that, I don't need to destroy your troops, I only need to find a weak spot I can use to defeat them. Second, I want access to Themiskyra. I want access to Amazon horses—a steady supply so I can sell them. I would, of course, share the profits with you, as its ruler."

"You want horses. And for this you would put me in place as head of Themiskyra?"

"No. Not just horses. Iron." Trusis needn't know—at least, not yet—that he also intended to take prime Amazon women to sell. "I see you are surprised. Yes. I have learned that the Hittite source of iron is Themiskyra. I want access to that same source. And I will share profits far more generously with you, as my ally, than the Hittites do."

"You apparently know nothing of Themiskyra. Our Amazons would fight to the death to prevent anyone other than our Hearth Queen from ruling there. And we also now have men under arms."

"Before we go any further, I want to know if ruling Themiskyra, and sharing in the bounty we could have through my trading resources, is something you want badly enough to spill blood. If not, our discussion can end."

Achilles studied the Themiskyran's face, weighed the silence fallen between them. Trusis did not immediately reject the proposal. That failure alone Achilles took as a resounding shout of weakness.

"Whose blood?" Trusis asked finally.

"The blood of any who choose to fight my forces."

"Fight? You have no troops at Themiskyra."

"I think you know that I do. Not at Themiskyra itself, but not far to the west in the Euxine Sea. By next summer, I will have many more. To be blunt, I am going to attack Themiskyra next year and take it. You can either ally with me and become ruler. Or you can be brought down with any others who oppose me."

"You propose to kill every Amazon there?"

"Only those, women or men, who choose to fight. Since you say that is the likely action of all of the Amazons, a lot of blood could be spilled. But perhaps you, as commander, a man known to them, would convince them it is better to co-operate with a force they can't defeat than to die. By accepting my offer, you could save many lives."

Achilles could almost see thoughts circling 'round in the Themiskyran's lowered head. Now was the time to add what the merchant had said would be the ultimate incentive. "What this requires from you is actually very little. I need to defeat your army here, now. Not destroy, I repeat. Simply a resounding defeat. I know how I can do that if I can get my hands on your commander, Damonides."

Trusis' head jerked up. "Damonides?"

"Yes."

"What do you propose to do? How can having him assure you of our defeat?"

"That I will not tell you. I will only say that he will not survive."

"What about Penthesilea? Do you propose to kill her, too?"

"That's not essential."

"I would insist that she not be killed. Not harmed."

"Insist?"

"Yes, insist. I will not help you unless you tell me, on your honor, that she will not be harmed."

Achilles had prepared for this demand. And honor must be served, so he had given care crafting his reply. "I give you my word, it is not in my plans to kill your Warrior Queen."

"She will be free to return with me to Themiskyra?"

"Of course. I will depend on you next summer to convince her, and her Amazons, to surrender rather than die. At that time, you will become king in Themiskyra." He paused, then added, "Lord Trusis. It has a fine sound."

"I need time to think."

Achilles' shook his head. Giving anyone time to think when selling them something they might later regret was bad strategy. "It is simply too difficult and too dangerous for us to meet again. You, also, are a man of honor. Take time, now, to decide. But a decision must be made before we leave here."

Silence. Achilles tolerated it, as he must, but he knew the outcome already. He had been virtually certain of what Trusis would do from the moment he learned that Trusis agreed to this clandestine meeting. Trusis was one of those many men who talked of honor but had none.

It was never pleasant to deal with such men. That reminded him. He must remember to double his payment to Muttalusha. The merchant had, at last, paid off grandly.

Trusis pondered a while, tapping his knee. He stood. He paced. He sat again. Finally he said, "I accept. We have an agreement."

They settled in to discuss specifics. Achilles beckoned to Automedon, who was waiting near the chariot, and Automedon brought wine.

❧ 57 ❧

DERINOE BOLTED TO FULL CONSCIOUSNESS OUT of a restless sleep. Someone had opened her front door. Every night, after tucking the children in and before retiring herself, she placed a small copper jug on a table in front of the door so that, should anyone try to enter from the outside, the pot would fall. She felt certain that she'd heard its tinny clatter.

Since the day Hektor had been killed and Andromache had hurled at Derinoe that venomous look, Derinoe had taken several precautions to reduce her vulnerability. In addition to the pot, she slept fully dressed, kept the sleeping room door closed, and left a tiny lamp lit within the chamber.

She leapt up from her pallet and in two steps knelt beside Leonides and Myrina. She covered his mouth at the same moment she shook him. His eyes flicked open. "Right this instant. To the roof!" she whispered. "Understand?" He nodded.

She had rehearsed this desperate measure with both children several times and now uttered a silent prayer to Artemis that she had done it often enough.

Leonides scrambled up, and as Derinoe awakened Myrina and whispered again, Leonides silently slid what appeared to be a heavy cabinet far enough to reveal the window behind hit. The wicker cabinet was, in fact, easily light enough for him to move because Derinoe had taken everything out of it. As she had taught him, he did not hesitate but climbed out the window.

A flash of pride, and hope, swept through Derinoe at how perfectly quietly her son acted. "Don't be afraid, love," she whispered to Myrina as she lifted her daughter through the window. "Just be very, very quiet. Just like we practiced."

Leonides was already at the roof. Myrina climbed up after him. Derinoe's heart pounding against her ribs, the words "Hurry, hurry" in her mind, she snatched up the bundle of the children's street clothes. She still had heard no other sounds, no footsteps, as she herself scrambled through the window and slid the chest back to cover it. But she didn't expect to hear anything. Andromache would use only professional killers, and professionals did not make sounds. They simply struck, did their work, and disappeared quietly back into the night.

Derinoe stood on the barrel she had placed below the window and raised her foot to begin the climb when she heard the squeak of the sleeping chamber door. She froze, pressing one trembling hand on her chest near her throat, as if to still her blood's racing. Soft rustling sounds came to her from inside. She rested her foot lightly on the ladder's first rung, remaining rigid.

Silence.

For agonizing moments she stood awkwardly, straining her whole body to hear the slightest sound. Her back and raised thigh ached. Finally, when she could no longer remain still, she crept, rung by rung with long pauses, toward the roof.

Someone had entered the house, and they would know by now no one was there. And surely they would immediately check the sleeping pallets and know by the warmth clinging to them that she and the children must have left only moments ahead of them. Her hope, her plan, was that they would think the three of them had left by way of the alley entrance.

Still not a sound. She began to doubt. Perhaps she was wrong. Perhaps the sound that awakened her was not the pot at all, but something from outside their rooms.

As the racing of the pulse in her neck slowed, she strained to hear anything from their rooms or on the street. Still nothing.

She reached the roof. Still no sounds. Leonides and Myrina stood looking at her. Leonides said in a whisper, "I saw them."

"Who?" she whispered back.

"Two men. I saw them from the wall." He pointed to the section of roof wall that overlooked their front entry. "Two men came out and ran away. While you were climbing."

She grabbed and hugged him. Then she said, "Hide under the blanket. We wait. It's too soon to go downstairs."

Leonides took Myrina's hand, led her to a blanket in a corner, helped to cover her, and then crawled under himself. Derinoe sat down her bundle of clothes and shoes and sat beside the blanket. She tucked the cover under their chins and stroked a stray curl away from Myrina's face. They settled in to wait.

What she guessed must be an hour passed. The children had fallen asleep. If she was to take them away, she must do it during darkness, and night was quickly approaching dawn. Finally she decided she must know one way or the other if someone waited below. For certain her life here was over, and much sooner than she had planned.

Derinoe climbed back down the ladder, and biting her lip, moved the chest aside and then listened for any movement within. Hearing nothing but her own breathing, she climbed into the sleeping chamber.

The lamp still burned, the chamber was silent and empty. But the door to their main room stood open.

She froze for a moment, then forced her feet to move. Their main room was empty, the front door ajar, and the copper pot lay on the floor.

She closed the door. This attempt had failed, but there would surely be another.

She wakened Leonides and Myrina, and well before Helios' arrival and a new dawn, she hurried the three of them away from the place that had been their refuge in Troy. Not far from the eastern gate she stopped and knocked several times on the door to a modest set of rooms. She knocked again.

"What is it?" came Nausicaa's familiar voice.

"Deri."

The door opened a bit, then wider. "Whatever are you three doing at my door. It's not yet morning."

"I—we—need a place to hide. May we come in. Just for a while. I don't believe there is any possible way Andromache can know that I know you."

"Ah," was all Nausicaa said as she took Deri's hand and led her inside.

Nausicaa's daughter come to the door of their sleeping room, treating the three early visitors to a sleepy and surprised face.

"A WOMAN WISHES TO see you," the guard said to Pentha, who had just sat down with Damon to grab a piece of fruit and bread for a quick lunch before they left to meet again with Aeneas. "She says she knows your sister, Deri," the guard added.

Damon's quickly raised eyebrows mirrored Pentha's own sense of amazement.

"Let her enter," Pentha said.

The woman was dark-haired and quite attractive in a plump, easy-going way. She seemed nervous, glancing around the tent's reception chamber with quick eyes, as if to assure herself she would not be pounced on. But she also came quickly to the point. "My name is Nausicaa, great queen. And I've come on my own because Deri is in trouble and you are not only a powerful woman, you are her sister."

"What kind of trouble? Why hasn't she come herself?"

"I told her she should, but she refused."

Pentha waited, tapping her finger. So Deri could be stiff-willed as well as compromising. Pentha glanced at Damon, who was studying Nausicaa intently. Damon was an excellent judge of character.

Nausicaa continued. "To be blunt, she fears for her life

and the life of her children. Especially for her children. Everything Deri does is for her children."

Damon said, "Who threatens her?"

"Deri told me that she told you she was Hektor's mistress. Myrina is Hektor's daughter. And Deri believes that last night the Lady Andromache sent killers to remove her and Leonides and Myrina from the city. You perhaps have no way or need to know that Hektor's wife is—was—extraordinarily jealous of her husband's affections."

Pentha felt a sudden uncomfortable shifting of her feelings, as if the ground itself had shifted. She had thought, for some reason, that Deri had been happy, content, and safe in Troy all these years. A pacified, tamed enjoyer of the benefits to be had by submitting to a man.

But Leonides was nine. Nausicaa did not say that Hektor was Leonides' father and Pentha suddenly felt certain she knew who was. How hard it must have been for Deri to survive, to say nothing of caring for a baby boy when she arrived alone and friendless in Troy at the young age of fifteen. What might she have had to do before Hektor entered her life and gave it some stability?

Pentha felt tears threatening. "Everything Deri does is for her children," Nausicaa had said. "You did not give her time to explain," Damon had said. Yes, life often required explanation if there was to be understanding and compassion between two people, even sisters.

"Please, Nausicaa, sit down." Pentha called to the attendant. "Joynene, bring our guest a choice of drinks."

Nausicaa took the chair nearest to her, but perched uncomfortably on its edge. "Deri says she has displeased you, and when I asked her to explain why she didn't think you would help her, she just said it was complicated. Something about an Amazon matter. But I'm here because I know her well. She is a fine mother. And I don't think things this serious are complicated at all. She desperately needs help, and you are her sister."

Pentha felt Damon's gaze on her. She met it. He smiled.

Pentha said to Nausicaaa, "And you are right. It's probably not all that complicated. Tell me where I can find her."

DERINOE TURNED FROM DRYING a plate toward Nausicaa's front door as it opened. Nausicaa hurried in, and behind her strode Pentha, dressed simply in tunic and sandals. Nausicaa had gone to Pentha!

Leonides and the two girls, who had been playing marbles, bounced to their feet, their eyes growing big as daisies when two more female warriors entered dressed in full battle gear, one with a chest the size of a man's and the other with a monstrous scar on her cheek. The modest room suddenly seemed tiny, filled from ceiling to corners with massive Amazons.

Stunned, Derinoe simply froze with the plate and towel in her hands. Apparently to fill the strained silence, Nausicaa said the obvious. "I've brought your sister."

Pentha strode across the room and stopped in front of Derinoe, her green eyes direct in their gaze. "I owe you an apology, Deri. I am profoundly sorry."

Deri was safe! Her children were safe! She felt her knees giving way. Pentha grabbed her and Deri hugged back, suddenly flooded with relief and joy. And gratitude—to the Goddess, to Nausicaa, to the Fates.

"I love you," she said. "And I am so glad you've come."

HER ARM LINKED WITH Pentha's, Derinoe strolled down a narrow street toward the temple to Artemis. Within moments of their reuniting they agreed that what they most wanted to do, in their mother's memory, was to sacrifice to Artemis.

And at last, Derinoe had some reason to feel totally secure. Behind them marched a contingent of six armed Amazons. Guards accompanied Pentha whenever she moved about the city. Not one person they passed failed to stop and stare at their party. Several times women on balconies fetched friends to come see the Amazons.

They reached the temple entry, a once proud set of bronze gates depicting laurel vines and stags. The dull bronze showed its age—dents and imperfections that, in the glory days of Artemis, would always have been kept at a lustrous shine. With Pentha, she halted at white marble steps. Derinoe said, "I have so much I need to tell you. Perhaps first of all, that Myrina is Hektor's child."

Pentha replied simply. "Nausicaa told me that."

"His wife, Andromache, wants to believe, or at least she wants the people of Troy to believe, that Hektor loved her alone. She is extremely jealous." Derinoe expected a great show of surprise from Pentha, but received only a level, thoughtful stare and the comment, "What peculiar thinking."

Pentha then added, "I apologize again, Deri, for what I said before. I'm so sorry. When you left us, Damon became quite angry. He said I gave you no time to explain anything. He was right. I'm ashamed."

"I had decided to take Leonides and Myrina away." Derinoe felt her skin warming. Embarrassment? No. The feeling was more like shame that she hadn't made the decision years earlier. "When I saw the women of Themiskyra enter Troy in such strength, I decided I want to go home. I want to take the children to Themiskrya. I want Myrina, especially, to grow up free."

Pentha broke into a dazzling smile. She grabbed Derinoe and hugged her. "I am so grateful we are together again." Pentha took her arm and they walked up the steps. Semele had apparently been advised that the Warrior Queen was at her door. She appeared at once.

After they sacrificed and prayed, as Derinoe and Pentha turned to leave, Semele said, "Penthesilea, when the day for battle comes, I would be honored to come to the battlefield and offer sacrifices for you and the women and men you lead."

"Semele, you honor *us*. I will let you know when and where."

She and Pentha stepped into the bright light of the sun. Derinoe's heart felt as light and bright as the sun itself. "It's so strange, Pentha. For years I did nothing but compromise—with Hektor and Cassandra, with the whole life of Troy and its cleverly disguised enslavement of women. I tried to pretend I was happy. Sometimes—the good times with Hektor or the children—I actually thought I was happy. But now that I know I can take them home to Themiskyra, my spirit is truly at peace."

"We all seek peace, every woman in her own way, I suppose."

"Word will spread quickly that I have sacrificed to Artemis. When Cassandra hears, she will disown me. I don't think she is vengeful. But I can no longer expect her help."

"We'll take no risks. We'll take the children to my encampment. Now."

❧ 58 ❧

"DON'T GET TOO CLOSE," DERINOE CALLED TO Leonides as her son ran to where Pentha's horse, Valor, was tethered. Myrina held Derinoe's hand lightly and dawdled as her bright little eyes soaked up every tiny thing they could about the tents, dogs, geese, chickens, artisans, pots of cooking food, and anything else they came across. For the first time in the two days since their arrival in the Themiskyran camp, Derinoe had time to take the children exploring.

The war stallions stood in rows, their halters secured to waist-high ropes strung in lines, far enough apart and on short enough leads that they could not get into trouble with each other. Derinoe rested her hands on Leonides' shoulders.

"He is quite fine," Leonides gushed. "I doubt Pegasus is any grander, mother."

The figure of a man moving down a lane of tents used by carpenters caught her attention. Damon. His brown, thigh-length tunic was belted at the waist with a thick band of bronze-inlaid leather.

Deri's hand moved to her chest, over her heart. Her sister's lover moved with commanding confidence. Damon was smaller than Achilles, but he possessed that same dominating presence: outsize shoulders and chest and powerful legs. And where Hektor's face had been as handsome, Hektor's eyes were almost always somber. Damon's eyes always seemed to twinkle, as if he was always looking for the humorous side to life. An easy face. A welcoming face.

Damon stopped to talk to a carpenter repairing a supply wagon's wheel. When he started walking again, she called out, "Damon."

He came to them. "Discovering the camp?" he asked.

"The children are fascinated. I must say, I'm still trying to adjust to the smell."

He chuckled, then said, "I walk the camp every day, and I also visit Valor." He considered Leonides, who was giving Damon the same look of awe she noted in the palace. "Would you like to feed Valor some apple?" he asked Leonides.

Rapidly nodded head from her son.

Damon held his hands out in front of him, empty palms up. He then swiftly swung his hands behind his back, and then out in front again, palms up, and in one hand he held an apple.

"Ooooh," Myrina gasped.

Leonides frowned. "How did you do that?"

"It's magic," Damon said, his eyes alight with deviltry. "I learned it from the same old and very clever centaur that teaches my friend, Bias." From a sheath on his belt, he drew a short dagger and cut out a quarter of the apple. He placed the piece in Leonides' hand. "Put it up in front of him, but be sure to keep your palm flat."

Leonides stuck out the apple, fingers curled. Damon quickly took his hand and flattened the fingers. "Keep 'em flat or he's likely to bite off one or two."

She said, "Do you have any word yet on the time of the battle?"

Valor lipped up the bit of apple and chomped on it.

Damon said, "Two days."

"That is so soon."

"The weather is favorable. I imagine Agamemnon's priest found the omens favorable. So we have two more days. Our spies will let us know when significant movement begins in their camp." He nodded to the apple. "Would you also like to offer your sister's magnificent beast a treat?"

Deri nodded, and he cut another quarter. He took her hand, turned it palm up and opened it.

His touch sent a shock, like unexpectedly touching heated iron, through her. She caught her breath, searched his eyes, but he wasn't looking at her face. He placed the piece of apple on her palm. "Don't forget. Fingers straight."

Her heart racing, she held out the apple. A velvet muzzle and hot breath—and then the apple was gone. She stood there, her hand poised in the air, her breath short. This feeling about Damon was a mistake. She didn't even want to put a name to so dangerous a mistake.

To Myrina, Damon said, "Would you like to pet him?"

"Yes, please," said her usually shy daughter.

Damon picked up the four-year-old as easily as Derinoe might pick up a pitcher of water. He extended one arm, bent at the elbow, and sat Myrina on it, as if she were seated in a chair, then brought her close to Valor. She extended her hand just as the horse threw his head up. Myrina jerked her hand away. "Don't be afraid," Damon coaxed. "Try again."

Her daughter, without hesitation, reached out and petted the stallion's muscled jaw. Derinoe's first thought was unbelief, but then she realized the effect Damon had on Myrina. With a child's instinct, Myrina sensed Damon's strength, and seated there on that powerful arm, she felt emboldened in a way she could never feel on her own.

Damon said, "Pentha's first cavalry commander, Bremusa, wishes we wouldn't use the Trojans. She thinks they don't have the discipline our strategy requires. She thinks in the heat of action, they will revert to the usual battle pattern here. The two forces simply surge forward and the men engage one-on-one."

She patted Valor's muzzle, to calm her racing heart. "I am sick that we all meet and what we face is battle. And maybe death. Why does it have to be that way?"

"I'm convinced Aeneas understands Amazons will only be effective if the Trojans follow Pentha's orders. If they do, we have a good chance. Of course, if Bremusa is right, we could face a disaster."

"Could Pentha— Pentha will be in the middle of all this?"

He returned Myrina to the ground and looked at Derinoe, all traces of humor in his eyes replaced by an ominous sadness. "Treasure every day you have with her, Derinoe. When an Amazon goes into battle, when a man goes into battle, there are no guaranteed happy outcomes."

"Why must this happen? Why did the Acheans have to come here?"

"I can't give you any satisfying answers. I can't find any for myself. But I agree with Pentha about one thing. Themiskyra's defense does depend in large measure on our Amazons' reputations for ferocity. If we accomplish nothing else here, we must confirm that beyond doubt. I accept that necessity. It has to be enough for me."

He cut the remaining half of apple in two, handed her another piece, and offered a piece to Valor, who snuffled it up.

She held out her piece to the horse. "I will pray for her. I will pray for you."

"You know, the Acheans have been bragging that Athena has promised them a great victory. We will deny their goddess her promise." To the children he said, "Don't get too close to the horse's backsides. A horse spooks easily and they kick like the mighty Pegasus."

Damon turned his attention once more to Derinoe. Light had returned to his eyes. He smiled, turned, and walked away. She could not take her gaze off of him. Finally he disappeared behind a tent.

"Come," she said, taking Myrina's hand. "It's time for lunch. Let's visit your aunt."

Leonides captured her gaze. "I wish I had a father like Damon. He's strong enough to have a pet wolf." Abruptly he turned, as if dismissing her after a scolding, and her son bolted at a run toward Pentha's tent.

His criticism, his yearning, stung her. And she was at the same moment sharply aware just how much she shared her son's admiration for Damon—much more than was proper that she should.

⇥ 59 ↤

D ERINOE FOUND PENTHA IN HER TENT, UNDRESSED
and wrapped across her breasts and down to her knees
in a large piece of white linen. The children rushed inside
and began exploring, Leonides drawn to a sword, and Myrina, to Pentha's white fur hat. "Whatever are you wearing
that for?" Derinoe said.

"Sweating."

"Sweating?"

"You aren't familiar with a sweat house?"

"I have no idea what you're talking about."

"Ah, then a great treat awaits you. You must join me. It
will clear your mind and refresh your spirit."

Pentha looked to Leonides. Her son had taken an arrow
from a quiver. Pentha dashed across the room and snatched
it away. "You mustn't trifle with that one," she said. "It's prepared for hunting, not battle. The tip is dipped in poison that
could make you sick."

Her sister replaced the arrow in its quiver, pulled an arrow
from different quiver, and handed it to Leonides.

He said, "How do you use the poison for hunting?"

"When the tip enters, the poison spreads within the animal and weakens it."

"Does the poison kill?" he said, his face intent on
Pentha's.

"No. That is left to the huntress."

"But could it kill?"

"My mother, Gryn, makes the poison. But, even though she could, she never makes it strong enough to kill. We want only to bring the animal down." Pentha touched Leonides' shoulder gently. "I once saw the death of a deer that I think must have been very susceptible. Like some people can be made very ill by bee stings. Her slow, painful death saddened me. We need food to eat. We don't hunt for the joy of inflicting pain or of killing."

"I want to learn to hunt."

"Then you shall. But for now, I want your mother to join me for a good sweat bath."

Pentha called to the guard, who entered. "Take the children to Gryn. Ask if she can feed them, and perhaps have her tell them stories."

After the children left, Pentha pulled out another long, white linen strip from a chest and handed it over. A screen stood at one side of the room. Derinoe stepped behind it, undressed, and wrapped herself as Pentha had done.

Near the tent, she had noted a strange little structure. Not much taller than her shoulders, it resembled an upside down bowl, entirely rounded, and covered with animal hides buried where they met the ground. She and Pentha stopped before what had to be an entry flap, although they would both have to stoop low to enter.

Pentha said, "Rocks heated there," she pointed to a woman tending a fire some paces away, "are brought inside. We pour water over them. It will be dark. Only one small candle. The idea is to enter a place where one can think clearly, commune with oneself and with the goddess, and if your spirit is troubled, pray for peace. It's a way to purify all of oneself, mind and spirit and body."

She stooped, unfastened the flap—which turned out to be a double thickness of hides—and entered. Derinoe followed.

She could see little but felt furs caressing her feet. Pentha said, "It's easiest to crawl."

Derinoe went onto hands and knees and felt her way forward.

She felt Pentha's hand on her arm. "Here is good."

Pentha unwrapped the linen and sat in comfortable nakedness. Derinoe followed her example. Her vision slowly adjusted to the faint light.

They sat quietly awhile.

Pentha took up a gourd, scooped water from a pail, and splashed it over rocks piled in the little hut's center. A great hiss of water and a blast of fresh steam washed over Derinoe. Sweat already beaded her skin and face.

She looked at Pentha and saw that, for the first time since their reunion, Pentha's face seemed relaxed and calm. Derinoe peered closer. Extraordinary transformation! Her sister obviously carried out her days, seemingly so competent, so in control, but with a weight on her spirit, carefully hidden, that was enormous. She had laid it aside briefly now, here in this dim and quiet place.

Derinoe reached out and held Pentha's hand.

❧ 60 ❧

D AMON APPROACHED THE CREST OF THE HILL OVER-
looking landscape open enough to fly Dia. Wolf paced
just behind his heel, between Damon and Bias. Bias carried
Dia in her travel cage. Trusis trudged uphill on Damon's
other side, and a contingent of twenty armed men followed.
Although he had promised Trusis this outing, Damon wondered once more at the man's motive. Trusis had so far
shown no real interest in Dia.

They were passing nearby a last, dense stand of oaks.
Bushes and brush smothered the slope ahead, but the hill's
crest was barren save for rocks and grass and a few sturdy
wildflowers, summer survivors. The soldiers brought food
on these outings and enjoyed not only watching the falcon
perform but also the chance to have some hours at ease. Trusis peered into the oak stand, then perhaps sensing that Damon had noticed, snapped his gaze once more toward the
crest.

Damon said, "Did you see something?"

"No. No. Nothing."

Damon stared at Trusis, an uncomfortable itch at the back
of his mind. "You don't seem yourself today. Why so quiet?"

An explosion of noise erupted from the woods, the sound
of broken twigs, sprung brushes, and running feet. Men in
Achean garb and brandishing weapons rushed toward them
at the charge. Damon didn't even have time to yell a warning

before the Acheans, who easily outnumbered his party two to one, were on them. He pulled his sword. A soldier leapt onto him. He fell backward, hit the ground, slammed the back of his head, and the world spun. Damon rolled the both of them, his head clearing, then backed onto his knees and brought his sword blade down and across the Achean's neck.

A warm blood arc sprayed Damon's legs as he bolted to his feet, only to be jumped again by two men from behind. They clung to him like lions on a stag's back. Damon swung them around.

At the edge of the struggle, he saw Bias drop Dia's cage and start running. Bias was unarmed. Escape would be his only chance. But even as Damon wished Bias' feet to sprout wings, a spear sailed through the air and slammed into the boy's back. Bias staggered and then fell to the ground, out of view.

Rage. Pure rage. Fired by it, Damon bellowed and thrust his elbow into the breastplate of one of the beasts hanging onto his back.

Trusis, sword drawn, ran toward Damon, and from one side, Wolf bounded toward Trusis. Clearly Wolf thought Trusis intended to attack Damon. As Damon grappled with burly arms around his neck—the soldiers appeared intent on pulling him to the ground, not killing him—he yelled, "No, Wolf!"

Trusis turned to Wolf, raised his sword, took one step toward the animal, and as Wolf was in a mid-air leap, shoved the sword's blade deep into Wolf's chest. The animal gave a great whine that pierced like a crude blade into Damon's heart, and collapsed at Trusis feet.

Around Damon, his Themiskyran men and the Acheans fought deadly struggles. At that very moment four more Acheans converged on Damon. He went down on his knees. In front of him he saw Wolf's body. And standing in the middle of all this chaos, Trusis. Trusis, doing nothing but standing there.

A blinding blow to the head, and he saw only blackness with a blaze of stars against it. Then nothing.

Trusis moved to where Damon lay on the ground, savoring the moment.

"Tie him well," Trusis said to the Achean attackers. "He's strong and he's clever."

He surveyed the scene. The only men now standing were Achean. A soldier approached him and said, "What do you want us to do with the two who are still alive."

"No witnesses," said Trusis.

PART III

DESTINY

❧ 61 ❧

STEAM HEAT DUG ITS WAY THROUGH DERINOE'S muscles down to her bones. She sighed. Not sure whether talking in a steam house was appropriate, or if so, what she should or could talk about, she waited for Pentha to break the silence.

Finally, Pentha said, her tone somber and with a direct gaze that probed deeply, "You told me Myrina is Hektor's child. You don't have to say, if you don't want to, but who is Leonides' father? He is a beautiful boy. He will become an extraordinary man in size. And we can hope, in character."

This was sad talk, but necessary. Derinoe said, "You know what happened. In Tenedos."

"Yes. And I've—"

"Let's not talk about it. Only one good thing came from that nightmare. My Leonides. But his father—I would gladly kill him if I could."

Pentha nodded. Derinoe noted a small smile curving Pentha's lips, as if it pleased Pentha to know that her sister had no love for Achilles.

Pentha said. "I suspected. That's all I need to know. If you don't want to, we won't ever speak of Tenedos again. Instead, let's talk of good things."

"Then let's talk about Themiskyra. Tell me what it's like?

"Ah, Themiskyra." Pentha used a corner of her wrap to wipe sweat from her face. "It is beautiful, Deri. Rugged, but

264 • JUDITH HAND

we have our comforts. At least there are comforts once one is no longer Amazon."

Deri licked her sweaty upper lip, tangy with salt. "Could I learn to ride? To hunt? Perhaps I'm too old."

Pentha chuckled "They say we are never too old to learn anything we want to learn badly enough."

Deri's thoughts suddenly turned serious. "What I want most is to have Myrina grow up free. Women don't have that here. You do. You're free to make the decisions for your life. How can anyone be truly happy without freedom?"

⊰ 62 ⊱

D AMON SNAPPED INTO CONSCIOUSNESS—AND FOUND himself blindfolded, sitting in something moving.

His hands were bound together at the wrists in front of him. A short length of rope tied him to a slat on what must be the side of a cart, it's wheels creaking like a great bull toad as they turned. In front and to the rear, he recognized the higher sounds of chariot wheels.

How long had he been unconscious? He didn't have a headache.

He felt no wounds.

So the good news, at least for the moment, was that whatever the reason for this capture, he wasn't wanted dead. At least not immediately.

But why? And what of the men who had been with him? Were they dead?

And Bias? Guilt struck. Behind the blindfold, his eyes burned. His throat tightened and he swallowed hard. He had promised Bias' mother to send or bring her son home, alive. How could a man bear living with such a failure?

And Trusis? What should he think about Trusis? Was he dead? Something about the way Trusis had been walking toward him—Damon had felt menace, and apparently so had Wolf. Wolf attacked. And Trusis had not been fighting. There were many things Damon didn't like about Trusis, but the man was no coward. Indeed, he was powerful and proud with a sword.

Trusis and his sword. The image of Trusis shoving his sword into Wolf flashed and fixed in Damon's mind. Wolf's cry. The pool of blood. Damon hung his head and bit his lip.

❧ 63 ❧

"**I** THINK WE NEED MORE STEAM," PENTHA SAID.
Derinoe felt already cooked.

Pentha thumped the leather side of the sweathouse with the dipper and within moments a young Amazon brought freshly heated rocks. Using iron tongs, she laid them on top of the still warm oval pile of gray stones, then used the dipper to spill fresh water over the lot. With a great hiss, clouds of steam billowed up and spread over Derinoe's skin. The girl left them alone again.

Pentha said, "Sometimes, when I am with Damon, I think it might be good to go to a new place. A different place."

Surprised, Derinoe said, "Somewhere other than Themiskyra?"

"I love our home, Deri. But sometimes Damon gets under my skin with his talk of a man and woman living together all the time. He makes it sound wonderful. It's something he yearns for, I can tell. They live that way here in Troy. What is it like?"

"I don't know. I was a man's mistress, not his wife. My best friend, my only real friend, was Cassandra, an unmarried woman."

"Damon talked more than once about a small place called Ephesus. A place away from battles. Good land, good hunting, favorable weather, good fishing. Just a village really. He says it sits on at a lovely location on the coast, many days south of here."

"Damon is a formidable man." Derinoe remembered Damon's touch on her hand, felt the pull of his nearness, and how she couldn't look away from him. The potential for danger and great unhappiness lay in her feelings for her sister's lover. If they were all to have a good future, she must find a way to avoid that precipice.

"I think now about perhaps leaving Themiskyra with him, Deri, because I'm nearly certain I am carrying his child."

"Pentha!"

"I have missed two bleeding cycles. Until we left Themiskyra a little over a month ago, I was usually with him twice a week."

"Does he know?"

"Not yet. I can't tell him until this battle is over. And until I am sure. He must have his mind focused only on fighting."

"I . . . I thought Amazons . . . well, how did it happen? Amazons are known not to have children."

"When we take lovers, we take a potion from the giant fennel, and another mixture is placed on a boiled sea sponge and put inside the body. They ordinarily prevent new life. But it doesn't always work. I am thinking, maybe Artemis gives me this gift as a sign that she will not be displeased if I leave with Damon. After I have served Her here."

"If you don't leave Themiskyra, what will happen?"

"A wet nurse. And my mother, Gryn, would raise the child for me until I become two and thirty. But when I think of a baby that belongs to me and Damon, I want to nurse it and watch it grow."

They talked more of Themiskyra and of children, then Pentha said, "It's time for me to return to the day's tasks." She took Derinoe's hand. "I want to invoke the blessing of the Goddess."

They looked upward, beyond the top of their little hide hut, into the heavens, to Olympus and Ida where the divine dwell.

Pentha said, her voice soft but firm, "We, your daughters,

Penthesilea and Derinoe, pray you will care for us fierce Artemis. I feel a great darkness in the world. A hungry, consuming darkness against women who love you. I'm afraid the darkness will consume all women everywhere. Even your daughters in Themiskyra. Mighty Goddess, give me courage. I must not fail." Pentha stopped, then with a choked voice whispered, "I will not fail You."

Derinoe listened with her heart's beats pounding in her throat, tears spilling down her cheeks, and Damon's words in her mind: "Savor every moment with her. When an Amazon goes into battle, there is no guarantee of a good outcome."

⊰ 64 ⊱

AFTER A RIDE THAT MIGHT HAVE TAKEN DAMON either as far as Troy or perhaps even the Achean camp, rough hands dragged him from the wagon. Rough hands on both arms guided him. He estimated that the day must now be in early afternoon.

The sounds were of talking men, clanging metal, and sawing. Much more nearly the sounds of a war camp than a town, and the men who had attacked had been Achean warriors.

The rough hands shoved him through a door into a quiet building. They forced him down a hallway in which they turned twice, a door was opened, and they shoved him inside. He tripped over something and fell to his knees.

AFTER SWEATING WITH DERINOE, Pentha's morning had been busy. First she spent time with the women and horses practicing lying-in-quiet. Then she watched the practice of the women and horses assigned to pull the log bridges. Finding their timing too slow, she ordered that another horse be hitched to each pulling team.

Now, having finished a midday meal, she must see to the fire. Pentha approached the tent of their fire carrier, Harmothoe. It was critical that the Amazon archers, both cavalry and infantry, have fire.

She passed Gryn and said, "Bias tried to steal my arm

bracelet the other day. He got it off my arm, but I caught him."

"He's determined, that one," Gryn said. "Always at it."

When Pentha entered the tent, two low-ranking cavalry saluted. She nodded. They returned to work.

She scanned the trestle tables and the hundreds of fire kits on them and the working men and women. Harmothoe approached and saluted. She was, for an Amazon, remarkably short, built like a block, body square with broad shoulders and hips. Her gift was a brilliantly inventive mind.

Harmothoe made fire kits by wrapping red-hot coals in dried peat, then enclosing the package in green bark and lashing it tight. The trick was to give the embers enough air to keep them burning, but not enough to burst into flames. When unwrapped and fed fine bits of dried dandelion fluff, a fire could be quickly started.

Pentha said, "How many are ready? I estimate only two hundred. That's not enough. Every two archers in the trenches must have one."

"You said you want five hundred. By the end of tomorrow, you shall have them."

"And the fire pits to make embers? I will put our warriors into the field tomorrow night."

"You have my word. The fire kits will be ready by tomorrow evening."

One of Gryn's serving girls burst into the tent. She dashed to Pentha and forgetting all formality, blurted out, "You must come at once, Penthesilea. Something terrible has happened."

Pentha ran with the girl to Gryn's tent. A large crowd already milled outside, perhaps a hundred men and women. She strode in to find Bias lying on his side on a table, facing her. Bremusa and Marpessa stood watching.

Gryn bent over Bias' back. The boy was filthy, his trousers torn in several places, and the pale look of his skin spoke of death.

"What?" Pentha said, looking at Gryn.

Bias opened his eyes. He tried to speak, a sound more like a groan.

Gryn said, "Spear thrust near the shoulder blade." She rinsed a cloth in a bowl of water.

Bias struggled to sit up. Gryn started to force him down.

"Let me sit," he said.

Pentha put an arm around him and helped him. She struggled to keep her mind focused, to keep her emotions calm, even as horrible dread threatened to shake her senseless. She looked at Gryn. "Can he have water?"

Her mother nodded.

"Fetch him water. Quick," she said to the serving girl. To Bias she said, "What happened?"

"Attacked. We were attacked, Lady Penthesilea."

The girl helped him drink a sip of water from a copper dipper.

"Did he come back alone?" Pentha asked Gryn.

Gryn nodded.

Bias took Pentha's hand and squeezed it, a weak gesture, almost a reflex, as if he were trying to muster energy. "Acheans attacked us. At the top of the hill. Maybe fifty or sixty."

"Where are the others?"

"Dead."

Damonides dead. Surely this was a mistake. *Stay calm!* "They are all dead? Including Damonides?" Damon could not be dead. She could not live if Damon were dead. Then another thought. "Trusis? Is he dead as well?" How could she wage a battle in two days without her two top infantry commanders?

"I'm not certain."

The boy gestured for more water, and in the moments it took him to sip it and lick his lips, she died a thousand times.

"Lots of chariots came out of the woods. I got hit pretty quick. Crawled into bushes. After they left, I found everyone dead. Don't really know about Trusis and Damon. Acheans must have taken them."

She laid his hand back on his thigh, took a step away, took a full breath. Perhaps Damon was not dead. Yes. That must be so. She had to believe that was so. He was only taken captive.

Gyrn laid a poultice on the wound.

"Lady Pentha," Bias said, his eyes brimming with tears and begging her for assurance and comfort. "Is it possible Damon is not dead?"

Pentha nodded. "I believe he's not. We'll know for certain quite soon. But in my heart I am sure our Damon is alive."

There were only six of them in the tent. She asked him, "Have you told anyone else what you just told us?"

"No."

"No one? Not the first people who brought you to this tent? No one?"

"No one, on my oath."

"Good." She looked to Bremusa and Marpessa and then to the serving girl and Gyrn. "No one outside this tent can know what Bias has said. Absolutely no one, unless I direct otherwise. Clear?"

Bremusa, Marpessa, and the serving girl said, "Yes," at the same time. Gyrn nodded.

"It is critical that our people not learn of this until I find out exactly what happened and determine the consequences. I'd like to think this camp has no spies, but I don't assume anything. Our enemies must also not know that we are aware of what happened."

She fell silent a moment, grappling with alternatives. Then she said to Bremusa, "Find Clonie. Tell her everything, and send her at once to Aeneas. She is to take her fastest mount and run him. She is to tell Aeneas this news—Aeneas alone—and ask him to find out from his spies whatever information he can that will be of use to me. I must have his response in no more than three hours. We must move tonight, Bremusa. While the Acheans still think we don't know what happened."

Bremusa left. Pentha patted Bias on the leg. "I am so glad, brave young Bias, that you survived. And I admire the courage it took you to return to us despite your wound. You could have waited until someone came looking for you. But it is very important that you returned to us with this news quickly. I will not forget your courage."

"I need to ask a favor." he said, looking down with a shyness so very unlike his usual cocky self.

"Ask anything."

"I was supposed to take care of Dia. But when I was hit, I dropped her cage. I tried to carry it with me. But . . . well . . ." He looked into her eyes. "I left her on the hill. I couldn't carry the cage and walk."

She hugged him, taking care not to squeeze where he was hurt. "You want me to send someone to bring Dia back?"

"Yes, please."

❧ 65 ❧

D AMON, BOUND AND BLINDFOLDED, LAY ON THE
floor where he had fallen. One of the men who shoved
him pulled him into a sitting position and pulled off the
blindfold.

Small room. A wooden stool sat in one corner.

And wooden rings in the wall opposite were a familiar
sight, rings where one might tie a prisoner, for punishment
or torture.

No windows. Illumination came from two oil lamps sitting on a shelf. Only one was lit; the room's corners lay in
shadow.

Legs moved in front of him, and looking up, he saw Trusis. Grim. And smug.

Trusis stepped forward and kicked Damon in the side. A
fire raced from Damon's ribs to his heart and snatched his
breath.

The soldiers looked to Trusis, awaiting orders.

Trusis seemed to be waiting for Damon's response. So
Damon simply stared at him, smiling, disgust putting a bitter
twist to the smile. Again, Trusis stepped forward, and this
time he smashed a fist into Damon's temple.

The small room reeled.

Trusis said, "That seems to have taken that smirk off your
face."

A cold rage sent chills rippling over Damon's back. "It seems you have found your natural place in life, Trusis."

Trusis squatted in front of him. "Yes. I am going to take my proper place. When this battle is over, I will return to our camp. My 'escape' from the Acheans will be quite impressive. And it is me, not you, who will go back to Themiskyra with Pentha."

"You've lost your mind."

"You think so?"

"What do you hope to gain?"

"I have Achilles' word that Pentha will not be harmed. I will explain our plans to him, and that will allow him to defeat us without killing her. Or too many of our troops, for that matter. It is not his intention to destroy us. He simply wants to ensure that the Trojans don't win."

"And then?"

"As I say, I return to Themiskyra with Pentha."

"What if, because of our absence, our troops are so disheartened we lose? What if Pentha is killed? You will have nothing to return to and no one to return with."

"Pentha will not be harmed."

What if the other royals overrule Achilles and decide to kill her?"

"Archilles assures me that he alone is planning to take Themiskyra. That none of the other royals are involved or even know of his plans."

"And what if Achilles is like you and can't be trusted?"

His face a twisted mask of hatred, Trusis stood. He said to the soldiers, "Tie him to the wall."

⊰ 66 ⊱

HER BLOOD RACING AND HER THOUGHTS SWIRLING so that she felt disconnected, Pentha strode into her tent, then stopped in place and clutched her head in both hands.

"Sweet Goddess, Pentha, what is wrong?" Derinoe asked.

Pentha dropped her arms and stared at her sister. Deri sat in a chair opposite the entry flap, a piece of embroidery in her hands. She laid her work on the low table next to the chair, stood, and rushed to hold Pentha by both arms. "You look ill. What can I do?"

"Damon may be dead." Pentha forced the words out, and the word 'dead' released the tears she had been fighting. They flooded down her cheeks.

Derinoe, her eyes widened in shock, released her. Pentha swiped at the tears. But they weren't going to stop. She rushed to her familiar chair, threw herself into it, and bending over, clasped her head again as the tears continued, her body heaving with sobs. She sensed Deri kneeling beside her, felt Deri's hand on her knee.

When her sobbing began to ebb, Deri said, "Please tell me what has happened. It can't be so."

Pentha nodded. She sucked in a trembling breath. "It's possible."

She took another breath, this one steadier, and took another swipe at her face.

"Here," Deri said, and handed her a piece of cloth from her sewing basket. Pentha sat up, wiped her eyes and blew her nose.

"Now tell me!"

"He had taken Bias and Dia, his falcon, to a hill to fly the bird. Usually Bias exercises her, but Damon goes when he can. They were attacked. Bias was wounded, badly, but returned. He says all who were there were dead. There is some hope. Damon and Trusis were not among them. It's possible they were taken captive." The tears started again. She brushed them with the cloth. "But it's entirely possible Damon is dead."

"I don't believe it. I won't believe it. And you mustn't either."

"I am terribly afraid."

Deri took both of her hands and squeezed them.

Pentha could barely speak, her words more like a whisper. "I cannot imagine life without Damon. When Bias first spoke as though Damon were dead, I emptied, as if all meaning poured out of me. This weakens me. This is exactly why no Amazon should become close to any man." She looked deeply into Deri's eyes. "I am so terrified of losing Damon that I can't think. When I most need to act, I am paralyzed."

"The paralyzing fear will pass. I had such fear once. When I was escaping Achilles, I thought I couldn't think, but fear of dying was greater. If anything, fear only sharpened my mind. Give yourself a few moments."

Deri let go of Pentha's hands, stood, and fetched a goblet of water.

Pentha drank it all.

Deri returned to her chair. Her face full of hurt and concern, she sat silently, watching.

Moments passed. The paralysis passed. Pentha rose and went to the tent opening. To the guard she said, "Fetch Phemios."

❧ 67 ❧

A ENEAS SAT IN PENTHA'S CHAIR. PENTHA IN-
sisted. She liked this Trojan commander and was especially pleased he had come in person and quickly to bring
her what information he had about the Acheans and Damon.

She herself paced as Gryn made Aeneas comfortable and
offered him drink. Others seated in camp chairs were Bremusa, Clonie, Evandre, Phemios, and Derinoe. Two other
Amazons she had selected for this raid stood, arms behind
their backs. It was late afternoon now, and before the early
evening they must be in the Achean camp, while they still
had daylight.

To her amazement, Marpessa entered the tent and approached. Marpessa saluted, then said, "My Queen, I know
you are making plans. And I understand why you didn't include me." She paused, and memories of their shared, not always pleasant, history hung in the air. "Now is the time for me
to tell you I have watched these months what you and Damonides have accomplished. I could never have equaled your
efforts. I would be deeply honored, Penthesilea, if you would
allow me to help you in this raid."

Pentha had rarely seen a gentle look on Marpessa's face.
Now she saw both sincerity and gentleness. "I accept your offer, sister."

Marpessa saluted again and moved to stand by Evandre.

Aeneas placed the goblet of mare's milk back on the stand

beside him. Pentha noted that he tasted little of it, and recalled Damon once laughing and saying that "Fermented mare's milk is something you must grow used to."

Just imagining Damon laughing brought the scratch of threatening tears, and she pressed her hands to her eyes to cut off the weakening memory at once.

The Trojan general said, "Although my instincts make it hard to envision you succeeding, since you are taking only women, I nevertheless like your plan. Indeed, the reason it has some hope of working is precisely because the Acheans simply will not expect women. As I already said, your men were taken by Achilles. Also, there is so far no word about them in any of the other camps. All the Acheans know you and your Amazons are here and that they will be fighting you day after tomorrow. But I doubt they comprehend the reality of fighting women any more than I can, including Achilles. The idea is something in our minds but not in our bones."

"Good. Excellent. We need every advantage. We will use every advantage."

Aeneas nodded. "It is also a great advantage that Achilles does not know you are aware of what he's done. They won't yet have put up any special defenses. But I warn again. Damonides and Trusis are in Achilles' camp, but my spies don't know where or for how long. The stockade, being in the center, is in the most secure area, but it's mostly for men who've gotten into drunken fights. Achilles may put your commanders somewhere else."

Pentha stopped pacing. "What is most important, and I am most grateful for your help, is that we know the camp's layout."

"We, of Troy, are grateful you have come to assist us. This information is little enough thanks." Aeneas stood. "I will await word of your success."

HEARING THE SOUND OF feet walking down the hallway, Damon called out, "Guard!"

The room had long since fallen into darkness.

It surprised him when the door actually opened and a

squinty-eyed soldier peered in. Light from windows across the hallway poured into the room. The guard took note of the leather rope that bound Damon to the rings in the wall.

"I'm thirsty. Will you give me water?"

From the quality of the light, Damon guessed it must be late in the afternoon or perhaps early evening. His ribs, where Trusis had kicked him, ached, but at least he had no pain breathing. He'd not had anything to eat or drink since early morning. And sitting in one corner was a bucket of water he had watched thirstily until the lamp flickered out.

The man leered at him. "Bein' thirsty's nothin' to what you'll feel when you can't stand any longer and hang from your wrists and the rope starts cuttin' in." He slammed the flimsy door.

"REMEMBER," PENTHA SAID. SHE sat, as if resting, with the four Amazons chosen for this raid—Bremusa, Clonie, Marpessa, and Evandre. Their party waited only a few steps off the narrow track leading into the Achean camp. "The secret is to feel you belong. If you feel you belong, you will look like you belong. Don't look any man straight in the eye and keep your shoulders down and you will be ignored." She grinned at them. "Though I will say, I think you all look just *lovely.*"

They chuckled.

All wore clothing of Achean slave women: simple, calf-length woolen robes and crude sandals. All but Pentha wore their hair in two braids over their shoulders. Pentha had stuffed hers inside a woolen cap pulled down over her ears, and on top of the cap she had stuck a felt, wide-brimmed sun hat used by slave women working in the fields. Her hair color was in itself distinctive, but its odd cut—short and in waves all over her head—was unlike anything worn by any women. It had to be disguised.

Each woman carried bundled firewood on her back. And strapped high on each Amazon's thigh was her dagger.

Bremusa said, "Gryn." She nodded toward the rutted lane leading into Achilles' encampment, an access used by the women and supply venders. Even the bridge crossing the moat here could not accommodate a chariot.

The path led to and from the spring where the women drew fresh water and washed clothes, and now, in the late afternoon, twenty or so figures plodded toward the camp on their day's last trip. Many carried water jars on their heads. Others toted firewood.

Gryn drove a narrow, wooden donkey cart carrying rushes and tins of olive oil, ostensibly for cooking. Hidden under the rushes were battle-axes and fire-starter packets.

The Amazons separated. Pentha, with Evandre and Marpessa, went first, falling in line not far behind Gryn's cart. In a few moments, Bremusa and Clonie would join the string of returning women.

Watching Gryn approach the narrow bridge over the yawning Achean moat—its depth that of perhaps three men and its width twice that—Pentha held her breath. Her mother reached the guard post, manned by two Achean soldiers. As Aeneas predicted, the guards paid Gryn no attention at all. Old women with gray hair didn't stir the smallest worry in their minds.

Nor did the guards say a word to Pentha or the two shy-eyed women with her. She stepped onto the narrow bridge and, looking ahead, watched Gryn and her cart pass through an arched doorway in the massive wall. Pentha estimated that the wall stood at least eight times the height of the cart.

In only moments, she and Evandre and Marpessa followed Gryn into the Achean stronghold.

Gryn headed the cart for the wooden building storing sail-cloth and sails.

The camp had been laid out in orderly fashion with enough space between the rows of tents and buildings so three chariots might pass side-by-side. Between adjacent tents, one chariot could pass. Gryn stopped the cart in the narrow space beside the sail shed, climbed down, and pretended to examine her donkey's right rear leg.

Pentha and her companions followed closely, but not so closely that they appeared to be with Gryn or the cart.

Pentha glanced behind. Bremusa and Clonie were also inside now, and headed for the lumber storage area.

Men and women came and went or were seated outside various tents at work or simply talking. Many more observers than she had hoped for. But it couldn't be helped.

"Follow my lead," she said.

She strode up to Gryn's cart, grabbed two tins of olive oil as if this were something she had been directed to do by someone of importance. She snatched up two rushes, and from under the rushes, a fire starter kit. She tucked them under one arm, and strolled around the side of the building and into the entry.

Openings high up near the wooden roof lit the good-sized room, a space about four times the size of her command center in the Amazon barracks. Because it was early evening, only dim light lit the interior. She stopped, letting her eyes adjust.

A soldier, stacking cloth, paused and turned to her. "What do you want?"

She sat the oil tin, rushes, and starter kit on the plank floor, stepped to him, put one arm around his neck, and as she reached under her skirt for the dagger said, "I've been watching you. I like you."

He started to pull back, and she plunged the dagger into his side. He fell to the floor writhing and moaning softly.

Evandre and Marpessa entered carrying their own supplies. Pentha turned to Evandre. "Gryn?"

"On her way to the lumber storage."

Another soldier came forward. Evandre dropped her tins and rushes. Seeing his companion on the floor and bleeding, the soldier stared wide-eyed at the three women. He sucked in a breath to shout but both Pentha and Evandre slammed into him, knocking him flat. Evandre leapt onto him and cut his throat.

"Be quick!" Pentha urged.

They spread out, draped sailcloth across large swatches of stored sail, opened the tins, and used every drop of olive oil to soak the sailcloth. Each Amazon untied the leather around the bark of her fire kit, broke the kit open, and using dandelion fluff, raised a flame. They set the rushes on fire and dashed from place to place, torching several sections of the oil-soaked cloth.

"That's it," Pentha called out. "Now to the stockade."

Together, the three of them walked out of the storage shed, not too fast, and headed toward the place where Aeneas' spies had said Damon would most likely be held. If all was proceeding as planned, Gryn had reached the lumber storage, Bremusa and Clonie had taken their supplies from her cart and were firing the lumber, and Gryn would soon be waiting for Pentha's team at the stockade.

❧ 68 ❧

ACHILLES LEFT HIS TENT, HEADING TO WHERE he'd secured his new prisoner. A meeting with the Themiskyran commander could be interesting, especially if this was the famed Damonides.

The merchant, Muttalusha, blocked his path. "Lord Achilles," the merchant said, smiling effusively. "I—"

Achilles walked past him. Muttalusha trotted alongside "You will be going into battle shortly. I really would like, I really think it would be prudent, if I might receive my payment. Now."

"I have something to attend to. Wait for me in my tent."

The merchant stopped. Achilles walked on.

THE DOOR TO DAMON'S cell opened. He had little doubt of the identity of the enormous man who entered, accompanied by a guard. The guard carried two lighted oil lamps, which he placed on the shelf.

Achilles strode to the center of the room, crossed his arms, and stared at Damon with critical eyes, as if judging the quality of a horse. He wore a red tunic belted at the waist with thick, beautifully worked, silver and gold inlaid leather. His massive presence seemed to expand into all the room's available space. The light entering from the hallway was that of early evening.

"I'm thirsty," Damon said.

Achilles gestured to the guard. The men fetched a ladle of water from the bucket and let Damon drink half, before he spilled the remainder down Damon's chin.

Achilles approached to within arm's length. He smelled of rose-scented oil.

In a deep voice, darkly tinged with muddy brown, Achilles said, "My best informant, the Hittite Muttalusha, says you are Achean trained. Are you the Damonides who fought for Iolkos?"

Muttalusha! The greedy little rat.

When Damon remained silent, Achilles said, "Knowledge of Achean skills and tactics won't be of any good to your troops. The day after tomorrow will be a Themiskyran slaughter."

The ropes on Damon's wrists seemed to tighten from the mere presence of the Achean legend. In spite of himself, knowing he could not get free, Damon clenched his fists and pulled against the restraints. If Aeneas was correct, here was the one man the Acheans most depended upon for their spirit. If Achilles could be killed, Aeneas was of the view that Agamemnon would eventually win over the other royals and take the Acheans home. If Achilles could be killed, at the very least the Achean fighting spirit would suffer a grievous blow and if Trusis was correct, if Achilles could be killed, the source of the Achean threat to Themiskyra would be eliminated. If Achilles could be killed. . . . And there Achilles was, only a step away. Damon felt his heart straining against his chest as his wrists strained against the ropes.

Achilles smiled. "So you choose silence. I don't suppose you would describe for me the defenses of Themiskyra. I'm going to mount a campaign there next year. I intend to control trade from Themiskyra in horses and iron." So, Trusis was right. Achilles was acting alone.

"With the kind of information you could give me," Achilles continued, "there would be less blood shed."

"You've got Trusis to help you."

The Achean's lips twisted in disgust. "Yes. More's the pity. I don't much like having to deal with dishonorable men."

A laugh burst from Damon's lips. "Honor. You talk of honor! Always this talk of honor and glory!" He leaned toward the Achean. "What you bring wherever you go, you bloated pig, is pain and grief. And then you talk of honor. There is evil in this world, and you and all those like you, are its beating heart."

Achilles face flushed red, his eyes slitted. He grabbed Damon by the throat and shoved his own face close. "As of this moment, your woman doesn't know why you have not returned. Tomorrow we will inform your Queen," his voice wiped dung on the word Queen, "that you are captive here."

He let go of Damon's throat. A smug smile slowly replaced the angry grimace. "I have no doubt she will try to save you. We use you to lure your Amazon lover. She will make a monumental sale, the Amazon Warrior Queen. I expect the Hittite Hattusilis will pay well to display her. After he has used her."

Damon spit in Achilles' face.

Clenching his fist, Achilles drew his arm back, then slammed his fist into Damon's midsection, a blow that felt like a bolt of lighting that ran all the way to Damon's heart and exploded there. Damon's legs failed. He crumpled. His arms yanked brutally at the shoulder sockets as he sagged against the ropes.

Another blow to the side of his head took his sight.

For a long moment he hung there, blind and unable to breathe. Finally he sucked in a breath as his sight returned, but his legs still could not lift him. The ropes tore into his wrists.

"Lord Achilles!" yelled a voice from the hallway. "Lord Achilles, there is a fire. In the sail shed."

Achilles bellowed, "Get Trusis in here!"

A rough hand grabbed Damon's chin. Achilles locked their gazes. "I have no further need of you!" He thrust Damon's head away with such force that the back of Damon's head hit the wall.

Achilles turned to leave just as Trusis strode into the

room. To Trusis he said, "Take him out and kill him. Do it well away from here. And dispose of the body so that no one will know how or when he died. No one! Ever."

Followed by his guard, Achilles stomped out.

❧ 69 ❧

WITH EVANDRE AND MARPESSA, PENTHA REACHED the stockade when, from the direction of the sail shed, she heard the first cries of, "Fire!" Fire was the greatest fear of any camp. Every person she could see stopped and turned toward the cries. Then they ran toward the alarm.

Gryn stood opposite the stockade, by the cart.

Pentha said to Evandre and Marpessa, "Wait until I say the way is clear."

She hurriedly crossed the space between the cart and the stockade. Several soldiers rushed out the door and off toward the shed. The guard posted at the door stared in the direction of the cries. Seeing her, he shared the obvious. "Sounds like fire."

"I have a message from the Lord Odysseus for your commander."

He turned his attention to her. "Give it to me."

"No." She gave him a bright smile. "I'm sure I could trust you. But I was told to give it only to your commander. Is he here?"

"Might be. Comes and goes by the back. That's why you should give it to me."

"Well then, at least let me see if he's here."

Now from a different direction, behind the stockade, came another cry of "Fire!"

The guard looked flustered. "All right. Hurry."

She stepped inside, where another guard lounged in a chair at the head of a hallway, rolling his knife between his hands by its grip as he stared toward the front entry. Seeing her, he stood.

"Please show me to your commander?" she said softly. "I have a message."

She saw no other guards.

"He's probably gone off to the fire."

"I was told to give him this message quickly, and that he would be here."

He hesitated, and she tensed to spring on him. He turned and started down the hallway. She let him walk her well away from the door. They made a turn into another corridor and at once she drew the dagger, threw her weight onto his back, and slid the blade deeply into the front of his throat, twisted it, then pulled it back out. With a hissing sound of escaping air, he slipped to the floor.

DAMON TRIED HIS LEGS again. They shook, but at least he could stand well enough to take the agonizing pressure off his wrists and shoulder joints.

Trusis walked across the room and took up an arms-crossed, arrogant stance a couple of steps from Damon. "I'm going to enjoy this," he said. To the guard with him he said, "Fetch another man."

"You are a fool, Trusis. Think what you are doing!"

"I know exactly what I'm doing."

"Do you think Achilles will let you rule Themiskyra? Do you think Pentha won't suspect what you've done?"

Two guards stepped into the room.

Damon said, "Achilles despises you."

"Cut him down," Trusis said to the guards. "Bind him well. He's strong."

PENTHA RAN BACK TO the stockade door. The guard stood stiffly, his attention now fixed in the direction of the sail shed. Again she threw herself against the man at the same moment she drove the blade deeply into the front of his neck, and as he started to fall, she dragged him inside, out of view.

She stepped into the doorway and gestured. Evandre and Marpessa dashed from the donkey cart, axes in hand. They stepped into the stockade and Evandre said, "Here," and thrust an ax into Pentha's hand.

With the two Amazon's at her heels, Pentha sprinted down the hallway, checking the rooms they passed, all but one empty. The single occupant of one room was asleep, perhaps from drink.

Aeneas said the stockade had a central room, the most secure. They found it. Empty. But with two still burning oil lamps and the smell of unwashed bodies. Someone had been here.

She said, "We have to try Achilles' tent. Pray Achilles is involved with the fires."

They dashed out the front of the stockade. Gryn ran up and grabbed Pentha's arm. "The back," she said. "They are taking Damon out the back."

⊰ 70 ⊱

THE TWO GUARDS TRUSIS BROUGHT TO DAMON'S
cell had quickly become an escort of six. Two men
pushed Damon—his hands bound behind his back—out a
door into an astonishing scene. Three goats and some pigs
ran past. A guard shoved him toward a cart where a handful
of chickens had alighted, all clucking or squawking.

To Damon's left, smoke and tongues of flame rose from
fires. Two big fires. The shouts and yelling from that direction suggested wild pandemonium. No wonder no people
were about.

One guard climbed into the back of the cart, and the
chickens, squawking even louder, scattered in all directions.
Another guard holding Damon's arms grunted, "Get in."

Damon hesitated. Could he break free? Run?

"Look out!" yelled a male voice behind him.

He twisted out of his guards' hands and spun around. Four
women ran toward them, battle-axes raised.

The guards, and Trusis, drew swords. Pentha attacked the
man on Damon's left. Damon threw himself against the
guard on his right. They hit the ground. Evandre bashed in
the man's head then spun to ward off the sword of another
guard.

Damon felt the ropes on his wrist being cut, and twisted
his head to find Pentha leaning over him. His ropes burst
apart.

A guard slammed blindly so hard into Pentha that she fell. She rolled onto her back. The guard spun around, raised his sword to drive it into her belly. Damon threw himself against the guard, wrenched the man's sword from his hand, and with a backstroke, cut him across the legs. He fell, screaming.

Damon reached to Pentha and pulled her to her feet. She turned and attacked a guard fighting with Marpessa.

From between two nearby tents, Muttalusha trotted into sight, obviously heading toward the closest fire. Seeing this brawling mess, the merchant stopped in surprise. Muttalusha, the informer!

He caught Damon's gaze, then ran toward the fire. "Amazons!" he yelped. He would bring down the camp on them.

Damon switched the sword to his left hand, stooped to the dead guard at his feet, pulled the guard's dagger from its sheath, took aim, and hurled the dagger. Artemis guided the blade. It found Muttalusha's back. The merchant screamed and fell on his face.

Damon turned to check Pentha and instead faced Trusis. Their swords crashed together creating a flash of white in his mind so vivid that for a moment it blinded him. By instinct he ducked, but still he felt the bite of bronze down his left side.

He switched the sword back to his right hand. He faced a Trusis with gnarled brow and barred teeth. "Aaarrgh!" Trusis yelled in frustrated rage as he swung his sword directly at Damon's neck.

Damon ducked under it, slid to his left, brought his own sword up toward Trusis exposed underarm, but Trusis quickly spun backward so Damon's blow chopped empty air.

Their initial awkward movements past, they faced off, breathing hard, but in better balance. Damon felt blood run warmly down his left side, but as yet he felt no pain. He charged Trusis, aiming a blow at the left shoulder. Trusis danced sideways and jabbed toward Damon's gut. Both thrusts missed.

Coming out of the stockade, Damon had seen tables with

stools around them across from the stockade door. He turned and dashed toward the tables and snatched up a stool. Holding it by one leg with the seat out, he could use it as a makeshift shield.

He tried to cut Trusis off from the table, but too late. Trusis grabbed up his own stool. Damon swung his stool at Trusis, who countered it with his stool, but Damon followed up with two sword thrusts that backed Trusis against one of the tables.

Unable to go forward, unable to maneuver, Trusis leapt onto the table. He chopped downward onto Damon, who blocked the sword blows with the stool.

Damon leapt onto the table, bringing him even with Trusis again, and they exchanged parries. Trusis backed up. He leapt to the next table. Damon followed, Again Trusis leapt to another table, and Damon followed.

He heard chariots. Perhaps Achean reinforcements. With renewed urgency, he slashed at Trusis three times, forcing Trusis to the ground. Chickens scattered, clucking loudly, their wings beating up dust.

Damon dropped his sword and the stool, threw himself at Trusis, using his right arm to push away Trusis' stool, and grabbing Trusis sword arm at the wrist. They slammed into the ground. They rolled. Rolled again. Now Damon was on top. He brought up his knee and rammed it into Trusis groin.

The traitor stiffened. Damon wrenched Trusis' sword from him, turned it, aimed the tip at Trusis heart, and flung his full weight onto the sword.

The tip slashed through bone and flesh and found the ground.

"Damon! Let's go!"

He felt weak. Sucked in a long breath.

"Damon!" Pentha pulled at his shoulder.

He scrambled to his feet. Bremusa and Clonie stood in the cars of two chariots. Gryn held the reins of a puny donkey cart.

The chariots were designed for two. Even if they rode a

tight three together, one person would be left behind. They would have to take the ridiculous cart.

Pentha shouted, "Evandre, Marpessa, go with Clonie! Damon and Gryn, get in with Bremusa!"

The Amazons swiftly moved as she'd ordered.

But Pentha stood staring at a fire raging in the stacks of lumber. Its acrid smell filled his nostrils. He heard the sounds of its oils snapping and pops filling the air. In the early evening light, Pentha's red hair also seemed to be ablaze.

⊰ 71 ⊱

DAMON SUDDENLY REALIZED IT WASN'T THE FIRE
Pentha was watching, but Achilles. Achilles, whose
back was to them, and who was shouting orders and waving
his arms. She seemed in a trance.

Damon grabbed her arm. "Don't even think it!" He
yanked her arm. "In two days, we have a battle."

She swung back into reality. She squeezed his hand then
dashed to the team pulling Bremusa's chariot and launched
herself onto the back of the right-hand horse.

Damon leapt into the car, pressing himself alongside
Gryn. "Here," Bremusa said. She shoved an Achean shield
into his hands, then turned and slapped the horses' rumps
with a willow goad. "Ha!" she shouted, as did Clonie and
Pentha. Side by side, the two chariots sped toward the wall
and freedom, honking geese frantically scattering to avoid
the chariots' wheels.

No men stood guard inside the wall, just outside, checking
the identity of anyone trying to enter. But Damon saw at
least ten men posted on the wall's top, all looking into the
camp, at the fires.

Their attention shifted at the sight of two careening chariots filled with women, and one with a red-headed women
astride a chariot horse.

He imagined their confusion. The chariots closed fast
with the wall, and still no arrows, no spears. Might the

guards be so baffled that he and the Amazons could simply ride away?

"Amazons!" someone shouted.

He brought up the shield. There was little room in the car to maneuver. With difficulty he held it in front of Bremusa. Gyrn hunched low.

Arrows and spears whistled around them. A solid strike onto the shield. Another. A spear glanced off. He noted now, as he strained to hold the shield in place, a burning sensation on his left side.

He couldn't see beyond the shield, couldn't see what was happening to Pentha. She was completely exposed, her only protection the speed of the horse.

They reached the gate and raced through it, heading for the Scamander river, its crossing, and then on to the Amazon encampment. An arrow grazed Bremusa's head. As she slumped into Gryn's arms, Damon grabbed the reins and took her place.

The guards on the outside, fully alerted, charged the chariots with swords drawn, but being on foot, they delivered not one vital blow. They immediately rushed to their own chariots. Within moments he and the Amazons fled in front of six Achean two-man chariots.

Their own chariots were overloaded. They could never outrun the Acheans. At some point, they must fight. They were seven to twelve.

Gyrn yelled, "Look! Ahead!"

They raced headlong toward another contingent of a dozen chariots, returning to the encampment.

Pentha pointed to their left, and Clonie turned her chariot. Damon followed. The well-maintained dirt road allowed chariots to pass three abreast, but now they bumped and rattled across open ground. Gryn held onto Bremusa to steady her as all three crashed into each other with every rock and ridge.

They could not outrun the Acheans. Nor was it likely he and six Amazons could defeat what he guessed must now be thirty Achean soldiers.

They clattered through a stream, water spraying up from the wheels and horses hooves. On they charged across the bumpy plain.

They approached a hill. Pentha pointed and Clonie reined the horses in a direction that would take them left of the hill. Chariots were notoriously unsuited for anything but level ground. They swung left, and he saw Pentha look back to see how fast the Acheans were gaining. To Clonie she yelled, "Faster or we die!"

He flogged the horses with the reins, and they responded, their legs pounding, their heads rising and falling, flecks of saliva flung from their lips.

The chariots rounded the hill and ahead he saw horses. Amazon horses. He looked behind. The Acheans were closing.

He and the women leapt off the chariots, and surrounded by a rain of arrows, mounted the waiting horses.

Clonie took an arrow in the leg. Bremusa, having regained her senses, rode up to her, took her arm, and slung her onto a horse.

Those days of riding with Pentha—Damon felt profound gratitude he had learned to ride at all. Now he must gallop, and hang on for his life.

Pentha led, and immediately he knew she'd made a mistake. He urged his horse faster, trying to catch her, to tell her that this way would only trap them, but there was no possibility of catching up with Valor. Damon was, in fact, the last in the racing line.

He yelled, "This is the wrong way!" His words jolted out of his mouth, distorted, and were, in any case, blown away by the wind.

At top speed they approached the canyon that separated this hill from flatland beyond. He knew the general lay of the country between the Achean encampment and their own, but he wasn't sure of the canyon's dimensions. But he did know it was too steep for horse or man to climb down and that a fall into it would be fatal. Pentha must have forgotten it.

He dared not look behind. He had all he could do to stay

atop the galloping animal, clenching his legs to the horse's heaving sides and clinging with one hand to the reins and riding blanket and with the other hand to the horse's whipping mane.

Perhaps she couldn't see the crevasse. He couldn't. She appeared to be blind, running at it full speed.

And then—Valor leaped it.

Then Clonie on her mount.

Then Gryn.

All of the Amazons were actually leaping the canyon. He was last. "Great God," he breathed, as his horse flung itself into the air.

His mount landed its front feet on the canyon's far side, but as it gathered its haunches to plant them on solid ground, Damon fell off. The horse, thrown off balance, missed with one rear hoof, lurched backward, lost its hold on the land and fell backward and went down.

Damon's legs hung over the cliff edge and his hands were slipping. He grabbed a rock. It pulled loose. He felt one toe dig into something solid, then slip away. Again sliding backward, he grabbed the thick, gnarled base of bush with both hands. His sliding stopped.

Kicking his legs, searching for a foothold, he heard one of the Amazons yell, "Pentha!"

Behind him he heard chariots rushing up to the canyon, the men yelling, a horse screaming as apparently at least one chariot couldn't halt in time and the horse and men went over the cliff.

Arrows whizzed around him. He felt a burning sensation on his left shoulder as one sliced him, but did not stick. Then at last, one toe found a solid footing. He shoved himself to the level surface and leapt to his feet just as Pentha swept up on Valor.

"Give me your arm," she yelled.

He swung up onto the stallion's back behind her, and they charged off, racing to catch the others.

❧ 72 ❧

LOOKS OF SHOCK AND AMAZEMENT GREETED DA-mon and the returning Amazons. He quickly realized that the rescue mission had been kept secret. Outside Pentha's tent they dismounted, the horses' grooms quickly coming to care for the animals. Clonie limped badly. Gryn said, "I'm going to care for that," and bustled off toward her tent.

Pentha hugged Damon, then pushed him back with a wide stare. "You've been wounded," she said.

He felt his left side. His tunic was slit open and soaked with blood. "I don't think it's serious. But it burns like fire."

"And your shoulder, too."

Phemios looked as though he'd slept in a horse pen, and the smile he gave Pentha was one of enormous relief.

And then Damon thought his eyes deceived him. Bias ran up to him and threw himself into Damon's arms. He hugged Damon fiercely.

Tears searing the backs of his eyes, Damon squeezed back. Seeing that Bias' shoulder was bandaged, Damon touched the bandage. "I thought you were dead."

The boy grinned. "It's been a royally fearsome day."

Damon hugged Bias again, thinking of the mother whose heart he would not have to break.

Gryn bustled up. "Here, let me see that."

But Pentha said, "Take care of Clonie, mother. And Bremusa has a head wound. I will care for Damon." To Phemios she said, "Talk to Bremusa. You and I will talk later." To Marpessa she said, "Have someone bring me what I need to clean and bind his wounds."

Damon patted Bias on his uninjured shoulder. "Tomorrow we'll talk."

He followed Pentha into her tent.

She stared at him, eyes glistening. Finally she said, her voice like a lover's caress, "If you had died, I would have died."

He pulled her into his arms, with one hand felt the soft touch of her hair. "Death is all around us. War is death. But for now, for this moment, we live."

Two serving women arrived with water, ointments, and cloths. Pentha pulled herself from his arms.

"Sit there," she said, indicating a stool by a table. She forced sternness into her tone, as though working to keep control, either of herself or of the situation.

The women left.

Pentha helped him pull the tunic over his head. She said nothing, but briefly touched the arrowhead.

As he had guessed, neither wound was deep. Her face— her beautiful face that he could not look away from had he wanted to—was set in a frown as she cleaned them.

"Jumping that canyon was insane, Pentha."

"No. Bold. It was the only way we could succeed."

"I nearly went into the drop myself. I can barely ride. And I've never jumped."

"But you are incredibly strong and agile. I counted on that."

"I almost didn't make it. The horse didn't."

"He was our best jumper, a great horse. If he couldn't bring you across, no horse could. Not even Valor. And, in spite of your lack of skill, he succeeded. His name was Wanderer, and many stories will be told to Amazon children about the day the great horse Wanderer saved Damonides."

She continued cleaning his side. He said, "The mess was not entirely for nothing. In fact, I learned some good news.

Achilles is acting alone in his threats to Themiskyra. He's kept the other royals in the dark. That simplifies things for us a bit."

She paused a moment. "Yes, it does."

He held up his arm while she smoothed on a comfrey ointment. When she finished, she shook her head. "I love you, Damon. And I am in terrible pain."

Joy swept through him. A warming flush rose to his face. Love. Pentha had never before said the word *love*.

But then, she'd said loving him caused pain. "What am I supposed to say? That I'm happy you love me, and sorry it causes you pain."

"The pain comes from fear of losing you."

"Love. And losing. I think to love guarantees pain, because eventually, no matter how long we live, someone dies. Someone is left behind. I love you. And sometimes it pains me when I worry for you. But most of the time, loving you makes me deeply happy."

She wound linen expertly to hold the poultice in place. Then she knelt beside him and took one of his hands, opened the palm, and kissed it. For a moment he thought to take her in his arms, to hold her, to tell her everything would be all right, but death *was* an unseen presence in the very air they breathed, and the thought of holding her suddenly terrified him. Within days he might lose her. Somehow his mind seemed to think that to hold her now would only increase the pain of loss.

With her gaze tightly fixed on his face, she said, "Maybe we could go now to that wonderful Ephesus. A place where no one would know me, and where men and women live together all the time. Ask me to leave this camp. Beg me to leave with you and go away."

Surprised, he pulled his hand from hers. "I don't understand."

"Just say, 'Let's leave. Now.'"

He stood. "I can't do that."

She sat back on her heels, looking up at him, the strangest

look in her eyes. Unreadable. He said, "And you don't actually mean it."

"Yes, I do."

Surprise shifted to shock, and when she didn't indicate she was jesting, shock turned to anger. He felt his neck and face warming. He glared at her. "What do you want from me? We are less than two days from what may be the biggest battle of any man's lifetime. Certainly of my life. A battle I've come to agree is crucial to defending Themiskyra. And you beg me to ask you to run away!"

She stood, put her hand on his arm.

He looked at it. She took it away.

She said, "For years now, to get through each day, I created a person that was a strong, invincible warrior. And as long as I can remember, I've wanted to kill Achilles. That would give me peace at last, I was certain. But the moment I thought I might lose you, I knew all that was pretense. If you were dead, killing Achilles would do nothing to make me happy."

"Now!" Blood pounded at his temples. He walked several steps away, then turned back. "You ask this now, when I have begged you before to leave. There was a time when we could have left. Honorably. But you wouldn't have it. Now you say this to me!"

A tear rolled down her cheek, followed by another. "I'm ashamed." she said. "But I love you. I want to live with you—all the time. Life in Themiskyra works. It's good. It's peaceful. I am frcc. But loving you has made me hungry for more." She bit her trembling lip. "I don't want you to die."

"How can you stand there crying and asking me to do such a thing? And why Achilles? Tell me that! What is this obsession you have about him? I don't understand you. Tell me!"

She straightened her shoulders and brushed away the tears.

She tightened a fist and struck it against her chest. "There are demons fighting in here!" She shook her head, her face a mask of conflict and pain. "Maybe being happy is not my fate."

He grabbed her by both arms. She was making no sense.

"You've said that before. Why?" He shook her. "Why do you say that? It's as if by saying it, you want to make it true. I tell you, you could be happy. But apparently you won't let that happen."

She wrenched herself free. "You should go! Let me be."

"I won't go away, Pentha. Ever."

In a long, silent, pause, she searched his face. Then she said, "I don't understand anything. Why have the Fates brought me to this place?" Her lips twisted into a bitter line. "Warrior Queen! I am a coward."

Once more amazed, he waved his hands in frustration. "What kind of insane thought is that? Your mind for battle is brilliant. And I've seen you fight and kill."

"Only when it really didn't make a difference to me if I lived. But everything is changed. I want to live, and I don't want to fight."

Not since Hippolyta's death had Pentha looked so sad, so defeated.

"When I was sixteen," she said slowly, "the Acheans came to Tenedos. Achilles came to our house. I was the one who had time to hide. I hid, and I watched him kill my mother. I watched him rape Derinoe. And the thing is—I watched, and I—did—nothing." She spit out the last words, a bitter self-indictment.

All the pieces that were Pentha suddenly fit together. He walked to her, took her hands. "Is this why you think you don't deserve to be happy? Pentha, you were sixteen. There was nothing you could have done."

"I could have tried."

He pulled her close, pressed her cheek to his chest. "You were sixteen, and not warrior trained. Surely you were terrified. Isn't that true?"

She pushed away from him again, turned her back to him and bent her head.

He put his arms around her shoulders and clasped his hands across her arms. "I don't know all of what you are. But I know you are *not* a coward. And I think you are finding out that you are a women who can love."

Pentha's wound was every bit as deep as his own, just of a different kind. He touched her hair, ran a finger along her chin. "You are being truly honest, not a coward, when you say you don't want to fight. That kind of honesty, recognizing and accepting who we are, not who others think we ought to be, may be the only way to find peace. It was for me."

"Sometimes fighting is necessary."

"Of course."

"I should have fought."

He went to the table and poured them both a cup of mare's milk and handed one to her. "I've met the great Lord Achilles. You would simply have been killed."

She sipped, her eyes lost in reflection.

Something she had said earlier suddenly conjured a thought. "Pentha. What about Leonides? Leonides—"

"He is Achilles' son." She took another sip of the milk. "I talked with Deri. She hates Achilles. But this obsession I have for Achilles, as you call it, has become not something merely personal, about me and my mother and Deri. It's about all of Themiskyra."

"You're instincts have been right. Deadly right. And depending on how much information Trusis gave him, Achilles may succeed."

"Trusis! Trusis! Great goddess. I had forgotten Trusis. Why did you kill him?"

"He arranged my capture, Pentha. Trusis betrayed us."

She sat her cup on the table and put a hand across her forehead. "He may have revealed everything. Our battle plans. Our defenses at home"

"I think not. He said to me, 'I will explain our plans to Achilles.' Not that he had done so, but that he would do so. I don't believe he'd yet had the opportunity."

Damon sat on the stool and continued. "The Fates picked you, Pentha. And they chose well. When I came down the mountain, I also accepted that the Fates picked me to help you. I have come to agree this fight is your duty. But I will beg you one thing. Promise me that under no circumstances will you fight Achilles in single combat."

She sipped from the cup.

Something frightening twisted his gut. "I mean it, Pentha. He may call for single combat. He would love to be able to brag that he killed the Amazon Queen. But he cannot command that you fight him and there is no dishonor in turning him down. Ignore him. You'll be no good to us dead."

Still she simply sipped.

Fear became an urgent goad. "He is huge, Pentha." Damon felt Achilles' fist slamming into his stomach. "You cannot beat him in single combat, as satisfying as you think that might be."

"I would be faster."

"Penthesilea, may I enter?" The voice was that of one of the serving women.

Pentha replied, "Enter."

The woman went into Pentha's bedchamber, and he saw the lights from lamps brought to life. She returned to the table and gathered up the salves, dirty water, and bandages. Damon stood and moved away from the table. The woman turned to Pentha. "Do you require anything else, Lady? Shall I prepare a bath?"

"No, Anna. In the morning. I am too tired now even to bathe."

The woman left and Pentha stood. "You must be tired too."

"I don't want to leave. I know we can't make love. What we both need is iron will, not softness. But I want to sleep beside you."

She smiled, touched his lips with a fingertip, and took his hand. She led him into the adjacent chamber, also comfortable and welcoming with furs on the floor and walls. They undressed, extinguished all the lamps but the one by the door, and slipped under the covers. She wriggled close to him, her hand outside the fur cover. He clasped it tightly in his.

He said, "Promise me you will deny any challenge by Achilles. Or for that matter, any of the royals."

"What will be, will be. Let's not talk of battle. Let's not talk at all. I'm truly exhausted."

He stroked her palm. Here was a woman who could wield

a sword with powerful blows, but her hand seemed small, her fingers delicate. He felt himself drifting off. "With you, my heart is always at rest. You are my peace."

Beneath her fingers, Pentha felt Damon's pulse beating in his palm. Apparently just being with her made Damon profoundly happy. She could imagine no greater pleasure than to marry Damon, have his children, and live the moments and days and years of her life with him.

They lay quietly a while, and then she spoke softly. "I envy you. That you are happy with who you are. You would excuse me for not fighting for Deri, but I should have fought, no matter what."

Pentha had another thought. "In a few days, when this is all over, I have something to tell you that has made me deeply happy. I think it will make you happy, too."

She waited, expecting him to say, "What?" and try to pry the secret out of her. And maybe she should tell him.

She rose on her elbow, studied his face, and found that he had fallen asleep. Still she whispered to him. "Deri says I'm free to choose. I choose you."

≫ 73 ≪

PENTHA AWOKE WHILE NIGHT STILL CLOAKED THE
encampment to find that Damon had already left her
bed. She felt under the cover, hoping to be able to touch a
trace of his warmth, but none lingered. She sat up and
dropped her feet to the floor and bowed her head.

Life was hard. Even brutal. And she must do today the
most difficult thing she could imagine. Not killing Achilles,
which she had longed to do for years. But offering him the
challenge to duel. Because a chance, a very real chance, existed that the Achean would kill her, and, brutal irony, she
now very much wanted to live.

THE EASTERN SKY SHOWED a faint, blue-gray rim of
dawn light. Only a short time now until the battle must begin.

Pentha turned from talking to Bremusa as a young Amazon rode toward her with Deri. Looking perplexed and still
in her sleeping gown, Deri sat on the horse in front of the
woman Pentha had sent to fetch her.

Pentha put her arm on Deri's leg. "I'm sorry to have dis-
turbed you so early."

"I wasn't asleep."

Pentha nodded to the woman, who slipped off the horse
and walked far enough away to give Pentha and Deri privacy. "I sent for you because it's possible I may not kill
Achilles today. I'm worried, and not only for Themiskyra.

For Damon. I don't want him to risk his life, perhaps lose it, for any reason. And certainly not to avenge me."

"Pentha. Please. I don't know—"

"Achilles must be killed. So if things do not go well, there is something important you must do. Something I couldn't do, but you can. For Themiskyra, and to protect Damon."

❧ 74 ❧

AN UNNATURAL PEACE LAY OVER THE PLAIN OF
Troy. At one hour past dawn, a morning fog hung
silently in the air, blotting out the sky but not the ground.
Damon gazed across what would be, in less than an hour, a
field of dead and dying warriors.

He strode to the chariot he had requested from Aeneas. To
the driver he said, "No matter what happens, stay close by."

"I'm ready, my lord."

"And keep a sharp eye for Achilles' pennant. As soon as
the initial skirmish passes, you must take me to him. No one
else should reach him before me."

"Yes, my lord."

Damon returned to where Phemios waited, and once more
studied the field. As he contemplated the gloomy calm, the
churning in his stomach eased. Surely the lack of wind was
an omen that the gods were with Pentha. Today, on this day
of battle, the notorious northern wind had failed to join the
gathered warriors, and gusts blowing against the arrows of
the Themiskyran Amazon horsewomen would have been a
serious handicap. They were already at severe disadvantage
for he estimated that the Achean enemy outnumbered
Themiskyrans and Trojans two to one.

Damon reached down the neck of his tunic and pulled out
the arrowhead. He closed his eyes, envisioned Pentha's

face—and the churning sensation struck again with force. He snapped his eyes open.

"There is enough light, Damon."

Phemios' voice startled him. He let the arrowhead fall against his armor.

Phemios continued. "I can finally make out their battle pennants. They appear ready to engage. All pennants appear to be up."

Behind Damon, forces four-thousand-strong waited at his command. Trojan troops, including all the chariots the Trojans could put into the field, covered his left and right. Although the raising of pennants did usually signal readiness to engage, Agamemnon's forces showed no signs of moving,

Phemios stirred again. Dressed in muscled cuirass, helmet, and greaves, he swept his hand forward to point as he talked. "Agamemnon and Achilles have taken the center, as we thought. They've put Nestor and Odysseus in charge of the left. Menelaus and Ajax to the right." He dragged his arm. "But I don't see Diomedes' pennant."

Damon felt a new flash of unease. He frowned and with the back of his knuckles, roughly stroked his beard. Why would Diomedes be absent? Could the Acheans be hiding forces, just as he and Penthu had hidden their own Amazon cavalry and archers?

Squinting, he scanned the plain. Although for the most part flat, scattered hillocks humped skyward here and there.

He scrutinized the five hillocks behind which lay five hundred Amazon horses and their riders, covered with cloth the dun color of the ground. Five hundred horses trained to lie silent for hours if necessary. As hard as he looked, he could see nothing, and *he* knew they were there.

The Acheans would not know. At least, they should not know unless Trusis had betrayed them to Achilles, and Damon didn't believe that was so.

No. On this day, the pivotal weapons of the forces under Pentha's command would be surprise along with terror and speed.

Aware that his anxiety for Pentha caused most of the churning in his gut, Damon looked right and contemplated the waist-high, cobblestone altar. Only a short time ago, Semele sacrificed ten white goats there. A diviner had examined the liver of the first goat slain and said the omens were right for battle. Fire still burned, and black smoke curled upward carrying the scent of charred flesh.

Damon strode to the altar, knelt, and took the arrowhead in hand. He struggled to force reverence to replace fear as he prayed. *"Divine Artemis, beloved daughter of Leto, great patron. I ask again, I beg you, protect Pentha. Give her your strength. Give her victory over the men that besiege this land."*

At the sound of hooves, he looked up. Pentha rode toward him along the line of solemn warriors who raised their spears and swords in salute as she passed. Admiration and love glowed on every face. She wore full Amazon battle gear, including the golden girdle and fur cap, the insignias of her rank. He bolted to his feet and slipped the arrowhead back under his tunic.

When Valor reached him, he grasped the halter's cheek strap. With his other hand, he rubbed the soft nose. "The horses are in place?"

"In place, down and covered, well before dawn."

He stepped closer and let his hand rest on her thigh—firm, and warm, and alive beneath his touch. She dropped the reins. With her left hand she covered his. "Give me time to return to them. Then attack."

He nodded and smiled for her, but dread kept his lips stiff.

She picked up the reins. Damon stroked Valor's cheek. "Keep her safe," he said softly. He let go of the halter.

With a light touch of her knee against the Valor's side, she wheeled the stallion, and he moved quickly into a trot that carried her away. Damon watched until he could no longer see the white fur of her hat.

He felt the men stirring, restless to be unleashed.

At last Phemios said, "She has had enough time now to reach them."

"No," Damon said. "Not yet."

The sun now cut patches in the fog, and where light fell on the Acheans, brilliant flashes from the bronze of their helmets, cuirasses, and shields shot across the plain. To the southwest, in the far distance, the increasing light revealed the dim outlines of the massive Achean wall.

Finally he felt certain she would be in place.

He strode out before the waiting men and their commanders, drew his sword and raised it. He raised his voice to spread as far as it might. "Do not forget," he shouted. "Pass the word. Approach slowly. Attack only at my command. We must lead them past our cavalry."

He turned. His aide handed him his helmet and then his shield. He secured both, feeling the hot rush of blood to his face, feeling the chest-tightening grip of battle fever. Beating his sword against the shield, he began a slow march forward. "Long live Artemis!" he bellowed.

"Artemis!" came the responding boom of thousands of male voices. The sound of swords, spears, and javelins beaten upon thousands of shields rose around him like thunder from Zeus.

The body moved forward, the first five ranks being expert spearmen and javeliners. "Slowly!" he shouted. He kept his pace steady, glanced left and right to be certain the Trojan charioteers were following orders and would not rush ahead.

At first the enemy made no response. Then he heard the distant sound of a trumpet, followed by the yammering of a battle cry spreading across the plain under the dismal gray fog. The Acheans advanced. They came quickly. He grinned, pleased.

"Slowly!" he yelled again, keeping to the same steady pace.

His heart thudded against his armor. His neck grew warm under his tunic. Soon enough the leading edge of Agamemnon's army moved into range of their archers.

"Now!" he shouted to Phemios above the sound of the beaten shields.

❧ 75 ❧

DAMON INCREASED THE PACE, FELT AND HEARD the lines of men behind him move as one with him. Within a heartbeat, the blast of a trumpet from behind shattered what, by comparison, seemed like calm. The shouting and beating of shields transformed to a wall of sound.

He watched with grim satisfaction when their archers, hidden in shallow trenches paralleling the enemy's advancing line, rose and fired volleys of burning arrows. He heard the hissing of the arrows' flight, watched the arrows arc and disappear into the low-lying fog only to reappear again as they fell and struck their targets in the front ranks of the Achean forces.

Trojan slings hurled flaming balls of oil-soaked grasses into piles of dried fodder. The fodder caught quickly. A wall of roaring red flames leapt up and across the field like a bleeding gash on the land.

Their arrows spent, the first squads of Themiskyran archers retreated at a run toward the Themiskyran line, seeking replacement arrows.

Chariots emerged on the Achean front. Attempting to turn too quickly in an effort to avoid the blazing barrier, some tipped over. Other drivers looked for a way through the flaming barriers. Horses balked or reared or ignored their driver's whips.

But pass through the fiery line some did, followed by the

infantry. The oncoming hoard swarmed like ants as they continued their forward rush. And the fires had distracted them. The Achean lines raced passed the hillocks behind which Amazons lay waiting.

The two opposed forces closed fast. "Javelins!" Damon shouted.

Immediately came the trumpet signal and waves of Themiskyran and Trojan javelins whistled into the air. At almost the same moment, Achean javelins began to rain around him. He dodged two. A third struck his shield. Its power jolted his arm, but the weapon streaked beyond and impaled itself into the ground.

"Attack!" Damon shouted. Again the trumpeter signaled.

He ran forward in a full charge. The front lines collided. The Acheans always sent poor fighters first. He knew this practice. Counted on it. He had seen to it that the best men of Artemis made up their front line, expert javeliners first, then expert spearmen and swordsmen.

Almost with ease he avoided the awkward moves of the first two Achean spearmen he encountered, and with a single sword blow each, gutted first one and then the other. The Achean tide kept advancing.

A giant of a man with a mace swung the huge ball at his head. Damon ducked, took the blow on his right shoulder, gasped, fell onto his left knee and lost his helmet. He brought his sword up in time to thrust it deep into the giant's belly, just under the man's cuirass. The man fell. Damon rose, put one foot on the body, and pulled his sword out.

A warrior raced toward him in a chariot, as if to challenge him to a single combat duel to the death. Damon was, after all, the Themiskyra infantry commander. His status guaranteed that his death could swing the tide of battle. And to kill him would count heavily. He loathed this revolting practice of the royals of both sides. Loathed the whole notion that the path to fame and glory lay in killing another man. How many men have you killed? Who? But in a short time he would use this foul tradition to kill Achilles.

So who was this challenger? The warrior in the chariot's car didn't have the enormous stature of Achilles.

Maybe Agamemnon? No. The warrior was too young to be Agamemnon. Then Damon realized the chariot did not carry a royal pennant. This was not one of the Acheans' royal heroes out for glory.

The charioteer, his body straining with the effort, drew his team to a halt. The warrior jumped from the car and rushed Damon, sword in hand. They exchanged fierce, ringing blows. White light shot through Damon's head.

Then he heard the sounds for which he had been waiting. A trumpet blast from the Achean rear, then the ululating cry of Themiskyran Amazons shrilled over the battling men.

The hair on his own neck stood, so uncanny was this sound from the throats of hundreds of women as they threw off their covers, urged their battle stallions to stand, leapt onto their backs, and attacked from the rear.

Hearing this skin-crawling sound, the warrior across from Damon froze, his eyes bulging. Damon gave the man a horrible grin. "Terrifying, isn't it," he yelled, and with one huge swing, took off the man's head.

Bodies sprawled now, all around him. The air smelled of blood and piss. Sweat poured down his sides.

He rushed the nearest man in his view. They exchanged two blows. He severed the man's sword hand. Blood, life, spurted warmly onto legs. At the thumping, creaking sound of an approaching chariot, he spun around scarcely in time to dive headfirst out of the path of a team running with an empty chariot car. He rolled and regained his feet.

He had lost track of Phemios. Lost track of time. He trusted that Aeneas' chariot and driver were still near. The quality of the fighters was getting better as the rear ranks of the Acheans, the better ranks, took over.

He, on the other hand, felt the burn of fatigue, age catching up to a forty-three-year-old man. But he sensed that they were pushing the Acheans back. His next blow he delivered with renewed zeal.

Now was the time to find Achilles. He spun around, looking for Aeneas' chariot. Not there. Bremusa caught his eye. She was on her knees and clutching Clonie's ominously limp body, and even in the heat of struggle, Damon felt a stab of horror.

Another warrior charged up in a chariot. Before he could dismount, Damon grabbed him by his sword arm, threw him down, and delivered a deep sword thrust into the throat. As the charioteer started to drive off. Damon leapt into the car. He shoved the man into the swirling melee of struggling warriors, saw someone thrust a spear into the charioteer's back. The man's warbling scream blended into the din of clanging metal, shrieks, groans of the dying, and the thundering of chariot horses and wheels.

Damon gathered the reins and aimed the pair toward the crest of a hillock. He needed height to find his quarry.

At the crest, he at first saw only confusion. There were many dead, Themiskyran, Trojan, and Achean. So much waste. Only steps away lay the dead bodies of Marpessa and Evandre. At the rear, though, the Acheans were retreating. Some had actually turned and were running. Mounted Amazons were running them down and finishing them with arrows or axes as their horses galloped past the stunned warriors. Damon doubted that any of these Achean men had ever seen a horse ridden in battle, let alone a horse ridden by a shrieking woman. A thrill of exultation raced hotly under Damon's skin. The Achean call for full retreat should come at any moment.

Where was Pentha? He scanned the field for Valor's distinctive gray color. Nothing. Damon's heart squeezed tightly and his breath shortened. Where was Pentha! *Don't let her be dead!*

PENTHA HAD ALREADY LOST count or any sense of how many men she had brought down. Around her the struggle still had the crazed feeling of midbattle, but she had decided before letting a single arrow fly that she would find and challenge Achilles as soon as possible and she had single-mindedly fought her way in the direction where she had first sighted his pennant. She saw a break in the Achean line at almost the same moment she caught her second glimpse of his pennant. She wheeled Valor, bent over him, and they raced toward the opening.

A downed chariot loomed ahead, then two horses on their sides, their legs thrashing. Valor leaped over them.

Pentha sensed that she was outpacing her second. It couldn't be helped. She had to reach Achilles.

Across the plain, she spotted the pennant and the chariot. She raised her sword arm and after sucking in a great breath, gave a ululation so loud it surprised her. Achilles' chariot almost at once veered in her direction. He'd spotted her. Doubtless recognized her cap. Now, at last, the mighty Achilles would pay—or she would die with the effort.

ANOTHER CHARIOT PULLED OUT in front of the Achean line. It sped toward Damon. And it carried Achilles' pennant. Yes! Damon thought. He reached for the reins— and saw Pentha. She came at a gallop from somewhere behind him, passed on his left, and raced forward.

Panic exploding in his chest. Scarcely able to breathe. *Please, my heart. Don't do this!*

Achilles' chariot halted. The legendary warrior dismounted. His charioteer pulled away. Pentha signaled Valor to a halt. The two warriors faced each other, close enough now to clearly see the expression on their opponent's face.

Word spread. The battle slowed, then ceased, with both sides in the immediate area separating, retreating in the direction of their respective camps to watch what would happen as the greatest warrior they had ever known fought the Warrior Queen of the Amazons. Residents of Troy would be watching in grim fascination, praying she would give them revenge for Hector. From shouts of rage and screams of pain and death, the plain of Troy fell suddenly, eerily quiet.

Pentha charged. Her first javelin glanced Achilles' bronzed shield and flew past him. Achilles was so tall that even mounted, she did not sit much above him. Damon noted, his heart rampaging with fear, that she had at least exchanged her wicker and leather shield for one of the tougher Achean ones. But compared to Achilles, bronzed from head to greaves, she was perilously vulnerable.

She wheeled Valor and charged again. This time Achilles' spear went up and he slashed at her as she passed. She deflected it with her shield. Her second javelin dug deep into the center of his shield. As she wheeled again, Achilles ripped the javelin away and thrust it to the ground.

Damon dropped the chariot's reins and stumbled out of the car. Without thought he ran toward where they battled, leaping or trampling over bodies and shoving men and women aside.

He burst onto the scene, his intent to attack Achilles. Two spears crossed in front of him at the same time that a pair of hands grabbed him from behind and yanked him to a halt.

"Release me!" he bellowed.

He looked behind. Phemios held him. "You cannot interfere, Damonides," Phemios said. "She challenged him."

Pentha once more charged Achilles. In their struggle, her cap had come off revealing her red hair, a short, fiery mass of waves that framed her exquisite face. Achilles half raised his spear, and as Valor charged, Achilles rammed the spear into the stallion's chest.

With great force, Valor's forward motion threw Achilles backward onto the ground, but the Achean quickly regained his feet. Valor staggered, squealing in agony against the spear. He went down on his front knees. Achilles ran to Pentha and, grabbing her by her hair, pulled her off her dying stallion's back.

Time slowed for Damon. He felt every beat of his heart. He saw every curve and line of her face.

⇥ 76 ⇤

VEILED, WITH BIAS BESIDE HER, DERINOE
climbed the stairs to Troy's northeastern tower. They
stepped onto the wall and turned to walk south.

"I'm glad you wanted to come," she said. "I have to see
what happens. I couldn't see anything from the encampment."

"I would give anything to be fighting. Damon should have
let me. I'm not too young. I've been practicing. I could at
least have carried a pennant."

"If after you see this battle you are still so eager to fight,
you will doubtless have many opportunities."

They reached the southwest section. The battle raged below. People milled about, edging themselves into the best
vantage points. Bias looked around, soaking up the mood.
"You'd think this was the games at festival."

"For some, there is a kind of sick pleasure in watching
death and maiming, But others are like me. They're here because someone they love might not return."

"Pentha will be all right. And Damon, too. No one fights
better."

He was so young, and so naive.

The battle sounds, faint on the wall's northern section,
were loud now. Cries and shouts, the whinny of horses, and
above it all, the clang of metal.

Bias said, "I smell burning grass."

Derinoe looked up at the roof of the great south tower and

could see that up there, there wouldn't even be breathing space. She saw Priam, and beside him Hekuba and Helen. But not Andromache. Was Paris in the battle? Or was he once again withdrawn somewhere else. She thought of Hektor, of his disgust for Paris, and of his own great, courageous heart. A familiar lump swelled in her throat.

"Here," Bias said. He grabbed her hand and, tugging her along, squeezed them between two fat men paying attention to two attractive women, but not to their place at the wall.

Now Deri could see. Her first impression was of churning chaos. Fires burned in the direction of the Achean camp. Horses and chariots moved about here and there on the plain with men, by the hundreds, either still fighting or lying on the ground. Her throat tightened and she pressed a hand to her stomach.

"We've won!" Bias crowed, his voice quiet so as not to capture attention, but greatly excited. "See there. The Acheans are fleeing."

This appeared to be true. In the part of the battlefield that lay to the south, in fact, in most of the field, she saw that Acheans were indeed fleeing back toward their encampment, in chariots and on foot, and were being pursued by Amazon cavalry. But there were bodies of men, women, and horses everywhere. Pennants lay on the ground, still clutched in the hands of the seconds of several Amazons, and some pennants she recognized—those of Evandre, Andro, and Harmothoe. Horrified by what this signified, she clenched a fist of one shaking hand and pressed it to her lips.

"There's the Trojan commander, Aeneas," Bias said, pointing to a spot where warriors had stopped moving at random. Several hundred of them, Achean and Trojan, had formed a huge circle, and in its center—

Derinoe's heart clenched and a great lump in her throat shut off her breath. Valor lay on the ground, a great bloody-red pool around his neck and head, his legs kicking. Damonides stood not far from the stallion, Phemios restraining his commander by the arms. And in the center of the circle, Achilles and Pentha. Achilles held Pentha by her hair.

* * *

DETERMINED TO BREAK FROM Achilles' grip before he could draw his sword, Pentha grabbed her head with her hands and wrenched herself to Achilles' left. Her hair pulled free and she spun away from him, her scalp burning. They circled, taking each other's measure, Achilles' now armed with sword and shield.

Damon had said Achilles was huge, but still his size stunned her. She snatched off her quiver and threw it down, grabbed up an Achean shield, drew her battleaxe from her girdle, and charged. She came in fast and low. She'd sever his leg at the knee.

He was also fast. His shield blocked her swing. She brought up her shield barely in time to take a fierce blow from his sword. She followed up with a backhand at his other knee. She broke skin, saw blood, but felt no meat.

But she had surprised him. He pushed her back a step with his shield, looking at her with wide-eyed amazement. As he swung his sword downward, she caught his sword wrist with the top of her shield. His sword spun into the air. The shouting and screaming and yelling from onlookers faded. She no longer heard it, fired only by that look of amazement in Achilles' eyes.

He ran to his right, away from her, and as she had snatched up a shield from the ground, he grabbed up a sword sticking out of a man's belly. Watching her again, his eyes no longer held surprise. Jaw clenched, he crouched, wary. Battle rage seemed to magnify the size of his eyes.

She dropped her ax and drew her sword. He attacked, hacking downward toward her left shoulder. Her practice with the Achean shield paid off when the shield took his sword's bite. His violent twisting of his sword to free it from her shield wrenched her arm like a bone being shaken by a dog. Off balance, her swing with her sword at his neck hit his helmet and glanced away.

He smashed his shield into hers, threw his whole weight behind his charge, and with a fist clenched around his sword's hilt, struck her on the side of the head. The blow lifted her off her feet. She dropped her shield, and when she hit the ground, her sword hand struck a chariot wheel and the sword spun from her grasp.

Achilles sprang toward her. She rolled. Snatched up her sword. Scrambled to her feet. As she rushed him, Achilles dropped his sword, grasped a spear from the ground, squared his body, and thrust the spear into her left side.

The force of the blow shoved her sideways. With her left hand she grasped the spear's shaft as she staggered backward and fell against Valor's belly. She looked down at her side and the spear sticking out of it.

Strange. Knowing the gesture was futile, she nevertheless pulled at the spear. It didn't budge.

I don't feel pain. But this wound. This wound I cannot survive. Like Hippolyta.

❧ 77 ❧

As Pentha fell against Valor, Phemios released Damon. Damon ran toward Pentha with
Phemios and Bremusa right behind him.

"Feed the bizarre woman to the dogs!" he heard someone
yell. "Throw her into the Scamander," came another cry.

He was entangled in a sudden rush in Pentha's direction,
with men shoving, pushing, and yelling. He fought with others to get to her. Then a loud, booming voice reached over
the throng. "Let her be!"

Damon pushed past two more warriors to find Achilles
standing not far from where Pentha lay against Valor, her
head lolled on the horse's belly, her eyes closed, her hands
lax on the ground. The ice-water chill of seeing death ran
waves of gooseflesh across his skin.

Achilles raised his arm, fist clenched. "Don't touch her!
Look at her. Look at a beautiful face. It would have been better for me to have possessed such a woman than to have
killed her. What arrogance to think she could defeat me!"

Sword drawn, Damon stepped forward. Phemios checked
him. "Damon! She challenged him."

Damon drove his sword into the ground. He wanted to
drive it through the Achean. Cut Achilles in half. Feed *him* to
the dogs. But, it had been a fair fight. He would not shame
Pentha. "Not arrogance." He spat the words at Achilles.
"Hate."

"Damon, she isn't dead."

He and Achilles turned. Bremusa, kneeling next to Pentha, had called out. Damon ran to Pentha. Bremusa moved aside.

He looked at the wound, huge and bleeding swiftly. Rage. Futility. His light, his joy, the center of his world lay bleeding to death on a filthy, stinking battlefield. "Pentha," he said softly

She opened her eyes.

At first she stared, then slowly focused on his face. "I don't feel you. Hold my hand."

He was already holding her hand. Now he pressed it to his chest. Biting back tears, he said, "We won. The enemy is fleeing."

"Good. Good."

"You were fierce. Magnificent."

"You were right. He's very big."

Her eyelids fluttered, her gaze became unsteady.

He choked out, "Pentha."

"Your hand feels . . . safe."

He tasted blood. He had bitten the inside of his cheek. "I love you. Always."

"You are. . . ." She struggled to snatch a breath. She searched for him with cycs no longer able to focus. ". . . my peace."

A small breath, but then no other. The profound stillness of death settled onto her.

Someone screamed, "Take the Amazon's girdle!"

Damon leapt to his feet, turned, drew his dagger, and spread his arms.

The shoving barely started when Achilles bellowed, "The right to claim her weapons is mine. And I say this woman fought with skill and courage. We will honor the Amazon Queen." He cast a fierce look at one of the Achean warriors, presumably the one who had shouted last. "Let the Trojans honor her with proper rites."

Bremusa pulled the spear from Pentha's side. Blood gushed out. Bile burned the back of Damon's throat. He turned away.

Aeneas stepped beside him and said, "I would be honored to take her to your camp."

Damon forced himself to turn to Pentha again. He lifted her, and with Achilles and the men and women from both forces watching, he carried her to the general's chariot and, still holding her, stepped up into the car.

❧ 78 ❧

SQUARING HER SHOULDERS, PRAYING THAT SHE would not start weeping again, Derinoe stopped outside Gryn's tent. Lamplight poured from the seams around the opening flap.

"Gryn," she called out. "It's Derinoe. May I enter?"

After a bit of stirring, Gyrn pulled back the flap. Her eyes were red-rimmed, her gray hair disheveled. She gestured Deri inside.

"I ask you to forgive me for coming to you now. I know your pain is fresh. But my purpose is urgent."

Gryn led to a pair of chairs, and as they sat she said, "It doesn't hurt to have my mind distracted. You just missed Damon." She nodded to the table beside them, on which lay Pentha's golden girdle. "He brought me her girdle. Heracles battled with Hippolyta—my daughter's namesake—over this girdle. And now it is in my care." She started to cry, but pressed her hand to her lips and stopped the tears. "Damon left to keep vigil with my daughter."

"My mission is urgent, so I will be quick. I come because Pentha asked me to. You make a poison for Amazon arrows. You can make it strong enough to kill a deer. I want you to make some of this poison for me."

Gryn frowned. "Why do you want it?"

"I can't tell you why." Gryn started to shake her head. "But Pentha asks it."

"No Amazon can use this poison to take human life."

"I am not Amazon."

The stillness of deep thought held Gryn. She bowed her head, clasped her hands. Deri waited. What if Gryn said no? What other choice was left if Gyrn said no?

Finally Gyrn looked up. "I loved her like my own. She was extraordinary."

Gryn stood. Deri also. Wise, kind eyes looked deeply into Deri's heart. With her face composed and solemn, Gryn said, "Come back tomorrow afternoon."

LIGHT FROM LAMPS INSIDE Pentha's tent escaped into the night's darkness. The guard pulled the flap open, and Damon stepped in. The outer room lay empty except for another guard at the entry to Pentha's bedchamber. He couldn't remember ever seeing so many lit lamps in a room. The resinous scent of frankincense created a sacred feeling in the space.

He walked to the guard. "Go outside. Keep watch there. And let no one enter here tonight except the woman who keeps the lamps lit."

She saluted and left.

He entered where only two nights ago he had slept with Pentha. She lay on the right side of her bed on top of the fur cover. This room, too, shown brilliantly with lamplight. On legs that felt like wooden stumps, he approached her body.

She had been cleaned and dressed in a red tunic. Golden sandals were laced to just below her knees. Her white fur cap lay on the pillow beside her. In two days she would wear it at her funeral.

A belt he had made for her cinched her tunic. He remembered the labor, the love, he had put into making the belt. Tears finally won their battle with his will. They flooded down his cheeks, dripped onto his chest. "Pentha," he croaked. His chest heaved as he fought to smother gasping sobs. An animal howl clawed its way up from his belly. It escaped. He fell to his knees and clutched his arms around his chest.

He stayed on his knees until the tears slowed, the heaving of his chest turned to normal breathing, the tears stopped.

He stood, left the room, went to the entry and said, "One of you bring me a perfume vial. A new one that has never held scent. Small enough that I might hold three in one hand."

He returned to the sleeping chamber, brought a chair to the side of her bed, and sat that way until a guard entered. She gave him a vial fashioned of pink quartz so finely thinned he could easily see the lamplight through it. The guard saluted and left.

Damon reached down the neck of his tunic and fished out Pentha's arrowhead. He untied the knot and took the arrowhead into his hand. For the first time he approached the bed close enough to Pentha to touch her. He didn't. He had touched the dead too many times. He did not want that memory of her—cold, still, spiritless.

Instead he took a lock of her hair and twisted it around one finger. Using her arrowhead, he cut off the lock. He sat in the chair, laid the lock on the bed beside her, and then used the arrowhead to cut a length of leather from its thong. With the leather, he tied the hair in a small bundle so it wouldn't scatter.

He started to put it into the vial, hesitated, put it to his nose and inhaled. The scent of her still lingered. Tears burned the backs of his eyes as he slipped the bit of Pentha into the vial and set it on the table beside her.

Holding her arrowhead tightly in his hand, he began the night vigil. At one point he realized he'd clutched it so tightly his palm was bleeding.

SOMEONE PUT A HAND on Damon's shoulder. He looked up. Gryn stood beside him, her gaze fixed on her daughter. They remained in silence for a while, then Gryn said, "It's morning."

"We had won the day. Why couldn't she let that be enough?"

"Dear Damon." Gryn patted his shoulder, then hugging

herself, she studied him. "When Pentha first came from Tenedos, she had many bad dreams. Rightly or wrongly, she lived with great guilt and great hate for Achilles. I don't think she could have stopped herself—not even for loving you."

"But we had won. I planned to challenge and kill him."

"In the morning, as my daughter dressed for the battle, she told me of Achilles' plans to attack Themiskyra. She said that Achilles must die. I knew then that if he did not call her out, she would challenge him. Someone had to kill him." Gyrn's face filled with sympathy. In gentle tones she said, "Do you think she would have left that risk to you when there was a chance she might succeed?"

For Themiskyra. For me.

Gryn squeezed his shoulder. "We came here not just to stop one man but to reaffirm our strength. If you will, Amazon ferocity. We have done that. Themiskrya is secure because of my daughter's vision and courage. None of this Achean hoard will dare to even think we are weak. Tales of Amazon strength are already spreading. In death, Pentha has the victory she longed for. She achieved the goal she lived for. Pentha grasped her destiny willingly. And you helped her. Don't let your grief hide that worthy truth."

He retied the arrowhead around his neck, rose, picked up the perfume vial. "I leave her with you, Gryn. And I thank you."

THIS EVENING'S TRIP WOULD be Derinoe's last journey into the citadel. Tomorrow evening, after Pentha's funeral, she would never set foot again in Troy. Troy was the past.

But there remained this one last task. She carried a special package, long and narrow, wrapped in green silk, tied with a dark green silk ribbon. A delicate-looking package.

After checking the public hallway and finding it empty, she stepped from the secret passage into it. She hurried to the door she sought and knocked three times.

Paris opened the door. He smiled and gestured for her to

enter. Nodding to a chair, he said, "Would you like something to drink?"

"No." She laid her package on the table.

Paris said, "I have been told that the Amazon Queen was your sister." Even his voice was soft and soothing. "I offer you sincere sympathy."

"Thank you."

"I am most curious to know how that could be."

"The story is not something I'm prepared to tell. It also has nothing to do with why I asked for this meeting. I prefer to come directly to the point."

"And that is?"

"You are a fine archer. Famous for your skill. I bring you the means to destroy your people's greatest enemy, Achilles. And of course, by doing so, you will win fame, glory, and the undying gratitude of all Troy."

⇥ 79 ⇤

DERINOE APPROACHED A LOW HILL OVERLOOKING a gentle bend in the Scamander River's course in search of Damon. He sat at the top, side-by-side with Bias.

As she climbed up, she studied Damon's back. His hair, tied with a thong at his nape. His broad shoulders. Soon, unless he granted her wish, her path might separate from his. The thought made her chest tighten with profound sadness.

They heard her, turned, and hurried to rise.

She said, "Gryn told me I'd find you here."

Damon's falcon perched on a leather glove on Damon's arm, her white head covered with the small leather helmet and its plume of red feathers.

She said, "I hope I'm not out of place or intruding."

Bias said, "We're getting ready to let Dia go."

Damon stroked the bird's nape. "We may as well do it now."

Derinoe watched the boy remove one and then the other leather jess from the bird's legs. Dia ruffled the feathers of her back, but still sat quietly.

Uncertain as to what was happening, Derinoe asked, "If you let her go, won't she just come back?"

Damon shook his head. "She really only comes back for food."

Bias, his lanky young body restless with enthusiasm, said,

"She's been stuffed, yesterday evening and this morning. Right now she's not even a little hungry."

Damon looked at Bias. "Ready."

The boy nodded.

Damon used his free hand to loosen the leather thong holding the tiny helmet in place. He lifted it smoothly off Dia's head. She blinked. Blinked again. But didn't move.

"Fly free," Damon said. He lowered his arm then heaved her skyward. Wings beating, stirring air that ruffled Damon's hair, the beautiful creature shot forward, swooped down the hill, banked, and wings once more in a flurry, gained height as she flew around them in a wide circle.

They sat in silence and watched the bird rise. When she had become a small dark speck, she stopped circling and headed inland to the east.

Derinoe asked, "Will she be all right?"

"Yes." Damon paused. "And more. She'll be free. Great things have to be free to find their destiny."

They stood and started back to camp. Derinoe said to Bias, "Gyrn has been taking care of Leonides and Myrina all morning. Please go ahead of us, and take them off her hands for a while."

"Sure." Bias thoroughly enjoyed Leonides' company. He took off down the hill at fast run.

To Damon she said, "I've come to ask for something."

He seemed not to have heard her. "The Acheans are smarting from their defeat. They are eager for another battle to change the score and purge the bitter taste they now have in their mouths. Agamemnon and Aeneas have set tomorrow as the day."

"Priam asked for a ten-day truce so we can have the funeral for Pentha in peace and then a nine day mourning celebration to honor her. This morning Agamemnon accepted. There will be no battle until well after the funeral."

"Fine. I will fight Achilles then."

"You won't need to."

"Yes, Deri, I do. Achilles remains a threat. We came here

to protect Themiskyra. To make absolutely certain, Achilles must be killed."

"Pentha has already assured Achilles' death. But a death in honorable battle at your hands is too good for him. He will have a different fate."

Damon frowned. "I will fight him, and I will kill him."

"Bring him honor? Burnish his name with glory because he dies in battle with the great Damonides? Or is it to win glory and honor for yourself?"

Damon's gaze flared with an angry fire, something she'd never seen in him before. "You don't know me or you would never use the words honor and glory in the same breath with talk of fighting or war."

"Well, isn't that the point of these duels in battle. Honor? Glory?"

He stopped walking, stared hard at her, his jaw muscles clenching. "I'm going to kill Achilles. He intends to attack Themiskyra next spring and he is so revered he may be able to overcome his men's present fear of our forces. Killing him will assuredly cut the heart out of any such plans."

"But I'm telling you, his death is arranged. He may already be dead."

"What you are talking about? What you say makes no sense."

"I won't—I can't—tell you details. But I have as much reason, maybe more reason, to want him dead than you. And I swear, Achilles will die."

She imagined his mind darting here and there to one idea after another, trying to solve that puzzle. He would never be able to. And she could never explain. Gryn had asked for, and Deri had sworn to, silence. Maybe he was thinking she had simply gone insane over Pentha's death. Or that she was the kind of woman who would put trust in a witch's curse.

She added, "Or is it revenge you want? Is it not enough that he die?"

He started walking again. When they reached the tent set aside for her and the children, he said, "When you came to the hill, you said you came to ask me something. What was it?"

She had annoyed him. Not smart when she needed a favor. "I perhaps sound like a crazy woman, Damon. I'm not. What I've said is true. Please believe me."

She waited for his response. He merely held a questioning gaze steady.

She proceeded. "I can't stay in Troy. This place, without Hektor, isn't safe for me or Leonides and Myrina. I was going to return with Pentha to Themiskyra. I would like to ask if you would let me return with you." For a second time she wondered if she should tell him before they parted that perhaps Pentha had carried his child, but once again reasoned that such news could only wound him—and Pentha had not even been certain. So that potentiality would have to be something kept to herself.

Damon smiled, that gentle smile that melted her insides like a gentle flame melted wax. "I would gladly take you back. I'm honored you'd ask my help. But I've decided I'll not return."

"You'll stay here?"

"No. Not here. There is another place I've wanted to see again, and I can't stand the thought of being in Themiskyra without Pentha." He put a warm hand on her arm. "But I am sure, absolutely certain, Gyrn will take you with her if that's where you want to go."

"Where are you going?"

"A small place to the south."

"Ephesus?"

He looked surprised.

"Pentha told me. They don't live the Amazon way."

"No. Men and women live together all the time as husband and wife. It's the life I prefer. Maybe the most important thing Pentha taught me is that I've lived alone too many years."

"I believe I would like that, too. I often wished I had been married to Hektor and could have lived with him."

"Bremusa comes with me. She doesn't want to return to Themiskyra without Clonie. I will gladly take you and the children."

"I will think about it." She turned to enter the tent.

He said, "I'm glad you came to talk. Your voice. It's beautiful like Pentha's."

Deri returned his gaze. "Will you trust me about Achilles? You needn't fight him."

"I, too, will have to think."

❦ 80 ❧

DRESSED IN A PURPLE TUNIC AND WEARING HER
white fur cap, Penthesilea's body lay on a bed of red
and white rose petals in Priam's own gold wagon, her bat-
tleax and quiver beside her and her body elevated high
enough that all might see her one last time. Drawn by four
horses, harnessed abreast, the wagon left the Themiskyran
encampment in the late afternoon.

Fifty Themiskyran drummers led. A hundred mounted
Amazons preceded the wagon, and a hundred followed it.
Damon was pleased with the preparations, grateful to Bre-
musa and Priam for making them.

He, along with the other surviving Themiskyran commanders, rode in a chariot behind the mounted cavalry.
Throngs of the entire Themiskyran entourage and the popu-
lation of Troy lined the road between the encampment and
the city, all of the mourners bearing charcoal-smeared faces.
And when Pentha's body passed, a great wailing rose, the
eerie sound tracing the path of the gilded wagon.

As they approached the Trojan grand south gate, he heard
Themiskyran singing offering a paean to Artemis. The
Themiskyran women continued their chanting as the wagon
drew up to the pyre, Amazon guards lifted Pentha's bier, carried it up a ramp, and placed it in the center.

On an elevated dais near the gate, seated in gold inlaid
chairs, were Priam and Hekuba, Helen, Andromache, Ae-

neas, and five of Priam's other sons and their wives. Two seats remained empty: one for Damon and one for Bremusa. Oddly, Paris was absent.

Semele lit four bronze incense braziers that stood at the four corners of the pyre. Amazon archers took their places, fifty on each side of it. They held bows and arrows, and in front of each woman sat a small tripod with burning oil.

Carrying Pentha's sword, Damon mounted the ramp and went to the bier, his chest tight, his feet numb. The lower rim of the setting sun touched the horizon.

He lifted her hand, wrapped it around the sword's grip, and laid the blade across her chest. Frankincense circled his head, singing voices filled the twilight sky, and memories flashed through his mind: Pentha hanging upside down in a simple loop trap, and red-faced after with embarrassment; Pentha laughing the first time he fell off a horse; the look of her coming to him naked by the stream on that cold winter day when they first made love; the fierce light in her eyes when they had performed their duel in front of all Themiskyra; her kissing his hands when she thought she had lost him. He fought back tears.

HAVING GIVEN HIS OFFERING of gratitude to Apollo, Achilles left the god's sanctuary, an ancient site not far outside the Achean wall. As this was sacred ground, and thus a safe place where no fighting was allowed, only a small contingent of men accompanied him. He would sacrifice next to Athena.

He stepped into the chariot car, and, at the moment the horses moved from the grove of trees outside the sanctuary, something flew past close to his left shoulder. He turned toward the grove. There was Priam's son Paris, also in a chariot and with bow in hand, nocking an arrow.

"Go!" Achilles yelled to Automedon. His driver lashed the horses. They broke into a run. Another arrow whistled past. Achilles pulled a bow from its chariot pouch and nocked an arrow of his own.

With six other chariots, he raced across the plain toward

the Acheans' beach wall and its safety. He looked behind. Paris was alone! No other Trojan chariots. Just Paris and his driver.

"Turn!" Achilles yelled. He shot the arrow, which hit the front of Paris' car. What kind of fool was Paris? He was outnumbered. Achilles and his men could slaughter him.

Another arrow from Paris flew past. Then, as Automedon had the chariot circled halfway around, a fourth arrow nicked Achilles in his bare, sandaled heel.

Now Paris also turned. His driver raced their chariot toward Troy, Achilles and the others in close pursuit.

Achilles felt a chill. He nocked another arrow. Shot it. It went wide as his chariot bumped over the rough plain. They weren't gaining much on Paris, who must have come with his fastest horses.

A wrenching pain twisted Achilles' gut. Then another. He dropped the bow. Another wrenching pain! His knees gave out.

He fell from the car.

Automedon reined in the horses, turned them, drew the chariot to a halt beside Achilles, and jumped out. The six other chariots raced up and stopped.

Achilles gasped. Automedon leaned over him, saying something Achilles could not understand. The pain in his gut—

"Help—" No other words were possible. The pain! Unbearable pain!

His insides were writhing and burning.

DAMON USED PENTHA'S ARROWHEAD to cut a lock of his hair. He laid it on the bier beside her, then strode back down the ramp, ascended the dais, and took his seat. Of Pentha's Amazon commanders, only Bremusa had survived. She ascended the bier, cut a lock of her hair with her knife, and placed it beside Damon's. Then came Phemios and four other surviving infantry commanders. Finally, Gryn and Derinoe.

When Pentha's body was once more alone, Damon stood.

He bowed to Priam, then Hekuba, and then faced the crowd. The singing stopped.

All faces turned toward him. Love. Pride. Grief. So many emotions churned within him. "In this battle, the women of Artemis led the warriors of Themiskyra and Troy to victory. The price was high. We, the people of Themiskyra and the people of Troy, have lost many courageous women and men. And we of Themiskyra suffer especially the death of our beloved Warrior Queen."

He took a steadying breath, deepened his voice, and raised it still more. "But in your grief remember, as long as people have memories it will be known that at the battle for Troy, the free women of Artemis fought, and fought with courage. Let it soften your grief, as it does mine, to know that from this time, into the distant and unknown future, the name Penthesilea lives forever."

He stepped back, the signal for the singers and archers. Once more voices filled the air with song, this time a newly composed paean to Penthesilea, Warrior Queen of Themiskyra.

Bremusa stepped forward. "Nock," she commanded, and the Amazons on either side of the pyre set the ends of special arrows, with tips weighted heavily and wrapped with oil-soaked linen, to their bow strings. "Light," she commanded, and each Amazon used her tripod's fire to set her arrow ablaze. "Aim," she said, and all one hundred archers bent back and aimed their arrows into the sky, seemingly straight up, but arched ever so slightly toward the pyre. "Release," Bremusa commanded.

A hundred burning arrows streaked upward into the twilight, reached the top of their flight, began to fall toward the pyre, their heavy tips tilting them over so that almost as one, a hundred burning arrows hit the bier. As the upper rim of the sun fell below the western horizon, oil and then wood caught fire.

✤ 81 ✤

LOOKING AROUND, WAITING FOR DERINOE AND Bias, Damon itched to leave. To go. To be on the road. Damon had said all his goodbyes and the call to something new had him shifting from one foot to the other.

Achilles was dead just as Devinoe had predicted, and under the strangest conditions—seemingly felled by Paris with a single arrow to Achilles' heel, of all places. Perhaps someday Damon would learn the full truth.

Gryn stood beside him, along with Phemios and a crowd of well-wishers. Earlier he had seen Bias, but where was the youth? Bias, like Bremusa, had decided to "see the world" rather than return home. Bias reminded Damon of himself at that same age.

Derinoe finally appeared, a large bundle in her hands and Leonides and Myrina running in front of her. The children ran to where Bremusa stood waiting beside her horse. Damon imagined that on this journey, Bremusa would always be the first ready—for anything the journey might throw in their path.

Derinoe said to Gryn, "It seems it's impossible to always remember everything one should pack. Look at this!" She gestured to her bundle.

Gryn took Derinoe's face in her hands and kissed Derinoe's cheeks. She shook her head and said, "Are you troubled? You have such a very long journey ahead of you. So many unknowns."

"Gryn, I can't remember when I've been more at peace." She looked to her children, Leonides assaulting Bremusa with questions about the care of her horse and Myrina petting the donkey tied behind the cart. Deri smiled. "If a woman with two children can ever be at peace."

Bias trotted up to Phemios. "You take care of yourself," he said to the commander. He stuck out his hand. In it lay a knife. Phemios stared. Bias shoved the knife toward Phemios, who reached to his belt, felt his knife sheath, and realized he'd been robbed. He grabbed Bias, thumped the boy on the back. "You devil!"

Bias skipped quickly to several Amazons: he produced an armband for Brie, a ring for Luna, and a bear-claw necklace for Aella. Each woman in turn, touched her arm, her finger, and her neck in amazement, so skillfully had the bandit done his work.

When he came to Gryn, she smiled. "It seems diligent practice has created a master." He held out his hand, and in it was one of the pair of delicate gold and amber earrings Damon now realized Gryn always wore. As he looked to her ears, she put a hand to them, and her eyes mirrored the surprise Damon felt.

Damon cuffed Bias on the ear. "You've become a dangerous man."

Bias turned to Gryn. His teacher smiled, and nodded.

Damon turned to Gryn. "Time to go."

She nodded.

Damon gestured for Bias to climb aboard the seat of the double-ox wagon that carried their supplies and belongings. He gave his hand to Deri, and she climbed up and sat beside Bias. Leonides jumped onto the back of the wagon, and Damon handed Myrina up so she could ride beside her brother.

Phemios clasped Damon's arm. "Travel safely," he said.

Damon unfastened the belt holding his sword and handed both to Phemios. "It's yours."

Phemios shook his head. "I can't take it, Damon."

"Yes. It's yours now. I intend to get by on my wits."

He turned to Pentha's dark chestnut mare, Dawn. Bremusa was already astride, leading her best brood mare.

Damon liked riding, and this was the beginning of a new life. A long journey lay ahead, and for long trips, there would be no more walking for him. No more wagons. And no more chariots. He did not have to follow Amazon—or Achean or Trojan—ways. This man would ride.

He did his best—he felt awkward—to swing himself onto Dawn's back. Bias taunted, "You'll be lucky if you don't fall off her ten times today alone."

The well-wishers followed them as far as the camp perimeter. Damon reached down the neck of his tunic and brought out the arrowhead. He embraced Pentha's spirit for a moment, then let the arrowhead rest once more on his chest.

The children waved and called goodbye to friends they were leaving.

Damon noted, though, that Bias and Derinoe—neither looked back.

MYTHOLOGY AND TRADITION TELL US THE FOLLOWING:

ACHILLES—WAS KILLED BY PARIS, WHO SHOT AN arrow into Achilles' right heel. That the great hero should be killed by a man generally agreed to be less than heroic and by such a seemingly trivial wound amazed many. It was explained that Achilles' mother had dipped the baby Achilles into the river Styx to ensure that he would be immortal. But she held him by the right heel, which the water didn't touch. Thus he had a vulnerable spot after all, hence the term "Achilles' heel." Achilles' body was burned and his ashes, combined with those of Patroklos, were buried on a headland overlooking the Hellespont.

It is historical fact that the Persian ruler Xerxes, Alexander the Great, Julius Caesar, Constantine, the Emperor Julian, and the poet Lord Byron are perhaps the most famous among the many who have made pilgrimages to the site in Turkey where this war was believed to have been fought, where the mighty Hektor fought the warrior Achilles, and where the great Achilles was said to be buried.

TROY—WAS NOT TAKEN by force but by cunning. Odysseus eventually devised a plan whereby the Acheans (Greeks) built an enormous wooden horse, the belly of which could hold hidden warriors. At night the horse was brought to the Trojan plain with Odysseus and others inside. The Acheans burned their camp and pretended to leave Troy, taking all their ships to sea and hiding behind Tenedos. In the morning, the Trojans found the astonishing horse. They also found a man who claimed that he had escaped from the Greeks. His story was that the Acheans had intended to sacrifice him to Athena to win her blessing for a safe voyage home. He also claimed the horse was left to honor Athena, and the Acheans (Greeks) hoped the Trojans would desecrate it, thus engendering Athena's hatred. The Trojans bought the lies. And further, they brought the horse inside the citadel in order to honor Athena. That night the Achean warriors, led by Odysseus, crept out of the horse, opened the gates, and the Acheans flooded in, massacring the inhabitants and looting and burning the city—hence the saying, "Beware of Greeks bearing gifts."

THE MEN OF TROY—all save Aeneas, his father, and his son were slaughtered. Paris died from an arrow in battle. Hektor's young son was thrown from the citadel wall. Aeneas fled with his father and son and according to one tradition ended up in Italy. According to that tradition, he was the grandfather of Romulus and Remus, the founders of Rome, and so in a way, also Rome's founder. It is historical fact that many Roman Caesars proudly traced their lineage to Aeneas of Troy.

THE WOMEN OF TROY—Cassandra was given as a slave and spoils of war to Agamemnon; Hekuba to Odysseus; Andromache to a son of Achilles who joined the Acheans not long after his father's death. Helen was returned to Menelaus, who took her back to Sparta where one version of the myth says they lived together again happily, Helen greatly regretting the folly of her youth.

THE ACHEAN MEN—AJAX committed suicide. After Achilles' death, a dispute occurred over who should receive his splendid armor, and when it was given to Odysseus, Ajax was so angry he threatened to kill some of the Greek leaders. When he realized the lack of honor in his threats, he took his life. He was also buried at Troy. Odysseus got lost for over ten years on his journey home and suffered greatly on his voyage (*The Odyssey*) before he finally made it back. Agamemnon returned home where his wife, Clytaemnesta, and her lover murdered him, and Cassandra as well. Nestor alone, of the most notable royals, returned home without tragedy or irony.

THE CITY OF EPHESUS was founded by Amazons. It is historical fact that the great temple to Artemis, built there hundreds of years later, was dedicated to Artemis and was one of the Seven Wonders of the Ancient World. When the Apostle Paul preached to the Ephesians in the city's great amphitheater in approximately 53 AD—roughly 1,300 years after the estimated time of the great war at Troy—the populace was enraged and are said to have shouted him down with the words, "Long live Artemis of Ephesus!"

THEMISKYRA ON THE RIVER Thermodon does not appear again in a particular story after Troy, but it retained its place as the ancestral home of the Black Sea Amazons. No place in modern Turkey has yet been identified as Themiskyra's location. Amazons were believed to have fought in the Peloponnesia War (431–404 BC). Thalestris, Queen of the Amazons reigning during the time of Alexander the Great (323 BC), was said to hail from the region of Themiskyra. It is claimed she came to Alexander and proposed that the two of them conceive a child together who would be the greatest warrior and ruler the world had ever seen. Alexander agreed to the plan and he and Thalestris spent time together, but Thalestris returned home to Themiskyra and died childless. The story is disputed. After Alexander's death, one of his generals, Lysimachus, is quoted as saying, "And where was I at the time."

ABOUT AMAZONS

CLASSICAL GREEKS AND ROMANS BELIEVED FIRMLY in the reality of these beautiful and fierce warrior women from their past. But at some point, Amazons passed into Greek mythology. The veracity of tales involving them became suspect.

We have no proof they ever existed. We have hints that it is possible. Burials of women with the weapons of a warrior—sword, arrowheads, or body armor—have been found in areas where mythology generally placed the Amazons. But while such finds suggest a tradition of fighting women in the region, so far the burials come from a much later period.

In the old stories, the Amazons were always at war with the Greeks, and the Trojan War—whether this, too, was real or simply myth—was no exception. The Amazons fought with the Trojan defenders against the invading Greeks.

Many people think of Amazons as men-hating women. It is sad but true, however, that we often justify brutality against an enemy by demonizing them. So it's not surprising that their enemies might have said that the Amazons were a race of man-haters and man-killers. That they not only lived separate from men, they ruthlessly killed their male children. Or that in order to better use their bows, they cut off their right breasts. One thing we do know: no paintings or statues from ancient times ever depict an Amazon without a breast. Quite the contrary. And while the sexes in a number of extant non-Western cultures may live fairly separate lives, we know of no culture where one sex lives totally separate from the other. This suggests that idea is also not likely true. When cultures clash, the winners live to tell the tales and write the history, and so our views about Amazons have been derived from the writings of patriarchal Greek and Western tales told hundreds of years after these extraordinary women, if they existed, passed from the world's stage.

In *Penthesilea* you will live with Amazons. But be prepared to let go of millennia of Western myth. Be prepared to see their world with a fresh view. This is a story about Amazons—but told with a twenty-first century sensibility.

ACKNOWLEDGMENTS

THE INSPIRATION FOR THIS BOOK STRUCK ME when viewing a sarcophagus from some ancient period in a museum in Turkey. Depicted there was the battle between the mighty Achilles and the great Amazon, Penthesilea. From that moment, I wanted the name of this woman of courage and beauty to live again.

I am especially indebted to my trusted friend and brilliant story editor, Peggy Lang. Her instincts about what works and what doesn't are invaluable. Others who have critiqued all or parts of the manuscript are Mark Clements, Chet Cunningham, Donna Erickson, Barry Friedman, Robert Holt, Pete Johnson, Bev Miller, Ellen Perkins, Ken Schafer, and Tom Utts.

In the book I recite the story of Actaeon and Artemis, which is a classic, and my version is modified from Geocities' website (www.geocities.com/Athen/Acropolis/4063/artemis.html).

Most important, my most profound gratitude goes to my editor at TOR, Greg Cox, a man who knew his history and mythology and has made my dream reality   to have Penthesilea's name live once more in the people's imagination.

ABOUT THE AUTHOR

Other fiction by Judith Hand:
Voice of the Goddess
Code Name Dove (writing as Judith Leon)

Judith Hand has made the transition from left-brained scientist to right-brained novelist. Before she began writing fiction some twelve years ago, she was teaching Animal Behavior and Ornithology in the UCLA biology department.

She is the author of several novels and two screenplays. Her epic of the Minoan civilization, *Voice of the Goddess*, has won numerous awards. Her contemporary romantic thriller, Code Name Dove, features a female spy whose day job is to lead adventure tours and whose great personal love is photography. In all of her stories, she writes of strong, bold women, women who are doers and leaders.

An avid camper, classical music fan, and birdwatcher, she currently lives and Rancho Bernardo, CA. For more information about the author and her books, see her website at www.jhand.com.